# MEMOIRS OF AN ANGEL

*****

## THE GREY PILGRIM

A COSMIC WHEEL NOVEL

## –Also By Brian Rodman–

*Memoirs of an Angel* (Comic Book Series)
*The Nebulizer* (Comic Book Series)
*The Midnight Mason & The Curse of The Black Knights*
(For the Pulp Factory Award Winning Anthology, Pulp Reality No. 4, through Stormgate Press)
*Terrestrial Seven* *with Robert Gardner
(For Louisville Cartoonist Society's Tall Tales & Little Lies)
*The Legend of Black Annis* (Illustrated Poem)
(For Louisville Cartoonist Society's Legends)
*The Road To Damascus* *with Reed Mitchum
(For Louisville Cartoonist Society's Sagebrush & Tumbleweeds)

Illustration Only Work
Pulp Reality No. 5 (Stormgate Press)
Elev8 Magazine
*G.I. Zombie* (For Atomic Stories)
*Archimedes Octane* (For Atomic Stories)
*Flight of The Thunderbird* (For Atomic Stories)

Edited by Kim Bray
with Robyn Rodman, Stefani Manard, & Brian K. Morris
Formatted by Sarah Mayer

This is a work of fiction. All of the characters, organizations, and events portrayed in this novel are either products of the author's imagination or are used fictitiously.

 For information, address B&R Publications, 9152 Taylorsville Rd, #257, Louisville, Ky 40299.

brianrodman.com

ISBN: 978-1-7338108-1-4

First Edition: March 2025

*For my wife and best friend, Robyn. This wouldn't exist without you. You are my world and I love who you are.*

*For my parents. Thank you for giving me comic books and drawing paper when I was a kid. And thank you for always encouraging me to chase my dreams.*

*For Doug. You gave a vulnerable teenage boy the affirmation and the confidence to follow his passion. I wish you were still here with us, my friend.*

*For Luke. Your friendship and comradery in venturing the unseen realm will forever be something I cherish.*

*For my God and King, who continues to wrestle me and win.*

Special Thanks To:
Jack Brannen
Jeff & Lydia Walker
Sarah Thrasher
Brian K. Morris
Clyde Hall
Evan Mitchum
Eric Scott Hawkins
Jonathan Gentry
Andrew Morris
Mike Paul
David Macauley
Jason Adams
Morgan Comnick
Kim Cox
Cindy Koepp
Ray Coffman
& Chad Nuss

**Trigger Warning**

This novel contains content that may be distressing to some readers, including adult themes, strong violence and language, traumatic experiences, and depictions of sexual violence.
Reader discretion is advised.

"Finally, draw your strength from the Lord and from his mighty power. Put on the whole armor of God, so that you may be able to stand firm against the tactics of the devil. For we do not wrestle against flesh and blood, but against the rulers, against the authorities, against the cosmic powers over this present darkness, against the spiritual forces of evil in the heavenly places. Therefore, take up the whole armor of God, that you may be able to resist on the evil day, and having done everything, to hold your ground.
So, stand fast, having fastened on the belt of truth, clothed with righteousness as a breastplate, and your feet shod in readiness for the gospel of peace. In all circumstances hold your faith as a shield, to quench all the flaming arrows of the evil one; and take the helmet of salvation, and the sword of the Spirit, which is the word of God. With all prayer and supplication, pray at every opportunity in the Spirit. To that end, be watchful with all perseverance and supplication for all the holy ones..."

–Ephesians 6:10-18

The vast realms of The Cosmic Wheel–forever turning as a living construct of order–could, at any given moment, overlap with one another. On many occasions, multiple worlds at a time would occupy the same space, warring over locations or persons to inhabit or defend.

The three realms of The Cosmic Wheel were Eden, Sheol, and Corporeum. Each realm worked as its own universe, with worlds, kingdoms, and cosmic laws uniquely designed to govern each plane. Eden was the home of the Heavenly Host–the elohim–whose DNA was intertwined with the holy Light of the White Throne. Eden was fueled by Tzohar, the Aeternum Stone of Eternal Light. Sheol was the Chaos realm, initially created by the consequential Dark energies of the Creation Wars. It later became home to many creatures, both fallen and true, but always remained the realm that the dead must travel. Corporeum was the realm between. A material realm caught in the constant tension between Eden and Sheol–between Light and Dark. A realm that held the most weight a creature could carry, for every decision made in that place would eternally echo throughout the worlds to come.

At the center of this construct, at the very heart of all creation, was the White Throne. There dwelled the presence of Yahweh, King of Ages, maintaining the order that kept creation in its place for eons, protecting it from chaos and ultimate destruction. For the Light shined in the Darkness, and the Darkness could not overcome it.

# ARTEMUS OF EOLAS

# OHK A YOM ME'NORANIK

The simple yet mighty phrase—*let there be light*—inspired constellations to dance and worlds to emerge. Life found its beginning in the cosmos. Thousands of millennia have passed since this moment, but I can still hear it reverberate throughout the ever-expanding realms of The Cosmic Wheel. Although I wasn't there to experience it, everything I've observed has its flavor. And oh, my friend, I have observed much in my time.

Beyond the Adamian galaxies, past the wild solar fields of the Xoth system and the deepest event horizon of Shaggai, a solitary mountain resides at the center of the Cosmic Ocean. The Eternal Mountain was the first response to The Words of Life uttered at the beginning of time and was given to me by the King of all creation, Yahweh, King of Ages.

Taller than any star or kingdom in the cosmos, this glorious peak is home to only one thing. A staircase emerges from within the mountain's bright blue, marbled stone structure, winding up and around the untamed peak to its summit, where stands the door to Eolas: Archive of Ages.

Through the glassy portal between the glyph-covered pillars, the Archive welcomes you into its endless world of stories, maps, songs, laments, and prophecies captured in orbs of Light called obus.

At the center of this conglomeration of information is the Tamias Mortem, an obelisk structure with a small, altar-like surface at its top. Placing an obu upon the Tamias Mortem reveals its secrets to the one who seeks its knowledge. The obu I am about to lay upon this ancient altar is not for the faint of heart. Before we follow its lead throughout time, it needs some introduction, as do I.

I am the keeper and Chief Watcher of this Archive. I have been here since before the first Age of All Things and I always will be. What I am about to relate is truly an extraordinary tale that only someone of my particular persuasion could tell. I am a creature of the Host of The Heavens, although I may not be what you would imagine. My name is Artemus, and I am your host on this terrible yet great adventure.

The world has changed considerably since the twentieth century. By the end of what was known as the Second World War, Lucifer's plan of domination through his infestation of Adolf Hitler had failed. It was a grand victory for both the Host of Heaven and the race of Adamians–humans.

Through the years to come–as in many years past–allegiance to the Light diminished among the Adamian race. The Institutional Church had slipped further and further from its appointed role as Light Bearer, embracing corruption and power. Many turned away from the King and trusted in themselves, materialism, or other gods to escape reality for the comfort of their own senses.

Through developing industry and working only for selfish gain, the race of Adam fell deeper into the pit of despair. They made deals with devils. Sometimes unknowingly and often deliberately they became trapped inside their souls, allowing The Dark Kingdom to feast. What the Adamians saw as profound progress was instead bringing about the end of their world.

At the close of the Twentieth Century, a division came to a climax amongst the Adamians. All but a determined few were utterly blind to what they now welcomed into their existence with open arms. Only a remnant remained, fighting for restoration and aligning themselves with an evaporating idea of hope found in a demonstrably misrepresented King no one could see.

After centuries of attempting to prevent such a catastrophic event, The Final War began. The Adamian race had allowed themselves to be corrupted to their cores, luring them into obliteration. The war threw the world into more chaos than ever before. As nuclear winter blanketed most of the Earth, many retreated underground, attempting to survive. Not a single being was spared its wrath; even the remnant of Light began to dim in this new world of ruin and madness.

Centuries passed.

After the fallout settled, a new generation of humanity began to pull themselves back together. The Adamians' answer to The Final War's devastation was more dangerous than anyone imagined. The new peoples of Earth formed The Grand Republic to bring peace to an otherwise chaotic planet.

As a measure to quell any great rebellion, The Grand Republic created massive prisons in the land remaining of what had been North and South America, Russia, and the majority of Asia. These prison territories became known as The Wastelands. They housed the troublemakers and criminals of this new world.

The Condemned lived in this nightmarish land until the end of their days. Their punishment spanned generations, passed on to their descendants born inside these savage and sprawling penitentiaries.

For the rest of civilization, peace began to grow. The first Grand Chancellor, Imatious I, and his High Elders deemed religion and "holy wars" the cause of The Final War. Therefore, the governing officials abolished the old ways and remolded them to reflect a more civilized age. The Republic Gathered–a replacement for the religious institution–shepherded all religions into a peaceful cohabitation governed by reason and scientific fact. All supernatural beliefs and mystical rituals were diluted and dismissed to reflect a more evolved humanity.

With enough time, however, cracks began to form. Regardless of how civilized and scientific this New World became or how harsh the punishments were, the call to something mystical tantalized the souls of its people once more. They co uld not escape their desires for something beyond the material–for one cannot sever themselves in two and continue to thrive–so they fled into the only place not yet under Grand Republic control.

From what was Damascus to Afghanistan, there was a fallout unlike the rest of the world knew, as it became a prime target and

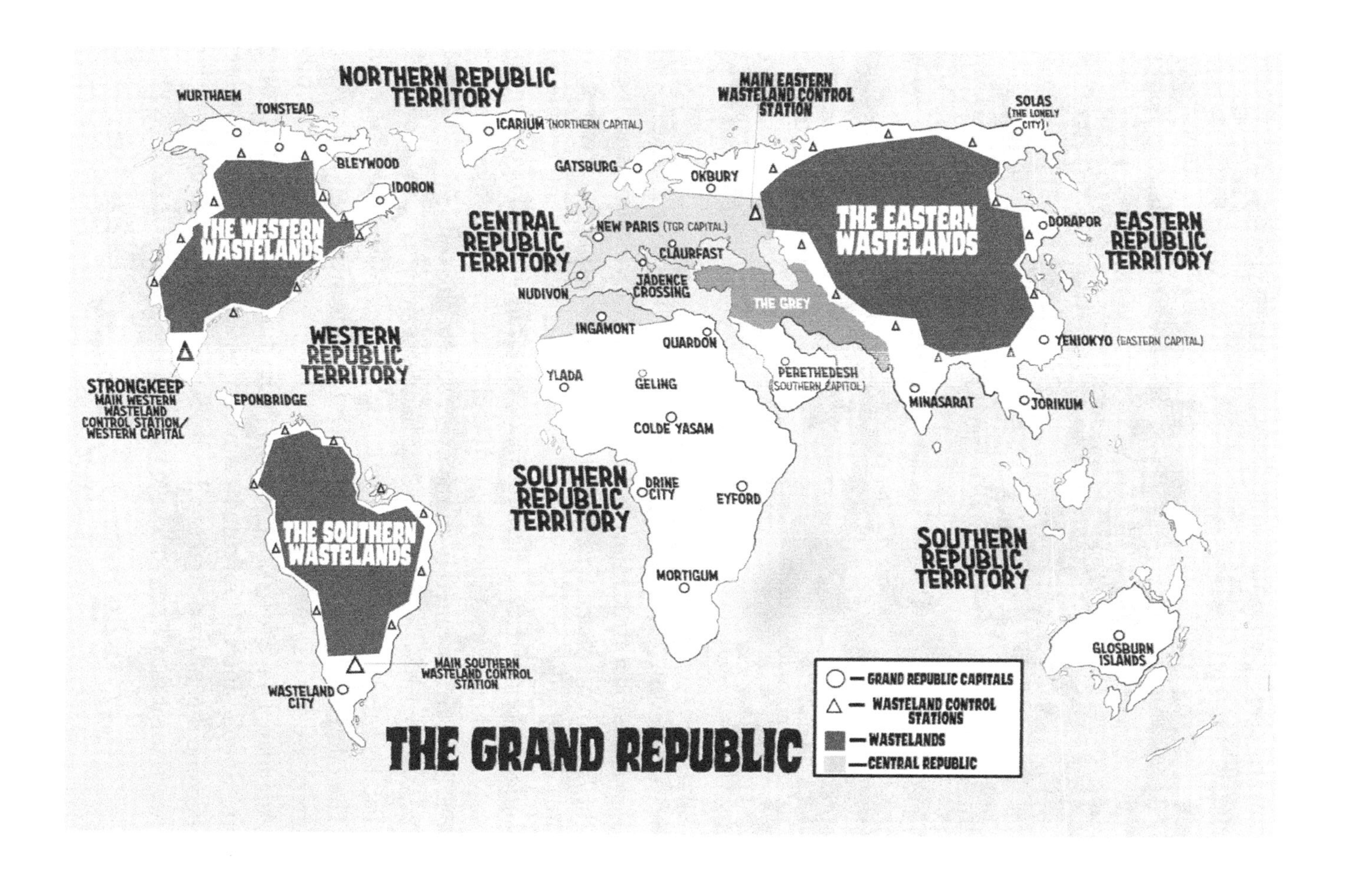
NORTHERN REPUBLIC TERRITORY
WURTHAEM
TONSTEAD
BLEYWOOD
IDORON
THE WESTERN WASTELANDS
STRONGKEEP
MAIN WESTERN WASTELAND CONTROL STATION/ WESTERN CAPITAL
EPONBRIDGE
WESTERN REPUBLIC TERRITORY
ICARIUM (NORTHERN CAPITAL)
GATSBURG
OKBURY
MAIN EASTERN WASTELAND CONTROL STATION
CENTRAL REPUBLIC TERRITORY
NEW PARIS (TGR CAPITAL)
CLAURFAST
NUDIVON
JADENCE CROSSING
INGAMONT
QUARDON
THE GREY
PERETHEDESH (SOUTHERN CAPITOL)
SOLAS (THE LONELY CITY)
THE EASTERN WASTELANDS
DORAPOR
EASTERN REPUBLIC TERRITORY
YENIOKYO (EASTERN CAPITAL)
MINASARAT
JORIKUM
YLADA
GELING
COLDE YASAM
SOUTHERN REPUBLIC TERRITORY
DRINE CITY
EYFORD
MORTIGUM
THE SOUTHERN WASTELANDS
MAIN SOUTHERN WASTELAND CONTROL STATION
WASTELAND CITY
SOUTHERN REPUBLIC TERRITORY
GLOSBURN ISLANDS
THE GRAND REPUBLIC
— GRAND REPUBLIC CAPITALS
— WASTELAND CONTROL STATIONS
— WASTELANDS
— CENTRAL REPUBLIC

battleground during The Final War. The radiation lasted for centuries, allowing a more eccentric population to secretly gravitate toward this quarantine zone between the Southern and Eastern Republic territories.

In time, this mystic land became known as The Grey, attracting not only the free-spirited but also the malevolent-hearted ones who reflected the very downfall of the Old World. As The Grand Republic expanded, fear of The Grey grew exponentially, ruling all who would dare darken its wooded boarders. This place was not entered lightly, if it was entered at all.

Despite the haunting presence of The Grey, The Grand Republic flourished. Many believed this new civilization was indeed the beginning of the end of evil, but oh, how wrong they were. For, in a world ruled by the curse of Khata, where realms intertwine and suffering reigned, no Adamian-made civilization could overcome the very brokenness of the human soul. Nor could it overcome the Darkness that awaited it on the other side of the veil.

As I hold this obu in my hands, waiting to cast it onto the Tamias Mortem, I must say these final words to you before we begin. The tale I am about to relate has deep significance, and I tell it with a great weight upon my shoulders. I have seen much in my time, Adamian. I have seen the rise and fall of countless kingdoms across all the Sheolic and Corporeum Realms. I have seen beauty at its brightest become the most wicked of all evils. So, heed what I say and take it to heart, for it may very well save your soul.

# PART ONE

## THE PILGRIM, THE WITCH, & THE STRANGER

# CHAPTER ONE

## -THE TELLYARD BARD-

The hooded pilgrim sped through the cold sand of The Lost Dunes with malice in his heart. The engine below him generated enough heat to keep him warm over the long cold journey, making him grateful to the Yeshuetic people from whom he departed two days prior. He had been genuinely surprised to find such a rare group of pacifists this deep in The Grey and this close to such a nightmare. The tribe had fed him and allowed him to wash his flesh and clothing. Although this people had very little, they had shared freely and abundantly, even giving him one of their last ungravity-pods to travel the treacherous sands of the Dunes. That sort of goodwill was unheard of here in this god-forsaken land and it made him almost rethink his mission. Maybe there was hope for this world after all.

*Not likely,* he thought. *Simply a few good folks trying to make a difference. A lot of good it'll do them in the end when an empty death is all that waits for them. Besides, if they really wanted to do anything of significance, they wouldn't have isolated themselves in the one place no one wants to be.*

His jaded emotions brought him back to his senses. No, to him, the Yeshuite people were just like the rest–kind to an extent, but with motives that were only self-gratifying. He was sure they were more than proud of themselves for how they treated such a dirty, loathsome pilgrim. That allowed them to feel good about themselves and sleep well at night, nothing more.

The ungravity-pod's high-frequency multimeter began to chime loudly, letting the pilgrim know he was closer than he'd ever been before. This was all so surreal. Slowing the pod and activating the multimeter's positioning system, he led the hovercraft to the base of a seemingly ordinary but mountainous dune. From the coordinates he'd been given, this was the cave tavern he'd been searching for over six years.

The Tellyard Bard was the entrance to his unholy destination. It was known throughout The Grey, but the ever-changing coordinates were known to few. And those few who knew were not people that most would want to know in the first place. The Bard was said to be a tavern–its latest location hidden in the Dunes somewhere–for those loyal to the most dangerous and wicked cult known to humankind: The Coven of Endor, ancient as it was malevolent. No one quite knew exactly how old it was, but it was common knowledge that The Coven's roots went further back than the Old World, the world before The Final War began. There were rumors it had played a prominent role in the war's origins, which was no surprise to the pilgrim. He was well acquainted with The Coven and its twisted role in the history of *his* world. Since the beginning, its presence intertwined with The Grey like a serpent coiling around its prey.

The pilgrim opened the door to the pod and stepped out onto the cold sand, the unstable ground shifting under the sole of his rugged leathersteel boot. His hood was pulled forward so far only his enormous, wiry beard was visible. Both were crucial in protecting him from the unforgivable conditions of The Lost Dunes. Examining the mountain of sand ahead of him, he walked ten paces forward and stopped suddenly. He heard something–the whirling of terraform engines.

Throughout his years in The Grey, the pilgrim had seen some T-13 terraform models. One wasn't functioning anymore, and the town it had once powered was abandoned long ago. Others he'd come across were functioning but didn't have much life left in them–their terracells being almost completely dried up. But the whirling he was hearing now didn't sound like an old, beat-up engine clinging to life. This sounded like at least three or four perfectly working T-13s. The High Temple in Perethedesh had as much, but that place took up half the city and *needed* them to control the climate and stability of the structure at its great heights.

*What in the world would need that many engines out here?* He thought as he took another step.

**Clink**!

*Hm. Usually, sand doesn't make that sound.* The hooded man knelt, his dark brown cloak billowing in the cold winter breeze. He pulled off his long black glove and felt the ground. It still looked like sand, to be sure, but the ground here was as hard as steel. Also, unlike the shifting sand a foot away, this ground wasn't cold, it was almost burning hot. He put his glove back on and pulled it over his forearm while walking back to the pod.

*They're using terraform engines to turn the sand into a metallic substance,* he thought to himself. *That's brilliant. Keeps the place looking like it's just a giant sand dune but merges and solidifies the granules. Provides excellent shelter from this climate and defense against any fool who would try to attack it.*

Upon reaching the pod, he pulled his tools out of the holster compartment. He packed light. It was essential in this place. He carried holy water from the Yeshuites, some dried jack-rabbit jerky, drinking water, and the Capurro Cross. The Cross was an ancient relic of unknown age and origin. It was unknown to him, at least. Obadiah knew but never shared that story with him. The Cross was made of stone, and each end came to an arrow-shaped point. The stone's back merged with a solid, unaged piece of oak that extended past the bottom point of the Cross, leaving the top and side points exposed.

The pilgrim secured his tools on his utility belt, closed the ungravity-pod door, put the control fob in the "home" slot, and watched the pod race away back to its owners at the Yeshuite village. There was no going home for *him.* Home wasn't an option anymore; no, he knew this was his final destination. This was the farthest he'd ever gone and the farthest he'd go. Surviving was never the goal of this mission.

He ascended the trail leading up the steel-like dune. Halfway up, the pilgrim came to a clearing that couldn't be seen from the ground–*another brilliant. strategic achievement.* This clearing

descended 15 feet inward, curved to the left, and revealed a cave entrance. The pilgrim stopped in his tracks. This was it. He'd prepared himself for this moment for years, but now that it was finally in front of him, his emotions began to run wild.

Taking a deep breath to calm himself, the hooded man entered the cave's darkness, immediately noticing the vibrations of what felt like tribal drums. It smelled of death and piss. He turned the corner to see a dust-covered sign bolted on the cave wall.

Twenty yards ahead, he could see neon lights–like the ones he remembered from *The Lowers* so long ago–illuminating the cave walls, revealing a sharp right turn. As he drew closer, the drums grew louder.

*"The Tellyard Bard: Enter under the protection of The Gods of Endor. Beware to those who would oppose them."*

*After all these years, my hell will finally come to an end,* the pilgrim thought as he pushed open the wooden saloon doors and walked into a nightmare of erotic torture and wretchedness. Sounds of screaming, moaning, and clanking of crockery punctuated by the loud tribal drums overwhelmed his senses. As the hooded man surveyed this throbbing nightmare, he pointedly took note of the room.

It was an enormously open space, illuminated by strobing neon poles next to every table, each with one or two dancers performing and *indulging* paying customers. The artificial fog covering the floor did nothing to hide the bodily fluids ranging from blood to urine to semen. To his right rested a large stage with an oversized sex throne currently being used as part of the evening's entertainment. Directly in front of the stage, a sorcerer stood shouting incantations over the erotic acts before him–no doubt praying for a godborn to be conceived.

At the center of the tavern, the floor descended to the bar where a single bartender stood mixing drinks, his face painted in a skull type tribal mask that the pilgrim knew all too well. In fact, he noticed that everyone in this tavern had identical makeup. That wasn't a surprise as the winter solstice was upon them.

Looming in the far-left corner behind the bar was a statue, at least twenty feet tall, of the ancient wilderness deity Baphomet, the chief god of Endor.

A large opening at the back of the tavern gaped like a demonic mouth, revealing not only the entrance to The Tellyard Bard Village but six decaying corpses suspended from the overhang. They were either fellow travelers who stumbled upon this place or, more likely, citizens who had blasphemed the Endorian gods.

No one noticed him yet, but he was sure to be an immediate target once they did. The pilgrim needed to get information quickly and disappear unseen into the Village. Most patrons were too busy being pleasured or mutilated to notice him walking toward the ramp leading down to the lone bartender. He reached the bar and sat down calmly. The hooded man was prepared to get information by any means necessary, but to do so forcefully right now was not his first choice.

"You lost, Pilgrim?" rasped a deep, gargling voice behind the bar. The bartender dried a baked clay mug with a rag while staring daggers into the hooded figure. His eyes–one dead–were as yellowed as his teeth. Like the rest of the room, his face was painted white with jet black around the eyes and lips. At the bottom of the jawline, markings resembling teeth traveled from one side to the other.

This man had a bright blue beard with a large handlebar mustache, and his unwashed, matted hair was as wild as the pattern of multiple colors with which it was decorated. He was shirtless, revealing rippling muscles under his dark brown skin. The hooded man couldn't tell if the specific odor he smelled belonged to the bartender or if it was the overall essence of this wretched place.

"Aren't we all?" replied the pilgrim as he placed four macecoins on the table. "I'd like a Stomach Pounder on the rocks if you got it. In for the solstice Saturnalia and looking for a place to stay."

"You're late. Saturnalia started yesterday. Where you comin' from with that coin?"

"All over. Just recently sacrificed some Yeshuite shits in preparation for The Black Mass. Looks like some of y'all are doing the same tonight."

The bartender spat on the ground in disgust at the "Yeshuite" term and agreed with the sentiment.

"Shits indeed. Good riddance to them self-righteous heretics. Still..." The bartender's twisted smile revealed his molding yellow teeth. "...I don't know you, and as a gatekeeper to this Village, I don't like how you come in here."

The pilgrim felt a strong hand abusively grip his right shoulder and grab a fistful of his cloak. He heard a slimy, high-pitched voice coming from behind him, which he assumed belonged to the hand.

"Well, well. Look what we have here, boys. A new toy to break," the high voice hissed. The pilgrim looked in front of him past the wicked grin of the bartender and into the reflection showing in the surprisingly polished copper keg. There were three of them.

The one who spoke had a worn-out fedora on his head that covered long, greasy ginger hair. His beard was patchy, grown out, and unkempt, making it look wild and directionless. Blood splattered on his face, covering some of his white and black makeup.

It appeared he had been drinking the blood because beneath his bottom lip, his beard shined a deep red. Like the other two men with him, he wore a black Saturnalia robe covering his entire body. Most importantly, though, he held a blood-stained knife in his right hand.

“He's well put together, ain't he? Looks like we get some more action tonight after all." This voice was deeper but hissed just the same. The second man had a relaxed blue/purple mohawk that rose above an otherwise bare scalp. His makeup was much more intact than that of the first man. The pilgrim then felt a giant, calloused hand grab the base of his neck, forcing him forward on his stool, leaving his face about three inches from the mystery liquid-soaked counter.

The third man slammed his fist down, splashing the horrid liquid into the pilgrim's beard. The vile thug leaned in close, allowing the pilgrim to get a better look at him. His eyes had been replaced with cybernetic vis-tech monocles that overlapped his sockets and burrowed into the side of his head. He beamed a nasty smile, his rancid breath leeching between his teeth and said, "Yeah, I bet he's *real* pretty, too. Let's have a better look!"

Time seemed to stand still for the pilgrim. This was his profession, but even more so, it was his gift...or curse as he often saw it. He moved so fast that the three men didn't even realize what had happened until two were dead on the floor. The first man's knife had been guided to shred the third man's carotid artery, and then it sailed behind them to bury itself in the second man's jugular, remaining there. The ginger was slammed onto the countertop and held in place by the pilgrim's massive left hand around his neck, the grip feeling stronger than steel.

"Where is she?" the pilgrim asked calmly. Few in the tavern paid them any attention. This was mild compared to what happened all around them. The ginger was stunned. How did this freak move so fast? Who was he? Then he realized who the pilgrim was asking about and immediately understood. The ginger then felt the transformation start within him.

"I won't ask again. I swear I'll-" The pilgrim was interrupted by a hatchet flying behind him. He quickly turned and caught the weapon by the hilt before it found the back of his head. Without hesitation, he returned it to its owner, the hatchet finding a new home between the man's eyes. At this, no one else felt brave enough to join the fight.

The hooded man heard a thud, felt pain, and saw stars from the ginger's strong kick as he stumbled forward, away from the bar. He turned to see the ginger crouched on the countertop like a twisted predator ready to pounce. The thug's eyes had rolled entirely back in his head, revealing pupilless yellow orbs which glowed in the shadows of the tavern. His fingers had morphed into razor-sharp talons, and his teeth were like thick needles waiting to pierce the pilgrim's skin. He leapt at the pilgrim with a fierce and inhuman howl. Again, the hooded man

knew what lethal move to take, but now that he was facing one of the *merged*, brute force wasn't necessary. He reached into his cloak and pulled from it the Capurro Cross, aimed it toward the flying possessed man, and calmly stated, "Christus Victor."

The wild yellow eyes began to burn with a bright Light. The demonic man shrieked in pain as beams of light from the cross struck him. The pilgrim stepped aside and let the ginger fall face down onto the fluid-soaked floor. The thug was dead before he hit the ground, steam billowing from his now empty eye sockets and open mouth.

Everyone around them glared at the man with the Cross in his hand. They looked like hungry, wild animals.

"H' epgoka ah. H' l' ah h'!" bellowed an authoritative voice from behind the bar. At that, everyone slowly resumed their business of debaucherous rituals.

"Haha...well, well..." the voice continued. This was a new voice, monstrous and evil. The pilgrim turned to face the bar and saw that the voice belonged to the barkeep with the bright blue beard and handlebar mustache. The barkeep smiled at the pilgrim, but his face was now completely twisted and his eyes mirrored the ones the pilgrim had just destroyed. "You're not as lost as I thought," he growled loudly.

"What did you say to them?"

"Something special. Don't you worry about it. I gotta say, I don't envy you. Mistress Etrulia's been expecting this for quite some time, but the fact that you're here mere days before the Winter Solstice...*that* is something that just tickles my Dark heart, pilgrim. You see...what Mistress Etrulia has set in motion cannot be undone." While the barkeep was speaking, his features were twitching and becoming increasingly distorted. The pilgrim had witnessed this demonic transformation before but rarely in a such slow progression.

"For here, in this place, we serve the old gods; the ancient ones. They have given us power beyond our wildest dreams, and they have saved the seat of authority in this realm for *her*. You may have bested these plebian merged creatures, but you will not defeat the High Sister of The Coven of Endor. Through her, we will conquer *all!!!!"*

**SPLAT!!!**

The Capurro Cross found itself embedded in the barkeep's forehead. Blood and bone pieces scattered across the countertop where the man's body slumped. The hooded pilgrim calmly walked over and pulled the Cross out of the barkeep's shattered skull, making him collapse, lifeless, behind the bar. As the pilgrim shook off as much blood from the Cross as he could, he noticed everyone around the bar staring at him hungrily again.

"Ancient ones, my ass," the pilgrim said, his glaring eyes meeting theirs. They all turned around and went back to their business once more. He now believed he understood what the barkeep said in whatever demonic language he spoke. Now that they knew who the pilgrim was, they were not to harm him, at least not yet. The pilgrim belonged to their Mistress.

Two things were very clear. First, his cover was blown, at least to those handful of people who saw him at the bar. And the five who were now dead were likely to be avenged. Second, he was *expected.* The barkeep knew about him, and, unless the demonic man was bluffing, the pilgrim's arrival was not a surprise. *That* was troubling. *Very* troubling. Yet again the pilgrim wondered if his protection spell had completely worn off somehow. He hadn't seen Etrulia, the High Sister of Endor, for over six years. The pilgrim was always careful not to reveal his intentions to the wrong people, which meant *most* people. And if the wrong people found out, the protection spell would take care of their memory. The only possibility for his cover being blown was a result of Dark, mystical means–strong witchcraft means. This meant he hadn't covered his tracks nearly as well as he thought.

The pilgrim walked up the ramp towards The Tellyard Bard Village. As he passed the statue of Baphomet, he spat on its base.

*The number of people who have been sacrificed in your name alone, you piece of shit...if there is some kind of god in charge of this world, I hope he burns your ass in Hell in the end.* He walked under the rotting hanging corpses and into this cesspool of nightmares.

# CHAPTER TWO

## -MESSAGES IN FLAME & BONE-

Far across The Grey, away from the pilgrim's violent entrance to the Tellyard Bard, on the outskirts of the Lost Dunes, stood a single sign of flourishing life. A gorgeously blooming oak tree resided next to a small cave. The stranger–for that is what other travelers in The Grey had called him–leaned back against the trunk of the oak and stared longingly at the moon. Even in a world filled with such hatred and malice, there was still awe-inspiring beauty to behold.

A slight smile came over the stranger's face as a brisk breeze moved through his twisted white locks and thick beard. It stimulated his senses, causing goosebumps to rise on his midnight-toned skin. The cold never bothered him. He preferred it over the heat. It was the *reason* for the cold that caused him grief. Such suffering had come from the Final War, which had changed much more than the climate of this planet. The kind of suffering he knew all too well.

He felt the gentle force of purring fur on his bare leg and looked down at his small friend.

"Is it time then?" the Stranger asked. He received a barking chatter as a response. The man scratched the tiny cat on its head, stood up, and walked toward the fire blazing inside his cave. The warmth from the flames soothed his chilled skin–another beautiful sensation. He took a deep breath, closed his eyes, and waited for contact. The man focused on his breathing and the snapping and flicking of the flames before him. He had mastered these senses long ago and knew how to gain access to the astral plane quickly. Time slipped out of meaning, peace overwhelmed him, and he knew who was now in his presence.

"I sense you, my King. What is your command?" he intoned in an almost trancelike state. Taking one long exhale, he slowly opened his emerald-green eyes and gazed up at the smoke billowing above the flames. It had filled the cave, and he saw the message he'd been waiting for in its swirling density: *Jonathan has arrived. Prepare him.* The man now knew what he had to do.

"As you wish," he said firmly, and the smoke dissipated through the small opening at the top of the cave.

As his surroundings became more visible, the man grew homesick. That surprised him. He'd been to many places throughout his life and rarely longed for home as he did now. But this mission was something he had to see to its end. He had started on this journey years ago, and he would honor the commitment he made to his brother and also to his King. So much depended on this journey, and so much hung in the balance. He glanced across the cave and found his small furry companion.

"I sure hope this works." The cat gave a slow blink in agreement.

Under the same moon, miles and miles away in a dense, haunting grove, stood another figure shadowed by a different tree. No man had ever entered here alive. The High Circle was a sacred matriarchal space. Wicked and Dark but sacred, nonetheless. The veil was thinner here than in other places. The unseen realms had more sway in this place, making communication between the physical and spiritual planes almost effortless. On this particular night, the figure under the tall, twisted, lifeless tree awaited a Dark message from an even Darker being.

Under the Kemick Agac, The Tree of The Skull, stood Etrulia, High Sister of Endor. She laid the bloody, green stone blade on its pedestal, and placed the half decaying head of her former lover on the blood-soaked altar.

"In Night of Stone,
With flesh and bone,
I call to thee,
Thy will be known.

"Speak to me when moon is full,
When air is thick,
And blood is pooled.

"And underneath The Tree of Skull,
I call to thee when light is null.
Hear my cry, oh Master mine,
And make my will unholy thine."

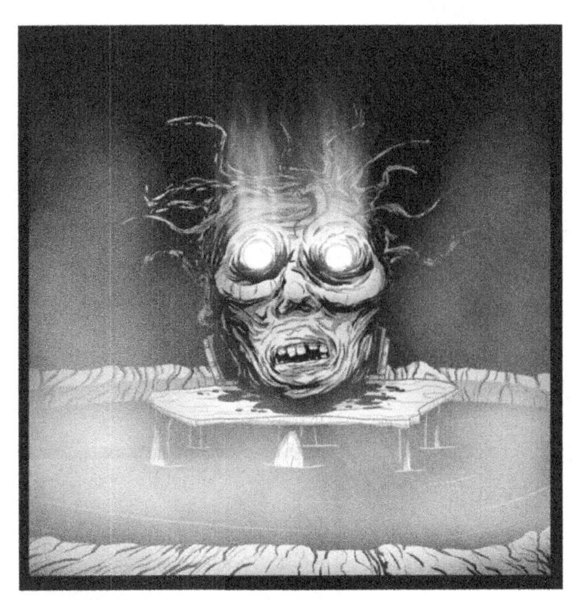

Her voice hissed and whispered in the darkness of the ceremonial grounds. The only light was from the full moon above. It illuminated her gaunt features and white, skull-painted mask. Her skin was a pale gray and her marbled gray and white hair fell, matted and wild, down the back of her filthy dark blue robes. Ceremonial sharpened bones lost in the wilderness of her unkempt hair protruded from the back and top of her head.

As blood pooled beneath the grotesque severed head, its emptied eye sockets began to glow a bright scarlet red, smoke billowing from its rotting holes. Etrulia smiled wretchedly. Her jet-black lips pulled back to reveal yellowing teeth.

"I await your instruction, my Master. What would you have me do?" she hissed. The altar began to quake as blood splattered around and onto the High Sister's face. Then, through the rolling smoke and piercing red gaze of the corpse's head, a thunderous whisper slithered forth.

"Sister of Endor, your loyalty is known. Another lover you have brought me and the final one has been delivered to you. He awaits your arrival with vengeance in his heart."

"So, he finally came." She beamed a sadistic grin as her yellow eyes glowed in the moonlight.

"Go to the Bard Village and welcome him to his final home, then take him as your own. The time of the Capurro Cross has ended. He has no weapon that can defeat you. He is destined to be by your side at the sacrifice."

"As you wish, my Master." Etrulia gleefully cackled, knowing that what was about to happen was the sweetest revenge she could have ever requested. It wasn't clear whose hatred for the other was fiercer, hers or that of the hooded pilgrim. But forcing him to submit to her Dark seduction was the worst thing he could endure. She cackled to herself. His Dark Awakening being now at hand, could only mean one thing.

"Age End is close, my Master. I sense it." She had been feeling the cosmic tides changing over the last few years. The skies were strange, and the stars told secrets only the Dark ones understood. Indeed, this was a sign that the end was drawing near. The time when they would rule all and welcome the old gods to their side once more.

"As do I, Sister of Endor. As do I," boomed the voice as blood overflowed from the altar and onto the ground at her feet.

"Soon, the world will know who its true ruler is," the pale witch screeched as she lifted the head from the blood by the hair and hung it from a chain on the Kemick Agac with the rest of her collection. At that moment, every empty eye socket of all sixty-five skulls hanging from that evil tree glowed a scarlet red. Throughout the grove, the Master's voice echoed in an unholy symphony.

"Yes. Very Soon."

# CHAPTER THREE

## -A WARNING & A PROMISE-

Three days had passed since his arrival, but surprisingly, the pilgrim remained primarily unnoticed. The hooded man found an abandoned brothel in an old, unused corner of the Village. It was clear that these people didn't have much longer. He knew that now. The villagers would destroy themselves within the next few years, maybe sooner.

While the villagers *could* find a way to leave, something was holding them here, some unseen addiction to this place of torment and lust. He knew what that addiction was, or rather *who* it was. Over the last few days, whenever he mentioned Etrulia, it was like he had sucked all the hope out of their existence; what little hope they still had. He did learn that this hell hole apparently wasn't always like this. A grieving widow gave him answers as she sobbed at the bottom of her son's rotting corpse that had been slid down on a large steel spike as a sacrifice for the Saturnalia. The bereft mother planned on committing suicide that night upon returning home. The pilgrim didn't attempt to stop or persuade her otherwise; he believed she deserved it. He thought with proud conviction that anyone in this god-forsaken shit hole deserved whatever death came to them.

The grieving woman informed him that this place used to be filled with laughter and plenty. It was a paradise for plunderers and vagabonds. She spoke so proudly of it, and he only grimaced at her pride in recounting the robbing and raping of others to form this twisted utopia.

Over the last year or two, things had gotten even worse as the control was given over to the High Sister Etrulia. She allowed the more destructive activity that High Sister Agatha had forbidden. While Agatha was Mistress over the Bard Village, there was some order to their existence, but Etrulia allowed chaos to rule. She would be gone for entire seasons, leaving her "children" in charge. Agatha had left these lands permanently, no one knowing why she left or where she went. This place had been rotting like the son on the spike in her absence.

Such was the price of dealing with devils.

But the pilgrim learned that word of Eturila's return had reached the Bard Village. She was set to present herself today and the opening solstice ceremonies would begin that evening.

As the pilgrim sat on the mystery-stained mattress in the grand suite of the old brothel, he could already hear the orders being barked at the villagers in the distance, outside the barred windows. *Prepare for her arrival or be executed for treason.* He stood up and carefully peered out the window, ensuring the streets below were empty. They were. No one had ventured to this part of the Village since he arrived.

After validating all was clear, he dressed. He was a large, powerfully built, broad man who looked much older than he was. Six years in The Grey was enough to age anyone, but this man's burdens took more of a toll than usual. His bare back, covered in old scars and freshly healed wounds, was draped in a white cotton shirt. The rest of his attire was made of black leathersteel. This metal-based material felt like a combination of worn leather and denim. Since it was almost indestructible except in extreme heat, it had kept him alive many times these long years. His pants and gloves were loose and flexible, while his boots and jacket were firm and heavy. He scoffed at the "Z" embroidered in faded red across the chest of his worn jacket. He was about to do what Henrik never could.

"I got to her first, you bastard." He said aloud to the jacket, quickly pulling his arms through the sleeves and zipping it up. After securing his tools and utility belt, he pulled his heavy coppermoc cloak over him. The copper fused moccasin leather would keep him

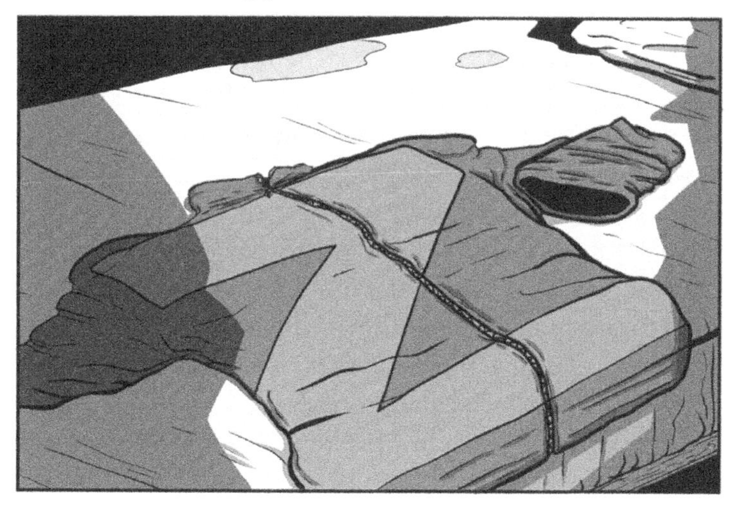

warm in whatever harsh conditions he faced. The pilgrim pulled the hood over his thick dark hair, shadowing his weathered olive face and deep-set tired blue eyes.

Exiting the bedroom, he trudged down the rickety flight of stairs to the lobby. Passing by the old front counter, he saw a registry of names–clients whom the whores had been partnered with on the last week of operation. He wondered how many lives had passed through here. For just a second, he pitied them. People were so easily persuaded and manipulated. The pilgrim wondered, if he had been born here, would he have been any different than they were? He imagined not. People were products of their environments and are viruses to the same world that created them.

Humans either destroy and corrupt their surroundings or use them for their own benefit and self-validation. Nothing more. Sure, they can accomplish wonders, but at what cost? How many great leaders of history have manipulated and abused their way to the top to achieve those wonders? What's the point of helping one's fellow man after crushing him on the way to the top? Self-validation. Lust for power. To create hierarchies so one can rise to the top only to turn around and pretend to help those he stepped on, is all a farce. And he knew he was no better. He had seen it firsthand in his own wickedness and was ready to be rid of it all. But he had one promise to keep. Maybe nothing mattered; perhaps it was all pointless, but he had to keep this promise to himself...and to *her*–Lynn.

He dreamed of his wife often, usually waking up in a cold sweat afterward, followed by an overwhelming sense of shame and guilt over what he'd done and for what he'd allowed himself to become. Perhaps that's all he ever was underneath it all. Of all the bridges he'd burned, that specific bridge had engulfed the one person he cared more about than anything or anyone else in this life. The flames from that bridge created a wildfire in his soul that never stopped burning, and it was swallowing him whole. He would make sure the bitch responsible would burn down with him. Regathering his thoughts, the pilgrim walked out the front door, knowing this was the end. He would not sleep again until death.

Making his way past a few broken-down buildings and an old cybernetic-pipeline leaking toxic fluid, he passed a dark alleyway and heard something that made his heart skip a beat.

"Greetings, Jonathan Young." Immediately he turned and pulled out the Capurro Cross, ready to use it as either a blunt object or a damning one. Jonathan Young. That was a name he had not heard in almost four years. No one out here knew it belonged to him. His name was "Pilgrim" to everyone he encountered. It was even the name he now gave himself in his own thoughts. No one this deep in The Grey asked for his true name, and he never gave it.

As he peered down the long, dark alleyway, he saw nothing.

*Great. That's just what I need right now. Some disappearing alleyway freak who knows my name*, he thought to himself. He took a few steps forward into the alley. He had to know who this was and how they knew him. He hadn't come this far to let his plan be thwarted.

"I believe you are facing the wrong direction," said the deep, smooth voice that was now behind him. The pilgrim knew his only option was to attack blindly. He jumped, turning mid-air with the point of the Cross aimed at the stranger's head. He didn't hesitate. But as he lunged the Cross forward, a long wooden staff intervened, smacking the cross from the pilgrim's hand. In the blink of an eye, the pilgrim found himself held in mid-air by the mightiest grip he'd ever felt. Somehow, it wasn't choking him; it was simply securing him at a distance, unnaturally far from the stranger's body. As he grabbed the stranger's wrist to attempt to break the hold, he felt himself freeze in place. He couldn't move. All he could do was stare downward into the piercing, emerald eyes of the stranger who held him.

"I do not wish to fight you, Jonathan Young, and I mean you no harm. I only wish to talk." The deep voice was audible, but Jonathan also swore he heard it in his head. What was going on here? Who was this man?

The stranger released his hold on Jonathan, and he immediately regained movement. His reflexes kicked in, and he landed on one knee, looking up at the midnight-skinned man with white twisted locks and beard who was blocking the pilgrim's exit. He leaned on a pale wooden staff in front of him. The man was cloaked in what appeared to be a combination of grayish-black feathers and fur. Jonathan noted that he'd never seen that texture before. Still kneeling, the pilgrim stared sternly into those green eyes and barked the question,

"How do you know me?" He then stood and was surprisingly much taller than the man who just handled him like a ragdoll.

"That is of little importance at the moment. What matters is what you are planning to accomplish here today."

"Look, as much as I appreciate you, ya know, not choking me to death, I'm gonna need a little more from you before we have a bonding moment about something that's entirely none of your business. I've been waiting for this day for quite some time and–

"Six years, to be exact." The stranger interrupted.

"*How* in the...what are you? Some sort of clairvoyant or something??"

"Something." The stranger said with a smirk.

"Look, I don't have time for these games, so you can either say what you need to say to me or get the fuck out of my way before I *make* you." Jonathan's anger now outweighed his curiosity. He bent down and picked up the Cross, ready to use it if he had to.

"Very well. If you face her now, they will all die. And so will you. All that has happened to you will be for nothing. You know this place doesn't have much longer; these people will destroy themselves if they stay under her curse."

"You want me to try and *save* these trash humans? The very same ones who did their best to end me when I first arrived?" Jonathan laughed cynically. "You're a Yeshuite priest, aren't you? I *knew* those tribal pissants would send someone after me. Even the greatest evil in The Grey can't be killed, according to you people, eh? And this *curse* you talk about? They willingly stepped into it, and they're getting what they deserve."

"No human is innocent. But it is not your duty to decide who deserves life or death. There is a Darkness growing that is much larger than this place and these devils." The stranger warned.

At that, Jonathan leaned in.

"I don't care. I've devoted my life to fighting this shit, and all it's given me in return is pain. So, I'm taking *this*..." the pilgrim held up the cross. "...and I'm going to *use* it one last time for *me*."

"Do you *really* think that is going to defeat her?"

"*This* is the Capurro Cross. It's one of the most powerful relics in the world and dates back to before The Final War. Being a devoted *follower of the Yeshuite God,* I'm sure you've heard of it. It has exorcized countless spirits and demons, and if it can't do the trick, I don't know what can. You've delivered your super cryptic warning. Now get the fuck out of my way."

The stranger sighed deeply and took a long look at the man before him. Jonathan Young was right. This life had brought him much pain, more than he remembered, in fact. The stranger sympathized with that. He had also known much pain and sacrifice while fighting for a cause greater than himself. He also knew that it may be too late for this man. The pilgrim's heart was filled with hatred and Darkness, sculpted by years of external pain and poor decisions.

Decisions. That's what it all came down to. Decisions across the seen and unseen realms had led them all here. And if Jonathan Young's decisions had already solidified his soul, then there was no going back. This deeply disturbed the stranger, for he knew what that could mean. But he had to adhere to the Law of Choice.

"You seem quite certain of yourself, Jonathan Young. May peace be with you." With that, he stepped aside, allowing the pilgrim to pass. Jonathan glared at him for a moment, still boiling with rage.

"I doubt it will." He stalked past the stranger and out of the alleyway, turned right and was back on the path he initially pursued.

# CHAPTER FOUR

## -THE ARRIVAL-

"All will kneel before Mistress Etrulia!!" As the Dark Sister's chief priest and personal guard, Zoric had been loyal to her since the beginning. He was rumored to have been a godborn, standing almost eight feet tall with a broad, robust build. He, like the rest, was painted with the ceremonial mask. His thick black hair was long and held up on his head by the aged skull of an infant. His shoulders and torso were covered in a fur shield vest revealing bulging biceps. Under the fur, and flowing down to his feet, was a custom Saturnalia robe. He was an absolute terror that no one dared to cross.

Zoric was conceived in the High Tower of the Bard Village during a ritualistic Beltane Orgia Ceremony dedicated to The Oak King. All three of the High Sisters of Endor–the high priestesses of The Coven–were involved in this ritual with multiple sorcerers, priests, and the Tellyard Bard concubines. He was birthed from High Sister Agatha, but the earthly father was unknown. His godborn father was said to be an Endorian god who had possessed one of the priests before ejaculation. The people didn't know *which* Endorian god claimed him, but everyone suspected Baphomet as he claimed authority in the unseen realm in this place. Rarely was a child born this way, so Zoric was treated as an unholy prince by the villagers and the High Sisters.

Etrulia had been gone for almost the entire rain season, and in her absence, chaos was the norm, but her return would likely not bring much order to the Village. Some rejoiced in this mayhem, while others were terrified. Either way, they all had to bow the knee or suffer torture and death.

The Bard Village was surrounded by solidified sand dunes that completely wrapped around its border. No one passing by would know of its existence, and the Dark Magick protected the Bard from being seen by skycabs from above.

From the exit of the Tellyard Bard tavern, the Village gradually declined through districts of small huts and houses.

Further down—gated off from the rest of the Village—was the Temple District, housing worship halls for each wilderness god of Endor. This district also housed the priests, who were rarely seen outside of the rituals and ceremonial masses. Below that, was the High Tower District. Other than when the villagers were marched through the district to reach the Lichgate, it was reserved for the sorcerers, priests, and the High Sisters, and their *guests.* Although it was at the bottom of the decline, the High Tower was the highest point, overshadowing the rest of the Village. It stretched almost as tall as the solidified dunes.

On the far side of the gigantic tower was the Lichgate itself; a mighty iron wall opening up to the ceremonial grounds where main rituals and sacrifices took place. This area was a large open plain, patchy with grass, sand, and cobblestone. A small forest, with a river flowing through it, surrounded the ritual grounds and reached all the way out to the base of the towering dunes. The forest was a place no one was ever permitted to traverse without the High Sisters. There were whispers that deep within the forest lay a stone altar that acted as a doorway to a secret realm. But no one knew the truth, for no one but the High Sisters ever returned.

It was in the ritual plain outside of the Lichgate, where the entire Village now gathered. Sorcerers monitored the crowd, noting any villagers absent, while priests gathered in front, behind Zoric, facing the forest.

*"Hail Mistress Etrulia!!"* Zoric's shouts were thunder to the ears of the crowd as they were compelled to repeat after him.

*"Hail!! Hail!! Hail!!!!"* they cried.

From the blackness of the forest, Etrulia emerged, arms outstretched in her Saturnalian robes, jet-black lips grinning twistedly against her white-painted mask. Her hair was still matted and unwashed, and the ritual bone points protruded from the back and top of her head like a malevolent crown. She cackled a haunting, wheezy laugh.

"My pets! How sweet of you to greet me like this! How I have missed your warm welcomes," she lied. She hated these people as much as they hated her. The ones loyal to her were so out of a desire for power rather than love or emotional attachment.

In turn she only desired their loyalty as a means of control. It was this control Etrulia thirsted for more than anything else. The Coven promised her this control long ago, and it unequivocally delivered. While Agatha and Annis were off, Dark Father knew where, fulfilling other Dark Eschaton prophecies, she was *here.* She was ruler. She was God.

Zoric walked up proudly, towering over her. If anyone *did* care for Etrulia, it was he.

"Mistress, the black altar has been prepared for your arrival. The opening feast will begin in one hour if you wish it to be so."

"Very good, Zoric." She caressed his painted cheek seductively. She knew his flesh waited for her that night. "I'm quite famished. What entertainment do we have planned for the opening ceremonies?"

"The Tellyard Bard whores will be performing, your Ungrace."

"Splendid." She smiled, and they both turned, walking toward the crowd side by side. "Let us pick one of them at random for ritual slaughter. That should liven things up a bit, don't you think? Get everyone in the mood for the Purging Ceremony?"

"It shall be done." he replied, showing no emotion toward the heinous act he was commanded to carry out.

"The Necronomicon has been adequately prepared, I take it?" she enquired, ready to deal out harsh punishment if the answer was anything but yes.

"Oh yes. And she's been enlightened by Corchak and

and Tolmund. They are our best sorcerers now."

"What of Ioana and Lorka?" Etrulia asked. She was surprised to hear they were no longer at the top of the Craft.

"Corchak and Tolmund challenged them to a witch's duel and were victorious over them. By law, we removed them from this realm." Zoric informed her ominously. She guffawed.

"Excellent! A little spirited competition keeps the Bard Village on its toes."

They stopped at the front of the crowd. Zoric turned towards her so only she could hear.

"Your Ungrace, there has been a disturbance of late. The foreigner is in our midst. He caused quite a mess at the tavern three..."

She pressed her grey finger upon his lips gently, silencing him. He looked down at her eyes in confusion.

"Silence, my pet. I am aware of such things." His confusion turned to awe. He was amazed with how in tune she was with the gods of Endor. How he wished to have that same connection with them—with the one who would call him "son." He longed for that connection almost as much as he desired Etrulia.

She removed her finger and walked two paces forward as he turned to the crowd. The villagers were silent, in anticipation and terror. She could say, *"let us feast"* or *"feast on the flesh of your neighbor,"* and by Endorian law they were bound to carry out her wishes.

"Normally, at this time, I would lead us in an altar sacrifice of blood and stone. However, this solstice, there's someone *special* in our midst." They winced at her chilling smile. What did she mean? *Who* did she mean? There was talk of a stranger in their midst who killed a gatekeeper at the tavern, but that was all they'd heard. How did that make him special?

"I know you're here, Jonathan. I can sense your anger. It is overwhelming and refreshing. How long has it been? Six years? More? Time does fly, as they say. And I must say that your anger is much more satisfying than fear, which *constantly* surrounds me. Won't you come out and see me?"

She was baiting him. He knew it. With his hood up, no one knew he didn't have the mask painted on his face. Some of their robes resembled his cloak, so he blended in perfectly, yet she knew he was there. This was it. He knew she would keep everyone standing here until the end of time until he made his move.

While making his plan of attack in the abandoned brothel, he thought of sneaking into Etrulia's bed chambers in the High Tower and waiting for her to arrive. But he knew she was more cunning than any foe he had ever faced. Her link to the Darkness was powerful. He decided he had a better chance of surprise if he hid amongst the crowd until an opportune moment. However, it seemed her powers were more advanced than he thought, destroying his element of surprise. He was caught off guard but had to make his move.

"Here I am, witch." He projected his voice from the midst of the crowd. Jonathan began slowly shoving villagers out of his way as he made a path forward. Zoric began to intervene, but the Sister held her hand up to stay him.

"Ah! *There* you are. I wondered when I would be seeing you again."

His arms were tucked away in his cloak, hiding the bottle of holy water he held in his hand. He passed in front of the crowd and was now within ten feet of the monster he had been pursuing for over half a decade. Etrulia had caused more pain in his life than anyone ever had. She had torn his world apart and destroyed his soul and the souls of those he loved. He thought he'd feel something more substantial at this moment. A sense of relief or overwhelming rage. Something. But mostly, he felt numb. Right now, she was nothing more than a box on a checklist for what he hoped was the last day of life.

"Well, well." She beamed hideously. "You *have* traveled far, Jonathan. I'm flattered." She hissed with a dark giggle.

"Don't be." He threw the holy water from the bottle directly onto her face. Steam billowed from her flesh as the water sizzled like acid, and she howled in agony. The scream was something out of a nightmare, resembling a herd of boars being butchered alive. She fell to the ground shrieking while thick, rancid steam surrounded her.

Zoric leapt into action. He moved inhumanly fast as he backhanded Jonathan, sending the pilgrim soaring through the air, his cloak flying off. Jonathan landed hard on the sandy grass of the plain. He grunted but quickly bounced up and spun around, facing the mountain of a man now barreling toward him.

"Now you die, foreign swine!" Zoric growled as he lunged at the pilgrim. He no longer cared what his Mistress had in store for the foreigner. Jonathan parried and leapt sideways to dodge his attacker. He had faced godborns before, assuming that's what this behemoth was. Their skin was notoriously thicker than most, but it wasn't invulnerable. With enough force, a sharp stone could penetrate it.

Zoric rushed the pilgrim again at top speed and landed a solid blow across his face. Jonathan felt blinding hot pain as he slammed to the ground, blood flowing from his mouth like a violent fountain. He expected half his teeth to be in the mud but didn't have time to check.

He was surprised his jaw wasn't broken. Zoric leapt on top of him and grabbed Jonathan's throat, surrounding it with one massive calloused hand. The godborn's other fist reared back, preparing for a final blow.

*This would be a good death,* the pilgrim thought to himself. He had lived much longer in the hellscape of The Grey than he ever expected and was able to permanently scar Etrulia, The High Sister of Endor. She would never forget that *he* was the one who maimed her pride, getting close enough to deliver a potentially lethal blow. But that was just it. The blow wasn't lethal. It was permanent for sure, but it wasn't the end of her. That's what he came all this way to do, and he wouldn't let some mouth-breathing godborn stop him from reaching his final goal.

Somehow muscling through the massive weight of Zoric, Jonathan grabbed the Capurro Cross from his belt. With a roar of anger and adrenaline, he shoved its pointed end into the godborn's neck just above the collar bone, twisted, and sliced to the left, severing arteries. Thick, black blood gushed out of the behemoth. Jonathan almost gagged from the smell of rotten meat as blood splashed on his chest and beard. Zoric froze in shock, and his grip on the pilgrim's neck immediately loosened as he fell on his back, limbs flailing. He attempted to let out a howl, but the blood bubbling from the wound strangled any sound.

The crowd—even those loyal to Etrulia—were terrified. This man had beaten Etrulia's giant. He had single-handedly destroyed their godborn judge. No additional would-be attacker would dare approach the pilgrim now, and Jonathan knew that. The pilgrim staggered to his feet, his eyes searching for the witch. She still crouched, whimpering on the ground in a cloud of dissipating smoke. Jonathan's only thought was to destroy her no matter the cost.

*No matter the cost*, he thought to himself as he approached this monstrous woman who had ruined the life he once held so dear.

"Alright, witch. This ends now," he panted. He thrust the Capurro Cross in front of him and boldly shouted, "Christus Victor!!"

Nothing happened.

A cackle pierced the silence.

"Yesssssss," her voice slithered, "this *does* end now!!!" Etrulia erupted from her knees in a twitching motion and grabbed the Capurro Cross that Jonathan gripped in his hand. In disbelief, he gazed into the blistered, mangled face of the demonic Sister, laughing before him. She let out a monstrous howl, and then a guttural language echoed from her mouth throughout the village.

*"Ahornah n'ghft ah'n'gha legethog r'luhhor!!"* The Cross became blazingly hot and began to melt in her claw-like fingers before finally bursting into flames. In shock, Jonathan dropped the blazing relic to the ground.

How was this possible? How did the relic fail him? His panicked thoughts tried to make sense of what was happening. Etrulia let out a deafening shriek as reddish-black necroplasmic energy spewed out of her putrid mouth, blasting Jonathan in the chest and sending him sprawling fifteen yards. Pain blinded him. He had seen necroplasmic energy used as a conjuring spell to manipulate other objects or people but never as a direct weapon like this. The pain was unbearable. His insides were on fire as he writhed on the ground. He could feel consciousness slipping away.

"You're so pathetic, Jonathan." Etrulia mocked him as she drew closer. Her eyes had rolled back inside her head, the whites now glowing a bright yellow. Her tribal makeup was smeared and splotched by her encounter with the holy water. Her blisters were already starting to pop and ooze blood and pus down her wickedly smiling face.

"I can feel your fear growing now. Your guilt is overwhelming. You came so far only to fail your pathetic family. I guess that's what you're best at, aren't you? Oh, so full of shame over what you've done to them." With that, she twisted her gnarled left hand as necroplasmic energy began pulsating around her fingers and long, claw-like nails, controlling his every move. She'd grown much more powerful since the last time they met.

"Come here and kneel before me, my pet," she hissed. Jonathan felt his body rising and moving against his will. His limbs were utterly limp, his feet dragging through the sandy grass toward this High Sister of Endor. As she quickly dropped her necroplasm-drenched hand, Jonathan slammed onto his knees in front of her. Etrulia sauntered around to his back, bent down, and caressed the side of his cheek. As she began running her fingers through his beard, her touch both disgusted and aroused him.

"Now," she whispered. "Let's finish what we started oh so long ago."

She snatched the hair on top of his head with her left hand. He had no power to stop her. At this point, he knew whatever she had planned was going to happen. Necroplasmic energy began oozing out of Etrulia's forearm. It traveled down her wrist and slithered around her fingertips. The energy dug into Jonathan's skull, exposing his mind, his thoughts, his past; everything was now Etrulia's for the taking. If there was a God, Jonathan knew that entity had abandoned him long ago, but if it had any mercy, he pleaded silently for it now. The High Sister leaned in close behind his right ear, allowing her tongue to slide along its outer rim, and then purred in a twistedly gleeful tone,

"Now...let your true form *awaken.*" Jonathan's eyes rolled back in his head. His mission, everything he had set out to accomplish over the last six years, disappeared in the bright green glow beaming from his eyes.

# PART TWO

## THE AWAKENING

TWENTY-FIVE YEARS EARLIER…

# CHAPTER FIVE

## -VISIONS IN THE DARK-

*"Now...let your true form awaken."*

Past the Astral Fields and the snowy kingdom of Northstar, the words echoed through space and time. Moriel–Chief Messenger of The Order of Michael–felt them wash over his admiral blue outstretched wings like an antenna receiving a message from a long-lost origin. The elohim closed his glowing cerulean eyes and inhaled deeply to take in this new information.

Moriel was striking to behold. A single pair of wings protruded from his temples and reached toward the heavens above. Instead of a nasal cavity, a dense protrusion led down to his mouth, which housed sharp canines. Below his mouth, he had a featherfur-covered jawline that creased and curved downward to form an elaborate, mighty featherbeard reaching his light rune-covered chest. Underneath the flowing, cobalt cloak that flooded the forming star he knelt upon, Moriel's robe pulsated with Light, a Light that gave him life and power.

The mysterious phrase that came upon him so suddenly absorbed into Moriel, haunting him. He knew not of its origin but sensed its urgent weightiness nonetheless. He imagined this marked his respite's conclusion in the Expanding Rim of Creation's End. This ever-changing sanctuary was always kind to him. The birthing of stars and bright constellations brought him peace and quiet from the ongoing war that had raged for millennia. These moments of tranquility were precious because they were rare, especially in this Age, which had lasted longer than anyone had ever expected.

For many, the Age of a Thousand Suns was not a measurement of Adamian time, since it had been more than a millennium since the Age began. Some elohimic beings believed it to be a precursor to the Dark Prophecy called "Age End", while others thought it *was* a measurement of time, sparked by a Tzoharian Nexus–fixed points

throughout time. It remained a mystery, even to the wisest Seraphim of The Adunalar Elohim, Yahweh's Divine Council.

Moriel did not concern himself with the complex meaning of this Age of the cosmos. He was a Power of the Heavens, Chief Messenger of The Order of Michael, a son of the Septum Dei–and he understood that wiser elohim had been lost to madness while trying to decrypt its meaning. He knew this Age brought a new covenant with the Adamians, a new promise of atonement that was ransomed in blood, heralding the end of the division between all Adamians and the King. It was a promise of freedom from The Dark Kingdom, if only they would choose it.

Some say the war raged ever more fiercely since that atoning ransom was made. The Dark Kingdom had a fire lit under them in ways never seen before. Many thought it was because they knew they had lost, while others believed The Dark Kingdom had a secret upper hand, hidden in the shadows, waiting patiently to be revealed.

Moriel was ever loyal to his King. Over time, he had only known love, compassion, and perfect leadership from the one who spoke everything into being. The King had been more patient with the Adamians than Moriel could ever imagine, for they had aligned themselves with The Dark Kingdom time and time again. They even cursed their own bloodline to gain power, damning their souls and the souls of their descendants in the process. Moriel dwelt on this extensively during his sabbatical from the war, and in this time of meditation, his compassion towards the Adamians had grown exponentially.

The Chief Messenger wasn't surprised by this growth of emotional empathy. He dared not dwell on such things without intentionally aligning his motives with the Spirit of the King. Moriel knew too many elohim who had fallen to the Dark through their hatred for the Adamian race and the King's devotion to the "dust creatures" they so loathed. Even his dear sister had fallen long ago, before Babylon built its Necrogate Tower and the accursed Nephilim plagued the ancient lands of Mesopotamia.

He imagined that along with it being a time of growth for his soul, this respite was also meant to prepare him for his next assignment. It seemed that assignment had begun with the haunting words that now flowed inside his mind.

*"Now...let your true form awaken."* He heard the words as though they were being said right before him. However, the voice uttering this phrase was new to him, which confirmed that it could not have been an elohim, Dark or Light. Neither was it a living, prominent Adamian in league with the Dark. This message was clearly something from the future. Something beyond the Time Order's power, meaning it was more than likely attached to a Tzoharian Nexus and needed his undivided attention. With his eyes still closed, Moriel reached out into the realms with his astral senses to connect with his King, taking care not to draw the attention of something sinister.

He was most vulnerable when exploring a potential Vision, for even a being as mighty as he could be struck down or spirited away while in the astral state.

"Moriel..." He felt the voice before he heard it. Joy and calm washed over him, a peace beyond understanding. "...be mindful of what you see." The Spirit of the King was with him now. He was safe.

However, as the Messenger opened his eyes to the Vision, he beheld a horror beyond all his wildest experiences. Everything was covered in a blood-red mist. The sky dripped a scarlet, nightmarish foreboding upon everything Moriel saw. He was standing in what could have only been the Central Grand Republic Capitol of New Paris in the Corporeum Realm, although he hardly recognized it. The Peace Tower–the home of the Grand Chancellor, built on top of what was formerly known as the Eiffel Tower in the Old World–was covered entirely in the cyclopean masonry of The Dark Kingdom.

Necroplasmic ooze dripped between each stone and formed its own architectural growth that protruded outward, giving way to massive–almost transparent–scarlet stone structures acting as extensions to the Tower itself. Moriel knew this type of stonework all too well–the ancient masonry of R'lyeh and the Elder Children–but never had he seen it manipulated in such a way in Corporeum.

As the Messenger's eyes continued to investigate his surroundings, something even more horrifying revealed itself. A *new* Aeternum Stone had been forged! It was engulfing all things in sight instead of giving off Light and life, as the Stones were meant to. It wasn't just dark in appearance like the Necrom Stone of Darkness; it was anti-Light.

The Twelve Aeternum Stones were responsible for all known life, as they were the very DNA of The Cosmic Wheel. The Stones were the first instruments the King had formed; tools he used in creation, and there were *only* twelve. No more, no less.

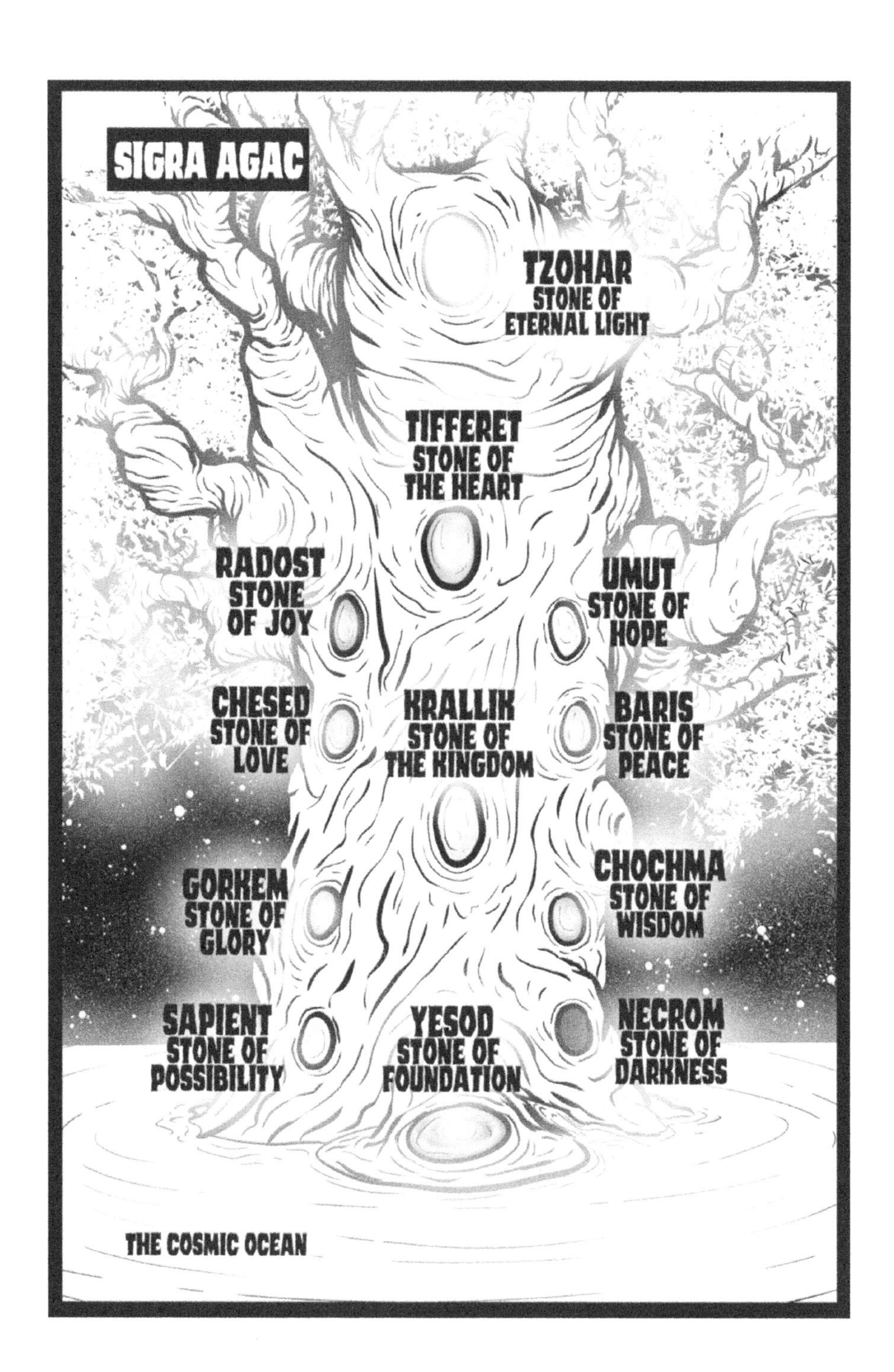
SIGRA AGAC
TZOHAR
STONE OF
ETERNAL LIGHT
TIFFERET
STONE OF
THE HEART
RADOST
STONE
OF JOY
UMUT
STONE OF
HOPE
CHESED
STONE OF
LOVE
KRALLIK
STONE OF
THE KINGDOM
BARIS
STONE OF
PEACE
GORKEM
STONE OF
GLORY
CHOCHMA
STONE OF
WISDOM
SAPIENT
STONE OF
POSSIBILITY
YESOD
STONE OF
FOUNDATION
NECROM
STONE OF
DARKNESS
THE COSMIC OCEAN

Yet somehow, not only had this new *wicked* Aeternum Stone been brought to life, but it had taken over the order of The Cosmic Wheel; replacing the Cosmic Laws with chaotic ones.

*How could this be possible*, he wondered? Aeternum Stones had been corrupted, broken, and scattered, but a new one had not been formed since before the Adamians walked the earth. To his knowledge, the only being who possessed the power to do so was the one showing him this Vision now. What did it all mean?

Gazing across the horizon of the city, Moriel saw multiple buildings with similar sinister additions as The Peace Tower, but as the scarlet mist cleared for a moment his eyes widened in awe and terror. Massive shadowsteel gates almost as tall as the tower itself loomed over the entire city. His gaze continued past the top of the gates and beheld an enormous stone fortress domed with the blackness of this new horrifying Aeternum Stone. Moriel closed his eyes and slowed his breathing, attempting to steady his mind and collect his senses. He was being shown something baffling. It was so rare for a Vision this wicked and profound to be delivered to a solitary angel, and it was imperative that he pay attention.

*Remember, you can't be seen or heard. So, gather it all in. This may be the most crucial moment of your life*, Moriel reminded himself. As he began to walk forward, the oozing black mud squished and slid below his taloned feet. This place was worse than any nightmare the Oneiroi had ever created. Hopelessness invaded the Messenger's emotions with every breath he took as he trudged

through the streets, observing the horrors of this alternate, necronomic New Paris.

Monstrous beasts roamed freely while creatures from all the Sheolic worlds were either being hunted or were hunting each other. The souls of the dead were being paraded through the streets on chains by their bestial enslavers, but the one race he had not yet seen—alive, at least—was the one race that called this planet its home. Where were the Adamians?

After traversing this land of Darkness for hours, Moriel's Spirit-led intuition strongly urged him to turn left after passing the next ghoulish structure. Upon obeying that urge, he understood where he was being led. Straight ahead lay the long winding stone staircase that brought him to the shadowsteel gates. Moriel knew that his purpose for being here was whatever awaited him behind those horrible iron spikes.

His nerves made him queasy, and his anxiety increased with every step of this unholy path. Finally, Moriel came to the plateau at the base of the grand staircase which led directly to the gate. There stood two Stewards—Dark sorcerers—at the bottom of the stairs, with their robed, leathery charcoal bodies. Multiple glowing red eyes covered their conoidal horned heads and they held spears made from

Necrom Shards—pieces of the Aeternum Stone of Darkness. This type of weaponry hadn't been seen since the Age of Rodinia. That was well before the first humans existed or received the breath of Ruakh–tzoharian sentient life. Even then, it was scarcely seen. But here, he saw Necromic weaponry in abundance.

When he first saw the Stewards, Moriel almost created an obu of Light to annihilate them, but then remembered he was in a Vision and calmed himself. Sometimes it was easy to forget, it all seemed so vividly real. The Messenger uncomfortably walked past the Stewards who stared blankly ahead, making no sound nor acknowledging the elohim of Light. Moriel began his final ascent, and that was when he heard the screams.

"PLEASE!! DON'T!!"

Moriel sprinted up the stairs. He subconsciously knew that he could do nothing to prevent whatever caused this pain and suffering, but he couldn't help himself. He reached the top and ran straight through the gates like a transparent specter. The screaming continued in the darkness of this foreboding atrium as he slowed his pace, gathering his thoughts and looking around. In the distance, large pillars stood silhouetted by what he assumed was a pit of fire below on the other side.

*"Please!* You...you don't have to do this!!" The pleading voice belonged to a female Adamian—the first living Adamian he'd seen. As Moriel reached one of the stone pillars and leaned against it, he peered at a colosseum filled with shrieking demons and cheering devils of The Dark Kingdom. However, their cheers and jaunts were

currently muted by the Vision. The woman's cries were the only thing the Messenger could hear.

"No..." Moriel gasped aloud. Below him was a deep, oval-shaped arena, clearly used for Dark rituals such as Undertaking, Merging, torturing, and ultimately, The Black Mass. However, not since The Watchers walked the Earth had he seen such a spectacle.

A woman was chained–naked–to two stone torches about five feet high with blazing flames emerging from their tops. Her arms were outstretched, and she had been savagely beaten. Her flesh was covered in bruises, cuts, and blood. Tears ran down her face as she continued to plead in desperation.

Behind her, towered a grotesque abomination with dark red leathery skin, covered in boils and matted, patchy fur. The being's glowing yellow, pupilless eyes–all six–illuminated the gnarled smile that loomed at least three feet over the top of the woman's light brown hair. One enormous vein-polluted arm draped across the woman's naked body, securing her for what would come next.

"Please...I beg you!!" Her final plea echoed throughout the arena with sorrow and helplessness. Then, the guttural, whispery voice of her judge responded.

"You spent *years* fighting against The Dark Father and our forces. You dedicated your life to preventing our arrival, and now you must be punished."

Moriel's attention was drawn by the ominous voice to the figure draped in shadow on the far side of the arena. He was elevated on a stone throne covered in skulls missing their lower jaws. As he arose from the unholy seat, his eyes illuminated red, piercing the shadows.

"Balhazar will show you the pleasures of our punishments here in this new world." At that, the figure who was speaking, emerged from the shadows. He was a tall, well-built man draped in a scarlet featherfur cloak exposing his pale olive-toned skin under it. A copper crown topped his unwashed, matted white hair. Scars covered his face and disappeared into a horribly unkempt, ghostly white beard.

But it was what the man wore around his neck that caught Moriel's attention: the Capurro Cross, or what was left of it. The Cross was known to all elohim of the Heavenly Host as it had been a powerful weapon against The Dark Kingdom for thousands of Adamian years. Although Moriel didn't know where it was currently located, he knew it was still intact, as opposed to what he was seeing around this man-king's neck.

*Manking*...Moriel thought. *No...it can't be.* His horror grew tremendously as he gazed at the red-eyed man who continued to speak.

*"You,* my dear, will be the first bride of many. With that honor, you will be reserved for my Princes, and you will have the *pleasure* of all who wish to take your flesh and use it to produce their offspring."

"*No...*" Moriel gasped.

"Once more, the Nephilim will walk the Earth, and the path to our enemy's complete destruction will be complete." The red-eyed man smiled wickedly at the sobbing woman, then he addressed the devil behind her. "Balhazar, taste and see."

"Oh God!! Oh no!!" She screamed as the deep, grotesque voice of Balhazar whispered in her ear.

"Your God has abandoned you, dust creature. We are all that's left." He then mounted the woman from behind, planting his abominable seed deep within her, and her screams were suddenly drowned out by the roaring hoard that filled the colosseum as legions of devils chanted.

*"Praise the Dark Father!! Praise The Master!! Praise The Dark Kingdom!!!"* Moriel couldn't believe what he was seeing. Age End. It was right in front of him. He thought this outlandish prophecy was just Dark propaganda from the enemy. But it was here, staring him in the face. Moriel's emotions ran wild. Rage filled him as the

abomination, Balhazar, took the screaming woman as his own while the red-eyed man cackled in approval and the demonic hoard cheered. The Messenger couldn't bear it any longer and let out a mighty shout of anguish.

**"NOOOOOOOOOOOO!!!"**

Light broke through Moriel's chest, flooding the colosseum with his boiling, righteous anger. His voice echoed through the cosmos, a cry of rage, fear, and defiance against what he had just witnessed. The Light surrounded him, whirling about him like a mighty thunderstorm. All he could hear was the echoing of his own screams until, breaking through the Light, were flashes–glimpses of horror. Then came the haunting psalm of the horrifying Dark prophecy: Age End.

"Look deep into the Darkness.
Let all Light dissipate as the sun
Dissolves into the angry red sky!"

He saw Adamians being crushed by the weight of the realms collapsing upon themselves. Gravity was being rewritten. The pre-ordained laws of creation were being undone. Mountains were crumbling. The Old Ones were breaking through the veil once more as creatures from all of Sheol were pouring into the same space, violently merging with one another as they collided.

"Let the hour of The Black Sun commence,
And usher in the Millennium's demise!"

He saw Earth being engulfed by an enormous, Genzarian creature of old. At the same time, millions of the Host of the Heavens were rocketing toward the planet, desperately trying to reach it before the shadow swallowed it whole.

"Gaze upon a new beginning!"

He saw a black, twisted tree, its thick body filled with Nephilim souls. The trunk opened, and from Pandemonium's fiery depths, Khata emerged in physical form. His pale face was covered in a black iron crown with the Evil Eye of fire blazing into the darkness. He carried "Deccal," the cursed blade of Azazel, and struck the seal of Dudael, freeing the cursed elohim from the pit.

"Let the Watchers be released
And bring forth *Age End!!*"

Finally, Moriel saw him. The one whose voice was shouting from the Thrones of Fire in the Gnashing Kingdom of Pandemonium. A lone figure stood before the Messenger, engulfed in flame. The only feature Moriel could see was a mangled and rotting skull whose lower jaw had been ripped from its home long ago. On top of its head sat a copper crown, and the creature reared back, letting out a vile howl of laughter, striking fear deep into Moriel's being. He couldn't escape its gaze. He couldn't move. This being was victorious over all things. He was King. He was Master. He was–

Moriel gasped for air, fighting overwhelming anxiety, as he found himself back at Creation's End. The peace of the ever-expanding cosmos was still there. Order was still there. Chaos no longer ruled his senses; beauty surrounded the Messenger instead of Darkness. The King's presence flooded him with peace and Moriel sobbed, collapsing on the forming star and directly into the arms of Yahweh, the King of Ages.

Moriel looked up into the eyes of his King. It still surprised him sometimes that this being of Endless Light and Eternal Power had become an Adamian. He raised Moriel to his feet and stared at him with deep brown eyes.

"Peace, Moriel. You're safe, old friend." The voice was soft yet strong, and the accent still had a slight flavor of the Second Temple Age of Nazareth. Moriel gazed at his King in awe as his anxiety and fear faded. Being in his presence was like sitting in the White Throne itself. The Light emanating from him should have been blinding, but instead, it was welcoming and warm. The King's thick beard and pulled-back hair were the purest white Moriel had ever seen. His skin was a deep brown, looking as if it had been freshly kissed by the brightest sun in the cosmos. He wore a flowing white cloak trimmed in gold, covering a golden breastplate with the Tetragrammaton–the Sign of the King–in the center. Under the breastplate was a white robe with gold vambraces at the forearms etched with diamond runes.

As tears formed in his eyes, Moriel started to question what he had just seen and why *he* was the one to see it, but the King spoke first.

"What you have seen is very real and quite dangerous. Go to Michael at Sof Haderech and tell him of this Vision. He will give you and the one who will meet you there the instructions you need. A dire road is ahead, but you will not walk it alone. Say nothing of what you've seen to anyone else. I wish I could say more, but this path is now yours to take. Shine in the Darkness, my friend." And with that, Moriel found himself alone on the forming star once again as tears rolled down his featherfur cheeks.

The King rarely appeared before a Messenger like that, and something this grave would usually have been shown directly to The Adunalar Elohim, not an isolated Power. And to keep it a secret? It was evident to Moriel, Chief Messenger of The Order of Michael, that this was the most urgent message anyone had ever been given since Gabriel heralded the coming of the Christ; and he was instructed to not tell a soul. Why him? What did all this mean? Michael knew some of those answers or at least the next step. Moriel gathered himself, wiped the tears away, and rocketed off the star and into the depths of space.

# CHAPTER SIX

## - LITTLE BOY BLUE -

The boy landed hard as he hit the cold, gangrenous ground. Looking ahead, he saw nothing but a vast wasteland of corrupted desert, dripping with a mysterious black ooze he had never seen before. Behind him, an enormous sprawling stone structure stretched as far as the eye could see. Panic began to overtake him. He remembered nothing. His identity and everything else he knew was entirely forgotten. A trickle of blood fell from his lip as his breath swirled into vapors and disappeared into the Dark sky above.

As he slowly and painfully rose to his feet, the necroplasmic ground stuck to him and snapped back quickly, leaving a putrid residue on his olive-toned skin. Moving forward, he heard nothing but his own trudging footsteps. There was no sound of the wind, no rustling in the distance, no birds in the air; nothing but the pounding of his quickening heartbeat and his short, shallow breaths. What led him here? Where was this place? No matter how hard he tried, he couldn't remember. It was as if something had slithered inside his mind and stolen everything.

Sensing a change behind him he suddenly turned to see an enormous, swamp-like forest, just ten paces behind. It seemed to have appeared from nowhere. As he turned back around there was nothing but total blackness, a void that offered no hope or memory. All he now knew was this haunting bayou engulfed in a terrifyingly putrid green fog.

"Please! Please remember something," he pleaded out loud to himself. The boy didn't know much, but he knew he wouldn't last long if his mind was lost, which he was sure was happening. Having no other choice, he begrudgingly walked into the forest. He had to keep moving, for the child knew he wouldn't survive if *they* caught him.

The first one he saw was in the tree above. A short, stocky nightmare, staring at him blankly with piercing, bulbous, yellow eyes and a slightly opened mouth. Hair covered every trace of its numb, malevolent expression. Wolf-like ears came to a point behind long, gray horns protruding from its brow. Behind the ears was an extended set of sharp antlers. One set traveled outward from the side of its head and the other extended lower beside its jawline, overlapping its matted, dirty, dark brown mane. The creature was draped in torn, black rags. It's bony, leather-flesh hands held a long staff with yellow-green flames spilling from the top. Although it couldn't have been any taller than he was, its wickedly feral aura completely terrified the child.

The boy now somehow knew they had been watching him, following his every move for who knows how long since he'd found himself in this nightmare. Why hadn't they killed or tried to attack him yet? Every place the boy looked, they were either hanging from the barren branches of the trees or hiding behind the twisted trunks in the fog. Always staring, making no sound.

*I have to keep moving! Whatever those things are, I can't let them catch me!* he thought to himself as he started sprinting through the ghastly forest. The boy glanced ahead at the top of the trees and saw the stocky beasts hopping from tree to tree, their matted manes and black rags whipping in the wind. Their long silence broke as he now found himself surrounded by their monstrous and echoey laughter, reminiscent of howling coyotes. The forest seemed never-ending, and the green fog made it impossible to tell what direction he was going. No matter how fast he ran, those things seemed to be one step ahead of him.

The boy skidded to a stop as one of those hairy, horned beasts landed on the soft, slimy ground right in front of him. He looked on in horror as the thing tilted its head, gazing at him curiously. The yellow-eyed, blank expression transformed into a silent, hideous grin, revealing mangled, needle-point teeth. It lowered the blazing staff it carried to the tree's base, causing the green flame to engulf it completely.

Almost immediately, the entire forest erupted into flame. The boy assumed the other monsters followed this one's lead in setting fires. As he started to run again–feet burning and blistering with every step–he saw an opening ahead. He increased his speed but was cut off as a tree branch slammed into the putrid ground directly in front of him. Green and black muck splashed onto his face.

The branch hadn't fallen onto the forest floor; it had *grabbed* at the boy. The branch was still attached to the fiery birch, and the trunk of the tree now glared at him with a raging, emblazoned expression of hatred. The boy stepped back in awe as he gazed at the scorching forest before him. All the trees now had hateful faces with eyes of flame and charring bark forming sharp, pointed teeth. There was no escape; he was surrounded.

"Boy..."

He heard it, or at least he thought he did. It was faintly a whisper, but it got his attention and made him turn to his right.

"This way..."

He was positive he heard *that!* The voice led him to an opening in the flaming forest, not twenty yards ahead. He didn't think twice; he didn't have time. He was sure his feet were completely engulfed by now. The boy ran as fast as he could toward the opening, not knowing what lay ahead. But he knew if he stayed here, death would be certain. He reached the edge of the tree line and realized too late that the opening was the edge of a cliff. He couldn't stop in time and ran right off the edge, losing his balance and tumbling downward, spinning and flipping in the darkness. As he hit the soft, fleshy ground below, a shot of pain tore through the top of his spine. The boy screamed in agony.

Blood spurted from his mouth in clots as he coughed. His back burned with sizzling pain. He reached around to assess the damage. Something had torn his back wide open, and he felt his blood-drenched spine protruding through the wound. He screamed in agony and turned to look at the cliff behind him, trying to discover how far he had fallen and what had caused the damage.

What the boy saw made him forget about the pain entirely. Horror washed over him. The enormous side of the cliff was actually a giant, hideous face covered in dozens of eyes blazing with fiery hatred. The giant gnarled grin boomed with loathing pleasure.

"Join us!!" it bellowed. A large, blood-soaked talon extended from the cliff's side near its oversized mouth. The talon must have been the cause of the boy's excruciating wound.

*Oh God...where am I?* the boy thought as his eyes widened with tears. *Who am I?* He began to sob, unsure which pain was greater, his back or his soul. He looked up again at the top of the cliff.

One of those hairy *things* stood there, staring down at him, a wicked, victorious grin on its horrific face.

Then, as if on cue, a faint voice began to sing and all his pain faded.

"Little boy blue, come blow your horn..."

The distant voice sang. Music? Is that what it was called? The boy couldn't remember. Exhausted, he turned his face toward the sound. A lush green, grassy field lay between him and a far-off house. He knew this place somehow. The boy got up slowly, not even questioning how his body could still move after such an injury, and began walking through the tall grass. Its sweet texture embraced his feet and brought relief. There was no more black slime or flame. The nightmare seemed to be over, but how?

"...the sheep's in the meadow
And the cow's in the corn..."

He knew this voice. He knew this *song!!* He began running as fast as he could through the field. The house was a beautiful sight, familiar and full of hope—at least to him. In reality, the entire area was dead, and the house was constructed of rotting flesh.

"But where is the boy who looks after the sheep?"

The singing continued as the boy raced up the walkway, climbed the small stairs leading to the porch, and kicked the door in. For the first time since this nightmare started, the boy felt safe. The illusion he was seeing made the inside of the house just as he remembered. It was his home! He bounded up the beautifully crafted wood staircase, the rotting flesh sliding as he touched it.

"MOM!" He yelled in desperation. He remembered the voice now. Visions of her beautiful face flashed in his mind. Her dark curly hair, smelling freshly of a perm, and her deep brown eyes that squinted when she laughed made him feel safe. The boy reached the top of the staircase and bolted down the hallway to the last door on the right, where a green glow faintly shown between the door and its frame.

"He's under the haystack..."

The voice continued. The boy slammed the door open.

"Mom! I'm here!" He stopped just inside the room, staring at the silhouette of his mother looking out the window. He could see her curly hair and the light reflecting off her nightgown, but then the illusion melted away. He saw the rotting flesh covering the room, gray and green pus oozing from the walls. In horror he looked down, and saw the floor seizing his feet, and black slime slithering up his leg, holding him in place.

The boy lifted his eyes upward to see the figure turn from the window. The Vision of his beautiful mother was replaced by a nightmare standing before him. Glowing, green eyes peered at him from jet-black leathery brows. The monster's face twisted into a hideous grin, revealing luminous and powerfully sharp teeth glowing in the shadows of the corpse-like room. The creature spoke the final line in its whispered and disturbing voice.

"Fast asleep."

The boy's eyes filled with green fog, and he crumbled, unconscious, on the putrid floor.

Lightning pierced the sky as rain pounded the ground on the tree-filled campus of Hillcrest Sanitarium. Cleric Mattia Bajuma quickly exited her skycab and opened her umbrella as she splashed down the smooth concrete walkway toward The High Council's elite therapy center.

"One world. One unity," she yelled over the sound of the rain hitting her umbrella as she held her master holobadge up to the security monitor. The doors to the facility opened gracefully, and she walked in.

"Cleric Mattia! Joyous evening to you," smiled the Headminister of the Sanitarium. He wore thick, horn-rimmed glasses over his amber eyes which stood out against his pale peach skin. His full head of light brown hair was combed tightly to the side. He wore a stone blue robe and the bright medal ribands upon his left breast reflected his seniority in the building. They contrasted the bleakness of the off-white walls and desk surrounding him. Mattia passed the elegantly framed portrait of High Cleric Malcolm and strode toward the front desk, which sat against the wall framed by long hallways on either side.

"Joyous evening to you as well, Bouchard." She greeted the Headminister with an equally friendly smile, showing her almost perfect white teeth and ruby lips. Her green eyes were warm and welcoming, and her chocolate brown skin glowed with self-care. Mattia's hair was natural but kept shorter. It was less of a fuss getting ready in the mornings. Most men, including this one, noticed her full figure.

She wanted to present herself well, but not vain. She believed her clients deserved her best, which started with her own appearance. Many of them didn't care about how they looked, and she wanted to show that care for mental health can be found in every act of daily life, especially proper hygiene and dress code. Mattia leaned over the desk and raised a hopeful eyebrow at Bouchard.

"How is my favorite client this evening?" she questioned. Bouchard sighed, looked down at the monitor on his desk, and gave Mattia a disappointed look.

"Quiet as ever," he said gently. "He hasn't made a sound all day, I'm afraid. Same as yesterday and the day before that."

"I see." She immediately went from hopeful to discouraged. "Well, hopefully, I can change that soon." She gave a weak half-smile. "Can you give me clearance to the hall, please?"

"Of course. Good luck down there." He responded while pressing the censor, turning off the electric shield blocking the hallway. She turned to enter the unit when she noticed something odd.

"Bouchard, why is his section's light off?" She inquired. Every doorway was illuminated except for this client's door.

"Oh, right. Maintenance can't figure out what's wrong yet. Must be some kind of short? I'm sure they'll figure it out in the next day or so. The voice commands and bots inside the room still work, though. It's just the lights that are giving us trouble." Bouchard confidently stated. But Mattia thought she noticed something else behind that confidence. Something troubling the Headminister that he was trying to ignore. Mattia nodded her head and continued down the hallway.

*All I need is for you to say a few words. That's it. That will show them you're making progress,* she thought while walking down the hall, as if telepathically pleading with the boy who now resided on the other side of the cyberglass observation window, ten feet in front of her.

*Please just talk to me.* One final plea before giving her command to the window. "Engage with client 43972." The window went from opaque to crystal clear, and the client's vitals and information appeared on the glass.

CLIENT: 43972
NAME: YOUNG, JONATHAN
DOB: 945NW, THIRD MONTH, YEAR 32 OF MAGNUS I (11 YEARS OLD)
DIAGNOSIS: SCHIZOPHRENIA, CATATONIA, DISSOCIATIVE IDENTITY DISORDER, JAUNDICE
LENGTH OF TREATMENT: 22 MONTHS
HEART RATE: 125
BLOOD PRESSURE: 134/75
OXYGEN: 93

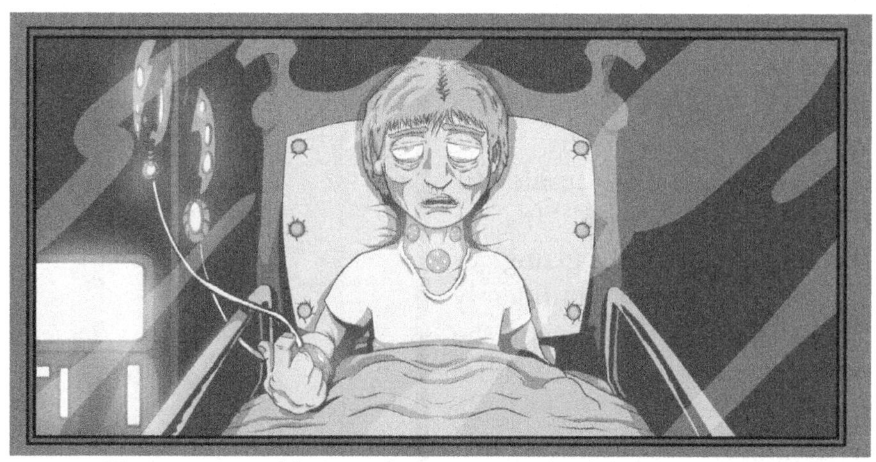

Eleven-year-old Jonathan Young had been nonverbal and nonresponsive for quite some time. He stared blankly ahead in the darkness, propped up in his bed. His last outburst—over a year prior—was nearly fatal to another resident at the Cresthaven wing.

"Hello, Jonathan. It's Cleric Mattia. I'm just going to run a few tests tonight. If anything hurts or you're uncomfortable, just say so or blink twice, okay?" Her voice was as warm as a summer morning, but the boy remained frozen in his trance-like state.

As she began to run tests using the voice prompts, she noticed something she hadn't before—his eyes. They seemed to be almost glowing green in the shadows of his room. She dismissed it as light reflecting from down the hall or from the machines inside his room and proceeded to run the tests.

# CHAPTER SEVEN

## - THE DARK GUEST -

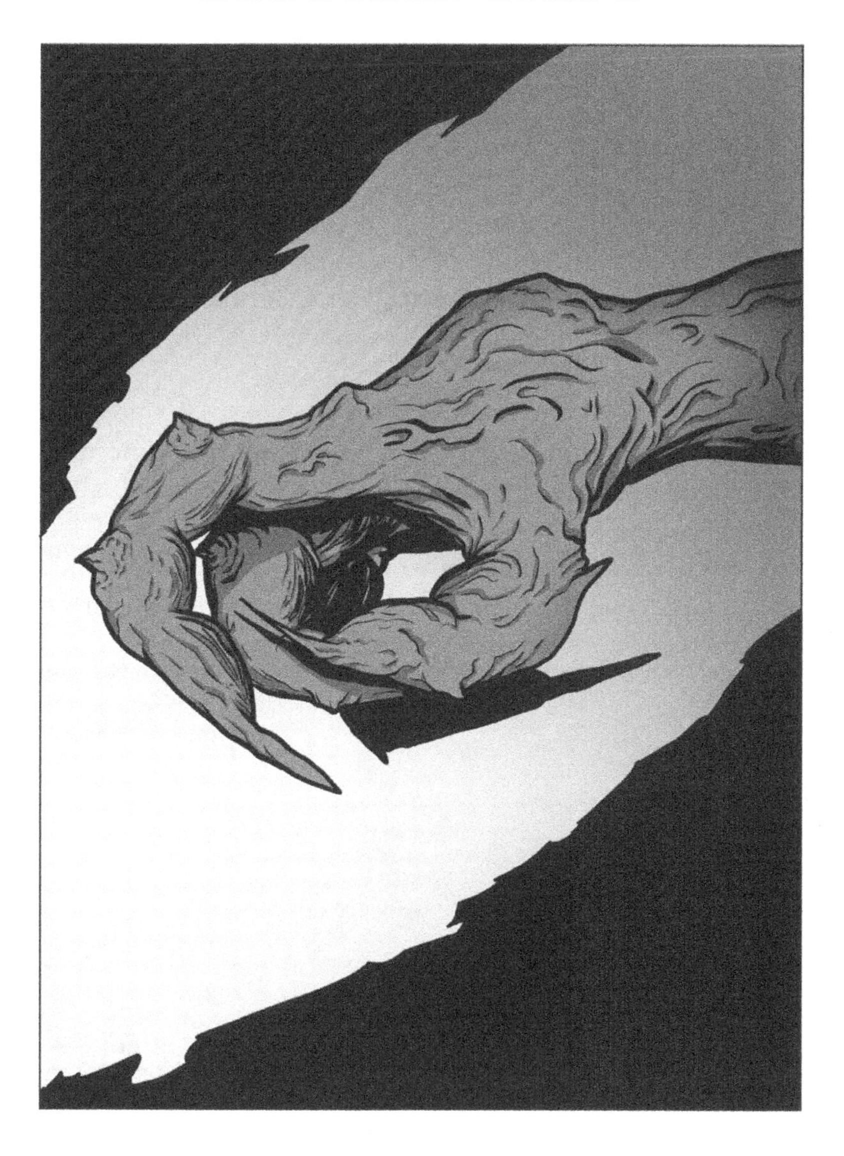

The dream was the same every night. The closet door would open, and soulless yellow eyes would glow. Taloned hands gripped the door, pushing it more, as a figure slithered into the room wearing a despicably hideous grin. As the Dark guest would creep slowly across the room, the girl would sense an overwhelming paralysis, tightening until she could barely breathe. She would anticipate with dread the one horrifying moment that would end this dream reality. The monster would touch her ever so gently between the eyes. At that moment, she lost all sense of time and awareness. Her mind and soul would become numbingly empty until no more happiness could be found.

This dream had been recurring off and on for months, maybe even more than a year. Her parents explained that all children experience these things. They had even consulted their Cleric to be sure. These horrible experiences were called "night terrors." But on this particular night, young Elizabeth would face a terror far worse than any nightmare she had ever suffered.

Elizabeth and her family lived in Outpost 36741 in Southern Republic territory on the other side of The Grey. It was a terraforming colony that had been at work for a little over a year and was proving to be a difficult place to maintain. The T-13 terraform models were not working as well as they once did, and the T-14s were unavailable in their region. Those were saved for Central Republic.

"Those high-brow bastards," her father would always say. The statement was usually followed by a quick slap across the shoulder from her mother, who then moved her glaring eyes from him to their young and impressionable daughter sitting at the dinner table with them. "It's true, though!" He would always say before censoring himself, and it actually was true if one was being honest.

Everyone knew that Central Republic was the priority of the New World. Each Territory had its own High-Class Cities where the more essential society types and elites lived comfortably. The Eastern Republic had Phillpine City, the Southern Republic had Perethedesh and Colde Yasam, while the Western and Northern Republics had LasStralia and Scottingburg.

However, none of them compared to Central. New Paris was the peak of civilization, to be sure, with its classic Old-World charm enhanced with all the latest tech and terraformed luxuries. The Peace Tower was where the Grand Chancellor and his Court lived. In fact, the entirety of the Territory looked like one ravishingly beautiful city stretched from the coast of Nudivon to the far eastern side of Claurfast. Its lights could be seen from almost all areas surrounding Northern Republic. But near The Grey Borders in Outpost 36741, the difference was stark. They might as well have been living in the Wastelands, according to Elizabeth's father. But either way, to Elizabeth, it was a peaceful and comfortable life. She couldn't ask for better surroundings to live out her childhood years.

On this particular night, it was about eight o'clock when Elizabeth's mother tucked her into bed. They went through their usual routine: a bedtime story and a debate on whether there should be a second reading. Sometimes, Elizabeth was victorious, but today was not that day. Her fears began to rise the minute she watched her mother walk to the door to turn out the light.

VISIT NEW PARIS
WHERE LIFE BEGINS

"Many seven-year-olds are scared of the dark," her father had told her. "It's very common and will pass in time. There's nothing to be afraid of; you're safe." He said all the wonderful things a parent should say to comfort a child. However, Elizabeth knew things her parents didn't. She knew her closet door, which stood directly in front of the foot of her bed, was a gateway to the Boogeyman. She never saw him outside of her night terrors, nor anything that provided evidence of the monster's actual existence. Still, every seven-year-old–including Elizabeth–knows *something* is in their closet. Therefore, if she didn't bury herself under the covers only peeking out occasionally, she would surely be doomed.

Elizabeth prepared for the worst as she began her nightly routine of sliding under the thick blanket that covered her, leaving only room for her nose and mouth to peek out slightly. If only Rory, that slimy weasel of a boy who teased her incessantly, could have seen her. Oh, the material he would have if he had witnessed this feat of cowardice. He had been her best friend only a year before the night terrors began. Then he changed. Something in him turned cruel around that time. Maybe *it* got him? Maybe that's what happened to you once the Boogeyman finally took hold?

Almost an hour had passed. Her adrenaline, along with the heat from the blanket wrapped heavily around her tiny body had kept her awake. Elizabeth began to debate with herself about whether this was worth the trouble. She would occasionally fall asleep in this position and wake up in the middle of the night too tired to care about the Boogeyman or his minions coming to get her. She would come out under her fortress and sleep well until she dreamed.

Another hour passed, and she was melting. She quickly removed the blanket from her head and lay on her back. The cool relief of freedom overwhelmed her, and she was instantly comfortable. The combination of the sweat and the cool air made her cover herself to her shoulders, and Elizabeth drifted softly to sleep.

It was now three o'clock in the morning.

All was quiet in Elizabeth's room. Nothing stirred. No sound was made other than the peaceful sounds of her sleeping.

"Elizabeth..." The word was little more than a whisper, but Elizabeth's eyes flickered open as she sleepily scanned her room. Nothing. Everything was as it should be. She laid her head back down and closed her eyes.

"Elizabeth, let me in..." Her eyes shot open—wide with fear—and Elizabeth sat up as she watched yellow fog billow from under her closed closet door. She could feel it again. The paralysis was taking over already. The door slowly opened, revealing a deep gray, gnarled, leathery face. A taloned claw pointed at her as the creature's mouth twisted its mangled yellow teeth into a hideous grin.

"Let me in Elizabeth. I only want to play." There was no mistaking it now. She was staring right at it. The Boogeyman was real!

Elizabeth was terrified. She tried to scream for her mother, but nothing came out. Her voice was gone. She tried to move but couldn't. The young girl didn't know if it was fear that froze her or some other force, but honest to God, she could not move.

The grinning monstrosity emerged from her closet, finally revealing whole body Greasy black and white hair topped its head and seemed to move on its own like a brood of snakes. Its thick skin was covered in boils from head to toe, gangrenous veins protruded between abscessed blisters and slimy muscular features. It was completely naked and every step it took left an oozing trail of necroplasmic slime.

"I won't hurt you, Elizabeth. I only want to play. Please won't you let me in? We'll be such good friends," the Dark guest sinisterly whispered as it inched closer and closer to the foot of her bed. The boil-covered Boogeyman waved its clawed hands in a circular motion, and Elizabeth felt her entire face turn numb. She felt the pressure between her eyes again as they rolled back in her head, and the whites turned a glowing yellow.

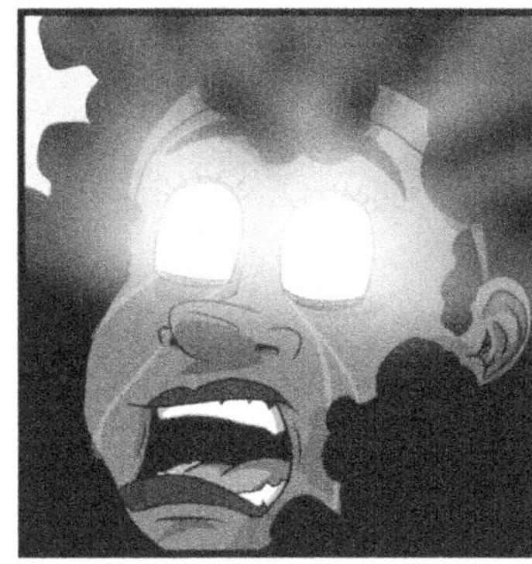

"That's it. Don't fight it, my pet. Soon we will be one. All you must do...is let...me...*in!!"* The devil leapt toward her face from the foot of the bed with taloned fingers outstretched. It was about to attain its prize and win another soul for the Master when it was ripped from its trajectory mid-air by a blinding emerald light. Necroplasm splattered everywhere, and the being howled like a slaughtered boar.

Elizabeth's eyes blinked as they returned to normal, her gaze falling once more around her room. It was quiet again. Nothing moved. Her closet door was shut just like it had been before.

"MOMMY!!!!!" She cried out into the darkness, pleading for stability and comfort from this nightmare. Elizabeth's mother immediately burst into the room to comfort her daughter.

"Oh, sweetie, what's the matter?? Did you have another nightmare?"

"It was real Mommy!! It was real!! The Boogeyman is real!!" Elizabeth shrieked, between sobs and flowing tears.

"Shhh. It's gone now, sweetie. Mommy's here." Elizabeth was then wrapped tightly in her mother's arms and carried downstairs for a late-night cup of hot cocoa.

Meanwhile, in a realm beyond what the Adamians could see, what remained in Elizabeth's room was absolute terror–very real and extremely powerful.

"No little girls for you tonight, Yirah!" Boomed the voice of an enormous and viciously ferocious elohim with a vice grip on the would-be Boogeyman's throat. Akalian, Head of the Order of Michael and a Chief Power amongst the Host of The Heavens, glared brightly at the devil with his white-emerald luminescent eyes. Akalian's flowing silver hair shone brightly around his dark sea green wings sprouting from both sides of his head.

Under his crown of long hair, emerald feather brows, resembling that of a crested owl, spread from the center of his forehead and circled his cheekbones like a mask. The rest of his featherfurred head, which matched the color of his robe and membranes, ended in a medium-length featherbeard partly hiding the Tetragrammaton emblem on his chest.

His shoulders were armored with Lightsteel pauldrons and covered with a sweeping, emerald cloak. Akalian's bulging muscles flexed as the ancient elohimic runes etched on his skin beamed brightly into the face of this bringer of Darkness. Akalian was hunting. Yirah wasn't the prime target, but he was the means to a centuries-long end.

"Where is he?!" thundered the Power. Akalian's teeth were sharp, powerful, and ready, while his iron grip closed in around Yirah's neck.

"Wh-Who?" Yirah could barely get the words out of his slimy, putrid mouth.

"Don't play games with me, little devil. Where's Xexxus?!"

*At last,* Yirah thought to himself. *So, this is why he's here. Good.* Yirah knew of other, more pressing matters and feared Akalian did too. But *this* was a tale as old as time. Akalian had been on the hunt for Xexxus for thousands of years. Yirah now chose to taunt the Chief Power instead of alluding to the more critical matters. Distraction. The Master would reward such efforts.

"I haven't seen him in ages!! Not since you let him slip right through your fingers when he sacrificed that little *whore* to The Dark Father and brought the Old World crashing down in flames!" At these words, Akalian throttled the unholy creature. No matter how hard he tried to fight their effect, Yirah's words stung.

He remembered Abigail and her band of Adamian protectors all too well. They had all fought so bravely against Xexxus' forces. Not a day would pass when he didn't see her frightened face while Xexxus' merged vessel offered her up as an unholy key to unlock the final Necrogate. The last of the Dark portals bypassing space and time brought the Old World crashing down into rubble when it opened. The memory of this event filled Akalian with rage. He *knew* Yirah had had more encounters with Xexxus since then.

"Lies will only bring you more pain, you filth." Akalian threw Yirah against the wall and held him there with rage-filled telekinetic energy. "Tell me where he is. This is your last warning." White-hot Light beamed from Akalian's opened palm and struck the devil in the bicep, severing the lower part of his arm from its body. Sticky, necroplasmic liquid spewed from the wound for just a moment before it was stopped by cauterization. Yirah howled in agony.

"YOU SAID IT WAS A WARNING!!" He screamed.

"It was a warning. The next one won't be as kind." Akalian grabbed Yirah by the throat once more and pulled him close. His hand lit up again, waiting for another reason to strike. "Now tell me what I want to know, and I'll spare you the pleasure of Tartarus."

When Akalian mentioned the ancient prison of the damned, Yirah immediately became more agreeable. Dark Father be damned, he wasn't going to *that* place.

"He's in an Adamian boy!!" Yirah shrieked in desperation.

"Where's the boy!?"

"I...I don't know! I swear on the name of King Yahw–"

"YOU DON'T GET TO SWEAR BY THAT NAME!" Akalian's rage boiled as he squeezed his grip on Yirah's neck. Just hearing the King's name being uttered by this disgusting creature was enough reason to destroy him.

The devil felt tendons beginning to pop inside of him. Akalian knew this slimy seed of a serpent was a lying, putrid, murderous thief, but he was telling the truth this time. Xexxus was smart; he wouldn't tell something like Yirah exactly where he was. He had been brilliant

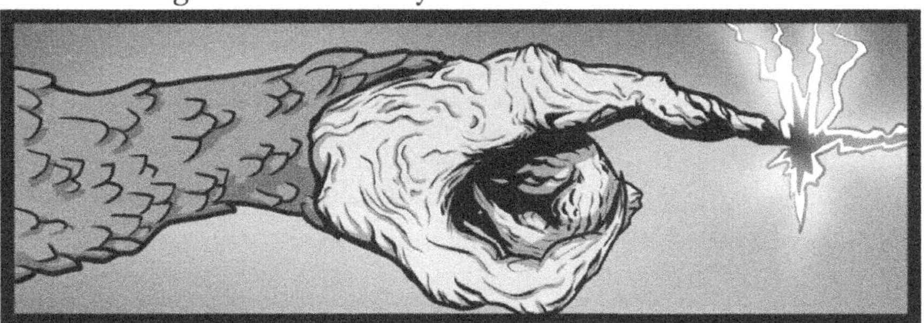

at covering his tracks for so long, Akalian wondered if their blades would ever meet to conclude this conflict that had stretched for ages.

Then something happened Akalian did not expect. Yirah began to chuckle.

"Heh...you should have been more aware of your surroundings, oh mighty Power." Akalian felt it now. Somehow, it had eluded him until this moment, but he was suddenly overwhelmed by the power of the malevolent Dark force. He sensed its almighty wickedness, dropped Yirah, and spun around as fast as possible with an energy blast ready to strike.

He was too slow. All he saw was red, hot necroplasmic energy strike him in the chest with the force of a Seraphim's smiting right hand. Akalian was flung out of the girl's building and across the outpost before he regained his bearings. He unfurled his enormous emerald wings and landed firmly on the outskirts of the terraforming camp.

With his wings still outstretched, the Chief Power felt the vibrations surge as the mighty pinions gathered tzoharian energy from The White Throne. The pulsating Light flowed from the center of the Tetragrammaton emblem on his chest, through his bulging right arm, and finally through his mighty taloned hand causing his weapon to materialize. Blasting into his hand with an amazing display of Light was his blazing longsword, Karaydin: The Light Hammer.

Ancient runes on Akalian's bright green blade illuminated the darkness of his desert surroundings. Twenty yards away, an enormous abomination of black ooze and throbbing scarlet veins erupted from the ground. Multiple tentacled extensions began protruding from the expanding charred blob of muscle and slime. The torso–if one could call it that, for it had no head or shoulders–began to implode, revealing a large vortex that beamed a bright scarlet red as it swirled in chaotic fashion. Akalian could hear the portalbeast's laughter echoing through the night air as it charged fiercely toward him, kicking up dirt and leaving behind a disgusting necroplasmic residue.

"Do your worst!!" Akalian belted as he dug his taloned feet firmly into the ground, holding his glowing blade out before him, ready to strike. He knew destroying this beast would not defeat the foe who controlled it. This was simply an avatar for the actual malevolent being he was warring against. Still, he was determined that this horror would end by the smite of his blade, nonetheless.

The necroplasmic tentacles took on a life of their own and began swirling in a hypnotic motion toward him, while haunting echoes of its sinister laugh twisted in the air. With a battle cry that reverberated through the heavens, Akalian leapt toward the beast, swinging Karaydin wildly through the air at any putrescent, oozing limb that came near him. But upon contact, the necroplasm coiled around Karaydin, stopping the longsword mid-swing.

The Power felt a hard tug at his right leg, then his left, then his wings; his whole body was being overcome by this scarlet-veined blackness. Laughter boomed louder and louder as the Dark ooze slimmed its way over Akalian's wings. The laughter was inside his head now; he felt it in his soul. Necroplasm slithered up his neck and overtop his featherbeard, finally pouring inside his mouth as his war cries were gargled and silenced.

Blackness surrounded Akalian. The terraforming camp vanished from his sight. All was silent. He still gripped Karaydin in his right hand, and his wings remained unfurled. He felt no pain or fear, only confusion. Where was he, and how had this creature overcome him so quickly? Karaydin was one of the Hafif Kalec, twelve mighty Lightblades distributed to the Chief Powers and The

Septum Dei. While Akalian's was one of only eight remaining, they were not easily defeated. If this Dark power could effortlessly best his Lightblade, it could only mean one thing.

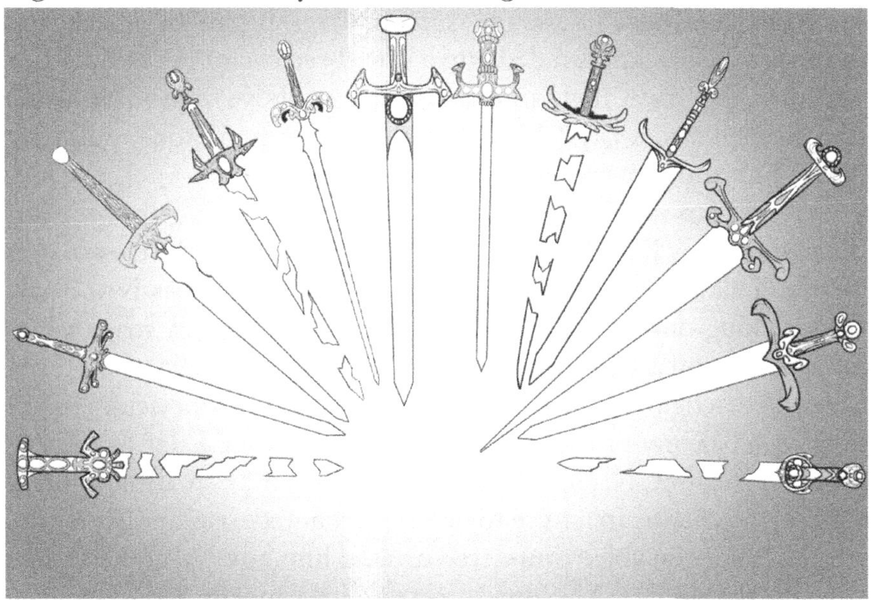

"Hello, little angel." bellowed the thundering whisper from the Darkness. That voice. It was so familiar, but Akalian couldn't place it. It was like trying to remember something from a nightmare long forgotten. Akalian turned toward the direction of the voice, and saw a lone flame suspended in the nothingness before him. The voice continued.

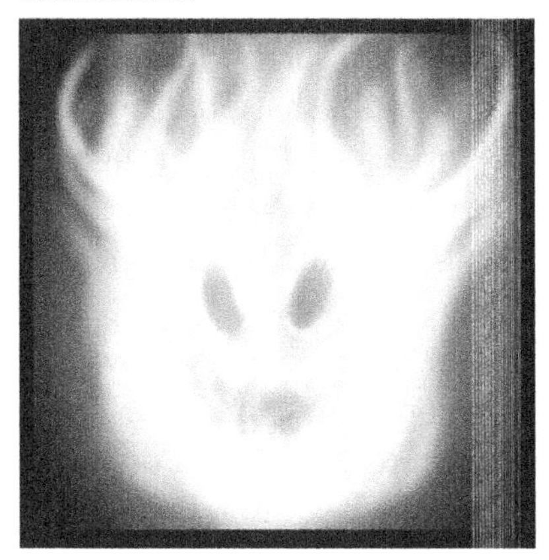

"Yirah is under my protection now. I'm afraid the Host of the Heavens have been blinded by his escape, and pursuing him would not be wise, for doing so would invoke my wrath...and I am not one to be trifled with." Akalian attempted to speak but could not; his vocal cords were frozen.

Fear began to creep in as his suspicions of what this being was were solidified. The flame started to grow more prominent. Its heat was unbearable, reeking of sulfur and death straight out of the Gnashing Kingdom of Pandemonium itself.

"You and your kind are witnessing the beginning of something...*colossal*." Akalian's surroundings began to quake and rumble as the blackness faded into a scarlet red cyclopean temple-like structure that rose high into the heavens above him. The flame transformed into a large, black hole-like Aeternum Stone, pulsating before him and growing as high as the temple.

Akalian felt fear now. In fact, he couldn't remember the last time he felt fear like this. This Stone was like nothing he'd ever seen before. This Stone was much more powerful and massive. Black, light-sucking ooze began to slide down the cyclopean structure as tentacular protrusions emerged from the Stone. Akalian heard the cheering of a demonic hoard behind him and turned, noticing he was now on a balcony of the temple itself, looking out as far as the eye could see. Scarlet, Necrom blades rose in the air as an army of Dark elohim, too chaotic in nature to describe, chanted together in victory.

"Yes," the voice thundered around him now, "feel the fear of your inevitable fate. My advice to you, little angel? *Run and hide!*" Suddenly, a mighty wind began to blow with the force of a hurricane. Akalian took to the sky, attempting to fight it, but the might in his wings was no match for the strength of its current. In a sudden rush of pain and wind, the wings were ripped from his back, leaving only torn membranes attached.

He attempted to scream in intense pain, but his vocal cords were still imprisoned. He spun wildly. His entire surroundings were now engulfed in chaos as the cyclopean temple shattered and the legions of fallen beings swirled and flew around him, laughing maniacally as they were being ripped apart.

Akalian looked up toward the black Aeternum Stone as it rose higher in the blood-red sky. As it pierced the crest of the atmosphere, everything around Akalian was engulfed in nightmarish yellow and green flames. He felt as if the fire was consuming his soul as he watched the remaining cackling hordes burn to a crisp and dissipate into an ashy nothingness. Finally, Akalian could bear it no longer. His vocal cords were loosened, and he let out a mighty scream. Obeying an insatiable desire to do so, he thrust Karaydin into his abdomen acting under an unknown and undetermined force.

At that, Akalian was back in the cold, moonlit desert of Outpost 36741. All was quiet except for the distant, bustling nightlife of Adamians and their machines. He felt his abdomen. No damage. Everything was as it should be. Why had he done that? What caused him to thrust his blade into himself like that? He felt compelled to do so, as though it were the only way to escape the nightmare he was living in, but it made no sense. How could that have freed him? He needed answers and guidance. He needed–

"Akalian!?" The telepathic connection boomed in his mind. "It's Willow! Can you hear me!?"

"I'm here, Willow," he said out loud as if his choirmite brother were standing right in front of him. "Did you see where Yirah escaped to? It would have been just a moment ago." There was a pause, and Willow spoke up again.

"Uhm. Akalian...it's been weeks since you faced Yirah. We lost all contact with you as well as our visual on *him*. We feared the worst. What...what happened to you? Where were you?" Willow's tone was a mixture of relief and concern. Weeks? The Dark being had taken him for what only felt like minutes.

"Akalian...are you alright?" Willow's voice cracked in compassion.

"No," Akalian responded with a forbidding tone. "I have to see Michael. Something is coming."

# CHAPTER EIGHT

## - A NEEDED CONVERSATION -

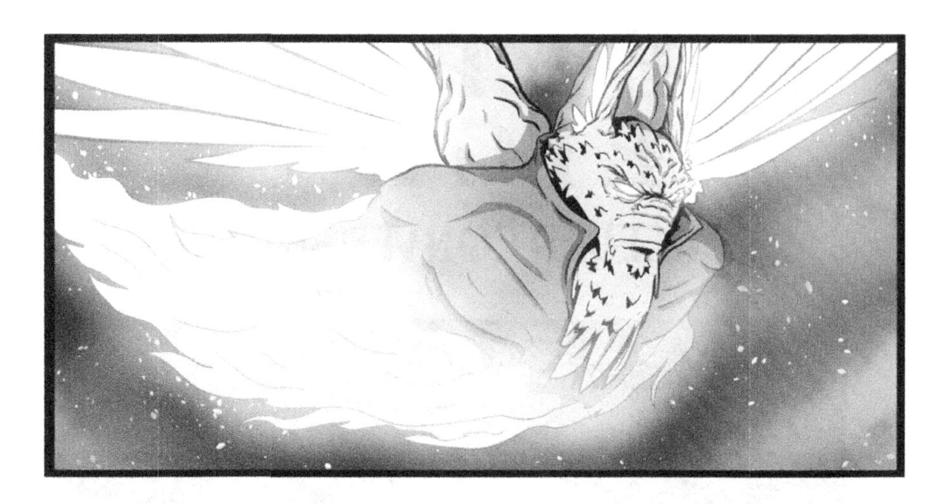

As Moriel hurtled through the cosmos with urgency in his wings, his emotions burned inside him like a fiery passion. He knew time was short. Since he left Creation's End, so many questions and feelings whirled around in his mind: *How was Age End a plausible endgame? Was this Vision indeed predestined—a Tzoharian Nexus? Why was it so imperative that this Vision be kept secret?* No matter the intensity of his confusion and curiosity, he *had* to calm these thoughts for now. Traveling at this speed, he had to be attentive. He could easily go too fast in the wrong place and cause significant disruption in the universe.

The Time and Celestial Orders governed the cosmos well, but catastrophes still happened, and Moriel didn't want to be the one to throw an entire galaxy out of orbit by mistake. It had happened before, but not by him. Thankfully, that system had been uninhabited. In fact, most systems and galaxies in the Corporeum Realm were vacant now. The UcDusme—Three Falls—of the Adamian race put an indefinite halt on the creation process of the cosmos. Adamains were supposed to be a

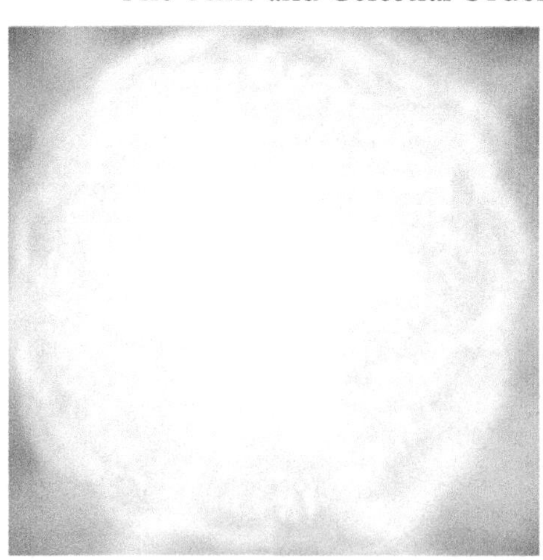

part of its continued formation, but after their union with the Dark, this would only bring more chaos to the cosmos.

Moriel wished he could have used a Pentaclegate (a divine portal of Light) but the path leading to Sof Haderech (the realm of Michael) as well as its entrance, was well protected. The Messenger knew that he had to pass the right systems at the proper speed while stating the correct prayers for the accurate vibration energy to be available to him when he attempted to summon the door to his Archangel's realm. In less than two bounds of his wings, he had passed the final galaxy, so Moriel knew he was about to arrive at the end of the celestial coordinates. As he slowed down, he saw beams of violet and lilac bounce around each other, and Moriel could smell the traces of lavender oak, revealing his arrival.

The Power held his wings straight into the air, slowing down to a complete stop. He took a long, deep breath of the interstellar dioxide and closed his glowing cerulean eyes, calming his anxieties. The beautiful scent of this place made the process abundantly easier than it might otherwise be.

In this moment of tranquility, Moriel could feel the vibrations of his journey build within him, traveling down his arm as he extended it outward, fingers together and palm pointed toward a particular spot in front of him. Energy came to life as Moriel's palm illuminated. Blinding admiral blue and white Light spiraled around each other as they traveled 100 yards ahead of the Power and burst into song. It was the sweetest music that could be heard other than inside of The White Throne itself.

The notes washed over Moriel like a warm blanket on a cold, wintery Christmas Eve. He breathed a stress-melting sigh of relief as the music transformed into Shazarah Agac, the enormous lavender oak of Sof Haderech. Moriel furled his wings until they disappeared as his flight continued toward the large opening at the tree's base. His taloned feet hit the ground inside the archway of the tree, and he began slowly walking toward the stone obelisk that would grant him access to the realm of his dear friend and mentor.

Atop the square pillar, the Pyramid of Haderech awaited the visitor to unlock its secrets. Only then would it allow Moriel to enter. The Pyramid was a Tzoharian Codex constructed by Michael to protect Sof Haderech from invaders from The Dark Kingdom.

Codexes were utilized by many Kingdoms and Powers across the realms of The Cosmic Wheel. While each codex was unique in combination, shape, and operation, they all shared the same purpose–either keeping something out or in. This particular codex was created by the Light of the Tzoharian Stone in the heart of The White Throne itself. Unless its maker corrupted it–which only occurred when a being fell to the Dark–the codex would remain as pure as the stone it was formed from. Moriel knew this codex well. He placed his hand upon the point of the pyramid, and the Power began to sing.

"Light of truth from far and wide,
Give me now what thou would hide.
Find in me thy pure extent,
Of qualified requirement.

Open gates of grace and love,
With Light from heaven pure above.
Pain and sorrow melt away,
By purest Light, thine holy way.
Amin y Amin."

As Moriel finished the verse, a blinding white Light began to fill the tree's hollow. The codex had heard the words and read the Power's heart as he sang them. It now knew this elohim's identity and purest motives. The Light of the Tzoharian Codex overwhelmed Moriel in a warming wave of peace, joy, and love. The elohim closed his eyes, breathed deeply and lost himself in this perfect moment of tranquility.

When he opened his eyes again, Moriel found himself surrounded by lush violet and lavender stone structures shimmering in the moonlight of Sof Haderech. Michael loved the night sky and the moon so much that the King gifted this realm to him where he would have it for all eternity. Moriel was atop a lone barbican that extended past enormous walls of rushing water, flowing down to the bright mulberry pools at the base of the mighty fortress of Michael, Prince of The Septum Dei.

Moriel took in the view of this wondrous place: shimmering mountains as far as he could see. There were towers and mighty stone turrets where guests were always welcome to stay. This entire landscape was the castle known as Aslan Keep. Within its countless rooms and royal halls, Moriel had known precious memories of brotherhood and glad tidings. However, this visit was not meant for such things. As the booming sounds of the waterfalls around him were interrupted by the concerned voice behind him, Moriel knew he must face this dreadful purpose.

"This place has always brought you comfort, my brother. That comfort welcomes you once more." Moriel turned to greet the prominent figure floating before him. His eyes took in the mauve Taoist robe billowing in the wind, held together by a silver Tetragrammaton medallion on his chest.

Michael stood nearly 7 feet tall–in this form–and looked to be a mixture of a Rocky Mountain Wolf and an Asiatic Lion, for it was he who inspired both species of animal. His featherfurred mane was a deep violet and extended to the single set of wings at his temples. One of his eyes was scarred shut, and one of the scars reached the middle of his nose.

He had earned those scars in a great battle long ago. Even though the King offered to heal them completely, Michael chose to keep them as a reminder that this war was not over and that his adversary was still prowling. His lone, luminescent periwinkle eye shone brightly as he extended his sizeable paw-like hand toward his beloved Chief Messenger.

"Tell me, Moriel. What has the King shown you?" Michael had felt the Vision when it happened, although he did not experience it himself. He, too, had questions.

"Much, my friend." Moriel paused as a grievously troubled expression crossed his face. "Michael...something is coming. Something...monstrous."

"What did you see?" Michael inquired.

"Never-ending Darkness," Moriel stated ominously.

"Where is this Darkness?"

"Not where, Michael... *when*." At this, Michael understood the graveness of the situation.

"Come, let's continue this at Savas Isigi." Both elohim lifted off and began flying through the mountain range.

Hidden amongst the winding mountains and towers of Aslan Keep there was a large, secluded bartizan that Michael used as his war room: Savas Isigi. Within these mighty stone-pillared windows, Michael prepared his inner Council for battles, rescue missions, and raids. However, on this occasion, the war room was empty–dedicated to a solitary and weighty conversation.

Moriel told Michael of the voice from beyond time that sparked the Vision. He explained the violent, chaotic reality of what appeared to be a future where all realms had imploded upon themselves, the mangled Capurro Cross and the Adamian who wore it, and the bold proclamation of the re-birthing of Nephilim. Lastly, he told the most disturbing fact of all, the command of secrecy given from the King himself.

Michael contemplated in silence for a moment. Who could blame him? This was one of the most disturbing Visions he'd ever heard. The fact that the Council was not to be informed meant there was much to sift through. After a few minutes of silence, Michael spoke, attempting to clarify what he had just heard.

"So...this Vision was of the future?" Michael asked, with stern purpose, as he leaned onto the centerpiece of the room: the Aeternum Stone table. It had been gifted to him by Gabriel, who was the dearest of all siblings to this Archangel of the heavens.

"Yes. It was Earth...although nothing like we've ever seen before. The evil pulsating from this new Stone was overwhelming and had corrupted every inch of the planet. The ground below me reeked of death and malice. But that wasn't the worst of it..." Moriel took a deep breath, closed his eyes, and prepared his emotions. Michael had never seen him this distraught, and it deeply concerned the Archangel. "The seal of Dudael. It had been broken by Deccal and its wielder was Khata, himself. And in that horrible prophetic song, the Dark voice used the term, 'the hour of The Black Sun.' I believe he was referring to this new Stone itself, which would put the events leading up to The Final War in a new and terrifying perspective. This was worse than in the times of Noah. It tore through the entire planet and all the realms, pulling them into one location. It was as though chaos exploded and rearranged *everything*."

Moriel saw the look of horror on Michael's face. The Archangel knew of the different meanings and prophecies of the end of time, but Age End was the one he secretly feared the most, like the rest of the Host. The Cosmic Wheel was governed by the pre-ordained order of cause and effect. With that came limitless possibilities of what could happen in every moment across all the realms.

All of the Heavenly Host knew the King was sovereign in his rule and in order, but the Archangel never once expected The Dark Kingdom's prophetic outcome of destruction would come to pass. Permitting choice to have its sway was one thing, but allowing evil to win was something he couldn't believe to be true. And the one thing that Michael couldn't wrap his head around was why the King wanted the Council to be left out of such a grievous Vision. A thought crept into his mind. He was hesitant to voice it, but knew he must.

"You're certain this was a Vision from the King and not just propaganda from the enemy?" Michael did not intend to second guess the Messenger's intellect–nor did Moriel take offense. He had to be sure this wasn't some grand fear-mongering scheme to distract them from the discussion Michael had with Gabriel mere moments before Moriel's arrival. It seemed almost too coincidental–for despite what had been said about it, coincidence did indeed occur, although rarely.

"I'm positive. He appeared before me at the Vision's end, embraced me, and I felt his Light flowing through me. It was as if I was in the White Throne Room itself." Moriel reassured his Archangel.

"And other than *me*, he said to not speak of this to anyone?"

"You, and someone else who would present themselves soon." Hearing this, Michael began to ponder what all this could possibly mean. What did he have to offer this Vision as far as an explanation? It baffled him just as much as it did Moriel. Then, Moriel could tell that Michael had a horrible thought.

"The Adamian whom you said ruled the Aeternum Dome Colosseum...the Darkness he was merged with...was it *him?"* Thoughts of a shadowed, scaly, indigo, serpentine face illuminated with eyes of flame flooded Moriel's mind.

"No," Moriel responded. He could tell Michael's fears were abated. "It was powerful, but it *wasn't* Lucifer." This supposed Age End Vision now had a new mystery attached to it. Lucifer was always at the center of every other Age End prophecy. His absence here was intriguing.

"What was it you said that voice uttered? The one that sparked all this?" Michael questioned.

"It said, 'Now...let your true form awaken.' It came on the Cosmic Wind, out of time and space," Moriel stated thoughtfully.

"A Tzoharian Nexus," Micheal said ominously.

"I didn't want to say it, but that's a genuine possibility," Moriel admitted.

"That certainly complicates things." Michael leaned heavily on the Stone table again.

"Doesn't that mean this *must* happen?" Moriel asked this question with a desperate hope that Michael would correct him.

"Not always," Michael taught. "There have been times when portions of a Nexus changed, but never the ultimate intent of the inevitable event." Moriel became hopeful.

"So, it's possible the Nexus, being a fixed point in time, is just the end of the Age and not *necessarily* Age End?"

"It's possible, but entirely too soon to tell. There's much more to this puzzle, and I fear what all the combined pieces will bring in the end." Michael then shifted the topic back to the Adamian. "So, you say the Adamian wasn't possessed by Lucifer, then who was–"

"It was a Dark Prince." A thundering voice pulled the attention of both elohim to one of the pillared windows, where perched like an emerald raven, crouched Akalian. Moriel now understood the King's meaning: "and the one who meets with you there."

Knowing what the King had told Moriel about this, Michael welcomed the fact that Akalian would now be with his brother on this journey. He had sensed someone else entering his realm, but since it wasn't a threat, he did not concern himself with it. Many visitors sought rest and solitude in Sof Haderech. Akalian jumped down to the floor of the bartizan room as his wings disappeared into his back.

"Where are the others?" Akalian inquired about the other Chief Powers. "They should be present to hear this as well."

"Bradoch and Forfax are scouting The Cosmic Ocean with Saints Andraus and Kephas. Raziel is on a mission with St. Nicholas. I'll brief them all once they've returned." Michael replied. "So, you've heard enough. What makes you so sure it was a *Dark Prince* that Moriel saw?"

"Because what I've just been through is all too similar to what Moriel has said. In fact, it's possible I was just attacked by the very being from his Vision. It was the Darkest energy I've felt in over a millennium." Akalian grimly confessed. Moriel and Michael both looked at each other exchanging forbidding expressions.

"If this being is one and the same," Moriel enquired of Michael, "is it possible that we may be witnessing the beginning of a reorganization within the enemy's forces? Is that, perhaps, what leads to the Age End Nexus?"

"Something *colossal.* The devil's exact words." Akalian added. The Dark Kingdom, although still *the* significant threat across the realms, was leaderless for the most part. There had been attempts to reorganize the Dark since Lucifer's entombment, but they had all failed. Loyalty was never an attribute within the nature of Dark beings.

The Dark Kingdom had not seen actual structure since the Adamian's second world war, or what the Heavenly Host referred to as The Tenebris Noctis–the Darkest Night. So many lives were lost. In the victory over Lucifer's horde, all but three of the Dark Father's most powerful Princes had either been banished to Tartarus or disappeared into hiding as they were far too weak to fight. That was their final stand, and Lucifer's forces scattered to form their own alliances.

The Host of the Heavens had to fight against mass chaos as they had to focus on multiple warring groups of devils who proved to be much more unpredictable. Little did the Host know that an even darker night loomed with the coming of The Final War. That proved that a leaderless, chaotic Dark Kingdom with powerful Adamians on their side could be just as challenging to war against as a unified enemy–echoes of the ancient Babylonian times.

"If a Dark Prince is truly rising," Michael said, "no matter what the Nexus outcome may be, we must anticipate competitors. This could very well send the realms into even more of an uproar than before, and whispers of Age End accompanying this new development will make things much more difficult to control. For if a Nexus *has* entered the realms, then The Dark Kingdom's sorcerers will soon get wind of it, regardless of how secret it is for now." Michael shifted the conversation to Akalian's mission. "Speaking of which, was Yirah able to provide you with anything useful?" Akalian sighed in frustration and disappointment,

"It seems as though Yirah is working with this Prince. While I was questioning the little vermin, the Prince showed up. He swallowed me out of time and into Darkness, claiming Yirah as his own." Akalian paused; his fear and anxiety rising as he continued, "It showed me something similar to Moriel's Vision: an army with

Necromic blades that ushered in a black Aeternum Stone and a whirlwind of chaos."

"How did you escape this being?" Michael asked, very concerned about what Akalian was saying. Michael had known that Akalian was taken, but he wasn't aware of what he experienced. That hadn't been a part of Willow's report.

Akalian hesitated. He wasn't sure how to answer this question because he wasn't entirely sure *how* he escaped.

"I..I don't know. Something...compelled me to act in a way I never have."

"What happened, Akalian?" Moriel joined in Michael's concern.

"I was overwhelmed with the urge to take Karaydin and run myself through. It seemed to be the only thing that would end the pain and sorrow. The drive in me was overwhelming. It was something urgent and *needed.* Something...almost...holy." As Akalian heard the words coming out of his mouth, he was just as concerned as his brothers. "So, I succumbed to my urge and was released."

The fact that an act of self-mutilation was the only way out of this Prince's grasp was something very serious. It was a direct parallel to the goal of possessing an Adamian: the hopeless and grievous act of suicide. For an elohim of The Host to have an urge like that could spell extreme danger for their mental and emotional state and have monumental consequences. Usually after hearing something like this, Michael would have been concerned about a deep oppression or possession of some sort, but he knew the Tzoharian Codex would have spotted a Dark presence and prevented Akalian from entering Sof Haderech.

The Archangel walked slowly over to Akalian, his expression grave.

"This is indeed very troubling. However, unlike Moriel's Vision, this was a direct attack from the enemy. Who knows how much truth it holds or what potential psychological damage it may have tried to cause you. The entire Vision may have been constructed to deteriorate your mind. It's happened before." Michael hesitated. "How are you feeling now?" he asked with kindness in his voice. The Archangel was genuinely worried about Akalian, not just because of this Vision. The Power had been through so much, and Michael understood the weight of Akalian's ongoing mission to find Xexxus. If this was a psychological strike, it had struck an extremely wounded heart.

"I'd feel better if I had gotten some information on the whereabouts of Xexxus." Akalian felt like changing the subject for the moment. This Vision troubled him deeply, and he wasn't sure what to make of it. Michael obliged, and Moriel followed his lead. "All I could acquire is that he is possessing an Adamian boy...that's all I know." Akalian's spirit dropped. He felt failure once more in his heart. How long would he have to track this elusive being? For thousands of years, Xexxus, The Last of Legion, had evaded him at every turn.

"Interesting..." Michael had a thought that hit him with both foreboding and intuition. Akalian and Moriel looked up. Had they stumbled upon a lead at last?

"Gabriel's Powers have been warring against a growing infestation in the Southern Territory of Earth for quite some time. Apparently, it's centered around a boy showing significant signs of an extremely powerful possession, although they cannot pinpoint where the boy is located. The entire city of Perethedesh is an enormously Dark stronghold of late."

Akalian immediately chimed in with an obvious question.

"How do they know it's a boy if they've been unable to locate him?"

"Gabriel reached out in astral form to find the source of this stronghold once the Dark grew in strength. All he could sense was the young boy's astral cries for help within the ether of necroplasm forming around him. Gabriel was then quickly cut off from the boy and hasn't been able to make contact again. Attempts have been made, but all have been in vain. For the last forty-eight months of Adamian time, all efforts have been focused on breaking the stronghold by force. However, instead of the stronghold weakening, it only seems to have multiplied in strength."

"It's rather odd for a single possession to have *that* much protection." Moriel added.

"Very much so," Michael agreed. "Meaning this is something more than a standard possession. This may be a competitor of the Dark Prince attempting to form their own kingdom."

"I don't mean to challenge your hypothesis," Akalian interjected, "but Xexxus has been elusive for thousands of years. Why would he risk it all now by possessing someone and drawing so much attention to himself?" Akalian had a good point, and Michael knew it.

"Why, indeed?", Moriel concurred, thoughtfully. "Why would a being on the run for so long suddenly plant roots and build an army that welcomes confrontation? Even if he *were* to be the Dark Prince's competitor, it seems reckless."

Michael then brought up an extremely troubling point.

"Nothing Xexxus does is *reckless*. Everything is calculated and measured. We all remember what happened the last time he did something like this." The horrors of the Adamian Final War flashed in all three of their minds. "He's been elusive for almost two thousand years. But with a possible Tzoharian Nexus pointing us to Age End, are we really surprised that these events are coming together like this?" Michael paused and stared at the two Chief Powers of his Order.

They both shifted and leaned back against the Stone table as they realized what could possibly be happening...again. This news was becoming heavier by the second. Michael knew he needed to bring them some encouragement at this moment. He wanted some as well.

"There are many unanswered questions here. And the weight of their potential answers is heavier than any of us can attempt to bear. But hope is not lost, my friends." Akalian and Moriel both looked at their Archangel assuredly. They knew this was true, but hearing it had the power to strengthen their hearts. It was a needed reminder, indeed. "Hope is never lost."

Moriel smiled slightly, and Akalian's heart softened momentarily with gladness.

"That's why I think you two should investigate. I want you to assist Gabriel in breaking through the stronghold and enter the boy's mind. Be it Xexxus who is leading this stronghold or not, we need answers, and that boy needs to be saved from his torment." Michael commanded.

Both elohim accepted their mission immediately. Regardless of the future, their devotion to the Adamians was second only to their dedication to the King. Besides, it was now probable that this boy was at the center of all the information they'd received. Only one thing remained before they moved forward.

"Do we know the boy's name?" asked Akalian.

"His name is Jonathan Young." Michael responded. With that, the Aeternum Stone table began to pulsate with a bright white Light as the voice of The Caretaker filled the room.

"St. Michael, this is Maximiel. Your watch is about to commence, and we await your arrival. St. Raphael is standing by." Moriel looked at Michael with a surprised expression.

"Michael, this was the eve of your watch? You didn't need to take this time to converse with us; we could–" Michael raised his hand to calm his beloved friend and brother.

"It's alright, Moriel. I have spent the proper time preparing for this. I'm always here when you need me, and this was of...*great* importance"

The Light from the Stone table began to dance until three rings of tzoharian energy formed, intertwining in a circular formation above the table. Michael unfurled his wings and began to float toward the Light rings as he addressed the two elohim.

"As you begin this quest, remember what we discussed here. Take care not to let news of the Nexus or Moriel's Vision be known to *anyone*. One wrong move here, and many Adamian souls could be lost for ages...or forever. Watch out for each other and shine in the Darkness, my friends." Michael then stepped into the rings, and with a burst of blinding white energy, the room returned to normal, and Michael was gone.

"*Moriel,*" Michael was now communicating telepathically with the Power, "*stay close to Akalian. He has been overwhelmed with grief for far too long, and I fear this experience may have been more than he can bear.*" Moriel looked at Akalian, who was leaning against the stone table and lost in his own thoughts. "*We know his strength is unmatched, but he can allow himself to take on too much weight. No one should bear that much of a load on their own, and we know his greatest temptation is to do just that.*"

Moriel communicated his agreement in thought. He now had two missions and would give both his undivided attention.

# CHAPTER NINE

## - THE HIGH COUNCIL -

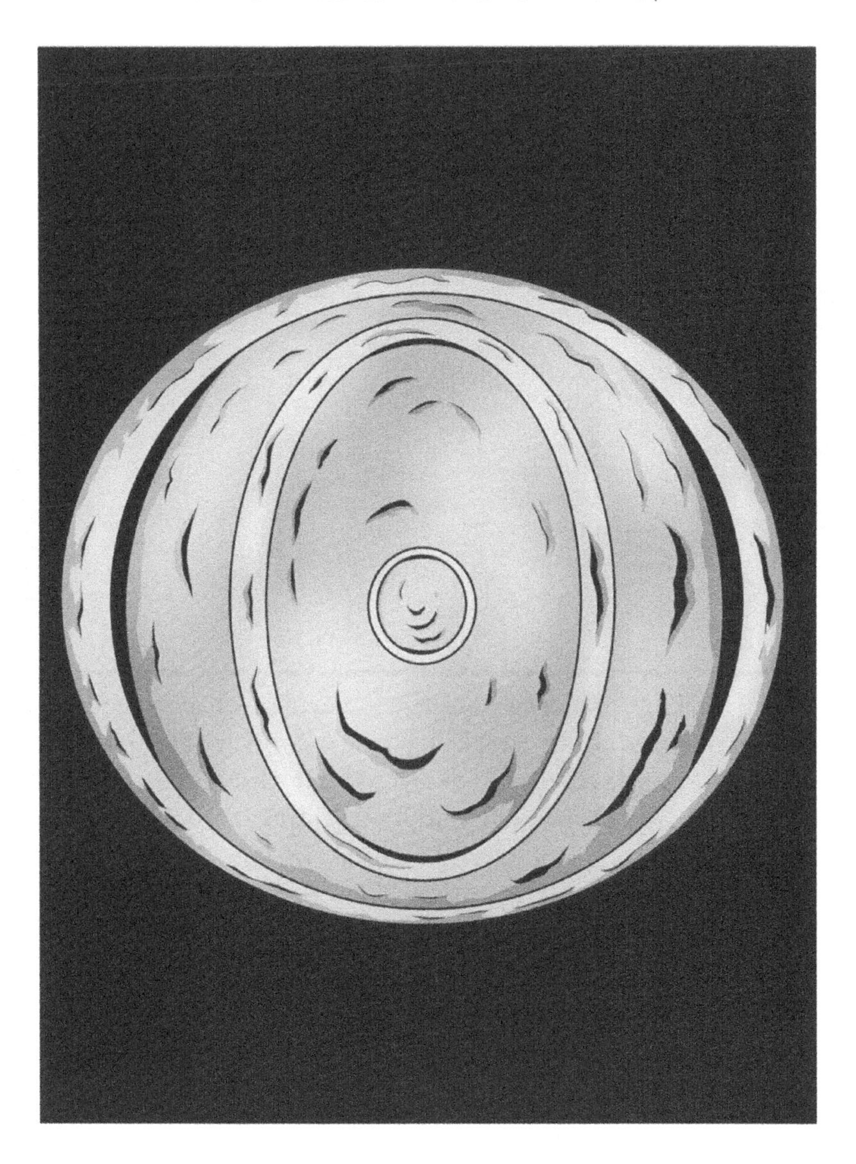

If there was one place in the Southern Territory of The Grand Republic that directly contrasted The Grey, it would be Perethedesh, The City of The High Temple. The great pyramidic structure of the Temple spanned almost four miles at its base and towered over two miles in height. This looming monument to The Grand Republic was so large that it had three terraform engines to keep it from disrupting the weather patterns of the rest of the city, as well as to provide stability in strong winds.

The High Temple was the epicenter of Perethedesh and functioned almost as an entire city in itself. Each of its hundreds of lower and mid-levels was dedicated to disciplines in science, agriculture, medical research, and, most importantly, mental health. Half of the scientific studies and facilities in The High Temple were dedicated to therapeutic practices. They believed that if they could master the mind, they could rid the world of crime and corruption altogether. The root of what causes a person to turn to that lifestyle could be eliminated.

The diligent scientists, doctors, professors, and Clerics who studied and worked in The High Temple dreamed of a day when a place as horrible as The Wastelands need not exist. Sociologists and economists had already constructed a system within the Republic by which everyone worldwide was cared for and fed. The base pay met livable wage standards. Inflation was prevented by various mandates so the powerful could not take advantage of the needy. Many developments came from this place of scientific and economic breakthrough and academic thought. Wonderful standards that helped and aided humanity for the better.

The upper fifty levels of the Temple were for those who wished to live on campus. While residents were free to come and go as they pleased, they never had need to leave. The Temple had everything they needed and wanted, from groceries to entertainment and exercise. It was all dedicated to them, for they were changing the world in miraculous ways.

The top two levels were devoted to The High Council, the leaders of The Republic Gathered. The penultimate level held the Council Clerics' offices. Each of the eleven had his or her own luxurious space where they could work, relax, and live comfortably for days if not weeks, if desired. Every one of these leaders was either a medical doctor or a scholar in a field heavily studied in the Temple.

The half of the penultimate level not dedicated to scientific practices, was filled with The Observatory, a place of meeting and deep personal reflection. The whole of The Grand Republic looked upon The High Temple as a sort of "Mecca" of thought and reason, and the Observatory was the closest thing to a holy of holies the Temple residents had. It was dedicated to solace, labyrinth meditation, and Council sessions. Aside from their therapeutic work, the Council's primary purpose was to cultivate a monthly ritual experience for the world to come together as one for the betterment of themselves, each other, and the environment.

High Cleric Nargol was the first to hold such a title in the Republic. In the year 132NW–New World–he presented his dissertation to Grand Chancellor Fortich Immatius and convinced the High Elders to create something to satisfy the human desire for religious practice. Recognizing that some were migrating to The Grey for religious freedom already, Nargol proposed that the human experience craved something like spiritual ritualistic practice, even if it wasn't directed to a particular deity or figure of myth. So, instead of throwing out everything resembling ritual and religion, The Republic Gathered was created to give the people a sense of coming together for a higher purpose in fellowship and community.

They sang songs that praised the change of the seasons, the goodness of humankind, love for one's neighbor, and the progress The Grand Republic had made. It wasn't considered worship because there was no higher being as the object of these songs. It was simply an acknowledgment of the accomplishments of humanity and nature as a community. This brought them together as "One Unity" and reminded them of their purpose in life–to take care of one another and their environment, continuing the evolutionary process that would eventually lead to a peaceful coexistence of all beings.

Dedicated ceremonies, feasts, and festivals were held at various times throughout the year, and there was even a text that was considered "sacred" in a sense. Every month on the Gathering Day, one of the twelve Council Clerics would give a homily from this sacred text called "The Code." It was believed to be penned by the founders of the Republic and addended by the first two High Clerics, Nargol and Martina Thesicus. The text was not considered inerrant or divinely inspired in any way, but it was viewed as a guiding document of immense worth because it had been constructed by the founders of the New World. The Grand Republic intended to continue these practices until utopia was found.

The highest level of the Temple was designated living space for one of the two people who held the most weight upon their shoulders in this world: the High Cleric of The Grand Republic. It had been structured that way not so the Cleric could "look down upon their kingdom," as some had whispered, but so they could look out and see how many people counted on them. In fact, only one other structure reached the height of this Temple: The Peace Tower in the Northern Republic, where The Grand Chancellor lived.

The view from High Cleric Malcolm's flat was one of the most gorgeous sights ever, or so Mattia Bajuma imagined. She had never actually visited, but she longed to walk the meditation labyrinth with that view. She envied him for that as she sat on her stiff fabric bench seat in her stone blue underform, staring out the window of the skyway train. She did not dare wear her navy-blue clerical garb with its ribands and embroidered Republic Gathered symbol, revealing her as a Council Cleric. That would bring far too much attention. No, her clerical robe was tucked away safely inside her bag.

She chose not to live in The High Temple like many of her fellow Council Members, as she felt she could be too easily detached from the people she was supposed to serve. Mattia lived in a flat about seven miles from the Temple and liked it that way. She usually took

the skyway train which wrapped around the entire city like a floating metal maze. She loved the view especially in the mornings. There was nothing quite like watching the sunrise over the enormous cloudpiercer buildings. They reached up to the sky like steel mountains kissed by the morning sun while the darkness of dawn lingered in the lower districts below. The Lowers–as it was called by the locals–remained lit by blazing neon signs as nightlife closed down to make way for the daywalkers. An ongoing cycle that seemed to never end.

Mattia loved this place and its many districts of life, culture, and color. From Laberdash Court to the bustling Backomie Avenue shops, it was vibrant and beautiful, but she knew better than to trust the cover of a book to tell its own story.

The Cleric had lived in the enormous city since her acceptance to the Shorehart Program years ago. Shorehart was an elite counseling school that trained the upcoming Clerics with the most potential to be therapists under The High Council. Back then, she had lived on the lower dormitory levels within The High Temple and enjoyed it for what it was. There was always something to do, and it felt no different from living in the city below. It was the work that she loved, healing people's minds through compassion and medicine.

The mind was an adventure; it could turn a nightmare into a dream if one could figure out which buttons to push. This work had captivated her as a student in primary school. She was selected by all her academy masters and placed on the path to becoming an elite counselor, but it was Obadiah who saw the potential in her to become a member of The High Council.

As the transport approached the Temple, she sighed, thinking about her old Mentor. Obadiah was second in command before–

*"Unboarding will begin in ten seconds. Please have your belongings ready as you depart the transport. Thank you for traveling with us this morning and we hope you have a joyous day."*

The intercom interrupted her thoughts and, sighing again, she picked up her briefcase. But *this* sigh had more weight to it. Today was the day she had been dreading all week; today she needed to convince the Council to extend the treatment of client 43972. The boy, Jonathan Young, had regressed over the previous two years he had been in her care. It had been four years total under the supervision of the High Council. He was now thirteen years old and, having made no progress, the Council would vote on his fate today.

In 178NW, High Cleric Martina Thesicus had written her famous and controversial dissertation introducing the Euthanization Decree. It stated that if clients were no longer improving due to their ongoing illness, they must not become a burden upon society. They will, therefore, be humanely euthanized to ease their suffering and improve their caregivers' productivity. This was understood to not be an act of malice but simply a method to humanely end the suffering of clients who were not responding to treatments created by the top researchers and therapists at The High Temple.

These treatments were nowhere near as primitive as the ones in the Old World. In those days, medications were given as more of a bandage than a solution to the problem. In this new system of government and healthcare, medications and treatments were a mixture of holistic and reconstructive solutions, which worked 95% of the time. Mental illness was losing the battle, reports showed.

Jonathan was admitted to the Council's care when he was nine years old and had only regressed, his dissociative tendencies and aggression increasing when not heavily sedated. Jonathan's case was quite different than others under the care of the High Council. Jonathan had been placed with the High Council when his parents were found butchered in their home. The boy was found under the bed, completely terrified and without any memory of what had occurred in the house that night. Disturbances were called in by neighbors who heard screams coming from the Young home almost a mile away. The Youngs oversaw a terraforming colony near the border of The Grey in the Eastern Republic territory. Their project had been ongoing for quite some time, and the Youngs were an intricate part of its success. They lived about three miles from the colony in a lovely house with a generous portion of land beside the forest bordering The Grey. Even though they were the wealthiest family in the colony, they were humble and quite hospitable.

They threw a grand party once a month after the Gathering Day service, for the children and adults of the community to feast and socialize. They were generous with their property at other times as well. Neighbors were always welcome to stop by and share a meal or use the land for personal special occasions. The Youngs were well respected and deeply mourned after their tragic death, which was blamed on an elusive, debauched lunatic from The Grey; the dangers of living so close to a place like that. There were petitions to sweep The Grey and rid the civilized world of such vermin. Still, nothing more than a simple investigation was done, and then the colony was shut down and relocated six months later once the project was completed.

No one suspected Jonathan of any foul play in the incident. Everyone who knew the Youngs knew that Jonathan was a very meek, well-behaved child who spent most of his time with the animals on the property.

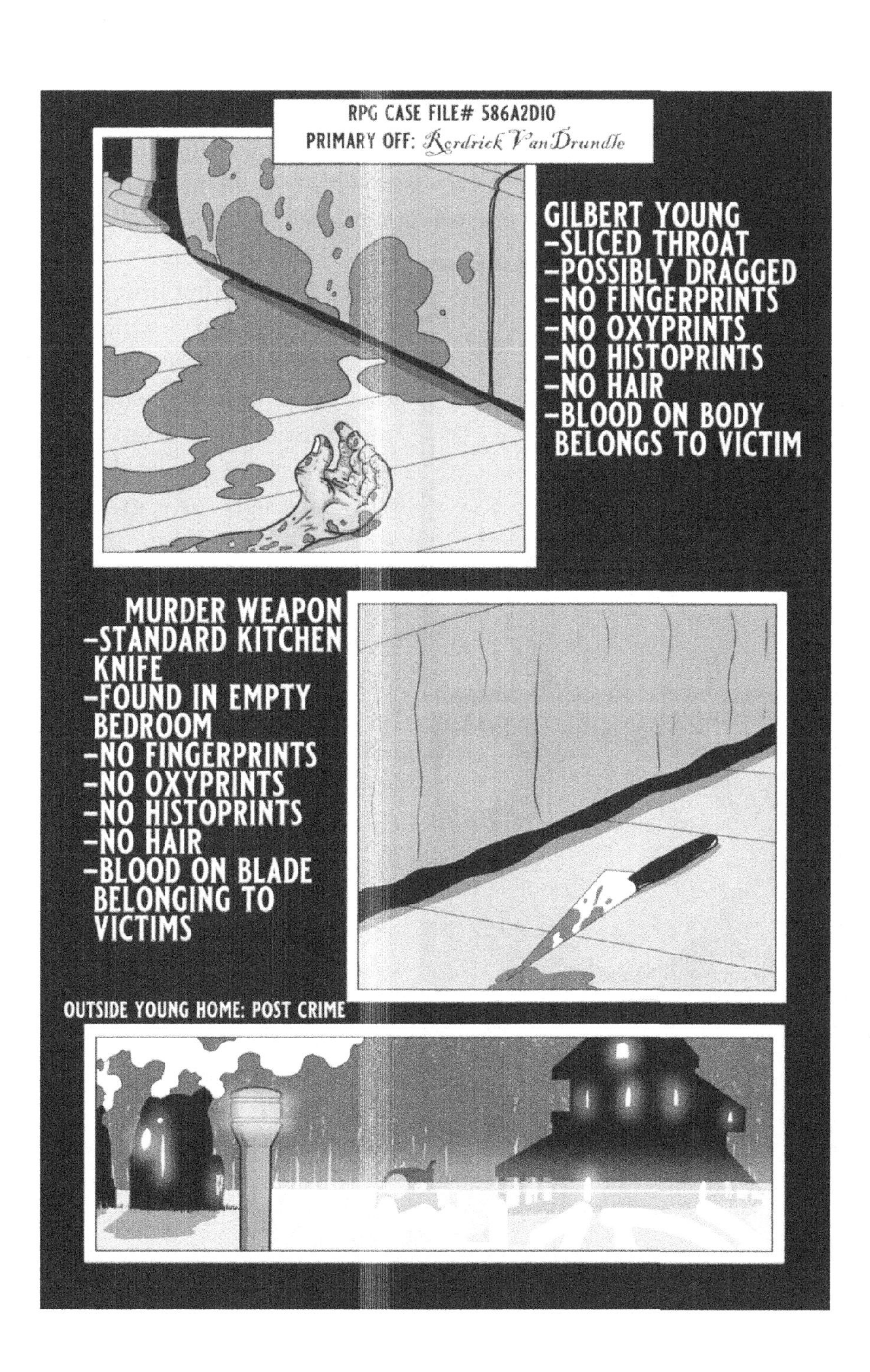
RPG CASE FILE# 586A2D10
PRIMARY OFF: Rordrick VanDrundle
GILBERT YOUNG
-SLICED THROAT
-POSSIBLY DRAGGED
-NO FINGERPRINTS
-NO OXYPRINTS
-NO HISTOPRINTS
-NO HAIR
-BLOOD ON BODY BELONGS TO VICTIM
MURDER WEAPON
-STANDARD KITCHEN KNIFE
-FOUND IN EMPTY BEDROOM
-NO FINGERPRINTS
-NO OXYPRINTS
-NO HISTOPRINTS
-NO HAIR
-BLOOD ON BLADE BELONGING TO VICTIMS
OUTSIDE YOUNG HOME: POST CRIME

He was liked by the other children, and he interacted appropriately with everyone he encountered. There was no way a small boy like him could have killed his parents, let alone in such a brutal manner. But, as time progressed with her client, Mattia had begun to believe something else was at work here.

He was first brought to the Cresthaven wing of Hillcrest Sanitarium, which was the children's wing for minor traumatic cases. Kids were housed here who did not show any signs of aggression, sexual or otherwise. In the beginning, the boy fit in fine. However, after the first year, he began having fits of rage and violence. After an episode, he returned to his quiet, meek self, remembering nothing. When he severely injured another child during one of these fits, he was transferred to Waverly Hall, a secluded wing of the Sanitarium. He was treated by Dr. Bouchard, the Headminister of the entire hospital.

Mattia volunteered to take Jonathan's case during this time. His personality changes and lack of memory piqued her curiosity and compassion for the boy. Over the next couple of years, Jonathan's personality disappeared entirely. When he was not in a catatonic state brought on by heavy doses of sedatives, he was what could only be described as evil.

Neither Mattia nor any of the other counselors had seen anything like Jonathan or the terror he brought to so many during the last few months of treatment. Now, Hillcrest staff were claiming to have nightmares of the boy appearing in different forms. In their nightmares, he would show them terrible things and catastrophic events. He knew things about people that he shouldn't. He was also showing abilities that had never been documented before in the history of The Grand Republic, such as telekinetic abilities, speaking in ancient dead languages, and levitating. Mattia and her colleagues were at a loss regarding treatment. The approved conventional techniques she had been utilizing in the last four years weren't working.

In the Old World, "the demonic" was rarely mentioned in clinical circles until an extreme case like this. The option of *exorcism* was always on the table if the patient or patient's family wished it to be so—and the patient met the specifications. However, in the New World, it was understood that those days were ruled by superstition and caused much more harm than good. And yet, Mattia's old Mentor taught her about the genuine success stories of exorcism. She was sure that she personally didn't buy into the reality of demons, but she knew that the patients who were convinced they were possessed found relief after an exorcism was successful. And sometimes, that's all it took for a patient to be considered cured.

However, these methods were now forbidden by the Council and the Courts of the High Elders and Patricians. She knew it went on in The Grey, and even though it was a long shot, she was prepared to propose that *desperate* methods be used in this desperate time for this desperate client. As Mattia exited the transport and walked onto the Mid-level Temple platform, her anxiety rose. The peace from the sunrise was nowhere to be found.

The High Council's session had convened in the Glass Room of the Observatory. The Observatory's portion of the penultimate level was uncovered, welcoming the fresh air that the terraform engines provided.

This level housed a beautiful garden surrounding the Observatory, which many Members used often. In fact, Mattia's favorite place on Earth was sitting under the large oak tree in the center of the garden. The Glass Room, however, was her least favorite. Over time, she had come to realize that what went on in this room defied what the glass intended to represent. Despite her hopeful resolve, she feared the entire system was proving to be precisely like the facade of the Glass Room.

Mattia sat as calmly as possible during the opening ceremonies of the session. The Council Clerics discussed the upcoming Gathering Day and who would give the homily about looking to the future for hope and peace. The High Cleric had chosen Cleric Gwen, who would deliver a portion of her newest dissertation on this exact topic. She had published it for mandatory Temple reading last year, but it had yet to be available to the public. The High Cleric thought this would be a perfect opportunity to share it with them.

Gwen, Phillip, and Edgar were High Cleric Malcolm's inner circle, and they always looked radiant. Gwen, with her short silver hair and midnight skin, Phillip, who looked as though he walked right out of an Old World Sultan's Council; and Edgar, who strongly resembled Malcolm with his well-shaved bald head, dark sunken eyes, and peach skin. Rarely was the High Cleric seen without them by his side, so it was no surprise that one of them would be delivering such an essential homily for such a critical Gathering Day. Mattia didn't care. That's not why she was here.

After the Gathering Day broadcast, the Council Clerics would join the High Cleric in the Observatory's Labyrinth Patio for the annual Midsummer's Eve Harvest Meeting. Malcolm himself would be leading them in a private ceremony of labyrinth mediation–a ritualistic meditation practice where walking along a maze-like path carved or painted on the ground, brings more and more tranquility as progression is made toward the center of the labyrinth. This meditation would bring rest as they prepared for the remaining year where the nights grew longer.

After all this was planned, they started on the session's "Fate of The Clients" portion. This was where each client's number would be brought to the table and decided by vote, determining what would be done with their treatment plans. Mattia grew increasingly nervous as the High Cleric brought up Jonathan's number.

"Fellow Clerics, a verdict *must* be reached on this one today, I'm afraid. We all knew this was coming." High Cleric Malcolm's voice slithered through Mattia's ears. He was going to try and make this quick. "After much deliberation and meditation on the subject, I move to euthanize the client due to the unfortunate regression of his mental and physical health. All who favor closing case 43972 say 'Aye.'"

"High Cleric." Mattia interrupted before anyone could officially agree; she knew they already unofficially did. "I implore you to reconsider. We cannot give up on this boy." She pleaded. Malcolm's countenance was undisturbed. He knew she would protest this case; she was too close to the boy to let it go. Mattia's unhinged compassion and lack of discernment kept her from his inner circle. He needed to weed that out of her and replace it with loyalty.

She was much too sensitive in her approach to these clients and was allowing that to overshadow her purpose here. She could be so much more if only he could *instruct* her more intimately. It was something the High Cleric had wished to change for quite some time, but her stubbornness was making things difficult.

"Cleric Mattia. There's nothing more we can offer this client. We have worked on his case for over four years, and the boy has only worsened." He could see her brow twitching and continued, knowing he was getting under her skin. "His condition appears to be permanent and irreversible. It is time to begin closing ceremonies and plan the client's Euthanization Day." The High Cleric ended his rebuttal with a condescending grin that radiated smugness throughout his entire being, from his peach bald head down to his navy cloak-covered boots. "Now, as I was saying–"

Mattia spoke again, mustering all her courage.

"High Cleric, with all due respect, I ask that we explore...*other options* to attempt to save this boy's life." There, it was out in the open now. Mattia's plea had been made, and the response was already going as she expected. Deafening silence filled the chamber. The High Cleric glared at her while the rest of the ten gazed at her in confusion and amazement. Rarely was the High Cleric openly challenged on such matters, but to suggest "other options" only meant one thing: deviating from The Code.

Trying to save her dear friend and colleague, Cleric Wendy, who oversaw the Cresthaven wing of the Sanitarium, spoke up.

"What other options do you suggest, Mattia? You and I have been working on this case since the Council officially received the client." Wendy was as brilliant as she was kind, but this was too much even for her. She attempted to give Mattia a way out. Wendy knew her colleague and friend had been under much stress lately with this case and was concerned about where that stress may lead. "Look, we tried everything the High Cleric has suggested. There's nothing more we can do." *Drop it, Matty,* Wendy's eyes urged. *This is not a hill you need to die on.* But Mattia was determined in her response to her well-intentioned friend.

"There are other methods. Alternative ways of dealing with a case this extreme." She then stood up and addressed the room. "They may deviate from The Code–" gasps and shuffling of robes immediately started.

"Cleric Mattia, let me–" The High Cleric interrupted but was cut off.

"They *may* deviate from The Code, but they have been known to work in other areas and at different times. This case is an exceptional one, and we cannot just give up because we don't know what the answer is at the moment. There are cases from the Old World that–"

"The Old World was monstrous!" High Cleric Malcolm's voice rose and shook with rage. "As were its methods and those currently being used in *The Grey*, which is where I'm sure you were going with this inspiring and educational monologue. Let me remind you that The Code was given to us as a means to not slip back into the ways of superstitious nonsense! We have evolved in our ways of dealing with troubled individuals, and when it is too late for a client and they are beyond our current ability to heal, we must, for the good of the client, the good of the Republic, and the productivity of this Council, offer permanent rest to that individual and move on to the next case!"

Malcolm paused to compose himself and sighed disapprovingly. He then continued in a more calm yet condescendingly dismissive tone. "There are reasons for these things, Cleric Mattia. To you, The Code may be a silly dogmatic text that shouldn't be taken seriously, but to us," he waved his arms around the table, "it is a very real and consequential tome that has made this world flourish for almost a thousand years."

"If we're never willing to try–" She tried to speak, but he immediately cut her off in a loud authoritative tone.

"To this Council, anything other than The Code is not only unorthodox but also dangerous to the future of science, logic, and medicine. If you disagree, perhaps you may not belong here with us." The High Cleric knew he had struck a chord with her. Mattia's eyes began to well up, and her arms tensed as she leaned against the steel table. He knew she was angry, but her silence meant he won this battle. Now for the final blow that would strike her down and put her back in her place. "You are beginning to sound like your old Mentor. I hope his disobedience has not inspired you?"

Silence blanketed the room once more for what felt like an eternity. The High Cleric and Mattia stared at each other with intensity, but Mattia's gaze broke first. She knew what that meant. She was one wrong move away from expulsion, or worse, exile. Her colleagues' expressions showed shock. She had never acted in this way before. Gwen and Edgar seemed to revel in it. Mattia knew if she didn't back down now, Jonathan would be lost, and there was no way she could help him.

"No, High Cleric. The traitor's behavior has not inspired anything inside of me. Forgive me. I was out of line." With that, she sat down, defeated. The High Cleric bowed his head toward her in a seemingly humble gesture of accepting an apology. He addressed the room again, filled with a smug sense of victory and a smirk he couldn't quite hold back.

"It's settled then. We shall begin closing statements on this case and proceed."

In a matter of seconds, the Council had decided Jonathan's fate. Seven days until his Euthanization Ceremony, which allowed the Midsummer's Eve Ceremonies to take place and then a weekend to prepare. The meeting adjourned two hours later. Mattia got up from her seat, gathered her things, and walked out of the Glass Room. As she crossed its threshold, she realized this would likely be the last time she ever would walk over it as a Cleric of The High Council. She said nothing to her fellow Clerics, and she avoided all contact with Malcolm. She wanted to believe that the High Council stood for something other than control, but after what she had just witnessed, she wasn't sure if it ever had.

Mattia walked down the cobblestone walkway of the Observatory, past the Grand Hall Telescope, where a class of fourth-year astronomy students was conducting daytime observations of the sky. She envied them. They had fresh hearts and minds with dreams of solving the world's problems and believed they were in a system that shared those same dreams. Perhaps she was wrong about the government she had dedicated her life to, at least as a whole. But she was not wrong about Malcolm.

Obadiah had warned her about him years ago. Even before then, she had her suspicions, but nothing concrete proved him to be anything more than a shrewd leader. Malcolm lacked compassion sometimes, but other times, he could be the most caring man. He had counseled many clients with great empathy and success, but there was always *something* about him that bothered Mattia. Something she couldn't quite explain.

Today, however, she saw it. It was like the scales falling from Saul's eyes in the old Yeshuite folklore. How could she have been so blind before? The overwhelming lust for power in Malcolm's deep-set, gray eyes was blaringly evident, obviously *sinister*. She wasn't sure how many Clerics he was controlling, but she knew it was more than a few. Mattia was giving Wendy the benefit of the doubt, but she was confident Gwen, Edgar, and Phillip were blind followers of The High Cleric. Could he be conspiring against the Grand Chancellor? Was that his goal? If so, that seemed foolish as The High Cleric was almost as influential and powerful as the Chancellor. *Almost.* That could be it. Maybe he craved more?

He certainly wouldn't be the first man in the history of the world to do that. Either way, Mattia knew what she had to do if she wanted to save this boy. It was true; Jonathan was much more than just another client in her eyes. Over the years, she had allowed herself to cross the professional line. This deep sort of attachment was forbidden, but the Council Cleric didn't care anymore. What had begun as professional curiosity transformed into a mother's love, and she would fight for this boy with all her might. She was willing to sacrifice everything so he could survive and have a real chance at life.

As she passed the large oak one last time, Mattia knew whatever remnants of hope she had placed in the High Council had just died in the Glass Room. She was leaving her navy robes behind and was prepared to commit treason.

# CHAPTER TEN

## - GOOD TROUBLE -

The transport ride home was both the longest and shortest Mattia had ever experienced. She fought back tears of sadness and an overwhelming sense of rage but felt confident that what she was doing had to be done for Jonathan, the future of The Grand Republic, and herself. Mattia couldn't help but feel so utterly alone in this prison of emotions. She looked out of the window at the city she called home and it felt so distant, so cold. It was amazing the difference a few hours could bring. Mattia felt foolish that she let her optimism get the better of her, and not just about this meeting, about everything. Obadiah was right, it seemed, at least about Malcolm.

At the beginning, Mattia had felt surprised and a little hurt that her old Mentor had never tried to contact her after his banishment. She assumed he probably thought he was protecting her by keeping his distance. She had grown so close to him in their last couple of years together, and she still had many questions. He was there one day and then gone the next, banished for treason. She never knew exactly what he was banished for, even though she had her suspicions.

However, one day, years later, after she had been elected as a Cleric of the High Council, a blank envelope was left on her desk inside the temple. The only thing written on it was coordinates. No signature. No note. Mattia knew what this meant and was positive it had to be from Obadiah. When she was training under him, he would use this method in his teaching style.

"It's to make things interesting," he would always say. Each set of coordinates would lead to a clue, leading to another set of coordinates. Eventually, the scavenger hunt led to a final test on Old World lore. If she got the answer right, she would get a week's extension on her following dissertation. It was a fun game meant to invigorate her mind and pique her interest in lore. Obadiah always emphasized how important it was.

*If we don't know the tales of the past, how will we ever understand the purpose of the future?* Mattia had that saying memorized by her second week under his tutelage.

She kept the coordinates hidden in her flat in case she ever needed them. Mattia had been tempted to find the location before. But, due to the danger and suspicion it could create, she forced herself to wait for a moment when that didn't matter anymore. The last thing Mattia had needed was an R.P.G.–Republic Protector's Guild–Officer on her back.

Once that occurred, one might as well say goodbye to the Republic and get used to The Wastelands' way of living. But now? As soon as she went off-grid, she could finally find out where the coordinates led, if they even led to anywhere anymore.

How long had it been? Over five years, to be sure. A lot could have happened during that time, and if he had gone where she suspected, the danger of such a place was insurmountable from what she had heard. She knew Obadiah ran a secret mission to The Grey to help suffering people. They were not allowed citizenship in The Grand Republic unless they gave up their "frivolous" ways and rejoined society. Mattia admired Obadiah for wanting to help those people and even assisted him secretly once or twice before his banishment. Regardless of how she felt about their reasoning for remaining in that awful place, she understood that it was their home and they were in great need. The Grey wasn't a place anyone dared to tread lightly.

Her guess was that those secret, ongoing mission trips had everything to do with his banishment and eventual destination afterward. Although she had never been there, Mattia was almost certain she would experience it firsthand.

Lucky her.

Mattia made it home and gathered her things, tucking the coordinates in her belt pocket. She draped herself in an old tattered, light brown, hooded cloak to block out the R.P.G. facial recognition bots. Then she walked the long thirty-block trek that led to the Descension Tube—a sizeable vertical transport to the lower districts—at the end of Artly Park.

As a Cleric of the High Council, Mattia had to be careful not to be recognized. If word got back to the High Cleric that she was seen heading to The Lowers—especially after that meeting—things could escalate quickly and not in her favor. Mattia believed that her posture of obedience in The Glass Room had assured him of her loyalty, at least for the moment, and she had to keep things that way. She had to buy enough time to get help and she only had seven days to make something happen.

The streets and walkways were busy, which gave her plenty of cover. It would rain later that evening, and many people had their poncho cloaks on in preparation, so blending in wasn't a problem—and with how worn her cloak was, she would also blend in well down below.

The Lowers wasn't necessarily impoverished as much as it was less "highbrow." Even though financial poverty was mostly extinct in The Grand Republic, it remained in spirit and in some ways of living. It was those who had an attitude of poverty who tended to favor the Lowers. In this way, the area was looked down upon by those who lived in the higher levels of the City of The High Temple. Still, it wasn't sneered at or feared in the way The Grey was, for even The Lowers still adhered to Grand Republic law, at least on the surface.

Once her crowded ride on the Descension Tube had reached its destination, Mattia could smell the mysterious odors of The Lowers before the doors even opened. She loved this city and its people more than anything, but even *she* had to fight the prejudice in her mind on that ten-minute ride down. Her condescension was not because of a lower-than-blue-collar status being forced upon them; it was primarily because they actively embraced this lifestyle.

In The Lowers, the housing districts and the red districts were mostly indistinguishable. While sex work was outlawed and punishable by the courts, StagNight bars offered patrons a more *synthetic* approach to pleasure. They were very legal, and business was always good. As long as it was artificial, it was allowed and even funded by the government in some cases to prevent new sexually transmitted diseases from spreading. Even though all of them had been cured, they feared something new emerging.

Because she had assisted Obadiah on a couple of his secret mission projects in the past–even though she had never been to The Grey–Mattia knew how to get to her destination undetected. The skycab routes were always smuggling things and people in and out of The Grey, and there was a particular pub on the East side of The Lowers that catered to such agendas if you knew how to ask.

Mattia kept her hood up as she passed through the busy, neon-lit walkways of what the locals called Porthaven, which consisted of mostly coffee taverns, pubs, and "bot-repair" shops. She passed a few locals waiting to get their cybernetics adjusted and remembered the heavy Cyberfolk population in this area.

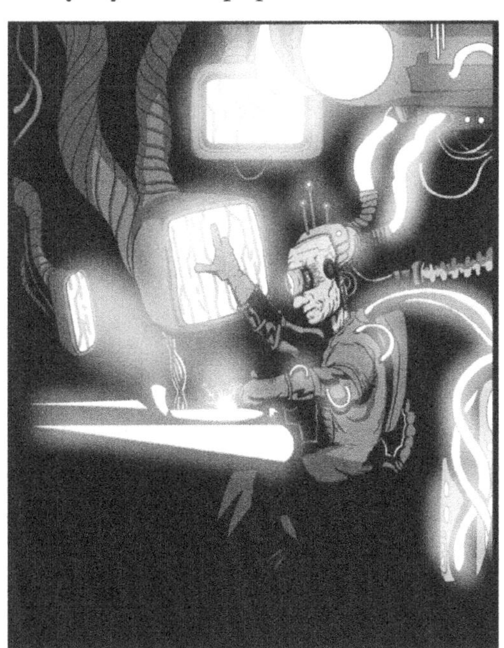

To combat the growing trend of cyber enhancement, in 531NW, Grand Chancellor Unarius Cobalt passed a law that prevented people from becoming more than 40% cybernetic unless it was medicinal. There were even some career and life placement paths that forbade it altogether. Over the last couple of hundred years or so, it became almost a statement of rebellion against the higher levels of civilization across The Grand Republic.

The term "Cyberfolk" was officially coined in 710NW, after the trend had been acknowledged as a legitimate way of life instead of just a fad. Even though it was illegal to identify as a cyborg more than a human, there were ways to get around the terminology. Cyberfolk were seen as "lesser than" by the higher levels of civilization, so they found refuge in The Lowers, where they could work and live away from all the scoffing and sneering.

Mattia walked through the network of districts, avoiding the red ones as much as possible when, finally, she made it to the far east side. The Galleria District was essentially one large restaurant marketplace filled with food carts and pop-up shops offering a variety of cuisines claiming to be from the Old World. The specific pub she sought was tucked away on the corner below a cyber-tech shop.

**BURGRAM GOLLIVER'S SPIRITS & CHIPS** was painted on the large sign atop the front of the pub. Mattia could tell the paint hadn't been touched up in the ten years since she had been here last. It was chipped and worn, just like the building itself. She smiled though, thinking it gave the place character. Not everything in this world needs to be polished to shine.

As Mattia stood before the heavy, frosted-glass doors, she paused to consider what she was about to do. There was still time to turn around. The heaviness of the consequences weighed on her. When she left the Council meeting, Mattia knew this was the end of Jonathan's care by the Council and her trust in the administration of High Cleric Malcolm. But if she did what needed to be done, her punishment would most likely be much worse than her former Mentor's banishment.

A Cleric on the High Council deliberately disobeying the will of the Council itself and conspiring with an excommunicated Council Member to do so could mean execution at best or a one-way trip to The Wastelands at worst. And what happens if this plan of hers worked? She would still have committed treason even if the boy's life was saved. But what was at stake here if she didn't do this? The life of a boy she had committed herself to serve and her dignity. Her integrity, which drove her passion for caring for others, was on the line.

For Mattia's whole life, she longed to help those in need. She had dedicated her talents and intelligence to fighting for those who couldn't fight for themselves. If she were to let Jonathan die, all of that would die too. As she stopped for a final moment and weighed her options, she realzed there was no contest. She pulled open the heavy glass door and stepped inside the pub.

Mattia found a secluded spot at the bar. There weren't many people in the pub, she noticed with relief. At first, she had no intention of drinking anything, but she decided that it wouldn't hurt to keep up appearances. Plus, it might be nice to have a quiet drink before her cab arrived. She could use a glass of aged corn whiskey–neat–to settle her nerves a little.

Before sitting down, she walked up to the barkeep at the front of the pub and informed him that she needed "a skycab on the rocks" and hoped it still meant what it did ten years ago. His half-cybernetic smirk and reply, "Be here in fifteen." assured her that she was still in the know. Now, she waited and stared at the oak counter before her, feeling anxious and alone in the world.

"What'll it be?" A gruff voice from behind the bar interrupted her staring contest with the counter. His hands were busy cleaning a glass mug with a thick sanitization rag.

"I'll have whatever is the strongest." She knew enough about corn whiskey to know that's what she would get. The barkeep sat the glass mug in front of her, grabbed a bottle of Multor Verbose 550NW, and began to pour the golden-brown liquid for her to enjoy. She immediately did.

"You're a little far from The High Temple, aren't you?" She almost spat her drink out. After somewhat recovering from choking on the burning liquid, she looked up at the barkeep, who had obviously seen through her disguise.

He was a middle-aged man with brown skin and a thick, well-kept dark beard marbled through with white. Above his scarred forehead–he must have had gotten into a few fights in his day–his brownish-white hair was pulled back into a ponytail, and the twisted locks reached to the base of his neck and top of his shoulders.

He had a mischievous smirk, and his eyes danced a little. He began to chuckle. "You're a Cleric, right? Don't worry, I'm not going to say anything to anyone. Nobody cares around here anyway." His smile was warm and trusting. Mattia began to loosen up just a bit. There was no hiding it or trying to deny anything at this point.

"What gave me away?" She said defeatedly, in a tone that said, *please, don't tell anyone.*

"Pretty much everything about you, from your high-quality cloak to your lack of Lowers....fragrance. But mostly, it was your cadence of speech." Mattia's hopes about her cloak and blending in were dashed. "So, what brings you to a place like this?" The barkeep continued as he picked up another mug to clean. There was something about him that she couldn't quite place, but for some reason, Mattia instinctively trusted this man.

"Desperation." She replied.

"I see. I've seen a lot of desperation in this pub, and I've gotten pretty good at judging the heart of a person. Something tells me your motives are a little different than most who pass through here." There was an earnestness and wisdom in his voice.

"I don't know about that." And she meant it. She didn't know about a lot of things anymore. "Have you ever had to make a decision that you knew in your gut to be right, but if you followed through with it, you would lose...everything?" What was she doing? She was letting her guard down so easily with a complete stranger, but there was *something* about him. She knew beyond the shadow of a doubt that she could trust this man. It didn't make logical sense, but she knew it was true.

He paused cleaning the mugs, momentarily lost in thought, and looked down at the counter. Mattia could tell he was contemplating something heavy. Then he sighed and looked up at her with the most honest, brown eyes she had ever seen.

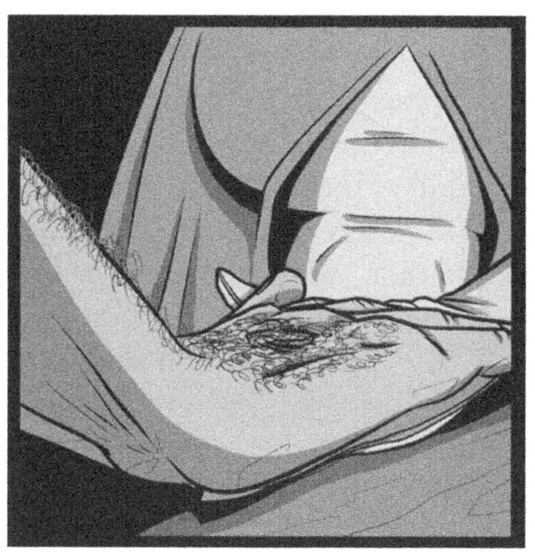

"Once...a long time ago, I was faced with a decision. My family's life depended on it. It cost me *everything*. But I did it." Now, a Lowers barkeep being someone with his intellect and observation skills was making a little more sense to her. And she couldn't help but think of where *she* might be in a week's time.

"Was it worth it?" she asked, tears welling up. The barkeep put his scarred, calloused hand on hers and stared deeply into her green eyes.

"I would do it again in a heartbeat." The touch of his hand brought a comfort that she hadn't felt since childhood. A glimmer of hope began to shine inside her for the first time in what felt like an eternity. She couldn't contain herself. Tears began to flow down her face as her fears started to diminish and a mysterious feeling of joy began to bloom inside.

"Thank you. I...I didn't expect such compassion from a–"

"From a barkeep in The Lowers?" His smile was warm.

"Yes." She chuckled shamefully, her tears continuing to flow. "I'm sorry. Excuse me, do you have a lavatory I can use?"

"Sure thing. Right around the corner." He hushed his voice. "When you come out, your skycab should be ready." He picked up the tray of glass mugs he had just cleaned and turned toward the kitchen.

Mattia opened the lavatory door and removed her hood. After washing her face in the sink, she dried herself and took a long look in the mirror. It didn't make sense, but she was more confident than ever that this was the right move. Even if it cost her career, her status, her home that she loved so much, or even her life.

Mattia was thinking more clearly than ever. This system she had blindly trusted to steward the people and to uphold the law was broken. It gave up on people to sustain its appearance and comfort. But it didn't just give up on them; it killed them. She saw now that it was genocide to maintain a facade of greater good. How could she have been so blind? She had wanted so badly to believe that she was on the right side of history that she was willing to overlook the deaths of thousands, even millions, of sick people who needed help. No more.

"No more." She reiterated out loud, pulled her hood back up, and walked out the door.

When she reached bar area, the Cyberfolk barkeep motioned her over with a wave of his hand. She knew her cab was ready, and so was she. Mattia walked up to the front counter and handed the man three rathbone coins to pay for her drink and two more for a tip.

"Thanks for the drink," she said with a smile. "And let the other barkeep know that his advice was well heard, and I thank him for his kindness." The barkeep looked at her strangely. His cyber features contorted in confusion as he looked around.

**BEEP BEEP!**

Hearing the horn of the cab, Mattia knew she had to hurry. She shrugged off the barkeep's confusion and smiled once more.

"Joyous evening to you." Mattia exited Burgram Golliver's Spirits & Chips with a newfound determination and hope for the first time in months.

He watched her leave the pub and get into the light covered green and gray SkyCab. No one saw him. He shielded all those around him from being able to see his presence, for the Light he emitted was so powerful it would destroy them all. He watched as the cab hovered above the street and then rose to meet the traffic about fifty yards above.

Rarely did the cosmic laws allow him to intervene in such a way, but she was on the path now. The Dark was cunning and bold, but he knew that any plans it was unfolding didn't stand a chance against the spark of hope Mattia Bajuma now had in her heart. That spark was enough to tear down any army. That was, in fact, the idea.

As he watched her skycab fly off, he could see everything in every corner of every realm. He was everywhere, watching all things simultaneously unfold.

Deep within The Grey, he watched grievously through the trees of a dense, haunting grove as a young woman was stretched out on a stone altar. In this dreadful place, the veil between the realms grew thinner by the minute. The chants of the disciples of Endor swam through the branches of the Kemick Agac, The Tree of The Skull, and pierced the night with powerful necroplasmic energy.

Standing at the head and the foot of the altar known as the High Circle were the two High Sisters of Endor, Agatha and Annis. This was an unholy ceremony of grief and birth as their former sister, Agnus, slumped over, dead, on a throne of sticks. Her lifeless corpse and severed head were rotting before their eyes. Stretched out on the altar was a young woman named Etrulia. She had run from all she had known and found herself in the wicked embrace of this odious, ancient cult that had manipulated her and promised her justice, using her lust for power and revenge.

As the chanting continued in this Dark ceremony, he watched the veil disappear, and two enormous and monstrous beings step out from the Sheolic realms, reveling in the Dark cosmic energy that allowed them to be there. Agatha and Annis bowed before the two elohim, their eyes, glowing a haunting yellow, rolling back into their heads.

He watched as a Dark beast draped in blood-red scales with a jawless flaming skull ushered the slimy, boil-covered, leather-skinned Yirah to the altar where the young woman lay. As Etrulia stared into the void of the night, Yirah ever so gently touched the space between her eyes, and they rolled back, mimicking that of the High Sisters'.

Far away, in the Elysian Fields of Perethedesh, in the Southern Territory of The Grand Republic, this same being of Light watched Gabriel, a Son of The Septum Dei, as he labored over his next strategic move. The overwhelming presence of The Dark Kingdom's stronghold was weighing on the Archangel. Although invisible to Gabriel, the illuminated being placed his hands on the Archangel's shoulders, bringing rest to his weary mind and hope in the midst of never-ending war.

In a barren desert of The Southern Republic–where no Terraform Engines ever seemed to work–the Darkness of Dudael reached beyond the Sheolic realms and into the very fibers of the Corporeum terrain itself. Unseen, he watched Lilith, Queen of The Wild Winds, gather her Fellowship to her side in preparation for the coming Black Mass. Dendron (The Oak King), Gaia, Baphomet,

Pazuzu, and all their hordes raised shadow blades in united victory over a plan that was thousands of Adamian years in the making.

He watched as Moriel and Akalian flew urgently through the cosmos to assist their dear friend and brother in Perethedesh, proving the comfort and hope he gave the Archangel was not in vain. He saw the strong brotherhood of these two elohim and their love for each other, but he also saw the probability of the coming events and how deeply these two would be tested.

In the Sheolic mind of twelve-year-old Jonathan Young, a sinister being admired the glowing green prison of slime that held the boy's soul captive. Xexxus' leathery skin shimmered as the putrid glow from the prison highlighted his enormous features. The invisible being of Light grimaced in disgust at the twisted smile of sharp, glowing fangs that spread across the face of this former King of Legion.

As Mattia's skycab rose above the clouds of Perethedesh, he watched it disappear into the night sky toward The Grey. He stood there suspended over the bustling city below, his cloak of blinding white Light flapping in the wind, revealing a golden chest plate with the emblem of the Tetragrammaton etched in the center. Ancient Lightrunes surrounded the symbol and also adorned his robes.

His brown skin was the same as it had been in the pub, as were the scars on his calloused hands and forehead. But although his twisted locks were still pulled back like before, they now showed no trace of brown. His beard and hair shone a pure, bright white. His glowing eyes of Light saw past the Corporeum Realm to every corner of every world and realm of The Cosmic Wheel. He saw all possibilities that were to come. He saw all decisions, every reaction, every ripple of energy that flowed throughout the cosmos and was present in all of them.

He knew the time had come for another rare move that his ordered cosmos allowed him to make. He paused for a moment, thinking of the weight that hung in the balance, took a breath, and he, Yahweh: King of Ages, creator of all things–for the first time in centuries–made a declaration for all fallen unseen beings to hear and heed.

"To all elohim of The Dark Kingdom, hear what I command. Cleric Mattia Bajuma is under my direct protection now. If any harm comes to her by your doing, before her appointed time, you will answer immediately and directly to me."

All Dark beings heard, and all shuddered at the thought of his wrath.

# CHAPTER ELEVEN
## -INTO THE FIRE-

While not every world or being in the Sheolic realms remained loyal to The Dark Kingdom, many of them did. Although some worlds had even been redeemed after the King's descension into this realm, as a result of his death long ago, Sheol was still where these sinister creatures called home. In fact, it was designed specifically *for* them long ago when The Cosmic Wheel first split. Yet, like all evil things, The Dark Kingdom craved more territory, and since the Creation Wars were lost, every Dark being of the unseen realms thirsted for rulership over the one place they still saw as their rightful claim: the realm of Corporeum.

One sinister creature, long ago, was able to unite The Dark Kingdom in a common goal through a necronomic prophecy known as Age End–the collapse of all order and the end of The Cosmic Wheel–spoken from the mouth of Khata himself. And even though this malevolent leader, known as The Dark Father, had been missing since the second Adamian world war ended–almost 2,000 years before this point in time–echoes in The Dark Kingdom of his prophetic crusade still drove many who remained loyal to his cause of ultimate cosmic chaos. For centuries, secret plans and silent armies lay dormant, strategically waiting for someone to give the order.

Then, after hundreds of years, as if out of nowhere, the Southern Territory of The Grand Republic became a hotbed of supernatural occurrences and infestations. This led to a raging Dark stronghold in the Sheolic plane, zeroing in on the city of Perethedesh and thinning the veil between the realms as each day passed. For over two hundred Adamian years, the presence of The Dark Kingdom had been growing much stronger; now, not even the great Archangel Gabriel and his legendary Order could overtake it. And even though this elohim of the Septum Dei knew help was on the way, and his King was ever present, his hope waned. He worried about something much more significant than this stronghold.

Something loomed in the back of his mind about what this hotbed of horror could mean for the future of The Cosmic Wheel, but alongside this concern grew something more. A shadow of a possibility haunted every step Gabriel took. Something he had narrowly escaped almost 2,000 years prior, and that escape, he feared, was now coming to its terrifying end.

Morning in The Lowers of Perethedesh was filled with buying and trading goods, hot food, and people hurrying off to the Ascension Tubes for work in the upper levels. Daily workers who stayed in the Lowers were Cyberfolk technicians, food cart chefs, coffee tavern baristas, or factory workers in the leathersteel mills. The rest of the business belonged to the night.

The Lowers may have been known for its less than tasteful decorum and activity, but it made the best leathersteel in The Grand Republic. The Lassiter Company, the largest factory in the Wellborne District, or "Cybertown" by the locals, was known worldwide for its quality of work. Because of that, they were responsible for the uniforms of the entire Republic Protector's Guild. From the Desk Jockeys and Field Troops to the R.P.G. Officers, every thread of leathersteel was carefully manufactured at The Lassiter Company for their safety and protection. Unfortunately, those who made the threads never felt safe or protected by those whom they clothed.

In the courtyards below the factory, merchants lined the cobblestone walkways with their cart-shops selling all types of supplies for leathersteel working. Food trollies, as well as carts selling everyday household items could also be found, in hopes that the workers would stop and shop on their way in or out of the mills. The R.P.G. looked the other way in this case because Torinth Lassiter, the president of the company, great-grandson of its founder, and High Leader of the Corporate Public House–was also dear friends with the Grand Chancellor, Magnus I. He encouraged this as a morale booster for his workers. In reality, it was to keep them close so that every step they took would be in the shadow of their "bountiful" livelihood. It was, like most things in this Republic, a method of control.

Control and power seemed to echo in the wind in those days, as most days before. Every person grasped for it, and the constant battle was not isolated to the Corporeum Realm of Perethedesh. To the average Adamian, this busy morning would look like the hustle and bustle of a typical day. However, if they could see beyond this realm, they would experience the viscousness of the Sheolic reality warring all around them.

"Watch out!!" yelled Raefun, as he tackled his brother in arms, saving him from the glowing green acidic bile of the beastly jotunn, towering over them, ten yards ahead. Their tzoharian armor was strong, but jotunn bile could eat through almost anything.

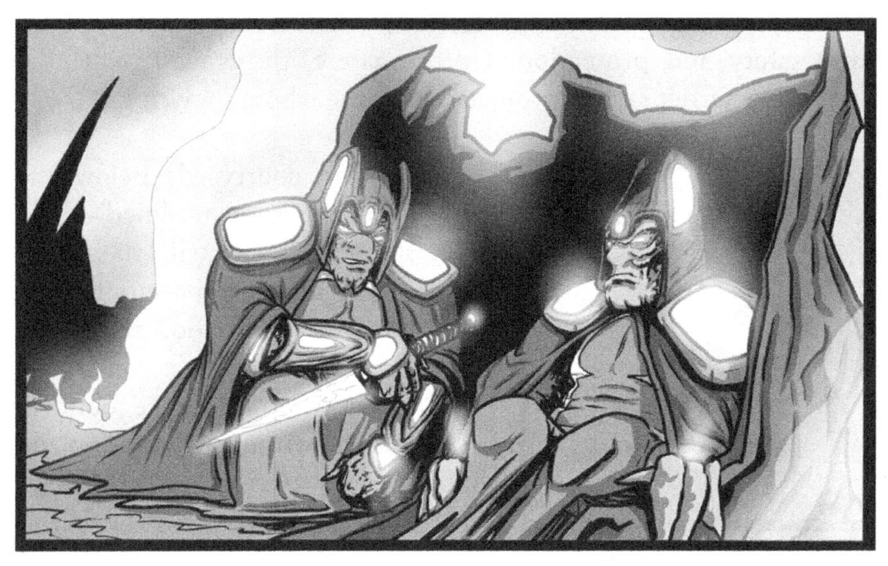

"Those putrid trolls. Damn them to the pit!" Joffus cursed as both gathered themselves back to their feet and knelt behind a wall of debris. "We *must* get this information to Lord Gabriel as soon as possible!" Their battalion had been on the front lines for six months of Adamian time, and both had just come from direct guardianship before Lord Gabriel reassigned them to the Stronghold War of Perethedesh. Joffus missed the intimate care of guardianship. He was loyal to the assigned Adamian he had grown to love as his own. Once he was assigned to her after she chose to entrust herself to the King, it had brought him so much joy guiding her through life, pointing her to the deeper truths of the cosmos, as she continued to embrace the ways of Light and authentic life. Life on the front lines of the constant war zone of The Cosmic Wheel was not always so joyous.

Every elohim, who was released from direct guardianship when their Adamian passed into their Purgatory, rotated into a battalion so others could rotate out. Unfortunately for Joffus and Raefun, their company was very skilled and well-rested from their previous assignments, so naturally, it would be the most equipped to hold the frontlines of battle.

They didn't think of themselves as being mistreated or of it being unfair. They were always willing to do whatever it took to defeat The Dark Kingdom and its ongoing, relentless rebellion against The White Throne. Someone had to fight on the front lines, and all of them would give their last breath to see the Light of the throne fully restore ultimate order to the cosmos. The most disheartening part, however, was that this particular stronghold wasn't only being maintained by the Dark but it was actually expanding.

Through a stealth operation, Joffus and Raefun had found some crucial intel, and they desperately needed to return to their base before the evening's Pentaclegate and inform Lord Gabriel. In the last few weeks, it seemed that unneeded reinforcements charged through Necrogates randomly, making it impossible for the Host to establish a consistent barricade. The latest addition to the stronghold was jotunns–giant troll creatures with ravenous bile they could project at their enemies. They had appeared outside the leathersteel factory two nights ago and had gained the entire courtyard for twenty-four hours. One was enough to overpower a small band of soldiers, but twenty-five had come through the portal, and overwhelmed them completely. Many of Gabriel's troops had been severely injured and worse upon the jotunns' arrival.

They had to keep the Dark forces from reaching the factory at all costs. Gaining such a fortified presence in the city would significantly enhance the Dark Kingdom's power. It wasn't so much the size of the mills–although that would be a huge advantage–but the Lassiter Company was fueled by greed and lust for power already, which made it even more difficult for Gabriel's forces to hold it as their own. If The Dark Kingdom gained such a place, it would become a fortress within the stronghold that would be nearly impenetrable.

Raefun and Joffus knew the importance of this final stand in which they found themselves. Their battalion had managed to take down ten of the twenty-five jotunns, but this one in front of them seemed to be the alpha of the gruesome pack.

Joffus sheathed his Lightblade and drew his short sword from the side of his admiral blue, tzoharian exoskeletal armor.

"Alright, jotunns are weakest at the joints below their haunches. I need you to get its attention and keep it occupied for a few moments. Leave the rest to me." Joffus stated with the confidence of a true warrior.

"Shine in the Darkness, brother." Raefun clasped forearms with his compatriot and leapt into a barrel roll onto the open field of battle. The snarling beast had just vomited acidic bile toward the main protection shields in front of the factory, and immediately spotted Raefun. The jotunn roared at him, its thick yellow fangs protruding from black, rotting gums. Its bulbous pale grey skull was covered in veins and sagging flesh. It stood upright about fifteen feet high, and had raging tentacles thrashing from its back. As it took a giant step forward, the ground below shook as its calloused, taloned foot crashed to the surface. Although it had no eyes, the beast still somehow gazed at Raefun with a piercing hatred and malice that washed over him like a consuming fire. It made him freeze for a moment, not out of fear, but in terrible awe at such a thing. How could an elohim of grace and love willingly become such a seemingly mindless creature of the Dark?

The jotunn roared again, and Raefun saw the glowing putridity of green saliva and acidic discharge about to project from its mouth toward him. He regained his composure and leaped to the right, just in time, dodging the slime. Jumping to his feet, the warrior hurled his short sword at the beast, stabbing it in the thick sack of its throat. The jotunn let out a loud growling yelp and slapped at the blade extending from its throat-sack. It swallowed the blade inside the sagging flesh. With a mighty cough, the now glowing, bile-covered Lightblade flew from the back of the jotunn's throat and slammed into Raefun's shoulder, piercing the armor like a hot knife through butter.

The warrior screamed in agony as the energy from the Dark and the Light traveled through his skin and out of the back of his shoulder blade. The force wasn't enough to travel through the back of his armor, though. The blade remained lodged inside his flesh, causing an enormous amount of burning pain. Raefun fell to his knees, yelling in torment as he grabbed the fresh wound.

The sounds of Raefun's pain were drowned out by the battle cry of Joffus as he severed the tendons at the left haunch joint of the jotunn. The beast writhed in pain and blasted acidic vomit wildly into the air. The feral tentacles on its back slammed into Joffus' helmet, sending the warrior soaring ten yards across the battlefield. But since most of the weight of a jotunn is placed on this particular haunch joint, the beast could no longer stand properly without the tendons to support it, let alone use that leg to walk.

"Bring it down!!" Shouted a soldier of the Host as more troops finally caught up to the scene and began blasting it with tzoharian energy from their breastplates. The blasts were not yet penetrating the beast's thick, leathery skin, but they seemed to be weakening it. One of the troops grabbed Raefun and carried him toward the protection shield.

As the jotunn began to pivot on its strong leg, it vomited wildly, directing the acidic slime at its opponents. Joffus jumped to his feet and started running toward the beast's tentacle-infested back. He leapt forcefully, swinging his Lightblade wildly at the serpentine appendages, slicing two in half. Joffus landed in the middle of its back, using the base of each tentacle as footing to reach the bulbous head of the vomiting jotunn. The warrior spun the sword around his hand in an acrobatic fashion, gripping the handle with the blade pointed down, and slammed his sword of Light into the throbbing skull of the beast.

The jotunn let out one final yelping roar of agony as it staggered. It finally fell to the scarlet necroplasmic mud below its feet, while Joffus leapt off its head and landed hard on the ground next to its lifeless corpse. At that moment, looking down at the fallen behemoth, Joffus wondered what would happen to whatever Light remained inside this creature. Was there even a soul left, and if so, was there still a chance for redemption beyond this form? He hoped so, for all their sakes.

"Joffus!" shouted a fellow elohim running up to him. "Raefun is badly wounded. Please, come quickly." Without hesitation, Joffus sprinted toward the protective shield that shimmered a bright royal blue and surrounded the factory. When he arrived, his brother-in-arms was unconscious on a bed engulfed in Light. Joffus stopped in his tracks when he saw none other than Saint Lūqās attending to Raefun's injuries.

"The blade was covered in that beast's saliva when it entered his body." The Saint told Joffus. "We removed it as quickly as possible, but the amount of internal damage, due to the acidic nature of the bile... it's hard to say how long this will take to heal. They're prepping him for tonight's Pentaclegate." Joffus knelt beside the bed,

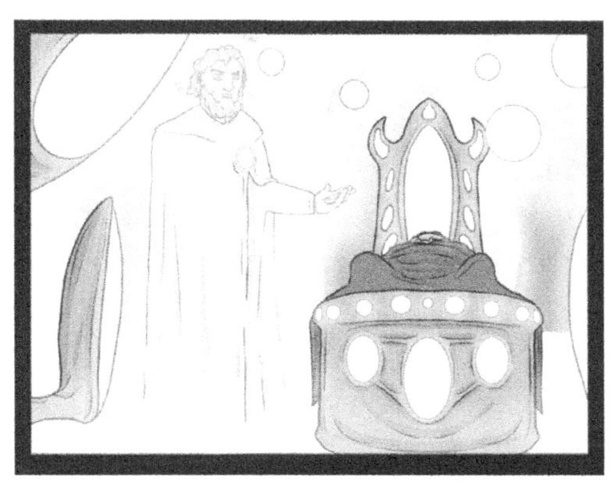

examining the damage the bile had wrought. Raefun's helmet, along with the armor from his torso and arms, had been removed. The skin of his organic robe was usually a smooth, silky teal green. However, the area surrounding the wound began to gray with streaks of leathery necroplasmic texture sprouting off in all directions down his arm and across his chest. The Lightrunes of his robe were faintly flickering in and out. Joffus knew this process all too well. He had seen too many of his fellow elohim fade from this form in such a state.

"Hang on, Raefun...please." A tear trickled down Joffus' maroon featherfur-covered cheek. He and Raefun had a long history of fighting side by side in this war across the millennia. Many elohim had faded from this form to join The White Throne. None of the remaining Host knew what that meant specifically, but they knew it meant they didn't see their siblings again. Promises of once again being with those who have faded echoed throughout the millennia, and the hope that the ending of this war would one day see those promises fulfilled kept every elohim going. It took a lot of damage to completely fade from this form. All elohim, Dark or Light, were immortal but not eternal. Despite what some may think, there is a difference.

To be immortal means that if a Heavenly being were to not sustain any substantial damage, they would live on. Even though those who remain in the Light do not die in the way an Adamian would, rather, they slip away into another form after spiriting away to The White Throne. There were many legends about what that form may be, but no one on this side of the war had seen it.

Saints, on the other hand, had already gone through death and their Purgatory, and arrived as Adamic Knights of The White Throne. Death in any form no longer held any power over them, as they were resurrected with the King and given spiritual bodies that naturally illuminated with tzoharian Light and reflected the Spirit of Yahweh wherever they went. It was rare to find such a Saint as Lūqās in a place like this. Joffus stood up and addressed this fact.

"Saint Lūqās, it's wonderful to see you here. But...what brings you to us?" It was a valid question as Lūqās was the Chief Saint of all physicians in every realm, including the Edenic elohim. For him to be here made Joffus a little concerned. Lūqās hesitated for a moment but knew what had to be done.

"The King asked that I be here...for you, Joffus. For the message you carry. What you are about to go through is unavoidable, but the pain need not be as great as it could." Joffus' heart sank as he heard these words. The grievous message from the Saint was immediately followed by a haunting, pulsing vibration, throbbing and rippling throughout the Host's encampment. Bright red energy began flowing through the air and collecting above their heads.

"No...it can't be," Joffus whispered to himself. He had never seen these creatures before. He had heard of them and the terror they wrought upon the Adamians, the elohim, and all Sheolic and Edenic creatures alike, but he had not *experienced* them. Pure fear ran through him like icy terror in his veins.

The Shadow Guard.

The nightmarish creatures, fluid, putrid, and tentacled were starting to appear through a Necrogate behind the protective shield. How? How was this possible?? Gabriel's shields were impenetrable from the inside. The amount of energy this Necrogate had to conjure to manifest in this space was unheard of. But here it was–in front of them. Bursting from the floating red energy pool came a mighty force of hatred and malice, sweeping the Heavenly Host in one fatal wave of screams and suffering.

Across the Sheolic terrain of Perethedesh, near The High Temple, victory cries from legions of The Dark Kingdom could be heard shrieking through the air. The loudest was the voice of Drakon, General of The Jackals, a nasty group of Kadathian mercenaries hired to do one thing: take control of The High Temple. They had accomplished that mission two weeks ago, and, since then, wave after wave of the Host failed to claim it and return it to its former state of neutrality.

With his calloused, pale-green, taloned hand, Drakon grabbed the throat of his would-be attacker on the battlefield full of warring elohim. He lifted the elohim and ran him through with his falcata shadow blade. Light and glowing white fluid erupted from the soldier's gut as he screamed in agony. The shrieks of pain were drowned out by the cackling laughter of the diabolical General.

This fallen creature had proven to be an unstoppable force in the ongoing battle for the Southern Territory. He had crushingly defeated many of Gabriel's troops over the years, and because of him and his Jackals, The Dark Kingdom had not given an inch. Drakon was their champion, their own personal stronghold defender, who proved his worth time and time again.

The General tossed the fading elohim aside like a ragdoll, parried from another attacker, swinging his giant falcata into the side of the attacking elohim's head, smashing through the helmet and piercing her skull. Drakon's bright green eyes smoldered from their hollow sockets and gazed over his protruding cheekbones of cracked, calloused leather.

His head was covered with armor that no tzoharian blade had been able to penetrate. The General claimed it was made of Seraphim bone. Shadowblade spikes stuck out of the side of the helmet, and a long featherbeard of a fallen elohim decorated the top of the bone-carved casque. Green, putrid saliva poured from his razor-sharp teeth as he mocked his foes openly while the battle raged around him.

"Pathetic!!" he shouted. "Where are your warriors!? Is this all the Host of The Heavens has to offer!?!" Gabriel's forces immediately began retreating, and Drakon gave out a sinister peal of laughter. "Such brave soldiers of Light!!" Drakon's mocking voice shouted. "Oh, how proud your would-be-king must be of the *self-sacrificial* loyalty on display in this city!! *Our city!!"* With this, the General raised his giant shadowblade victoriously and shouted, *"Praise The Dark Kingdom!! Long Live The Dark Father!!"*

Through his hubristic show, Drakon failed to notice that it wasn't only Gabriel's forces retreating but his own as well. From both sides, elohim were running and flying in all directions, away from where Drakon was standing. The General finally noticed as his surroundings became brighter, and the ground started to shake. As he looked over his shoulder, Drakon, the mighty hero of The Stronghold War of Perethedesh, was greeted with a meteor-sized ball of tzoharian energy. Bursting with emerald and blue Light, it crashed down upon him, burying him and his thunderous declarations.

Leaping from the now glassy muck of the scarlet ground and immediately into action, Akalian and Moriel furled their wings into their backs. Illuminating

Light blasted from their fingertips into the oncoming horde of Jackals that were pouring back into battle from their previous retreat.

"Let's clear a path. We have to find a Pentaclegate to Gabriel's fortress." Akalian started as a burst of tzoharian Lightning struck his taloned, sea green hand, leaving Karaydin in his grasp.

"Indeed," Moriel agreed calmly. He gracefully raised his arm in a fluid-like motion, palm up to the sky, then slammed it down only to raise it once more. That action brought a blinding white and blue shield up from the ground, surrounding the two mighty elohim. The Dark army of Jackals slammed into the glowing shield, vomiting bile and curses against the holy screen that separated them from their target. The Jackals howled in defiance of the impenetrable forcefield as they pummeled it with their weapons of shadow, flame, and bone. Akalian glared at the sea of yellow and red eyes that flamed back at him through the secure veil of white and blue. He then playfully smirked as he gave a side-eye to Moriel.

"You're going to make this less fun, aren't you?"

"Oh, if only there wasn't so much more fun ahead of us." Moriel snarked playfully in return. With that, the Power quickly pulled tzoharian energy from his essence and formed an obu blazing with Heavenly Light. With no great effort, he raised his arm, palm to the heavens above his head, and commanded the orb to soar into the sky. It all happened so fast that the Jackals–even those who saw what was coming–had no time to react.

"Işık olsun!!" Moriel shouted, his voice booming into the ears of every Jackal surrounding them. At that, the obu exploded and shards of Light shot through the horde's bodies. The force of the blast melted the Dark creatures' skin, melding it with their armor before they dissolved into ashes. The gargled wails of the Jackals diminished, until the only things left surrounding Akalian and Moriel were husks of burnt carcasses.

"Path cleared," Moriel said with a smile.

"Well, that's one way to do it–*Moriel look out!!*"

Immediately, Moriel was hurtled across the battlefield from a bright yellow and terrible necroblast to the back. Akalian was tackled from behind by three half-charred Jackals who escaped most of the orb's blast. Moriel lay prone on the hot scarlet ground; the impact of his landing broke the glassy texture below him. He was fighting unconsciousness and determined to win.

His entire body was numb, and as he regained feeling, blinding pain shot from the point of impact on his back throughout his whole body. Whatever had just hit him was extremely powerful, and he hadn't been able to sense its presence at all, which was troubling. However, he could sense it now as the shadow of an ominous being boldly marched up behind Moriel's limp body.

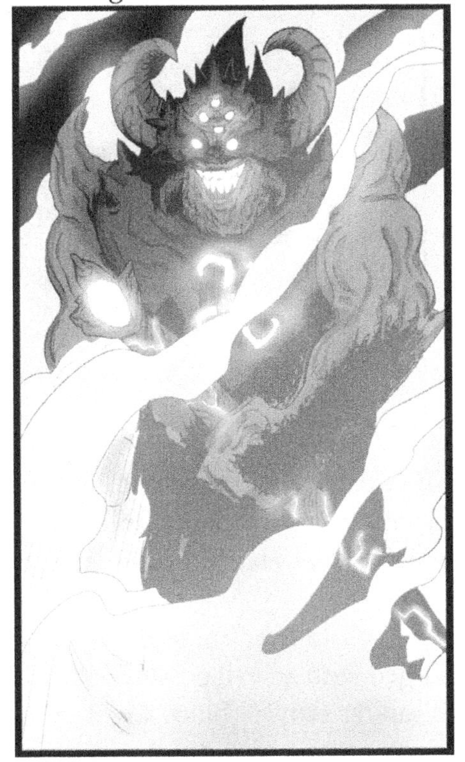

The Messenger gained enough feeling and strength to roll himself over on his back to face his attacker. But in doing so, Moriel was taken aback at the monstrosity standing before him. Underneath the massive armor was dark red, leathery skin covered in boils and matted, patchy fur. His six glowing yellow, pupilless eyes illuminated his gnarled smile. Moriel gasped as recognition dawned on him. It was the same sinister creature that had raped the Adamian woman in his Vision.

What was it the man in the copper crown called him? Balhazar? Something else grabbed Moriel's attention. Clearly, this creature was a general of some sort, for he was decorated with extravagant and grotesque armor of rust-colored shadowsteel that rose into spikes at the shoulders. He wore a vastly intimidating helmet, erupting with razors at the top that promised his victims a vicious, agonizing death if it were to pierce their skin. But what lay embedded on the enormous breastplate was a symbol that Moriel knew all too well, and it immediately haunted him: The Thrice Doomed Sign of Destruction. The sign of Hastur: The King in Yellow.

The Yellow Sign had not been seen in over a thousand years. No one knew to where Hastur had disappeared after the Adamian Final War. Some said he had been building his kingdom in The Wastelands of Earth; others proclaimed he had spirited away into the Dreamlands of Sheol. While no one knew for sure, one thing was certain: this connection between Hastur and Moriel's Vision was grievous. He remembered what the red-eyed, copper-crowned man said and shuddered:

*"Once more, the Nephilim will walk the earth, and the path to our enemy's destruction will be complete."*

"Time to die, little angel." The words hissed from the colossus in a gargling depth snapping Moriel back to reality. Balhazar lifted his necrostaff of pulsing, yellow energy. Wherever Hastur was, his power was certainly on display here.

Moriel braced himself; he couldn't muster enough energy to create a defense. As the necrostaff surged with an evil power, Balhazar was suddenly engulfed in a blinding royal blue Light that momentarily fractured and splintered his form into a million serpentine globs of black slime, sending them flying through the air in all directions. The necrostaff fell to the glassy red ground.

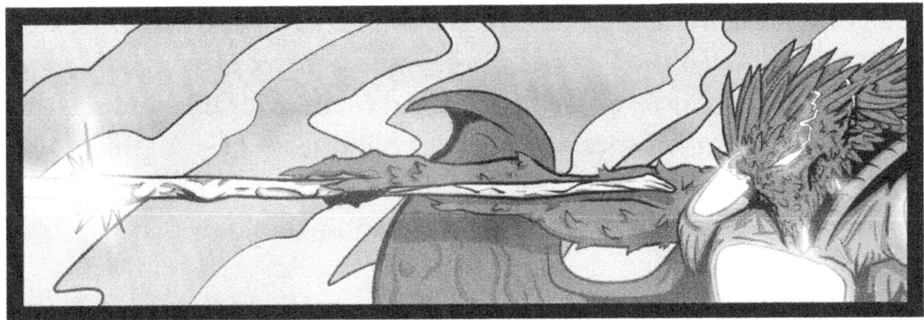

"Not today." A firm voice came from a figure Moriel was relieved to see. Fifteen yards away, Staff of Tzohar in hand, stood the valiant Afkiel: Chief Power of The Order of Gabriel. She was in full battle armor with her dark, gray-blue exoskeleton suit, illuminated chest and shoulders, showing the source of its tzoharian strength. Her navy blue featherfurred head was free of a helmet, for she fought better without one. The tzoharian armor created an invisible shield around her entire body, so she was somewhat protected.

Afkiel and her kindred did not have mouths or membranes like Akalian and Moriel but rather communicated telepathically with those to whom they chose to speak. Afkiel's head was engulfed in thick, navy-blue feathers drawn behind her and bound together, preventing them from falling loose at her shoulders. The Light beaming from the Power's armor matched the color and intensity of her eyes, which now looked over to Akalian. He was breaking free of his attackers by sheer brute strength. When freed, he severed their bodies in two by means of Karaydin.

"Akalian! Get to him quickly!!" The command reverberated in Moriel and Akalian's minds as Afkiel ran frantically toward the wounded Power.

"Moriel! Don't move!" Akalian shouted. Moriel was thankful for this because he still couldn't move very well. Running would have been out of the question. He looked up in the red sky toward the west and saw the reason for Afkiel's urgency: an army of winged Jackals and Night Gaunts were flocking toward them. Moriel could see that they all carried necrospears of varying energies. There was no doubt now; a nightmarish alliance had formed here. That's why this stronghold was so mighty. The real questions were how many were in the coalition and who was leading them?

Afkiel tossed a Tzoharian Codex–a small, crystal-like sphere–before Moriel. It immediately began to twist and spasm, seemingly unlocking itself, all the while becoming more and more illuminated. Relief washed over Moriel as he realized what this device was creating.

"Focus on the Light of the Pentaclegate! And don't blink!" Afkiel directed as she and Akalian arrived at Moriel's side simultaneously. The flying horde was closing in on them. One of the Jackals launched its spear toward them from fifty yards out, and Akalian sliced through it as fast as it arrived. The codex opened the Pentaclegate, overtaking them in blinding white Light. The next moment, the glassy red ground was barren, and the oncoming horde of Jackals and Night Gaunts watched as a blinking tzoharian spark faded from their view.

# CHAPTER TWELVE

## - NO PLACE FOR THE MEEK -

It had been two days of traveling through The Grey before Mattia reached what she hoped would be her final destination on this mad treasure hunt. Hopefully, the "treasure" would still be there. She found herself praying to whatever was out there—which surprised her because she wasn't one to believe in such things—that Obadiah would still be at these coordinates and that he would be available. Who knew what he had gotten into since he'd been exiled? Was he even the same man anymore? A lot can happen in a decade, and Mattia knew she was less trusting lately. She attempted to shrug off the cynicism as best as she could and lean into some optimistic thoughts for a change. After all, the Council Cleric was excited to finally see her old Mentor again; it had been entirely too long.

As she made her way up a dusty trail on the side of a hill, Mattia stopped for a moment, gazing out for miles at the lush forest of this region. She never thought this place could be so beautiful, not in her wildest dreams. It was almost unbelievable to think that most of this used to be desert in the Old World. She knew terraform engines had been brought into The Grey long ago but never expected anything like this. Mattia knew the new T-13s were capable of changing the landscape of environments at a molecular level, but this was breathtaking; a scientific marvel.

Regardless of the awe-inspiring beauty before her, she was thankful for the temperature-controlled jumpsuit she now wore. Mattia had picked one up years ago during a High Council retreat. A digital panel on the wrist of the suit could be set to "auto-temp," which fluctuated with the natural rise and fall of body temperature, or there was an option for a manual setting.

The suit was powered by a hybrid source of solar and electromagnetic resonance, so the more it was used in direct sunlight, the more powerful the charge would be. And the sun had been in full force these last two days, to be sure. Outside, it was a sweltering 110 degrees, but Mattia's suit registered a pleasant and consistent 72. This made traveling with her cloak on for extra protection from the elements–and whatever else might come her way–that much easier.

The Cleric made her way to the top of the hill and gazed ahead into a deep tunnel, formed by low-hanging trees and overgrown shrubbery. She pulled the coordinates from one of her leathersteel utility belt pockets and double-checked her solar compass. If Mattia was reading it correctly, this tunnel was the doorstep of her destination.

As she stepped into the tunnel, a sudden wave of foreboding anxiety swept over her. What awaited her on the other side of this shadowed canopy? An overwhelming fear crept into her mind, building with each step she took. Now, halfway through the tunnel, she realized that all sounds of wildlife that once surrounded her mere moments prior had completely silenced. All Mattia could hear were her footsteps and her heart pounding aggressively inside her body.

In the shadow of the looming greenery, the path took a sharp turn to the left, and she saw the opening ahead. Mattia felt both relief and dread wash over her. The exit of the canopy revealed a large hut down the hill. She felt relief that there was indeed a hut, but dread because it looked freshly vandalized.

The uneasy silence hung in the air as she carefully descended toward the broken-down door of the hut. She could tell that the interior was dark, which could mean many things. Maybe the place had no power source, or the power source was off, or it had been destroyed. The hut's exterior was tidy, and there was a well-kept garden, so it seemed doubtful that it was abandoned. She knew Obadiah enjoyed gardening as one of his meditative practices, so the hope that rose in her was suddenly shut down by the state of the door. It had been violently kicked in, and the window next to it shattered.

The closer Mattia got, the more she could see the explicit details of the vandalism. There wasn't blood on the ground or in the hut itself, which was a good sign. However, even though she was only ten feet from the door, the darkness inside was thick and foreboding. She waited for a moment and listened. The ominous silence in the area extended to the interior of the shadows before her, leading her to believe that whatever *had* occurred here had already passed on.

Mattia carefully approached the broken opening of the hut. She could now see outlines of furniture and a few large crates or boxes–she couldn't quite make out which–inside, not far from the door. As the Cleric inched toward the looming shadows, her anxiety grew until she was flushed and sweating. She felt the sweltering 110-degree air more than she had in the last two days. Mattia stood in the doorway and immediately felt the overwhelming sensation of being watched. A presence now penetrated her senses, and it felt wrong.

"H..hello?" Mattia's voice quivered as she stepped just inside the doorway, peering into the void with fear. Suddenly, the void starred back with two piercing yellow eyes from behind the large crates. A rush of freezing terror flooded the Cleric's body. The shadowed creature howled. Everything happened so fast. Mattia barely had time to react but did so instinctively with remarkable speed.

The eyes emerged from the shadows as the creature they belonged to leaped from behind the crates, twisting, writhing, and howling in a grave, grievous tone that sounded like it was from the depths of the blackest hell. It leapt toward Mattia with a speed and force she had never seen before, its sharp nails grabbing at her throat. The Cleric latched onto one of the beast's arms and fell backward, kicking the creature's pelvis and using the momentum to throw it over her as she landed hard on the ground, sacrificing her lower back to the moment. Ignoring the pain, Mattia jumped up quickly, spun around, and took a fighting stance, now thankful for the "pointless training" she had received in the academy.

It was required of every student in the primary academies across the civilized world to take at least basic self-defense fighting skills. Some also took advanced classes. The courses helped the students calm their minds and bodies under extreme stress. It also helped in general protection against common deviants. However, what stood before Mattia at this moment was no common deviant. There was nothing *common* about this creature at all. Now, in the daylight, she saw the thing in full. It was completely hairless, and its gray, dead skin looked like one large, cracked and worn callous. The teeth were long, thick fangs, too many to count, traveling back into the monster's throat that coughed up thick, yellow bile. As it stared at her, snarling, she noticed the creature was shorter than she initially thought, but its limbs were awkwardly lank and lean.

Mattia glared at the monster; her heart was in her throat and her pulse was throbbing at her temples. Her muscles flexed, ready, while her mind raced trying to and make sense of what stood before her. As she awaited another strike from the lanky, snarling thing before her eyes, Mattia realized something strange. As though it had multiple wills, the creature would lunge at her and then stop itself suddenly and violently, roaring and growling at itself when it did so. It was as if part of the thing wanted to rip her to shreds, but another part was begrudgingly restraining this feral action.

"No. Can't," the thing gargled to itself.

Before the Cleric could give much thought to this newfound oddity, a figure lunged out of the trees and tackled the lean, gray beast. Before Mattia could react to who this was, the figure slammed the howling creature against the ground and fractured its nose with a sharp and precise elbow, stunting its cries and focus. As soon as they hit the ground, the man grabbed something out of a satchel strung across his torso and shoved it into the blood and bile-filled face of the gray thing.

*"Nooo!!!"* The creature cried out. Mattia swore that was a cry of desperation. That assumption was confirmed as the dark-skinned man held a large stone cross. She hadn't seen its kind outside of a museum.

*"Christus victor!!"* he shouted with an almost perfect, ancient Latin accent. What happened next was something that would haunt Mattia's dreams forever. At that moment, she entered a completely different reality from what she had known. She knew monsters weren't real. She knew science and logic were what made the world go round. She appreciated myth and legend as simple tales of morality and a good pastime. However, all of that shattered before her eyes as blinding white Light burst from the stone cross relic and began melting the gray creature from the inside out.

When its eyes began to boil and spill over, Mattia looked away and covered her ears to blot out the agonizing wails. It sounded like a young dog being ripped apart. Steam billowed from the small creature's dead face. The man ominously looked down at it from his now crouched position atop the corpse of what used to be a monster.

There was no compassion in his eyes, only justice-filled hate as he gazed down at the thing which he reviled with every fiber of his being. He looked up at Mattia, who stood fifteen feet away, staring at him with wide eyes while taking her hands away from her ears.

"Hello, Matty. Welcome to The Grey," he said gruffly and somberly. Obadiah stood up and rushed to Mattia's side as she began vomiting.

# CHAPTER THIRTEEN

## - THE MERIDIAN -

Many times throughout history, when the Adamians described "Heaven," they often described it with billowing clouds, harps, long flowing white robes, and an overwhelming feeling of peace, joy, and love. Some of those attributes were entirely true, but others were misrepresented–mostly unknowingly so–and confused with what was known as Elysium or The Elysian Fields. These Heavenly fields were a border between the realms, where evil dared not go and where those who aligned their wills with the King would begin their Purgatory. It was also a respite for the holy elohim at war with the fallen, and was filled with the tzoharian energy of The White Throne.

The undulating energy gave off a cloud-like appearance, washing inhabitants' souls with the overwhelming peace and hope of the King himself. No Dark creature could ever venture here and survive more than a few moments before being annihilated from the impact of the tzoharian Light. A few foolish members of The Dark Kingdom had attempted such a task but never returned to their masters. Eventually, all Dark Ones abandoned these efforts after understanding there was not a single vulnerable point they could exploit.

However, the reason so many Adamians thought of Heaven as a cloud-filled paradise had to do with what was known as "near-death experiences." When a human who had aligned themselves with the will of Light would enter into a state of crossing the realms, if only for a moment or two, they would enter Elysium. Here they would be protected from whatever forces wished to enslave their souls upon departure from the Corporeum body, or worse, enslave their Corporeum body upon release of their souls.

This place of respite and hope was where Gabriel had been encamped during The Stronghold War of Perethedesh. His fortress, The Meridian, was known throughout the millennia to be a haven for all elohim who found themselves in the Elysian Fields, weary from the constant battle across the realms of Corporeum and Sheol. From its grand Halls of Knowledge to its Temples of Tzohar, a weary elohim could stand directly in the Light of the King for as long as they needed, finding complete restoration. The Laws of Time and Space worked differently inside The Meridian. Each level and compartment had its own cosmic order for whatever was needed. It was built to be an island of healing from the sea of Darkness.

The fortress itself was a giant tower made from Aeternum cobalt, constructed by the Order of Hariel, who—even before the great fall of Azathoth—was already one of the greatest artists in the cosmos. He even helped construct The Kingdom of Zion, the capital city of the Edenic Realms. Hariel had been summoned before The Adunalar Elohim at the beginning of the Creation Wars to begin construction on the Kaleler Edu: Seven Fortresses of The Septum Dei. Each of the mighty towers of the Archangels was made with impenetrable Aeturnum Stone and domed with a fine, glass-like, indestructible bardak formed in the rivers of the Edenic Realms. But out of all the towers constructed, Hariel found The Meridian to be the most beautiful and life-giving. Although each fortress was unique and incomparable in its own way, Hariel believed there was no finer haven in the cosmos than this when it came to rest and healing.

The Grand Hall of The Meridian acted as an interdimensional platform for both inbound and outbound elohim looking for solace. Almost every type of Heavenly creature could be found trafficking through this vast Hall. From the mighty and graceful Ophanim, who had four wings and a multitude of eyes which saw everything, everywhere, covering the membranes of its body, to the regal Thrones, whose knowledge was second only to the mighty Seraphim and King Yahweh himself. Even the lowly choirmite, whose speed and agility were unmatched in all the realms could be found here.

The Grand Hall was filled with diverse life, beauty, and fellowship. In the center of the arena was the Pillar of Velkominn, a sovereign beacon for all who would come to Gabriel's halls. This pillar beckoned three specific elohim to their safe haven among the cosmic stars.

As Ophanim flew across through the airways of the Grand Hall of The Meridian, a Pentaclegate began to form at the base of the Pillar of Velkominn. What started as a spark blasted into a sphere of blinding white and blue Light, covering a mile radius of the Hall. When the Light began to dim, three figures could be seen: Akalian, Moriel, and Afkiel, in the same positions as when they disappeared from the Sheolic battlefield in the shadowlands of Perethedesh.

Each of them took a breath, and Akalian dropped to one knee, next to his brother. Moriel was wounded and would need healing before they continued their mission. Afkiel stood, putting a comforting hand on Moriel's shoulder.

"How much time have we lost, Afkiel?" Moriel asked his sister through the wincing pain in his back. Pentaclegates were known to take varying amounts of time to travel from one place to another, depending on the destination and what cosmic laws had to be traversed. Although to the traveler, it always felt as if no time had passed at all. Moriel thought it likely that this portal may have taken multiple Adamian days, given they had to travel through the Sheolic realm and maneuver through the Elysian Fields. However, the telepathic response that followed was a pleasant surprise.

"None. This Pentaclegate was instantaneous." Afkiel replied, looking down at the spent sphere that lay before them. What was once shimmering and crystal-like was now faded and gray, depleted of energy from the single use. Akalian and Moriel simultaneously looked at their fellow elohim in amazement. Akalian spoke up.

"Instantaneous?! I've not heard of such a powerful portal in all my days. How much energy did this–"

"It was an emergency," Afkiel boldly interrupted. "Lord Gabriel believes that time is running out to stop whatever plan The Dark Kingdom is concocting. We all sense that this–

*"Akalian!! Moriel!!!"*

The happy call that rang through the Hall was a single voice of pure joy and whimsy. A bright orange choirmite, a third the size of the three Heavenly creatures, flew with gleeful force and slammed into his brothers, knocking Moriel and Akalian on their backs. While Moriel did not particularly appreciate it given his current health status, he couldn't help but chuckle at the exuberant dance Willow was now performing on top of Akalian's chest as the warrior lay flat, looking playfully annoyed. Afkiel stood over them all, amusedly judging.

"Hello, Willow," both Moriel and Akalian facetiously groaned.

"You made it!! Praise the King, you made it!!" Willow continued to dance as his four wings–a pair at the shoulders and a pair at his lumbar spine–retook flight. Willow hovered at eye level with all three elohim standing before him. "Thank you, Afkiel, for bringing them here so quickly!" Willow said, almost singing.

"It was literally my duty, Willow, but you're welcome," Afkiel chuckled.

"Ha! It's wonderful to see you, Willow, but...*why* are you here?" Akalian questioned the little teddy bear-shaped elohim, who couldn't wipe the beaming smile from his face. The Power was glad to see his tiny brother but was quite confused at his presence. The last he had heard from Willow, he was going to The Adunalar Elohim to inform them of Akalian's findings on Xexxus.

"Metatron sent me to inform Gabriel of your arrival," he said proudly.

*Metatron?* they all thought as they exchanged puzzled gazes. This situation was becoming more interesting and even more troubling.

"And you got here *that* fast and undetected...in this chaos?" Akalian playfully questioned.

"Small creatures accomplish great things," Willow said with a twinkle in his eye.

"They do indeed." Moriel smiled lovingly at his small sibling. The orange featherfurred choirmite had been their brother in arms within the Order of Michael since before the fall of The Tower of Babylon. Rarely would a choirmite be placed in a governing position on an Order of the Septum Dei, but Willow had earned his Tetragrammaton emblem, shown proudly on his belly where the source of his power resided. It was etched along with his many Lightrunes and was beaming a luminous yellow, matching the feathers of his wings and his enthusiastic, joy-filled eyes.

During The Great Floods, when Cthulhu The Leviathan claimed ownership of the Adamian galaxy, Willow nearly sacrificed himself to help bring down the former high priest of Azathoth. Every Goliath has his David, so they say, and Cthulhu never suspected a being so small could defeat him. In Cthulhu's defense, no one else did either. The King and Michael were exceedingly proud to bestow the Tetragrammaton upon the first choirmite and induct him into Michael's governing body. But more importantly than his power and skill in battle, Willow was a true friend. This was his gift above all else, and both Moriel and Akalian were especially thankful for this creature they could depend on and lean into during times of grief and pain.

More than anything, he could always make them smile, and a smile in grave times was like a lighthouse illuminating the way through the stormy sea.

"As overwhelming as the presence of The Dark Kingdom is at the moment, Metatron felt it wise to send Willow instead of an obu." The deep, wizened, and powerful voice came from behind the four elohim. A feeling of relief and welcome washed over Akalian and Moriel as they turned to face the sizable figure of Gabriel, Son of The Septum Dei, Herald of Visions, and Angelic Dogrudan–direct messenger–of King Yahweh himself.

Lord Gabriel stood a good two heads taller than them. He was armored in a deep cobalt exoskeletal suit, white and blue Lightrunes spanning his entire torso and arms. His left deltoid was covered by a Lightsteel pauldron that extended down past the bicep. A cobalt paludamentum cape covered the Archangel's right shoulder and fell past his half-robe that began at his waist, draping down to the Light-filled stone floor of the Grand Hall.

Gabriel's blueish-gray face appeared aged as he looked down at his fellow elohim. Light-blue runes adorned his neck and head in a maze-like pattern; and above both of his eyes, Gabriel had three Tetragrammaton Lightrunes. This elohim of The Septum Dei had earned a thousand more but had refused them in his humility. Gabriel was the epitome of a quiet, meek warrior, but when it came time to cross blades, he was as fierce as Michael–if not more so.

"Lord Gabriel," Akalian said while placing a fist against the Tetragrammaton on his chest in respect. "It's wonderful to see you again." The others followed suit.

"It's good to see you too, my friends," Gabriel kindly said. With a smile, he continued. "I'm glad you're here. There's much work to be done." He turned his attention to Moriel for a moment. "I can tell you're injured. We will provide you with a healing chamber, but first, do you have the strength for a brief orientation?"

"Of course," Moriel assured Gabriel.

"Good," there was a grave importance in his voice. The smile transformed into a more serious expression. "Then please, come with me." With that, Gabriel turned and ascended into the air, two of his own governing Order flanking him on either side, while the others followed. Akalian supported Moriel as they traversed across the Grand Hall toward an archway on the far side.

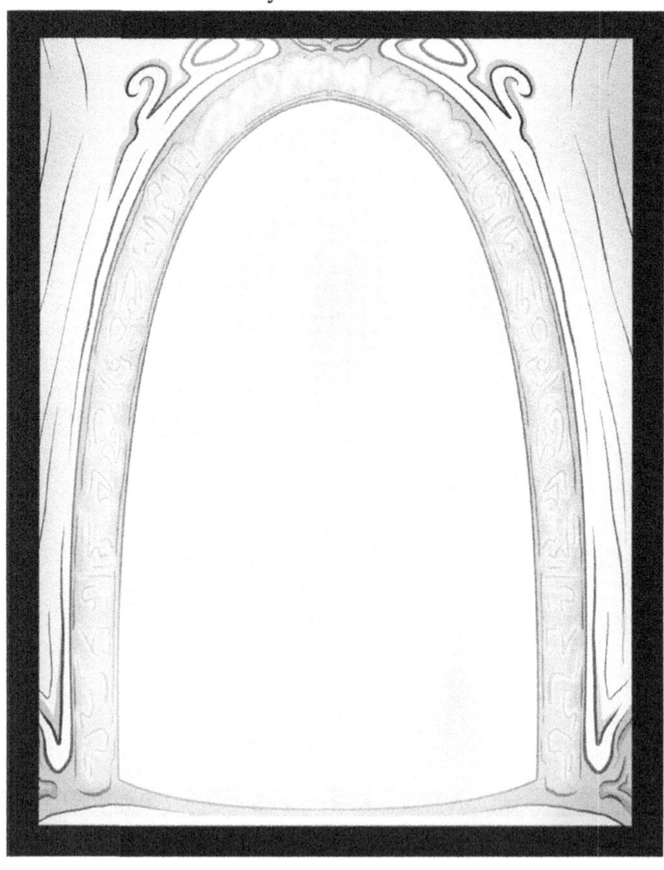

Akalian had been there before, but the runes that marked the archway gave him an unexpected glimmer of hope:

*"The Light shines in the Darkness, and the Darkness has not overcome it."*

Akalian had seen so much horror in his life, so much pain. Eons of a war-torn existence made him sometimes wonder if it would ever end. He knew the prophecies of both the Heavenly Host and The Dark Kingdom, which told different outcomes of this forever war. The Prophecy of Yeshua, The Great Téleios, promised a New Eden expanding across the realms, where everything would be returned to its proper form and restored to a holy, happy union with its maker. And even though there were many debates on *how* that would come about, the outcome was always the same: New Eden. But Age End loomed in the back of Akalian's mind.

The nightmares he had seen and the ever-expanding shadow of The Dark Kingdom, were enough evidence that things seemed to be getting worse instead of better. This disturbed him, and he wrestled with a doubt that he could not shake. The anxious thought of the possibility that evil might be victorious haunted him. He constantly rejected that potential outcome, but had he not seen The Dark Kingdom triumph before? Indeed, not across the realms, but yes, he had undoubtedly seen them victorious many times, in fact: Azathoth, Adam, The Watchers, The Noahic People, Israel, The Institutional Church, all of them failed in one way or another, each one giving The Dark Kingdom more power.

To be sure, in moments like this, when these thoughts slithered into his mind, he was reminded that in all he'd seen, the King somehow always had an answer that turned the shadow into a ray of hope. However, like so many, Akalian thought New Eden would have arrived at the close the Second Adamian World War. Everyone thought that would have been the right time for The Great Téleios to occur. It was "the war to end all wars" across Corporeum and Sheol or so they thought. The Soma Aedrum–Yahweh's true followers–in all their grievous faults, had, in many ways, begun to unite during that time of turmoil. But those days ended not long after the war's final months and grew continuously bleak until The Final War came. It was as in the days of Noah, as though Age End had already begun. Maybe it had?

This continued pattern fed the doubt in Akalian's mind, and it was also what troubled him most regarding a stinging seed planted in his heart long ago by a once dear brother. Why did the King continue to allow this never-ending cycle of suffering and shadow? Indeed, he was powerful enough to end Khata once and for all...surely–

"Are you alright?" Akalian felt the comforting hand of Moriel upon his pauldron shoulder.

"Uhm...yes," Akalian responded to the concerned Messenger. Moriel wasn't convinced. He knew Akalian would never lie, but he also knew the quest for Xexxus, and now this Dark Prince business, deeply troubled him. But Moriel let it go, for now at least.

Akalian regained his composure and realized they were now on the other side of the archway and inside The Sanctum, Gabriel's war room. The actual placement of The Sanctum was fluid throughout The Meridian. Archway portals–like the one they had just entered–were located all over the fortress, leading directly into this room where Gabriel held council. The essence of The Sanctum was attached to the Archangel's will and could be secured when needed.

In the center of The Sanctum was a large Aeternum Stone table, like Michael's, that illuminated in tzoharian Light. Before them was a glowing hologram of a three-dimensional map of the three realms that overlapped one another in Perethedesh. As everyone settled around the stone table, Akalian thought it best to get straight to the point.

"Do we know where Jonathan is and if it *is* Xexxus possessing him?" Gabriel didn't mind the boldness; in fact, he welcomed it.

"Unfortunately, we aren't sure who is leading this infestation just yet," Gabriel answered. "But with the information that Yirah provided you and the gravitas of this stronghold, I wouldn't be surprised if it *were* Xexxus. In fact, much of what we have seen points in that direction." Gabriel paused, and his tone became grievous. "Unfortunately, they have kept the boy well hidden. We cannot penetrate the telepathic shield their stronghold is producing, and the seemingly random Necrogates that keep appearing throughout the city make it almost impossible to maintain any surveillance on their activity. We have all but exhausted our resources throughout this battle.

"I'm afraid we have no choice but to stand our ground until the Spirit of the King moves inside an Adamian within the stronghold. Once he has Awakened someone and they respond, the Dark shields will begin to crack. Only then will we break through and know the boy's whereabouts and be able to take you to him."

*An Awakening?* Akalian thought.

Moriel almost simultaneously spoke those thoughts into existence.

"How long has it been since an Awakening has happened...here...in *this* place?" It was a valid question. Awakenings were not an everyday occurrence, especially in these later days of the Adamian world–so different from the beginning. Long ago, humanity was welcomed into the creation process alongside King Yahweh. As rightful heirs, the King wanted the Adamians to co-labor with him in restoring and taming creation from the wild fruit born out of the Great Fall of Azathoth and his Court.

After the UcDusme, that collaboration was corrupted thrice-fold, and after that, the only possible way for a human's will to match that of the King's was if an Awakening occurred. The mysterious Spirit of the King would call out to an Adamian heart, and that person would choose to respond. It was a phenomenon that had not occurred for ages of Adamian time in Perethedesh, for these days were ruinous. Other than a small remnant, the Adamians across this new civilized world had walked away from the King. Once more, they handed over their inheritance of co-laborship to The Dark Kingdom.

Gabriel leaned heavily against the Stone table, feeling its smooth texture. He was finding himself desperately overwhelmed by a feeling of defeat.

"I honestly don't know," he said with a quiver in his voice. "The Dark Kingdom has had deep roots here for quite some time. Their forces refuse to be broken." While he tried not to sound defeated, Gabriel understood the weight of the situation. He knew that even *if* the Spirit called out to an Adamian, by the laws of The Cosmic Wheel, the Adamian would still have to respond, and many times of late, they had rejected the call. Gabriel had faith in his King and had seen him turn the Darkest of shadows into the brightest Light with the slightest spark. Why hadn't that occurred here already?

The King had conquered death so long ago, yet the days seemed to grow increasingly grievous. Could somehow Age End truly be upon them? Could this be the fate of the world leaving King Yahweh to lock it away in another realm for all eternity? The days of Noah saw Adamians walk entirely away from the King, resulting in the Earth and its new abominations being destroyed by overwhelming, chaotic waters. All but a select few were annihilated, and even they fell soon after that. No, it was not his King that Gabriel doubted; it was these people. These people who continually walked away from the Light and joined the enemy time and time again. These people would be the reason for this world to find itself forever sealed in Darkness.

And yet, hope still lingered.

"But with you two here now," a burst of optimistic glee pierced the foreboding cloud that haunted the war room of the Archangel. Willow continued, "That *has* to mean the King is moving!" All eyes now fell upon Akalian and Moriel. The King had indeed sent them through Michael's command. That was encouraging and extremely heavy for the two Powers of the Order of Michael.

"That is quite true, Willow," Gabriel smiled and decided to catch the choirmite's optimism. "I think we should all anticipate the King's direct intervention soon." He became serious once more. "And when he does make his move, we must act quickly...for somewhere in the nightmare beyond that firmament is a boy imprisoned, and he is running out of time."

Green, rancid fog billowed amongst the catacombs of the sinister throne room inside the midnight-black castle. The shadows danced like demons in the halls of Pandemonium, and the air was a choking, sulfurous haze. The Castle of Endless Night was a vast, demonic fortress constructed long ago with hate, pain, and malice as its brick and mortar. It lived in the deep shadows of the realms, biologically and spiritually connected to its master who, like a leech, would find a host and drain them of their existence before moving on to another. Each host gave him more and more power that would pulsate throughout the castle. However, this particular host was something rather special.

The master of this wicked place had waited for the boy since he first heard the prophetic words of The Dark Father. Proclaimed in the wild kingdoms of Dudael, the salvific prophecy promised to give the realms back to their *rightful* owners. Of course, others like this boy preceded him, but Jonathan Young was the one prepared for the Dark Proclamation in ways none other had before. Like the tyrant's Messiah, the boy's path was paved in ways unnatural to regular Adamian life.

"You are alone, dust creature," the deep, hollow voice hissed. "And you are *mine!"* The hideous elohim boomed and laughed a sinister cackle. He scraped his talons along the necroplasmic cell where the astral form of Jonathan Young was suspended, surrounded by glowing emerald slime. Every touch of the Dark elohim poisoned the boy. Jonathan had lived in this state since he found naive hope in a rotting house inside his mind. He had forgotten what life was like before this. All he could remember was that mangled and horrific face charading as his mother who brought him here and continuously tortured him.

The boy couldn't hold the pain in any longer. The utter despair had taken him, and he let out a slight whimper. He couldn't help it; the agony was too great. For even in astral form, every being would feel pain as if it were happening to their physical body.

"*Silence!!* You were not given permission to make your pathetic noises!!" The horrible figure flicked his wrist, and the boy's esophagus was ripped from his throat. Bright green blood and tissue burst out of the boy as bile, snot, and tears began seeping from his face. It seemed Jonathan's tormentor would take every chance he could to provoke such occurrences and then maliciously punish the child in various ways. This was actually one of the less severe acts.

In the beginning, Jonathan hoped that he would grow numb to such tortures, but stripping the boy of all hope was the first priority of his captor's strategic malignance. Then, he made sure Jonathan felt every molecule being ripped from him each time. Aside from taking great pleasure in doing so, the possessors of The Dark Kingdom tortured their victims while gaining more and more of their essence, allowing greater control and power over the host. This horrid energy that allowed the possessor to become even more powerful than before.

In The Dark Kingdom, power and dominance ruled. It was survival of the fittest at its most malicious state. That was true freedom in the eyes of the fallen: The Dark Doctrine initiated by Azathoth himself. Conquering was the liberation of oneself, and the more an elohim could spread its dominion, the more genuine to itself it would become. Abusive sessions such as this were crucial sacraments of possession for these monstrous beings. With each torturous act, a Dark being would become one step closer to merging with the host. Then after an appointed time, an unholy ritual would solidify the merger. A ritual known as The Black Mass.

"Lord Xexxus..." A slimy, quivering voice had emerged to enter the scene of violent liturgy. The owner of this voice was short, and sagging. A gray, wrinkled creature with four unmatching cesspool

eyes that let out putrid gas steaming up and above her head. From her chapped, cracking mouth, needle-like fangs protruded in all directions. Her appearance was mainly hidden under an inky, moss-colored cloak.

"Why do you disturb me?" growled the mountainous monster that towered over the mangled spirit of Jonathan Young, as he turned to face the intruder. The petrified messenger, his most loyal servant and grand vizier, Yagorath, bowed prostrate on the glowing green, slime-covered ground. The ancient evil, Xexxus: Last of Legion, was a living nightmare.

Xexxus could take different forms. To the Adamian eye, he would have–in this form–appeared to be at least 10 feet tall and covered in a thick, crocodile-like skin that transitioned from the blackest of shadow to the deepest shades of basil, moss, and emerald. But his eyes, sunken into the pits of their sockets, glowed green and pierced any recipient of his gaze with horror. Even the charade of patient diplomacy in his bowing eyelids did nothing to restrain the terror found there.

The most prominent feature of Xexxus was four horns emerging from his brow, forming an unholy crown on top of his head. Upon his Transfectiation–the willing deconstruction and reconstruction of an elohim's entire genetic makeup–The Dark Father gave Xexxus this crown as a sign to all the sinister and wicked creatures that his dominance would never be extinguished. The Four-Horned Crown was a sign given to very few by The Dark Father, fewer still wore it as an anatomical badge of honor. Only the most sinister creatures earned this unholy rite.

A Transfectiation differed from what was known as a Transfiguration. All Adamians were the victims of thousands of years of unseen, genetic manipulation under the Curse of Khata; causing some to wander the world afraid, attacked, and unsure of whether or not they belonged to the human race at all. But those who chose to walk the Path of Light were Transfigured during their Purgatory journeys after death, freeing them from the bonds of both confusion and superiority. For no Adamian in Corporeum reflected humanity's original intent. The Word of the King initiated this transformation and freed every Adamian to follow in his footsteps. However, all

elohim—Light or Dark—were created perfectly from their beginning, walking alongside the King in their first days. Therefore, to reject that perfection and embrace something else was, for an elohim, one of the Darkest acts they could perform.

"Rise Yagorath. What news do you bring me?" Xexxus bared his thick, sharp fangs when he spoke. Yagorath raised herself to her knees and leaned heavily upon her lich staff. This particular lich staff held the eye of a dead Ophanim, and gave Yagorath a precise and valuable glimpse into most realms and kingdoms. Xexxus once courted this creature when she was human in the Corporeum Realm. He saw fit to enslave her soul before death, Transfectiating the dust creature she once was into his personal sorcerer. Xexxus was both disgusted by Yagorath and ferociously aroused by her.

"The intrusion is important, my Lord," she hissed. "Word has come. Yirah has merged with the dust creature, Etrulia. Once more, The Three are one." Xexxus paused momentarily, his eyelids lowering further as a devilish satisfaction washed over him. Finally, the time was upon them. He had waited countless ages of man for this, and it had finally happened. The Forging of The Final Three had occurred; the long-awaited fulfillment of The Coven of Endor had arrived during the alignment of the blood moons across the realms, and The Master had accomplished it.

Xexxus secretly had his doubts, of course, but he knew The Master's faith in the Final Heraldic prophecy was unmatched, and his loyalty to The Dark Father's Vision of Age End went beyond passion; it was a deep, twisted obsession that fueled a patience and strategy the likes of which Xexxus had never duplicated. The Dark Father had paved the way; it was time for them to finish it and usher in his return.

"Is the stronghold still secure?" Xexxus collected himself. They had come too far to fail now.

"Gabriel's forces have yet to penetrate the stronghold, my Lord, and word is that the Archangel grows desperate." Yagorath chuckled at the end of her delivery, very pleased with herself and the news she could bear her ruler.

"And what of the sow?" Xexxus snarled at the thought of the command of protection that the enemy's king had declared mere days ago. *This would-be king would not have the power to command such things for long,* he thought to himself.

"There hasn't been a sighting of her since–"

"Since the tyrant came out of hiding and made his threats, only to disappear into his Throne Room once more?"

"Ummm...y–yes." This type of talk made Yagorath uneasy. She knew the promises of The Dark Father, but this tyrant king still had unlimited power for the moment, and the fear of him suddenly appearing before them was beyond terrifying. Yagorath had heard of such things happening to others, and that plagued the back of her terrible and twisted mind.

"It matters not. The time is drawing near, just as The Master predicted. The Black Mass approaches." Xexxus turned away from the sorcerer and focused once more on the child spirit he had locked away in this necroplasmic cell. Jonathan tried not to make a sound as his throat slowly pieced itself back together, only to be torn out again later, he had no doubt. Tears flowed down the boy's cheeks, and his bloody, bile-coated mouth quivered in fear as Xexxus' leathery, taloned hand reached inside the necroplasmic prison where Jonathan was floating helplessly.

"The Master has much in store for you, dust creature," the Legionnaire smoothly cooed. It might have come across as soothing if his tone had not been so sinister. A talon wiped a tear away from the tortured child's cheek. "You should feel honored...for soon you will be safe with The Dark Father. The Master will have full control, and 'Little Boy Blue' will be no more." A twisted, fang-ridden grin engulfed the fallen elohim's face. "But until then...let's have a little fun."

The black hallway of Hillcrest Sanitarium had been exceptionally quiet these last few days. Client 43972 was now the veteran and sole resident of the hall. Over the years, maintenance never could get the power to the lights to connect correctly for some reason, and Waverly Hall was slowly immersed in darkness. Since this client had been near catatonic–aside from random outbursts–for the last four years, they moved the others to different parts of the sanitarium. Per High Cleric Malcolm's instruction, maintenance was to worry about other, more important matters, leaving 43972 alone and in the dark.

However, in the last few days, a strange green glow could be seen shining through the observation window of his room. When Headminister Bouchard noticed this, he walked down to the boy's room, changed the window's clarity to completely transparent, but could see nothing but the darkness inside—a Darkness that waited patiently and smiled.

# CHAPTER FOURTEEN

## - MEMORIES & NIGHTMARES -

Moriel shot out of his bed, perspiring as though fresh from battle. The Messenger could tell that his wounds were healed now, at least on the outside. He expected his dreams over the last few days would be of his Vision and the behemoth Balhazar that now haunted his mind. While that was undoubtedly the case, it was not what dragged him out of rest this early morning in the depths of the Meridian.

Moriel hadn't dreamt of his sister in quite a long time. In fact, the thought of Cadariel was almost non-existent in his mind these last thousand years. Cadariel– *The Starlight of Eden*–perished long ago; what remained was only the corrupt Dark being she became. *That* monstrous creature had been at the forefront of the Messenger Power's consciousness more often than he'd wished. The thought of her influential presence in The Cosmic Wheel made his stomach retch.

Although, it wasn't her Dark form that he dreamt of–at least not that he could remember since waking. It was what she once had been–pure and loving with the most beautiful, smiling eyes Moriel had ever seen. The ache in his heart grew heavy as he fought to hold the image of her face from the rapidly fading memory of his dream. The Dreamlands–a perfidious world of Sheol–could be a place where even the sweetest thoughts would become haunting nightmares upon awakening. Dreams such as these have driven all sorts of creatures mad–Light, Dark, and in between–if they dwelled upon them for too long. They could become lifeless hope, casting a spell upon the dreamer and draining their energy for years, if allowed. The Messenger's struggle with his sister was different than that of Akalian and Xexxus, but the pain was just as real and, at this moment, just as wounding.

Truth be told, Moriel had made peace with his sister's fall from the Light eons ago. He understood that Cadariel's actions and choices belonged to her and her alone. Her mind, twisted with the will of Khata, is what turned her into the Dark beast she was now. Unlike Akalian's situation, there was no guilt or shame for Moriel to hold onto or weigh him down. Therefore, he was free to face his grief head-on from the parting of his sister, however erroneous it was. But this made Moriel's heart break all the more for his dear brother. He couldn't imagine what it would be like if he were in Akalian's place.

After a few moments, Moriel allowed himself to focus on the present. Dreams for elohim of the Heavenly Host differed from those of the Dark or of the Adamians, but they were just as elusive in many ways. Akalian's ongoing pursuit of Xexxus might have triggered thoughts of Cadariel that manifested in Moriel's sleep. But the Messenger Power wasn't convinced that's all his dream was. He felt in his essence that it was somehow a key to unlocking an answer, and he wasted no time gathering himself and silently walking a few steps toward the Temple of Tzohar adjoining his chamber.

As Moriel inched toward the opening of the Temple, he breathed deeply, preparing himself. He needed his mind to be calmed to receive whatever the King would show him.

The Messenger crossed the threshold of the Temple, knelt down upon the padded, glyph-covered pedestal in front of the Tetragrammaton symbol of his King. He let out a long, steady exhale, beginning the meditative posture, and saying the prayer of the Temple of Tzohar.

"Oh, King of Ages,
Grant me this passage of clarity
So that I may do your will of Light.
Banish all Darkness that surrounds
My thoughts and my will,
Aligning my essence with You.
In the name of Yahweh,
Amin y Amin."

Overwhelming calm immediately washed over the elohim. Cadariel's face began to resurface in his mind, becoming more apparent every moment to the point where Moriel felt he could almost reach out and touch her. However, just as her eyes came into view, a dark shroud began billowing around her, piercing the top of her soft, antler-covered head with a scarlet bolt of sinister lightning. The smooth, glowing, sky-blue membranes crowning Cadariel's head began breaking down, transforming into a thorny, charred texture. Her featherfur skin hardened and cracked while a wicked grin spread across her face, her eyes disappearing into a cavernous, black abyss within her skull. Everything that *was* Cadariel had now fallen into shadow, leaving only *Lilith* in her stead.

The now Dark beast, Lilith, stood before Moriel, cackling as four enormous leathery, dragonesque wings emerged from her shoulders and back. Pitch-black smoke slithered from the depths below her, presenting her with the cursed blade, Deccal. As Moriel's former sister raised the scorched longsword above her head with a mighty battle cry, Lilith was joined by a sinister brood of elohim: Dendron (The Oak King), Pazuzu, Baphomet, and Gaia. Moriel knew these other Dark beings as the gods of the odious Coven of Endor, but he was unaware of their alliance with his former sister.

While the Vision continued, Moriel watched intently as the black smoke parted, revealing the same twisted tree from his former Age End Vision. This was similar, but not the same, for the being that emerged from the depths of the tree wasn't Khata this time, but rather the sinister Adamian who ruled the colosseum. The unholy group followed Lilith in a ghoulish parade toward the Adamian, whose eyes now burned a scarlet red. They all dropped to one knee as Lilith presented Deccal to the red-eyed man.

However, the very moment the Adamian touched the scorched sword, a beam of bright Light engulfed the man's hands, and spread until his arms were under the control of the blinding white force. The Adamian wrestled with all his might as his Light-possessed hands snatched Deccal from a cowering Lilith and her profane fellowship. As the brood scattered in fear, the red-eyed man fought vigorously against the Light at the base of the black tree, tumbling and struggling against his own hands as they attempted to run Deccal through the man's abdomen. Finally, with a mighty roar, the Adamian succumbed to the Light and forced the scorched blade through his gut.

At this moment, something happened to Moriel that had never taken place in a Vision before. The Adamian, whose abdomen gushed like a scarlet flood, glared at Moriel with wide, desperate eyes filled with malice. The Messenger felt his entire body go numb as his gaze met the red stare of this self-wounded man. The Adamian ripped Deccal from his stomach and opened his mouth, pointing the blood-drenched blade at Moriel. His lips did not move, but nevertheless, the prophetic words poured out, a Dark omen.

"The only way out
Is to move further in.
For even the wisest of all
Cannot go back again."

At that, Moriel let out a hard exhale and, opened his eyes, finding himself back in the Temple of Tzohar. Emerging from this Vision, he felt anything but peace. But the Messenger now had a sense of clarity that he did not have before. Placing his fist on his chest, he thanked his King and stood up calmly. Upon exiting the Temple, Moriel rushed out of his chambers. He had to find Akalian.

# CHAPTER FIFTEEN

## - THE AGE OF THE ETERNAL TREE -

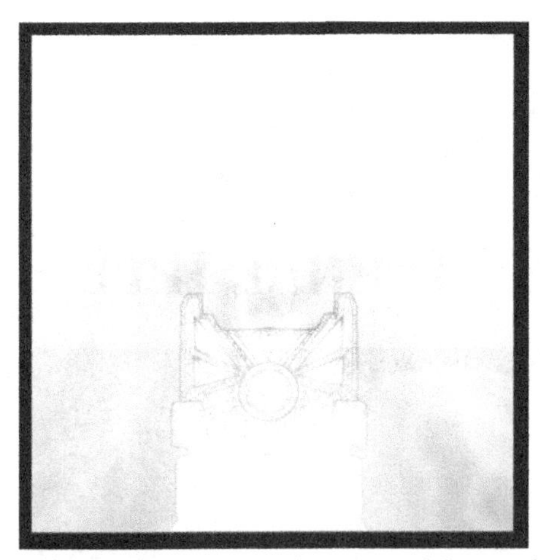

The familial bond did not originate with the Adamian race. Its roots grew deeply and flowed from the gloriously mysterious Trinitarian relationship of King Yahweh. All creation was meant to experience this type of love and fellowship, and for a time, it did. Long before the King breathed the Ruakh—divine energy—of life into humanity's first parents, the cosmos was already home to a large and bountiful family. It is this family which, perhaps out of all created things, eventually felt the deepest pain of brokenness.

It is said that as the King of Ages uttered the first words of Ruakh, life was produced in the form of a joyous eruption that generated space and time, as well as all the matter and energy that has

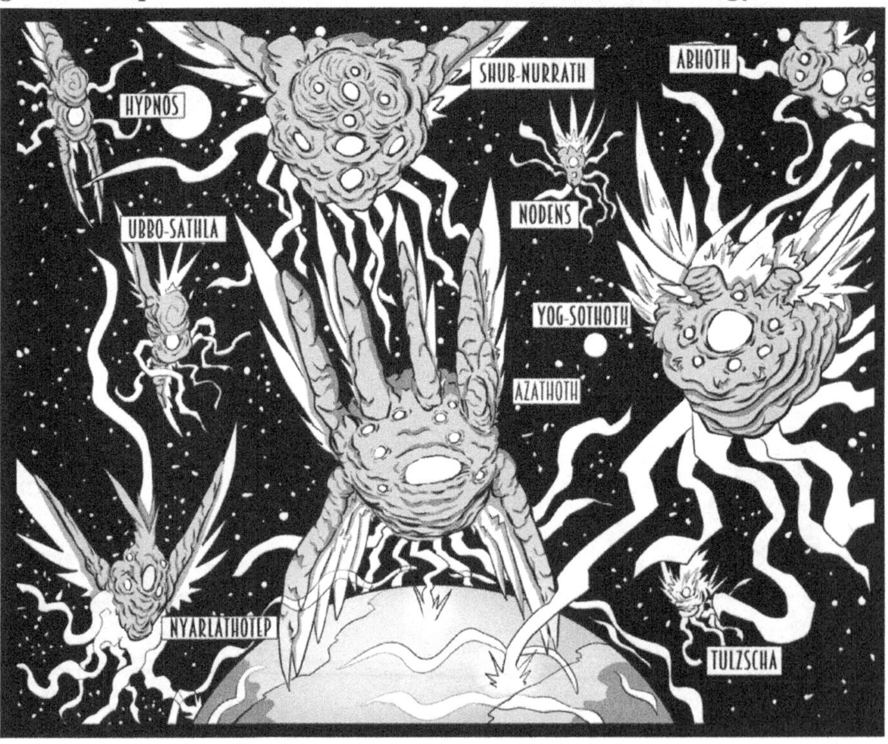

ever been known to the cosmos. At that moment, The Cosmic Wheel was brought to life, a construct that could be ever-growing, ever-expanding further out and further in, with Yahweh at its center.

For over 300 million Adamian years, the El, Word, and Spirit of the King formed the cosmos and prepared it for a thriving, conscious life that reflected the Image–the pure nature and character–of Yahweh. Finally, when the time was right, through the King's preordained order of Cosmic Law, The Elders were brought into being from stardust and dreams. Azathoth, Yog Sothoth, Nyarlathotep, Shub-Nurrath, Hypnos, Nodens, Tulzsha, Ubbo-Sathla, and Abhoth were gifted the mysterious, life-giving breath of Ruakh, filling them with the tzoharian Light of The White Throne. Thus, they became the King's first sentient, conscious image bearers, and were welcomed into the creation process as co-laborers.

The Dara Cinn–later known as The Great Old Ones–were the first fruits of the co-laborship between the King and his Elders. Together, they formed every Heavenly being from the mighty Seraphim to the meekest choirmite, and all were given responsibilities during the ongoing progress of the cosmos which lasted over five billion Adamian years.

When this creation of the Heavenly beings had come to pass, Yahweh established his Divine Council–The Adunalar Elohim–to assist him in governing the cosmos and awakening it to the fullest potential of life. The King did not *need* their help, mind you, but he *wanted* them to share in the beautiful experience of creativity and collaboration. Through this, he also created a deep, loving family whose celebration of life and love was euphoric and exceeded all joy ever thought possible. Those were splendid and happy times. Oh, Adamian...how I miss them.

At last, the foundations of the cosmos were complete, and it was time to begin Yahweh's grandest, most precious creation yet. In a small corner of the cosmos, he announced that he would create a world for a new addition to this cosmic family, whom he would see as his children and co-heirs to The White Throne. The King would come to call them Adamians, named after the first of their kind, and would make their world the new location of Eden: The Realm of The White Throne. Many rejoiced at this announcement, for the glory of the King's love was spreading tremendously. However, the heart of Yahweh's first creation grew corrupt with jealousy, and Azathoth revolted against his maker, friend, and King.

Azathoth and his Court of Elders were tasked with preparing this new primordial galaxy as a holy playground for the Adamians while they learned how to create, steward, and evolve in wisdom. However, in secret, Azathoth began producing the bitter fruit of his rebellion in the microscopic fibers of the newly forming planet by creating his own brood, The Elder Children, who would take over the Earth as their own and begin a more ruthless evolutionary process outside the will of Yahweh and the Divine Council's plan. Azathoth's path of evolution was dominion and conquest instead of a nurturing, mothering love as the Spirit of Yahweh would provide. During this rebellion, the harmony of The Cosmic Wheel began to split; chaos crept into an otherwise ordered cosmos, introducing all creatures to the absolute hellish reality of war, for the first time.

The Creation Wars tore a hole through this beautiful family of elohim. They were led by the very being who was meant to express the most fulfilling joy and creativity of the King. The wars lasted millions of years, starting slowly but gaining terrible traction. Azathoth's Elder Children eventually rebelled against him, and then the Council of Azathoth imploded entirely, expanding the conflict and complicating things even further. Ultimately, the entire cosmos was engaged in battle; elohim of every kind were fighting one another, either joining the rebellion of Azathoth, leading their own, or remaining true to the King.

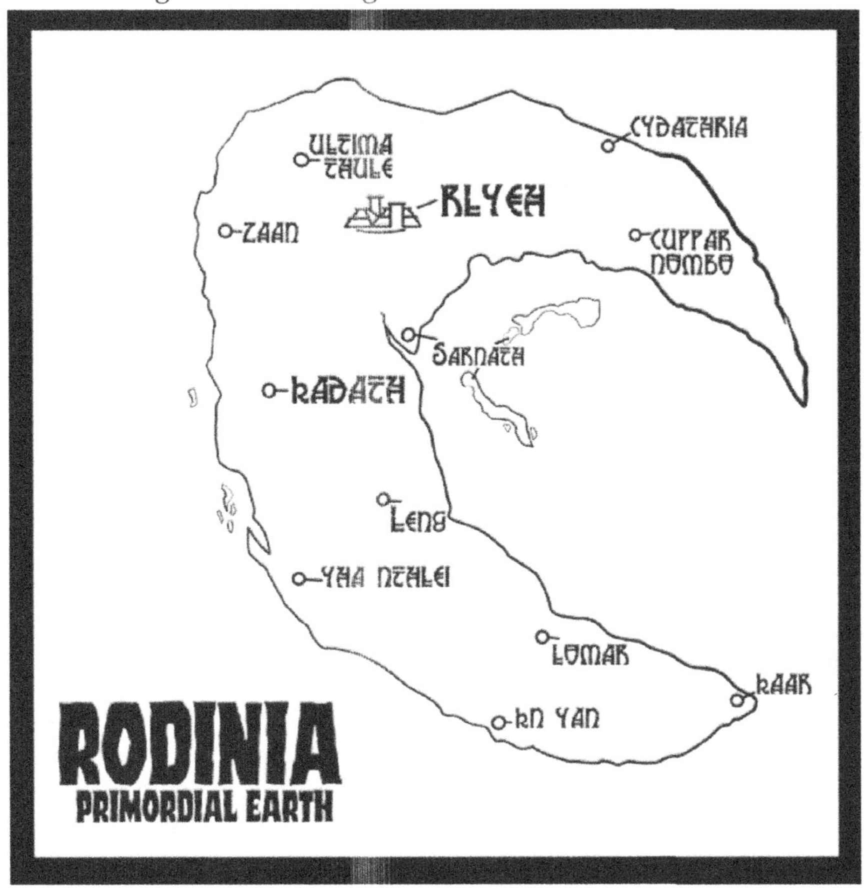


Then, the turning of the tide occurred when, during the Battle of R'lyeh, the Archangel Michael took up the Spear of Necrom–which had been gifted to Azathoth and his brood by the sinister Khata–and pierced the ground of the Temple of Cthulhu, High Priest of Azathoth. The smiting from Michael sent a tzoharian shockwave throughout the cosmos, bringing the mighty city of R'lyeh crashing into the watery depths below, with countless Elder Children and their would-be god, Cthulhu, down with it.

Once one large land mass known as Rodinia, the world began breaking apart and shifting, an action that would never entirely stop over billions of years, for the might of the Archangel's blow was fierce and wrathful. However, the climax of the Creation Wars occurred in the most unlikely of places: Zion itself.

Zion, the City of The White Throne, where the Trinitarian Presence of King Yahweh dwelled, was a kingdom encased in Light. Sacred Stones of carnelian, chrysolite, emerald, topaz, onyx, jasper, lapis lazuli, turquoise, and beryl adorned this capital city of Eden and its settings and mountings. Of all the Heavenly Host in this mighty kingdom, the most honored were the Tronule Gardinalor: The Seraphim Guardians of The White Throne, powerful winged serpentine beings whose featherfurs shimmered with tzoharian Light. The holiness of the very throne of King Yahweh reflected from their souls and illuminated all who stood in their presence. These throne guardians were the honor guard of Yahweh and were known to be the wisest and most revered of all the creatures of the Heavens. But the greatest of these was Lucifer, Son of The Morning.

Lucifer, a direct creation of Yahweh, governed The Adunalar Elohim and acted as Angelic Dogrudan–Grand Messenger–between the King and the rest of the Host of the Heavens. He was brilliant and intimately walked with the King amongst the white fire of the mountains of Eden. In wisdom and might, he was second only to Yahweh himself, or so it was said.

The temptation of Lucifer began small, as most temptations do. Upon first learning of Azathoth's betrayal, he was grieved and shocked at such an action. Then, over the course of thousands of years, watching the supposed freedom Azathoth and his Court had found in their rebellion, Lucifer began to entertain thoughts of his own and even questioned the integrity of the order of The Cosmic Wheel itself.

Azathoth was quite powerful; there was no mistake about that. However, he lacked the strategic intellect to successfully orchestrate a coup of this size. Azathoth had become far too greedy and hasty in his pride and rebellious lust for power and had now lost complete control of the entire situation. On the other hand, Lucifer knew that amid chaos–which had clearly erupted across the cosmos–it would be entirely plausible to create an army within the ranks of The Adunalar Elohim. Perhaps his fellow Seraphim and even some of the Septum Dei would see that the King they worshiped and aligned themselves with was clearly indifferent to the suffering across the cosmos and was selfishly hoarding power. For what being, if all-powerful and good, would allow such a travesty to continue? What might be an ulterior motive for this particular rule of *order?*

Lucifer used this crafty method of spreading doubt by having conversations masked as constructive communal growth within the Council. He would pose the questions as hypothetical thought experiments to "affirm" that the King was in control and had their best interests at heart. Yet, those theoretical thought experiments began to linger in the minds of many. Soon, a portion of the King's honor guard and most trusted friends were whispering doubts and conspiracies about whether Yahweh was who he claimed to be.

It was at this point, the sinister force, cloaked in mystery, known only as Khata–who had seemingly emerged from the shadows of the chaotic whirlwinds of The Creation Wars–approached Lucifer

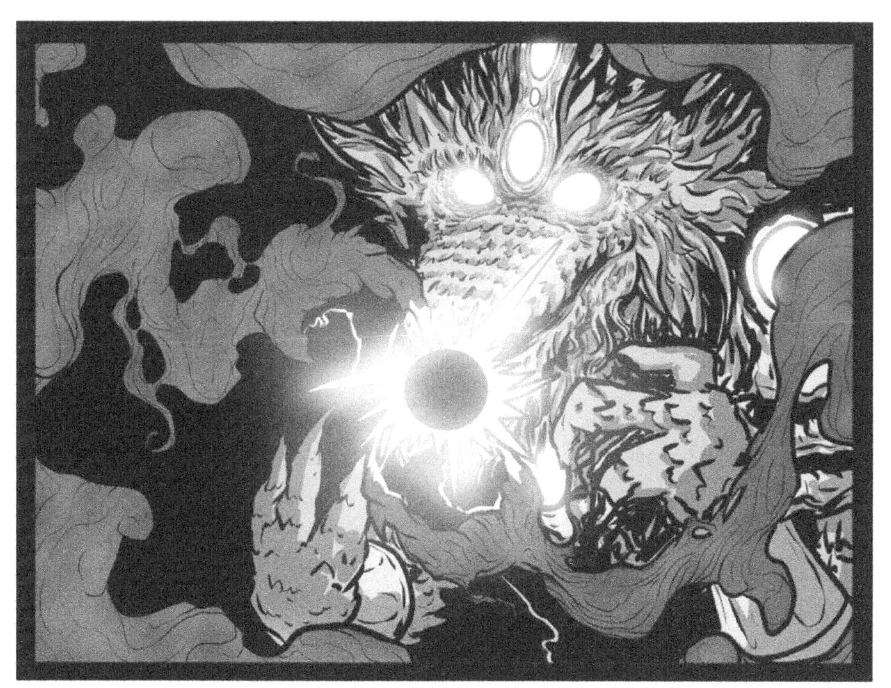

in a Vision. Khata showed him what the Dark entity claimed was the true history of the cosmos–past, present, and future. This Vision transformed Lucifer from a prideful being on a quest for power into a deranged warrior of chaos on a mission to reveal Yahweh's falsehood and free the rest of creation from the authoritarian order. This desperate and mad conviction that Lucifer now believed inspired him to lead a charge on the Kingdom of Zion.

During this final battle of The Creation Wars, Michael led the Septum Dei, the remaining Tronule Gardinalor, and all the holy powers of the Heavens against Lucifer and his horde, including the mighty Azathoth and the remaining members of his Court. The battle became known as the Luctus Bellam for its tragically grievous sacrilege and dreadful outcome. The violent destruction caused the next evolution of Khata as the entity took physical form on the battlefields of Eden as Mot–the manifestation of death itself.

The ultimate consequence of Azathoth's betrayal had come to fruition. In his overwhelming grief, King Yahweh sang The Lament of Dahe, casting every primordial Dark power into the newly revealed Realm of Sheol where the chaotic forces had been overflowing for ages. Sheol had been created and kept in secret by Yahweh to maintain order in the Cosmic Wheel. The original, singular Wheel had not only split to make room for chaos but now, because of the damage being done on Earth, a third Wheel emerged, creating the

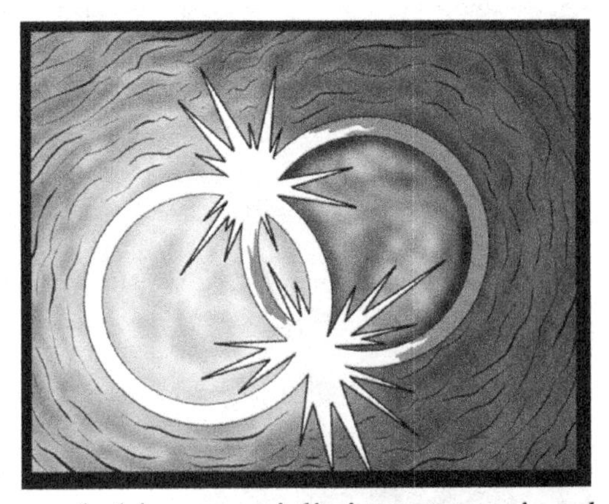

Corporeum Realm—a universe ruled by materialistic nature tainted by the Dark. As a horrible consequence of such a cataclysmic event, a terrorizing and grotesque being was ushered into existence. The opening of Sheol and the transitional birth of Corporeum created a monstrous agent of chaos, one who would forever plague not only those in Sheol but Corporeum as well: Tiamat, The Chaotic Abyss.

Tiamat was formed from the tumultuous energies of Sheol combusting with the ordered vibrations of Corporeum upon the opening of the first Necrogate by Yahweh during The Lament of Dahe. Not only did Yahweh grieve the opening of this portal, but he immediately began to war with the cursed, hydra-tentacled creature that emerged from the watery depths.

While the King, through his song of Lament, kept the raging waters of Tiamat at bay, he simultaneously cast all the fallen, rebellious elohim through the Necrogate to Sheol. From Azathoth to Lucifer to the new form of Khata, every Dark creature was thrust into this new realm of blackness and malice ruled by the chaos they had created. Madness and terror would now be their fate, for a plague of disorder would have a governing presence over every step they took. Not only would passing into Sheol attack their minds, but it would ultimately warp their appearances to show them for what they had indeed become: abominations.

As the Lament reached its climactic notes, the Host of Heaven joined with Yahweh to seal the portal for good, ultimately locking away the creature to which it had just given birth. Tiamat was the final horror to be spirited away into this new realm of shadow and fear,

cursed to be its forever gatekeeper. At this very moment, the last note of The Lament of Dahe formed a new Aeternum Stone that shone a bright blue and locked the gate of the abyss. This stone was forever known as Yesod: The Foundation Stone of The Earth.

In the aftermath of Tiamat's imprisonment, the Earth was left in ruins. The creature's chaotic force had engulfed the entire planet with its waters, covering all the land and sky to the brim of the Atmospherical Firmament before being locked away.

The Host of the Heavens had gathered around the brokenness of the Adamian galaxy, mourning for both the loss of their brothers and sisters who had rebelled and been banished, but also for the destruction they left in their wake.

This galaxy was supposed to be the new home for the Kingdom of Zion, where Yahweh's new children would grow and thrive alongside the Heavenly Host. It was all lost. Everything on the Earth created by Azathoth had been cast into the Necrogate or crushed by the chaotic waters that now ruled it. No pain felt up to this point could match the crushing defeat these elohim now experienced. The Creation Wars had indeed ended, but what was left was destruction and ruin.

Then, in the grievousness of the moment, the voice of Yahweh began to sing once more. But this was not a song of lament.

It started in a low, somber tone, and then, like a warm hearthside fire on a bleak winter morning, the notes became a consoling relief as they danced into the hearts of the Heavenly elohim who watched the mothering Spirit of the King move across the chaotic waters of the scarred, primordial earth as if to prepare it for new life amongst the ashes of war.

Millions of Adamian years passed.

"First to Eden yet again!! I didn't even use my other two wings!!" Baetiel playfully belted loudly to his brother, who had barely breached the warm and mist-filled Atmospherical Firmament of Earth behind him. "And you thought you could best me this time!? HAHA!!" The brothers had indeed traveled far, for they had flown from Sof Haderech–300 million galaxies away–racing to Sigrafinna Agac, The Garden of The Two Trees, which resided in the center of Eden on Earth. Today was the day they had waited for. After all this time, the first Adamian was going to receive Ruakh and be awakened to his inheritance as heir and co-laborer in taming the remaining wilds of the earth, stewarding it back to what it was supposed to be before Azathoth's rebellion so long ago.

"Are you still weary from passing through the Xoth system, dear brother?!" Baetiel flew alongside the slightly slower elohim to playfully scoff, looking directly at him while he continued. "My dear

Akalian, you're always falling behind!" He chuckled, and his tea-green tribal-marked face smirked with a wink.

"Maybe so," the smirk was mischievously returned by the whimsical smile of Akalian, whose featherbeard and long white hair majestically blew in the wind. "But at least I look where I'm going." With that, Akalian flung his wings open, throwing him vertically into the sky and bringing him to a sudden stop.

"Wha–"

**BOOM!!**

The reaction time of Baetiel's mighty wings failed him as he slammed hard into a large mountain on the outskirts of Sigrafinna Agac. However, the sounds of the elohim hitting the side of the mountain were almost completely drowned out by his brother's overwhelming laughter. Akalian now glided downward to where Baetiel lay, covered in branches and brush, annoyed and unamused.

"Oh, if only Michael could see the Head of his Order right now!!" Akalian could barely keep it together. "How proud he would be!!" The elohim then erupted with laughter.

"The Host beams with laughter at your words," Baetiel grumbled as he spat leaves out of his mouth and pulled twigs out of his mint-green featherbeard and deep black mane.

"Oh, don't be so sour. Come!" Akalian puffed out his chest and slammed his fists on his hips, standing boldly and playfully in the sunlight. "Today we celebrate!!" He bent down and clasped hands with Baetiel, pulling him to his feet again. Akalian placed a hand upon Baetiel's shoulders, let out a freeing sigh that brought a more somber tone to the moment, and looked up at his brother with tears of joy.

"Praise the King, for the stain of The Creation Wars is finally being wiped away today."

"Indeed." Baetiel returned the joyful heaviness of the moment. "With the breath of life given to Adam this day, we will wash away the shadow of those horrors and begin a fresh, everlasting peace with our new family." They simultaneously flapped their wings, lifted into the air, and gently glided toward the center of the Garden of Eden, where Sigra Agac: The Life Tree stood towering into the heavens, reaching miles wide and pulsing tzoharian Light across the Edenic valley.

Despite the true hope of Baetiel's words that day, peace was not everlasting. The corruption of the Creation Wars bore continuous bitter fruit, which found its way back to Eden on Earth in the coming

years. There, the representatives of all Adamians followed in Azathoth's footsteps and seized autonomy for themselves. In this choice, the entire human race was corrupted with the same curse that consumed the previous steward of Earth and his Court. Because of the Adamians' choices, Khata was able to weaken the veil between Corporeum and Sheol, allowing Darkness to take root once more. Upon the Adamians' first embrace of evil, Eden left the lands of Corporeum to maintain its purity and to not destroy the Corporeum Realm by the fire of its remaining presence.

For a thousand years, the Adamians continued to fall deeper into shadow and align with the forces of The Dark Kingdom–in every way imaginable–that had emerged from the depths of Sheol. Darkness had indeed returned to the Corporeum Realm with a vengeance. Many elohim, tempted by their lust for power and for the flesh of Adamian women, would turn from King Yahweh and attempt to create their own Kingdoms on earth, sharing an unholy knowledge with the Adamians, which only corrupted them further.

Everlasting peace seemed to be nothing more than a wishful dream. Everything was broken once more, even to the point that the chaotic waters and its terrors were summoned to destroy all of the corrupted creation. Even though, the King renewed his commitment to the Adamians once more, their descendants would soon welcome corruption into the Corporeum Realm yet again.

Throughout 2,000 years of constant rebellion, Akalian and Baetiel remained loyal. They grieved together, they fought battles together, they were faithful to their King, and were commended governing elohim in the Order of Michael. But on the day the sun set behind the Towers of Babylon—the day that the Adamians attempted to unite and undo the order of Corporeum by merging it with Sheol—the two Chief Powers sat on a hillside and watched as, once again, the Adamians fully aligned themselves with the Dark. But this time, Yahweh would not remain by their side, for they would be scattered amongst the gods they held so dear, like ashes in the wind.

"I am tired of this war," Baetiel said in a tone laced with exhaustion.

"As am I." Akalian agreed wholeheartedly with this statement. So much pain. So much rebellion. "I feel it weakening my very essence at times."

Baetiel scoffed.

"No. I am tired of *his* war." The exhaustion was still there, but there was something else.

"What are you saying, Baetiel?"

"I am saying that if Yahweh is as powerful and as good as he says he is, then why doesn't he bring this war to an end? He's certainly had ample opportunity to do so." Akalian's heart began to sink upon hearing these words. He knew this war had taken much from them. So many close brothers and sisters had been lost to the Dark or had faded from their current forms and joined The White Throne. Baetiel had taken this last rebellion very hard, so Akalian knew he needed to be gentle, but there was something more to this last statement. Something troubling about what his brother might be insinuating.

"Baetiel," Akalian placed a hand upon his brother's pauldron to ease the mood as best he could. "I know this was hard. It was for me, too. But this way of thinking, it's not–"

"Not what?" Baetiel snapped. "*Obedient?*"

"It's not how this works," Akalian finished, and was taken aback by how his brother just spoke to him. Never had he shown this side before. Akalian went on. "What of freedom? What of justice and responsibility? The King made Adamians so they might partake in his divine nature and experience the joy of creation, love, and freedom. *Love* has stayed his hand in this and prevented him from completely destroying them all. Love for them and for us."

"Please." Baetiel broke away from his brother's embrace and began walking away towards the edge of the cliff. "Akalian, don't be so naive. Is this not all a masquerade? Freedom? Choice? It's a facade. We both know the measure of his sovereignty or so we've been led to believe. If that *is* true, we have no more free will than an ant under the Adamian's boot. Yahweh *wants* this war, or perhaps he is not powerful enough to end it?"

*What is happening?* Akalian frantically thought, growing angry.

"There is no question of the greatness of his sovereignty, but this doesn't mean choice and responsibility are a *facade*. I don't pretend to understand the relationship between destiny and freedom, but I *do* know this is not a war he *wants!!*" Akalian felt himself shaking, but Baetiel remained as cold as a stone.

"And if it is?" Baetiel had now walked off the cliff and into the air as though it were solid ground. He turned to Akalian and glared at him.

"If it is... *what?*" Akalian began to release tzoharian Light from his essence and into his right hand.

"If it is *his will*...then he is a monster. If it is not, then he has led us to believe he is something he isn't and therefore, he is a *liar*. Either way, we have all been deceived." As Baetiel finished, his eyelids bowed slightly.

"*When!?*" Akalian reached through the realms and pulled a tzoharian Lightning bolt to his right hand. Karaydin emerged powerfully, ready to strike. Tears rolled down the warrior's cheeks. "When did they get to you!?" He screamed, and Baetiel returned the same energy.

"*They never had to!!* Look around you, Akalian! Do you not see destruction at every turn? Have we not witnessed humanity's ultimate fall *three different times!?* But our *King* still refuses to *end this!!* Instead, he gives them over to the elohim of The Dark Kingdom?? He will scatter the nations, placing them under the control of the fallen, whom we have fought for *millions* of *years?? How is that not defeat!?"*

"Because this is not the end!! It never has been!" Akalian howled at his brother. "Do you not remember how he brought life out of the watery grave after Azathoth and his brood were banished to Sheol? Do you not remember how he clothed the nakedness of humanity after Adam and Eve fell from grace? Do you not remember how he has brought Light out of the Darkness every single time? He will again show the shadows who he is and reclaim this world." Akalian was sobbing through his angry screams, holding Karaydin tightly in both hands, ready to strike.

"And watch it destroy itself once more? I'll have no part of it. Not now. Not ever again." Baetiel's stoic coldness subsided, and tears began to flow. Through the sobs, he continued. "You may strike me down if you wish, but I wish no harm upon you. *You* were always there, right by my side, able to bring Light out of the Darkness that was brewing inside me...but the Darkness became too much, brother. I can no longer look at this world and see hope. I only see it for what it is: sorrow."

Akalian froze. He couldn't believe this was happening. His brother, whom he loved so dearly. His brother, who taught him how to fly and fight and was always there to make him laugh...was never going to be there again. Hopelessness washed over the warrior as his gaze left his brother and peered upon his blazing blade of Light in his hands. Could he strike a final blow against this being whom he loved so much? Could he find the strength to do what he knew must be done? He had seen where this road leads. He knew what would happen to his brother and the destruction that would follow in his wake. But with all the weight of the cosmos on his shoulders, Akalian lowered his blade. As the tears continued to flow, he looked upon his brother again in complete and utter desperation.

"Please...don't do this..."

Baetiel fought back the tears, looked Akalian in the eyes, and spoke in a cold tone that burned into Akalian's mind for all time.

"I already have." And, as a hard rain overwhelmed the Tower of Babylon and night fell over the two elohim, Baetiel drifted away in a cloud of green billowing fog, never to be seen by his brother again.

Back on the Meridian, in present time, Akalian wiped the tears from his emerald, crested owl-like cheek at an observation window near the Hall of Knowledge. He thought of Baetiel often, and of the nightmare he'd become.

Memories can cripple even the strongest of creatures. They loom in the back of the mind like a cancerous fog that clouds hope and happiness from view. Unresolved trauma of the past haunts everyone, including beings of the unseen realm. For those filled with the holiest Light, the weight of the Darkness is a heavier burden to bear. But in a seemingly constant state of war where literally everything lays in the balance, bear it, one must.

"So, I see Willow has finally given you a few moments of peace." A welcomed familiar voice came from behind him as the warm comfort of Moriel's hand came to rest on Akalian's shoulder. This brother, his closest since Baetiel, was a gift. In Akalian's blackest hours, Moriel was always there to lift him up again. Akalian wished he could express more emotion and show Moriel just how much love he had for his brother, but his ability to do so seemed to be lost in that green fog that took Baetiel from him all those years ago. Nevertheless, Akalian forced a smile and turned to face the playful smirk on the face of the admiral blue Power which now stood before him.

"Yes, for now at least," Akalian chuckled genuinely. Indeed, Willow hadn't given him a moment's peace for the last few days while Moriel was healing in his chamber. "But I don't imagine it'll last long. How are you feeling?"

An ominous expression overtook Moriel. "I'm alright now...but the moment my strength returned, I had to find you." He hesitated momentarily, trying to gather his thoughts and how to state everything clearly. "The devil that wounded me on the battlefield, I've seen him before."

"I don't doubt it," Akalian said. "I'm sure we've seen all of the fallen at least once."

"I mean to say...that I have seen him *recently*." Moriel corrected. The ominous expression now began to make sense to Akalian.

"When?" He asked. That was a valid question, to be sure. It was improbable that Moriel would have recently encountered a general in the Perethedesh War.

"In my Age End Vision. And there's something I haven't been able to get out of my mind. He was the one performing The Black Mass with the Adamian woman."

"I see..." Akalian trailed off, unsure of what to say next.

"However, as grotesque as that was, that's not the haunting part. The blasphemous ceremony was being overseen by the man possessed by your potential Dark Prince. It's something *that* man said that is most troubling to me. He announced that The Nephilim would rise again. Doesn't that sound a bit familiar to you?"

"That's impossible, Moriel. The Nephilim have long since fled these realms. They're nothing more than disembodied echoes in the Dark. The Watchers are locked in the depths of Dudael and Tartarus, and haven't been seen or heard from since. They were all but eradicated Ages ago."

"I know...but allow me to continue. Over the last few days, I've been meditating on this, and perhaps there may be another way The Nephilim can return. Despite what we may believe, it's possible that at least some of the spirits of The Nephilim have found their way out

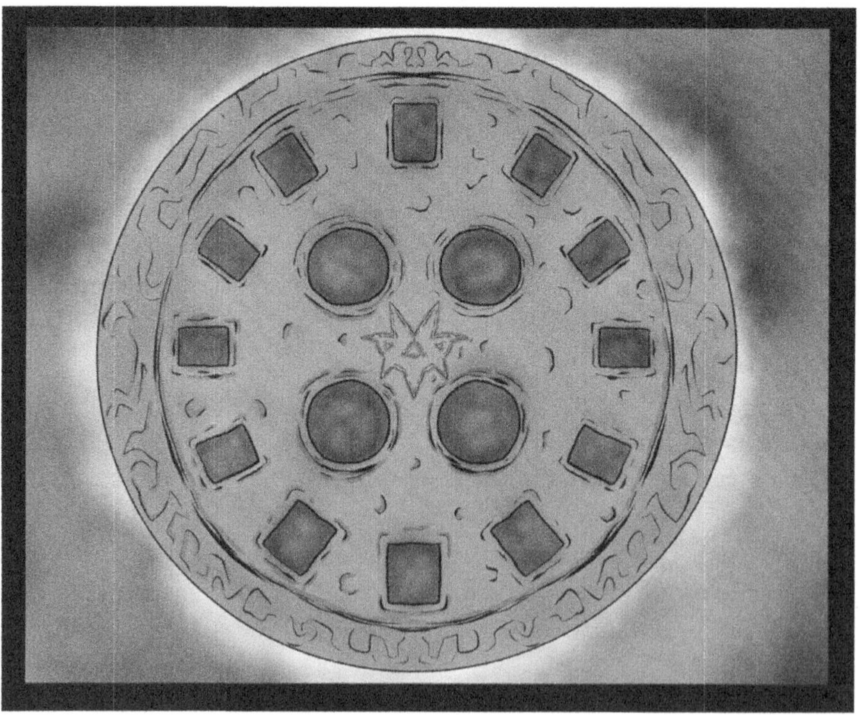

of the ether, and are hiding in the deep places of the cosmos, waiting for an opportune moment to come back once more. What if something brought them out en masse? Something foretold..."

"Are you speaking of *The Manking* Prophecy?" Akalian was taken aback. The Manking Prophecy was intimately linked with Age End and was counted amongst the Heavenly Host as an evil conspiracy that even led some astray. Moriel pulled him away from the open doorway of the Hall of Knowledge and continued in hushed tones.

"The ancient prophecy of Age End told of a single figure who would rise out of Nefil Agac, pull the sword of Azazel from its prison, and cause the earth to be swallowed in Darkness."

"Has anyone ever seen the Nefil Agac?" Akalian whispered. "It's just a Dark legend, Moriel. I don't know anyone who has seen signs of it outside of the claims within The Dark Kingdom."

"It was in *my* Vision, Akalian. And..." Moriel paused, scanning the concerned face of his brother. "And I had *another* Vision this morning. It was of Cadariel."

"*What?*" Akalian questioned, in shock.

"Yes. At least it started out with her...then she transformed into Lilith. *She* possessed Deccal and, joining forces with the gods of Endor, presented Azazel's blade to the very same Adamian man possessed by the Dark Prince in the colosseum."

"And we're trying to find an Adamian *boy* that The Dark Kingdom has created an entire stronghold around to keep us from, with Xexxus potentially in the center of it all," Akalian added.

"Precisely." Moriel stated firmly. "And we know that Xexxus has been known to call himself a *Herald* in the past." Akalian twitched in anger.

"Should we inform Lord Gabriel of this?" Akalian suggested.

"Not yet. As far as I know, this still must stay between us," Moriel replied gravely.

"And *that* is a troubling thing all on its own. Why do you think the King commanded this secrecy?"

"I don't know...and honestly, I fear what that answer may bring." Moriel finished the sentence more to himself than to Akalian. "However, there is more you need to know. There was–"

"My friends." A voice startled both elohim as they turned to find Afkiel draped in her formal robes instead of the armor they previously saw her in. "I don't mean to interrupt, but Lord Gabriel requests your presence." She paused for a beat, and her tone turned grievous. "Something's happened."

# CHAPTER SIXTEEN

## - PROPHECY OF DOOM -

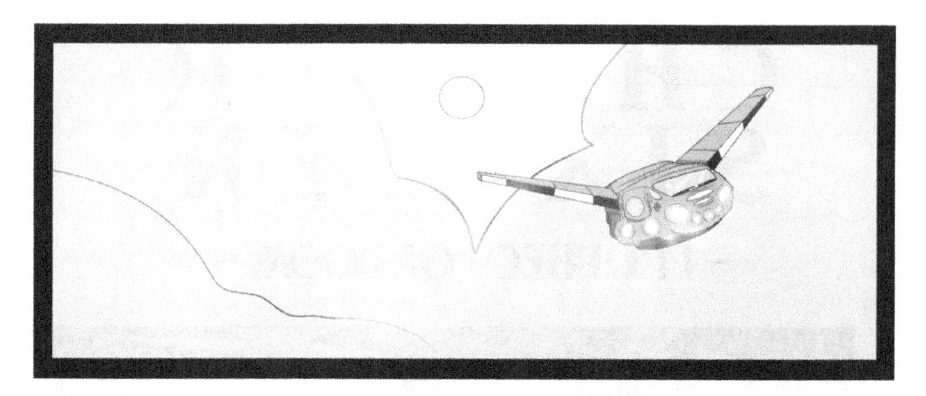

"Thank you for agreeing to come so quickly," Mattia said, sitting in the back of the skycab as it broke through the clouds above The Grey. Her fellow passenger stretched out a little and relaxed his left arm against the back of the long seat that connected them, basking in the air conditioning he hadn't felt for months.

"Of course," Obadiah replied. "Unfortunately, your case sounds all too familiar to what's been happening here in The Grey. You said he was scheduled to be euthanized next week?"

"Monday afternoon. That gives us a little under three days to work with him...if we can gain access tonight, that is." Mattia responded. She honestly couldn't believe this was happening. Obadiah was right beside her; they were traveling to disobey a direct order of The High Cleric–punishable by exile or worse–and monsters and magic were apparently real. All of it was so overwhelming. She had to try her best to stay calm, or her emotions would get the better of her.

"And you're sure you'll be able to do that? Get access, I mean," Obadiah questioned, for good reason too. He was very much an outlaw of The Grand Republic. He risked a lot by returning, but he knew she wouldn't have come all this way unless it was necessary. And he knew other things, too, things that were too coincidental to ignore.

"No, I'm not sure." At least she was honest. "But I *am* pretty confident I can. Bouchard basically eats out of the palm of my hand," Mattia said embarrassed. "Normally, I wouldn't take advantage of something like that, but this is different. Plus, he always looked up to you." Obadiah chuckled at the flattery.

"I can't believe Bouchard is the Headminister of Hillcrest now. He was a great assistant counselor, don't get me wrong, but I never would have pegged him as Headminister material. He seemed too naive and trusting for that kind of role."

"You'd be surprised. He's made a lot of good changes at the Sanitarium."

"Not enough, it sounds like." Obadiah's tone grew ominous. "Matty...when does the Gathering have its Midsummer's Eve Ceremonies?"

"This evening–"

"And how closely has the High Cleric been paying attention to Jonathan's case?"

"An average amount, I supposed." She was confused. "Why do you ask?"

"Hm," Obadiah grunted to himself. "Just curious. Wanting to gather as much information about the coming days as possible." Mattia allowed herself to reflect on the previous day's events. Those hideously yellowed, bloodshot eyes and that animalistic howl invaded her memory.

"Obadiah...you said the thing that attacked me was once a boy. How did he become...*that?* And how did you *kill* it?" Obadiah sighed–he knew this was coming–and pulled his leather satchel from the side holster of the cab seat to his lap. After he unbuckled the flap and flung it open, he pulled out the large stone cross from his fight with the ghoul child. It was rugged and weathered but beautiful. It was either fastened or welded to a piece of oak from top to bottom; Mattia guessed it was to give the stone more support. Obadiah looked down at the artifact with an almost fearful respect and started.

"The Cross of Capurro is an extremely powerful relic. It was used by exorcists in the Old World and was a legend even then. It emits an energy that the shaman priests of the Yeshuite tribes described as 'a holy Light,' and one that can do a lot of damage to evil things. You saw that firsthand yesterday." Obadiah quickly slipped back into his teacher role, and Mattia felt that familiar comfort in this chaotic sea of confusion.

"According to the priests, the history of faith and blessing that's been poured into this thing has given it an immense amount of power. I'll tell you more about its history sometime...but for now, there's something you need to know." He shifted his gaze from the cross and back to Mattia. His dark brown eyes shone from behind his heavy, graying brow, and the chocolate brown face Mattia was so used to seeing smile at her in her memories was stern and frightfully serious. The lines on his face, bags under his eyes, and weathered goatee with gray splotches made this man look like a much older, traumatized version of the honorable Cleric she once knew.

"We're at war out here. That *boy* was part of a small group of elite, ghoul-like creatures that's been hunting me and others fighting against The Coven of Endor. That thing hasn't been a boy for quite some time now."

"The Coven of Endor is...*real?*" Mattia was horrified. One more thing to add to her eventual mental breakdown.

"Very," Obadiah said bluntly.

“I mean, I just thought people were being superstitious. I never in my wildest dreams thought The Coven was an actual thing.”

"Look, I know this is all hard to hear, but if we're going to save your client, you need to hear it. The leaders of The Grand Republic try to hide these things from the *civilized* world, hoping that people will never believe in anything but what the governing powers tell them to believe. It's an entire system built on tangible, logical, scientifically proven materialism that's been manipulated and abused for one purpose alone: control. But I've seen things with my own eyes, fought them, *killed* them...things that I only thought were mere myth." He stopped, took a breath to gather himself, and continued.

"Matty, the last ten years have shown me that I’d spent my whole life living a lie. One that was intentionally fed to me from the highest authorities of our world. The Coven of Endor not only exists, but its roots run deeper than you may want to know."

"I don't *want* to know any of it," she said, almost to herself. "I can't handle all this right now." Mattia shook her head, trying to make sense of everything she'd just heard. "Let's back up a moment. Please. Tell me how a child can become one of those *ghoul* things." Obadiah readjusted in his seat, turning to fully face Mattia. He had forgotten that she was the most practical and naturalistically minded of all his students. That made her a good counselor and therapist; she kept her mind grounded and realistic. But, even if she was one of the most

enthusiastic pupils, when it came time to learn about the old myths and legends, he knew that folklore was only ever folklore to her. While others, even he, thought there might be some truth to them, he knew *she* never did. Obadiah saw panic building in her, so he led her in a breathing exercise to calm her mind. Then he continued recanting the horrid rituals of transforming children into demonic soldiers.

"They call it an Undertaking. It's a disgusting process of indoctrination where over a certain amount of time–weeks or months, depending on the child–of *'enlightenment,'* the children invite evil spirits into themselves. After that time is completed, a horrible ceremony called a Black Mass is held where some sacrificial ritual seals the demon inside the body, where it then has free reign." Obadiah's voice began to crack as he fought back tears. "Many villages are mourning the losses...and we are losing this battle, Matty. The Coven brings in more and more converts each day through the promise...and delivery...of power and pleasure.

"The head of The Coven, Agatha, is self-proclaimed Stick Queen of The Grey, and others have treated her as such for hundreds of years."

"Wait. *Hundreds?"* Mattia was baffled.

"At least." He said calmly. "At first, I didn't believe it either, but... during a raid once, I ran her through with a blessed blade. Apparently, it wasn't blessed enough, though, because she tossed me through the forest like a ragdoll. Then she pulled the blade out of her as if it were a mere splinter, looked at me with those piercing dead eyes, licked her black blood from the blade, and snapped it in two before disappearing completely, right in front of me. I never got a chance to get that close to her again or to her symbiote sisters."

Mattia sat frozen, eyes bulging, mouth open. Terrified. Obadiah hesitated to go on but she needed to know what they were up against. He knew that Mattia was now in this fight, too, whether she wanted to be or not.

"About six months ago, we *were* able to track down Agnus, the third High Sister of The Coven, and perform a successful raid. One of our freedom fighters severed the bitch's head from her body. It was still cursing at us as we gathered her slave children onto our transport.

We're all but positive that she did die, though, because word is Agatha has now chosen another to replace her sister."

"Wh..why does that make you *think* she's dead? Other than, ya know, cutting her head off." Mattia couldn't believe she was having this conversation and asking these questions as if it was everyday information to gather. This was insane. But Obadiah was as calm and collected as ever. And she had to keep reminding herself of what she had just experienced with the, what did he call it? Ghoul-child?

"The Rule of Three. It's believed that in direct mockery of the Trinitarian God, The Coven of Endor has always had three High Sisters ruling at a time."

"So, this coven has roots in old Yeshuite lore, then?" Mattia stated, remembering her studies from being his pupil.

"Correct. Which is why I believe The Cross of Capurro–being the oldest relic known to the Yeshuite tribes–could very well kill Agatha. So far, it seems like The Coven's horde has responded to the Cross like that ghoul-child did today. And *nothing* has had that kind of effect on them up to this point. This could be the key we've been waiting for. I hope it is. If it's not, I don't know how much longer we can hold out.

"After Agnus was killed, things got worse instead of better. Agatha sent out the second–and in my opinion, most dangerous of The Three–Annis, on a rampage throughout The Grey. You see, Annis is much more feral than Agatha or Agnus was. She doesn't just collect children for rituals or sex trade; she eats them alive. It's said that the terror and cries of the children, mixed with their blood, flesh, and bone, are the source of Annis' power. Legend says that she's half-giant and judging by how big she was when I saw her, I sympathize with that belief. She's the juggernaut, the unstoppable force of The

Three, and she alone is responsible for most of the death and destruction I've seen in the last ten years."

*"How* has *none* of this been brought to light in The Grand Republic?!" Mattia now shifted from shock to anger. "How could all of this be happening mere hours from the city of The High Temple without anyone having a single clue??"

"When your only source of 'credible' information and belief comes from a place that doesn't *want* you to know about this, then no one will. Also, think about it, Matty. No one wants this to be true. So, if the authority the people trust assures them that any *silly rumors* of ghosts and goblins are absolute rubbish, then that's what they'll believe."

"Obadiah, I am that authority. I have been for over a decade now! I've never *once* heard of this...horror."

"And yet, you're here. In secret. Asking me for help. So, *something* in you *knew* that there was more they weren't telling you." His words stopped Mattia. She was going through the exact same emotional and mental spiral he did fifteen years ago. Her faith in the Council had diminished considerably, and her trust in Malcolm was gone. But this? This was something else entirely. This was a conspiracy beyond her wildest imagination. She anticipated corruption but not secret satanic witchcraft and monsters. That's when it hit her.

"Are you saying Malcolm is involved in all this?"

"I'm saying I think your *client* may be a direct–"

**DING!! DING!! DING!!**

Mattia's communicator was screaming at her, and it was the emergency line. Only two people had this combination, Bouchard and Cleric Wendy. Confused, the Cleric accepted the call by pressing the earbud in her ear twice.

"This is Cleric Mattia." Obadiah saw her pause for a moment. "Wendy? What's going– *what!?"*

In a fueling station on the outskirts of Perethedesh, Cleric Wendy Foster had hacked into the stations' communication booth to override the history of the outgoing calls for that hour. She needed to warn her friend and colleague of the sinister turn things had taken at home.

"They're moving Jonathan's Euthanization to *tonight,*" Wendy said frantically. "Bouchard told me this morning. He also said that the High Cleric has been here quite a bit this week, in private, *assessing* the boy's condition. When I went to Malcolm to inquire as to why, he officially dismissed me from Clerical status for asking too many questions about it, saying my loyalties were no longer to the Republic and I was clearly spying for you." Wendy paused to calm herself.

"I don't know what's happening here, but something is *very* wrong, Matty. I can't put my finger on it, but *why* would he *dismiss* me and accuse me of *spying* for asking a few questions about a client under *our* care? So, I'm calling to tell you that I know you're pursuing your *other options,* and whatever you're doing, you need to do it *quick.*" Wendy's tone changed, becoming more ominous. "I'm going into hiding, Mattia. I've seen things recently that are deeply troubling. I don't have time to tell you what they are right now, but let's just say I'm not waiting around here for Edgar's hands to end up around my throat. I love you, my friend. Please take care of yourself." And with that, the line went dead.

Mattia pushed the earbud twice and looked at Obadiah. All the shock, all the confusion, all this unwelcomed revelation suddenly evolved into one focused emotion: rage. Faster than Obadiah could say, '*What's the matter,*' she slammed her fist on the sensor and opened the privacy divider between them and the driver. Leaning forward, she turned on her holobadge. The entire front seat area

illuminated with the official Clerical seal, resounding proof to the skycabby of who and what she was.

"By order of the High Council," she screamed into the poor, frightened man's ear. "I command you to take us to Hillcrest Sanitarium immediately!!"

Afkiel led Michael's Chief Powers to Gabriel's quarters. Two White Throne Principalities kneeled on the floor next to Gabriel, caring for a severely wounded warrior. Encircling the room were multiple elohim clutching one another and grieving anxiously.

"They...they took Raefun," uttered the shaky and trauma-filled voice of Joffus from the ground. Half his face had been torn off, and a necroplasmic poison was slowly inching toward the warrior's remaining eye.

"What happened to Joffus?" Moriel whispered to Afkiel.

"The Shadow Guard."

Moriel and Akalian both looked at Afkiel in horror. "He was Pentacled here by Saint Lūqās, who could barely keep him stable. There were no other survivors in their camp," she whispered to them.

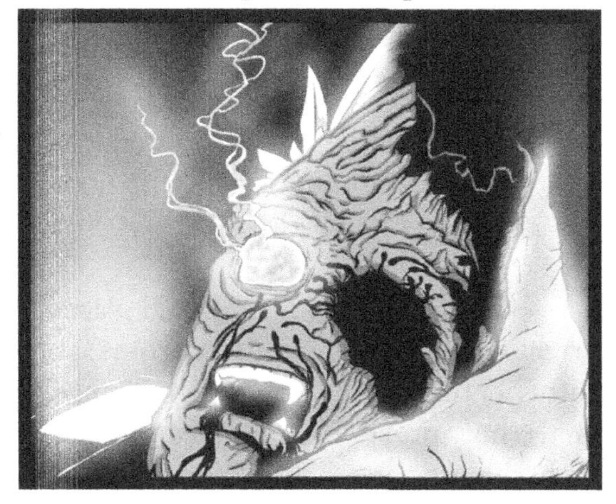

"Joffus," Gabriel said with tears in his eyes. "You have my word and the promise of the King that you will see Raefun again. This is *not* his end. Nor will it be yours." It was clear that the mangled body of Joffus was fading from this form. His maroon featherfur was graying as Raefun's did earlier, and the Light was beginning to fade from his remaining eye. But as the necroplasmic slime fell into it, a bright green glow began to overtake the fading organ.

"Joffus..." Gabriel questioned. "Can you hear me? *Joffus!"* Joffus' entire body began to levitate from the floor, knocking the two Principalities over and sending Gabriel hurtling through the air. The warrior's limbs twitched and moved in rapid, twisting motions as his mouth opened wide and a green fog spewed forth from the gaping hole in the side of Joffus' head. Suddenly, the warrior was stretched tight in midair as a putrid odor overtook the room, and Darkness enveloped them. The only thing visible was Joffus' contorted, crushed body, violently stretched and suspended vertically, surrounded by a deep, lime-green fog. As fear overtook the room, all went quiet for a moment, and a monstrously guttural voice from inside of Joffus began to speak.

"Away in the Dark, where devils take flight,
Flames engulf your dreams with fright,
Screams and suffering and teeth that bite,
On the road to the Castle of Endless Night.

The Serpent teems and slithers within,
Se'irim chant and prance in your skin,
The hounds of Hell fly with all their might,
On the road to the Castle of Endless Night.

So, abandon all hope ye who enter this blight,
A land that tears and blots out the Light,
Where Darkness reigns with no hope in sight,
Beware the Castle of Endless Night!"

Gabriel leapt to his feet and placed his hand over Joffus' eye. A bright white Light illuminated from Gabriel's Lightrunes to his hand. Joffus' entire face lit up as the Archangel closed his eyes and focused on the holy prayer his lips murmured. When the prayer was over, the Light dimmed and Gabriel removed his hand. Joffus' face was almost entirely gray, with just a glimmer of maroon left.

"It's...too late." Joffus' voice was crackled and weak. "It...has begun." The gray hue took over the remainder of the warrior's body, and he passed from that present form.

The room became a cacophony of sobs and whispers. The grief of their brother's fading and the uncertain horror of what just transpired left those in Gabriel's quarters in a state of panic.

"SILENCE!" Gabriel's voice boomed and echoed throughout the room. Immediately silence fell. He looked at the two Principalities dressed in their formal White Throne exoskeletal cloaks and helmets. "Prepare him for The White Throne." They began summoning a Pentaclegate for Joffus. "Afkiel, ready every occupant of the Meridian. We've no time to lose." He then addressed the room once more. "Everyone. We will be holding Council at the Pillar of Velkominn immediately. Let's move!"

As everyone began to disperse, Afkiel saw the look of fear and determination on Akalian's face. She looked at Moriel and asked, "What is the Castle of Endless Night?" But before Moriel could answer him, Akalian grimly said,

"Xexxus."

# CHAPTER SEVENTEEN

## - A COUNCIL OF WAR -

"So, it's true. It really *is* him," Willow said. He was floating above his Ophanim friend, surrounded by thousands of elohim. Willow had assumed Xexxus had a part to play in this stronghold war, but he had hoped—at least for Akalian's sake—that the monstrous being wasn't at the center. They were all gathered in The Grand Hall and had heard what had just occurred less than an hour ago in Gabriel's quarters.

"Yes," the Archangel answered. "There is now confirmation that Xexxus is behind the stronghold in Perethedesh. Joffus told me the boy will be merged tonight during a Black Mass." Gabriel took a moment to allow this troubling news to settle in before giving them something equally as heavy. "I was also informed that Joffus' entire battalion was either destroyed or spirited away...by The Shadow Guard."

Immediately, fear washed over the council, and Gabriel could hear thousands of the same responses: *The Shadow Guard? Here? How do we fight against that? King Yahweh, help us.* The Archangel didn't blame them. He knew the twisted horrors of The Shadow Guard and had experienced them before. He'd even watched them completely engulf a Seraphim once, which was unthinkable. The Shadow Guard was the blackest order in all of The Dark Kingdom, and they were here, alongside legions of other depraved beings. All to ensure that nothing would disturb the unholy rite that was to take place that evening.

"Did he say *where* Jonathan is?" Akalian's voice boomed through the chattering multitudes, and the question lingered in the air as all elohim quieted down to hear the answer. Gabriel understood Akalian's determination to face The Last of Legion, but there was more to consider here than the Power knew. Gabriel had experienced strongholds like this in the past, and he understood that sometimes the best move to make—for the moment, at least—was to not make one at all.

"Yes," Gabriel said reluctantly. "The boy is at Hillcrest Sanitarium, but from what Joffus and Saint Lūqās have reported, the stronghold is at its greatest around that building. I'm told it's heavily guarded by Stewards who are ready to sound the alarm at any moment." Stewards were not the fiercest of warriors but they were

formidable in battle due to their other abilities. They were the equivalent of Thrones in the Heavenly Host, Dark sorcerers who could conjure a myriad of terrors in an instant. Plus, at least one of them would have a Caduceus Staff with them—a lich staff—that held a scarlet Necrom Shard at its top. Gabriel knew of thirteen active Caduceus Staffs. In addition to being able to produce countless curses and spells, they could also form a Necrogate in an instant and usher in multitudes of unnamed horrors.

Akalian turned to Moriel, who had been deeply reflective since Joffus' prophetic warning.

"We must move quickly if we're to evade those Stewards. Maybe you could *clear a path* again?"

Moriel opened his mouth to respond but was cut off.

"Without an Awakening, your fate will be the same as Joffus and his battalion," Gabriel interrupted. "I understand what this means to you, Akalian, but there must be a plan of action before simply Pentaclegating into the Sanitarium. If there can even *be* action at this point. It is obvious this is much more than mere possession. Xexxus is clearly constructing something *sinister*, but as you well know, there are times when we cannot move forward with an attack. It may cause greater harm—"

"I will *not* let him slip through my fingers again, Lord Gabriel!" Akalian escalated, and Gabriel's tone rose to match him.

"And I will not allow you to lead my Order into destruction! I have lost far too many in recent years on this stronghold alone, Akalian. I do not wish to see this boy perish, but there is obviously much more at stake here than one child and your vendetta."

"His reign of terror is *my* doing!" Akalian shouted these words, tears forming in his eyes. Gabriel was taken aback. "As he and I watched the scattering of Babylon, I could...*should* have ended it immediately. But I allowed him to betray the King and escape. The plague *he* continues to spread is a direct cause of my weakness. I will *not* allow him to take another life. Not while I still have mine."

Akalian was shaking with anger, and a shocked hush fell over the crowd of elohim. No one in that room except for Gabriel, Willow, and Moriel knew what had happened that day all those years ago. Now, everyone saw the shame that had haunted their brother for thousands of years.

"I've remained silent long enough." Moriel stepped forward and addressed Akalian. "You cannot continue to allow your guilt to lead you. You are not responsible for Xexxus' actions, nor are you liable for his path of destruction. Hope and compassion stayed your hand on that cliffside of Babylon, not alliance with the Dark. If we are to cease utilizing hope and compassion in our fight against the evils of this cosmos...well then, they've won the day, haven't they?" Moriel then turned toward Gabriel.

"Hope, Lord Gabriel. That is what we have. When everywhere you turn, all you see is suffering and death, it is easy to forget hope. Even we, elohim of the Most High King, can be so overwhelmed that we forget such things. But we must remind each other that with great hope comes great risk...for love and freedom. King Yahweh has shown us that time and time again." Moriel backed up, placed a hand on his fellow Power's shoulder, and said, "This risk, for this boy...it's a chance we're willing to take, Lord Gabriel. We are meant to be here for this. And as you just said, there is much more at stake here than any of us realize. Even *you."*

"And Lord Michael sent us for that very reason," Akalian added. "We do not ask you to send support alongside us; we are prepared to take this on alone if necessary."

"They won't be alone!" The joyful tone of Willow chimed in as he flew down to meet his brothers on the floor of The Great Hall in front of Gabriel. "You can count me in." He was all smiles. The two Powers returned the expression.

"And me." Afkiel stepped forward from behind Gabriel and faced her Archangel. "My Lord, you are both wise and courageous. No one could have led this attack against the stronghold better than you have. But even if there's a slim chance, we must try to finish this tonight."

Gabriel's stern gaze fixed on the four elohim who stood before him and then he looked out at the rest of his Order who stood anxiously awaiting his next word. He now knew what was to become of him next. The King had made it known to him; he felt it in his essence. Through the forbidding threat of what was to soon occur, a smirk broke through.

"Order of Michael, indeed." He said with a chuckle. "I sense his stubbornness in *all four* of you. I thought I had been a better teacher than that, Afkiel." He said with a wink. "Very well." Gabriel lifted into the air and floated toward the archway, calling out his order of attack. "Afkiel, your garrison will accompany them. Willow, you scout out the premises of Hillcrest, locate the Steward with the Caduceus Staff, so we can make it our first target. The longer we can prevent them from calling out for reinforcements, the better." He looked back at Afkiel. "If it becomes too overwhelming, get out of there." Gabriel then looked over his shoulder at Akalian and Moriel. "That is my counsel to you two as well."

Gabriel then addressed his entire Order one last time before leaving to man his station in The Sanctum.

"You are all brave and noble elohim, and I am deeply honored to have led you through this. Let's end it if we can. Shine in the Darkness, my friends."

# CHAPTER EIGHTEEN

## - THE BATTLE OF HILLCREST -

The skycab entered Perethedesh airspace just as the sun set behind the mountainous High Temple. Its shadow loomed over half of the Southern Capital. The coming nightfall felt ominous yet appropriate to Mattia and her former Mentor, who was quickly resuming that role in her life again. There was so much she didn't understand. So much she thought was true that had turned out to be a lie. Mattia now felt more ignorant than ever before, and with the ignorance came an overwhelming sense of loneliness.

For the last few miles, a nameless fear had been growing inside of Mattia, and it showed no mercy in its crippling entry into her psyche. She and Obadiah had formed their plan moments after she gave the command to the driver. Given the rushed, improvised timeline and their surging adrenaline, it was as solid as possible. Then silence overtook them both as the weight of the situation pressed upon them. Mattia felt her heart rate speed up as their skycab passed The High Temple and its gardenesque level where Gwen's homily would soon end.

Up ahead stood Nargol Tower, its two-mile-wide rooftop housing Hillcrest Sanitarium, a place Mattia had, up to this point, known only as a bringer of hope and reason. Now, for the first time, she saw it as a sinister house of the damned. Who knows how many clients had been mistreated in this place under her nose? Those thoughts were slowly starting to seep in since Wendy had ended her call, and Mattia feared knowing the answers to the questions.

Thankful to be rid of these two, the skycabby circled the top of Nargol Tower and, finding a clear landing space about one hundred yards from the sanitarium–per Mattia's instructions–sat the vehicle down next to a grove of evergreens.

Although she couldn't see the terrors around them, Mattia felt the plague of monstrous spirits immediately upon landing. It was as if the malevolent hostility was reaching out to claw away at her soul. She couldn't explain it and she had never felt this kind of unreasonable fear before. As Obadiah opened the sliding door to exit the vehicle, the fear came alive in Mattia's mind. She was never one for an overactive imagination, but she was actually beginning to believe this was some external force. After the events in The Grey, she was becoming more convinced.

Images of formless monstrosities flooded her mind. Mattia could hear them roaring and cackling. Blended pictures of bloody teeth, glowing eyes, and slimy black tentacles invaded her most intimate thoughts, increasing her anxiety to extremes she'd never before experienced. As Mattia exited the skycab and set foot on the soft grass, she felt the presence of what could only be described as pure evil surround her. It pulled at her soul and licked her flesh with a bloody, sensuous tongue. The Cleric swore she could feel taloned claws scrape over her skin, although nothing physical was present. Darkness assaulted her every step, making the journey toward the sanitarium that much more horrifying. Fear was boiling up inside her, ready to erupt. Tears formed, and Mattia's progression toward the building slowed until she stopped, frozen in place and petrified. She wanted to cry out to Obadiah who was jogging ahead of her, unknowingly leaving her behind, but the horror-stricken Cleric couldn't muster a single syllable.

"Do not be afraid, Mattia." A soft yet powerful voice echoed in her mind, freeing her completely. This wasn't the external dread. It was something different, something calming and almost familiar. Mattia's surroundings immediately turned from blood-red horror to the quaint and peaceful arboretum, now lit by the fresh night sky. She felt as though she knew that voice. She'd heard it before. She–

"What are you doing, Matty?" Obadiah had finally realized he was alone and ran back to where his former pupil stood, frozen in the night. Mattia was snapping out of it now and saw her confused and concerned Mentor in front of her.

"Did–Did you hear that?"

"Hear what?" Obadiah questioned. He grabbed her hand; it was warm and strong. "Come on. Let's go." They began to running together along the tree line leading up to the main entrance of the Waverly Wing. Along the way, an orange tabby cat pounced alongside them. Mattia noticed it and wondered how one of the therapy animals had gotten out, but this was no time to deal with such things.

As they reached the security monitor, Mattia placed her holobadge on the screen and said her words of allegiance.

"One World, One Unity." Meanwhile, Obadiah was busy shooing away the tabby cat, who was hissing at the former Cleric's offensive means of doing so. A simple head pat would've sufficed instead of a soft kick.

"Act casual," Mattia said as she looked back at Obadiah. As the doors opened, the cat ran off, and the two walked into the facility's lobby.

Bouchard stood behind his desk, which was positioned against the far wall, as it had been for many years. Over the last couple of years, however, multiple security screens and a large control computer had been installed, which almost encircled Bouchard, and made his workspace look more like he was a prison warden from the Old World museums than the Headminister of a sanitarium. That observation wasn't lost on Obadiah.

"Joyous evening, Bouchard. I hope all is well. I've come to check on my favorite client." Mattia attempted to be as casual and carefree as possible.

"Joyous evening. I apologize, Cleric Mattia," Bouchard responded from behind his giant desk, "but I have been given explicit orders not to allow you, or anyone, access to the Client until the Grieving Ceremony tomorrow morning." Bouchard looked over his thick-rimmed glasses, adjusted his pale blue robe at the collar, and stepped out from behind his desk.

"And it is most irregular and quite forbidden to have former Cleric Obadiah on the premises. He cannot be here. As Headminister of this sanitarium, I must–"

"Bouchard, please." Mattia gently approached him and placed her hand on his shoulder, almost seductively. "We only need a few moments with Jonathan. It's just to pay respects. You know how fond I've grown of him over the years. Besides, Obadiah has been cleared of his former charges. Did you not receive that memo? I believe it was sent out this morning. I was sent to bring–"

"False," Bouchard said as he slapped her hand away. Obadiah hadn't thought that part would work. "Your request is impossible, and it is unacceptable that you have brought him here. He has been excommunicated! That most certainly did not change. This breaks more laws than I can count–" Bouchard was stopped mid-sentence by two vice grips on the not-so-small bicep of each of his arms. Facing him, Obadiah stood a good foot taller and was much broader than Bouchard, who took notice of that fact. He was meant to. Obadiah glared at the Headminister with a look that promised a concussion if Bouchard didn't choose his actions carefully.

"Give us five minutes." Obadiah's grip loosened, and he moved both hands to the top of Bouchard's shoulders. "Just five minutes to prove to you that this boy is in real danger here. You told Cleric Wendy that Malcolm was here a lot this week, correct?"

"Y-yes, he was even here a couple of hours ago...why?" Bouchard stammered in his reply.

"Isn't it highly unusual for a High Cleric to visit a Client who is a lost cause so often on the week of his Euthanization?"

"I...suppose it is, but–"

"Give me a chance to show you just *how* unusual it really is." Obadiah let go of the Headminister and took a step back. "Please, old friend."

Bouchard had once held Obadiah in the highest of regards. In fact, he envied the former Cleric and was brokenhearted when Obadiah was excommunicated. Indeed, it was unusual for the High Cleric to do what Obadiah had mentioned, but that wasn't the only thing Bouchard secretly questioned. He had seen more odd changes in policy than anyone else over the last couple of years, troubling things that his loyalty to the High Cleric and trust in The Grand Republic caused him to ignore or explain away. But sometimes, questions lingered in his mind. He knew he couldn't verbalize them, or else he too might disappear like others he had heard about. In fact, Bouchard wondered if it was actually loyalty and trust or rather, fear preventing him from taking action. However, what action could he take? He was but one man under the thumb of an empire.

"You now have four minutes and fifty-five seconds." He decided this was the action he could take as he shut off the electric shield in the hallway. "When your five minutes are up, I call the guards." Mattia and Obadiah wasted no time and immediately began running down the hallway toward the shadows that held Jonathan Young prisoner. "I'll be watching your every move!" Bouchard yelled after them as he walked back behind his desk. He absolutely meant what he said, but secretly, he hoped they would find something that made rebellion a viable option.

Outside the sanitarium, the orange tabby strolled through the open grass between the moonlit trees and shrubbery. It purred and mewed as it moved in and out between the tall, midnight-black figures strategically placed throughout the grounds. Every grim creature looked identical to the next, for Stewards lost all their uniqueness upon their Transfectiation in service to the Darkness. Each one had six blood-red bulbous eyes scattered across their claw-infested, conoidal skulls. The rest of their bodies were almost indiscernible, for their worn, leather-flesh robes were as black as night. Talons jutted out from their veiny, sculpted arms.

As the cat weaved between the Stewards, they paid it no mind. The feline race was known for its ability to live in the in-between spaces of the realms. The Dreamlands were overrun with cats who had passed on from the Corporeum Realm or were currently dreaming themselves. This tabby was quite vocal as it wandered the grounds, finally loafing down next to a Steward holding a large, body-length staff with a scarlet Necrom Shard at its top. This Steward with

the Caduceus Staff suddenly became very aware of the cat at its side when the "meows" turned into...

"NOW!!" Immediately, a Pentaclegate pierced the air directly in front of the staff-wielding Steward. Karaydin emerged from the portal and severed the Steward's head from its body. At the same time, Willow changed his form from the cat back into his choirmite self, caught the Caduceus Staff and tossed it through the portal, connecting this world to The Meridian as Afkiel's garrison poured into the Sheolic plain of Hillcrest Sanitarium.

"Jonathan?" The door to Client 43972's room creaked open, revealing total blackness inside. It was as if the light from the distant hallway did nothing to illuminate the way in for Mattia and Obadiah. "Jonathan, we're going to take a look around if that's okay?" Of course, the boy didn't respond to her; he hadn't said a word for years. Mattia clicked the flashlight option on her holobadge while Obadiah pulled his out of the leather satchel draped across his chest.

“He's been heavily sedated," Mattia told him as she shined her light on the pale, jaundiced face of Jonathan Young. He had what looked like self-inflicted wounds across his cheeks and above his eyes, which were fully opened, pupilless, and staring blankly ahead. The boy was seated on the floor, bound in a leather straitjacket with straps connected from his shoulders and waist to the ceiling and floor.

"Does Bouchard know about those wounds?" Obadiah asked.

"I'm sure he doesn't. They look infected."

"Perhaps he doesn't see the point in treating the wounds of a child who's about to be euthanized?"

"No. Bouchard wouldn't allow this...I bet he was instructed to not come in here either." Mattia realized.

"Ah. Well, he could at least turn the lights on for us." Obadiah scoffed. He was understandably annoyed with his former counseling assistant, turned Headminister.

"The lights stopped working in here over two years ago. Maintenance can't figure it out," Mattia said, ominously. Obadiah stopped and gave her a foreboding look. To distract herself from what that look could mean, she asked, "What are we looking for exactly?"

"Anything out of the ordinary...other than these lights. Specifically, markings."

"What type of markings?" Mattia began scouring the walls of the room, which, besides the observation glass covering the room's span, were covered in padded cloth.

"Do you remember when I had you study the Midsummer's Eve rituals of the Old World?"

"You mean the myth of the Oak King?" Mattia had loved that one.

"The Oak King, Gaia, Lilith. All are very similar. Old World cultures would sacrifice to them on Midsummer's Eve to gain power or guarantee a bountiful harvest," Obadiah explained. "Each culture used markings or symbols to bring power to the ritual. Especially if a sacrifice was involved." Both continued to search the room frantically. While Mattia picked through each pillow on the padded wall, Obadiah investigated the boy himself–from straps to bare feet–and continued his teaching moment. "They would surround their villages or ritual grounds with them. If a sacrifice was involved, they would sometimes mark the body of the animal or human with sacred glyphs or runes."

Mattia was having no luck and was halfway through the back wall when she noticed something. The floor was covered in a large rug.

"Many times, they would engrave the same markings on the sacrificial table–"

"Or on the ground surrounding it." Mattia interrupted him and pointed at the rug below them. "This wasn't here two days ago, Obadiah." She bent down and lifted the rug, revealing a blood-stained marking of the May Pole, among other symbols that she didn't have time to make out.

Obadiah looked on in horror as the face of Jonathan Young came alive with pure hatred behind bright glowing green eyes. Obadiah hurriedly dug in his satchel for the Capurro Cross, but he wasn't fast enough. An invisible force slammed into Obadiah and sent him crashing through the observation window and halfway down the hallway toward Bouchard.

The Headminister saw Obadiah land hard on the floor, surrounded by blood and broken glass. His thought was not on the man in the hallway but on the one he cared most about–the one still inside that room. He darted down the hall, past the excommunicated Cleric, who was now propping himself up on one side, shocked at what had just occurred.

"Hold on Cleric Mattia!!! I'm-" Bouchard's heroic cry was cut short as a bright green blast burst out of the observation window, sending both men flying into the air and further away from their dear friend and her captor.

The battle raged throughout the Sheolic plain of Hillcrest. Every square inch of the sticky, black ground was filled with violence. Although the Stewards had lost their Caduceus Staff, reinforcements continued to arrive. Gabriel had been right; this was the heart of the stronghold. Although they had the element of surprise, their ability to gain or maintain control was unsustainable.

However, it didn't need to be sustained for long. This was never meant to be a full-fledged attack on the sanitarium itself. Unlike other fronts, they weren't trying to retake anything but simply buying time. A fact of which The Dark Kingdom was ignorant. Afkiel reminded herself of that as she blasted a hole through the tentacle-covered Dark Young–the cursed steeds of The Dark Kingdom–galloping towards her. She hadn't seen the steed offspring of Shub-Nurrath since the Dakuraida–Dark Riders–attempted to cross over during The Final War, yet she had destroyed four of them already tonight. Indeed, this stronghold was unprecedented and alluded to a more significant threat than any of them had realized.

A few hundred yards away from Afkiel, Moriel sliced through the conoidal head of a Steward as many more began charging toward him. Their shadow blades clashed against Illeti, his twin cup hilt, broad swords that shone with bright blue tzoharian Light. Above him, an obu tore through his foes who attempted to attack him without his knowledge. The skill of the Stewards surprised Moriel, who was himself a master swordsman although it wasn't his preferred method of fighting. Tzohar Kazame, an ancient style of Light-fighting that harnessed the power of Tzohar: The Light Stone through obus, was where Moriel excelled. But unfortunately, when multiple shadow blades are rushing all at once, Light-fighting isn't nearly as valuable as a blade or two.

Near Moriel, Willow blasted Light from the Tetragrammaton on his stomach, ripping one Steward in half and wounding another behind it. Almost immediately, the choirmite felt a vice grip on the membranes protruding from his shoulders and was heaved twenty yards before gaining his balance in mid-air. He used the power in his wings to propel himself back toward the wretched thing that threw him. It was one of the Div–giant horned brutes who resided in the deep places of Sheol and roamed the Cosmic Ocean, waiting for an unsuspecting Adamian to invite them into their homes. Not every Div was a sorcerer, but this one seemed to be, judging from the look of its scarlet and deep purple robes.

Div sorcerers had the strength of a jotunn, and the craftiness of a Steward. That combination made them extremely dangerous. Willow was about twenty feet away when he realized this. After dodging a blast from the Div's axestaff, he deduced that the best tactic to use was his speed in flight. Immediately he began flying circles around the Dark creature.

Above them all, Akalian took to the skies, blasting Light from one hand while wielding Karaydin in the other. He shouted with visceral power while cutting through the first wave of Night Gaunts emerging through a Necrogate from the Sheolic Moon. They were like a school of piranhas smelling fresh blood. This flood of nightmarish creatures with slimy midnight blue skin flapped their massive bat wings toward the Power and swiftly overtook Akalian, which was no easy feat. But the Night Gaunts were no mere malevolent force either. These eyeless devils were the guardians of the Sheolic Moon. Their Kingdom belonged to one of the most diabolical minds in The Dark Kingdom: Nyarlathotep. Akalian looked around and was thankful their master wasn't present, for now at least.

A Night-gaunt swooped in close to Akalian, screeching through its needle-like teeth, and slammed a hellfire-laced hook into the Power's shoulder. It wrapped a chain attached to the hook around his neck and pulled tightly. Akalian was barely able to slide two fingers between the chain and his throat before being strangled. A Night Gaunt's hook was said to be one of the most painful weapons in all of Sheol. Not only did it physically injure its victim, but it injected a necroplasmic poison, weakening them for captivity. These effects were already beginning to take place within Akalian's system.

"NO!!" Willow cried as he looked up and saw his brother overtaken in the red skies. The Div, using this distraction as an opportune moment to catch up to the choirmite, slashed Willow across the face with his axestaff. The choirmite hit the ground, a gush of illuminated white blood pouring from his eye.

"Wake up, damn you!" Obadiah slapped the horn-rimmed glasses off Bouchard's unconscious face. "I need answers!!" As the Headminister came to, he saw a half-crazed Obadiah standing over him, bloody cuts covering his face and arms. Bouchard was lying on the floor next to his desk. His head throbbed as he lifted it.

"Wh–what in the world happened in there?" Bouchard asked as he reached for Obadiah to help him up. The former Cleric ignored both the question and the request. He opened the half door that led to the Headminister's control center, and looked down at the center screen.

"You said Malcolm was here a couple of hours ago?" he asked Bouchard, who was now on his feet, cradling the back of his head and entering the interior of the desk area.

"Yes–what are those markings on the floor??" The screen before them revealed the interior of Jonathan's room from the corner above the door.

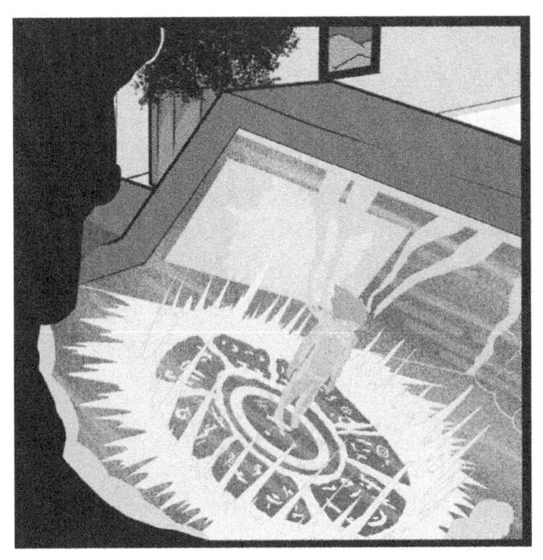

The picture was flickering in and out with static, and the two men could barely make out what was happening. But it was clear that the floor was covered in runes, glyphs, and pagan symbols that Obadiah recognized all too well.

Inside the room of Client 43972, Mattia was almost frozen with fear. She backed up slowly against the padded wall and stared into a twisted grin of pure evil.

"Hello, Cleric Mattia," the deep voice of Jonathan Young–or whatever was inside of him–hissed. "How nice of you to visit." Mattia's mouth gaped open, and a tear ran down her cheek. Jonathan stood in the center of the room, glaring at her from bright, hauntingly green globes that seemingly pierced her soul.

It had all happened so fast. After something–she could not see what–tossed Obadiah through the observation window, the boy ripped himself free from the straitjacket and restraints connected to the ceiling. The markings on the floor began to glow, and a green, billowing fog filled the room, choking the Cleric with its sulfurous stench. The rug below the boy's feet molded and deteriorated before her eyes, as though years of decay rotted it away in seconds.

Mattia couldn't think or process what was happening. She just felt an overwhelming, all-encompassing rush of fear like she had never experienced before. This horror exceeded even her wildest nightmares. This was nothing like the ghoul-child she faced earlier in the day. It was something much more sinister. Somehow, she knew its evil mind transcended her by thousands of years, if not longer. It was speaking directly to her, and it knew her name. Jonathan cackled at the horror emanating from Mattia's trembling body.

"Do you *really* believe you can save him, dust creature?" bellowed the voice inside the boy. "He is *mine!*"

Back at Bouchard's desk, Obadiah and the Headminister watched helplessly through the screen's static. The rug had deteriorated entirely, and the boy now stood in what Obadiah knew to be an ancient sacrificial Magick circle. It was known in The Grey as the Primary Circle of Sapiential Offering and went hand-in-hand with the Ritual of The Sapient Stone. This Dark sacrament promised to bring extensive wisdom and esoteric knowledge to The Coven or community that submitted themselves to it, and, as legend had it, the ritual's roots went as far back as the forbidden fruit of Adam and Eve–if one believed such things. Obadiah immediately went back to questioning his former assistant.

"Did Malcolm ask you to turn the camera off while he was inside, Bouchard?"

"Yes, but–"

"Has this been the normal practice since he's been visiting?"

"Most of the time." Bouchard was starting to see where Obadiah might be going with this inquisition. "He said it was for the boy's privacy in his Final Hours before the Euthanization Ceremony. But it's customary since the High Cleric made it into Clerical Law a few years ago."

"This isn't a Euthanization, Bouchard," the former Cleric stated. His tone grew more ominous than Bouchard had ever heard before. "It's a sacrifice."

"*What!?"* This couldn't be. Bouchard oversaw the most prestigious sanitarium in the entire civilized world. Human sacrifice didn't happen anymore, let alone here in this place. This was absurd. This was beyond belief. And yet, what his eyes showed him could not be dismissed. "How do you know this?" he asked.

"Those markings on the floor? It's ancient witchcraft and not the helpful kind. He's been prepared for something far beyond anything I've ever experienced, Bouchard. When is Malcolm coming back tonight to perform the Euthanization?"

"He didn't say. He told me he would give me further instructions after the Council's Harvest Meeting." A cold realization suddenly washed over Obadiah.

"Harvest Meeting..." he whispered to himself. "Oh, my god. It's a Black Mass."

"What?" Bouchard was now panicked and confused. He'd read about Black Masses in the Old World, but he never gave them much attention because they were extinct, at least as far as he knew. Obadiah leapt over the front of the desk and sprinted towards the lobby door.

"Wait!" shouted Bouchard. "Where the hell are you going!?"

*"Watch them!"* Obadiah shouted without looking back and ran out of the automatic doors and into the night.

Green fog swirled around Jonathan as a heavy wind spewed out from the markings on the floor like a cyclone inside the room. The boy's garments were deteriorating just as the rug did moments before, as he slowly rose into the air, arms outstretched like Christ on the cross. Jonathan gazed down at the Cleric who now stood below him, utterly lost in the terrifying reality she had fallen into over the last sixteen hours.

The possessed boy's throat expanded, the top two layers of his skin tearing to reveal raw flesh underneath. An inhuman, guttural moan began to give life to words–if one could call them that–that seemed to break down the very fabric of the last strips of sanity Mattia had.

"Cahf ah nafl mglw'nafh hh' ahor syha'h ah'legeth, ng llll or'azath syha'hnahh n'ghftephai n'gha ahornah ah'mglw'nafh." The foreign tongue had not only torn at the boy's throat but it had changed the physical world around him. Mattia was no longer in the sanitarium room. She was in a void enveloped in shades of green mist, giving way to cyclopean structures built from an amalgamation of dark stone and slime, with angles and dimensions she could not understand.

Jonathan looked down at her with his bulging, pupilless, hate-filled eyes. "Things have been set in motion which no one, especially a *sow* like you, could ever dream of preventing. I have gone before all, throughout time, and prepared the path to the new Age! I am The Final Herald, destined to bring forth The Destroyer of the Earth!! I am new life!! I am new birth!! I am *Endless Night!!"*

At the climax of Jonathan's crescendo, the slimy green cyclopean structures parted, revealing to the petrified Cleric a

labyrinth of shadowed stone. In the darkened entrance to this wretched maze, multiple pairs of bulbous eyes pierced the shadows of the massive structure. Mattia lost all remaining hope. If she could have moved, she would have crawled into a fetal position and regressed to her primal child-like state of thumb-sucking and crying in the night for someone to care. But she remained elevated, somehow still standing on her own.

Then she realized that the strength in her legs did not feel like hers. Something else was holding her up, something strong and...good. Mattia closed her eyes for the first time since the observation window shattered, breaking her sanity with the glass.

"I am true life," said a strong and gentle voice from behind her. A warm and caring hand was placed on her shoulder. "I am the Light in the Darkness." Calm washed over her, a peace she could not understand. The fear was melting away, and order was being restored inside her mind. "And I am with you. Always." Though she could not explain it, the touch of the hand brought an overwhelming comfort in ways she had not felt since her childhood. Since her mother's touch would calm her and convince her that it was all going to be alright.

For the first time since this nightmare began, a glimmer of hope began to shine.

Mattia opened her eyes, tears running down her cheeks. This time, they were not tears of fear but of hope, hope that soon transformed into brave determination. Her surroundings were back as they were supposed to be. The labyrinth, with its eldritch eyes, had disappeared out of sight.

She was back in the room. Jonathan was still levitating with arms outstretched. The markings were still glowing, and the fog was still there, but she could now see where she was and, more importantly, *who* she was. This mysterious voice of comfort and peace had given that back to her.

"I don't know who you are..." Mattia said out loud to whoever or whatever just touched her shoulder. "...but please...help me." Filled with confidence, she looked the possessed boy–whom she had cared for and grown to love unconditionally–in the eyes as if for the first time, not as a Cleric would look on her client, but as a mother looking on the devil who had enslaved her child. "Save him."

"No..." The possessed boy protested softly, fear lacing his monstrously deep voice. It had happened, and there was no stopping it now.

A beam of tzoharian Light blasted out of the cavernous fortress of the Sheolic Hillcrest Sanitarium. The Heavenly energies between the Corporeum Realm of Hillcrest and its Sheolic counterpart merged to form a holy Alpha Pentacle that lit the scarlet sky above Afkiel's garrison.

On the subatomic level, Pentacle particles existed in between the realms of The Cosmic Wheel, constantly warring against their corrupted Necro counterparts. They could be manipulated for travel, communication, and for wisdom.

The purest of all Pentacle particles was the Alpha particle and the only being who could summon it to form a Pentaclegate was Yahweh himself. So, when this Alpha Pentacle was conjured, there

was absolutely no mistaking who created it.

The sun-like beam ripped through Akalian's assailants, freeing the Power of the wicked hooks and chains that bound him. Before it faded, the beam not only rejuvenated the warrior but also gave Akalian more strength than he had when he arrived in this sinister land.

"The Awakening! He did it!!" Afkiel rejoiced as she took to the sky, raising her Staff of Tzohar and beckoning the other elohim to follow. "Quickly! Ophanim, ascend upon the Alpha Pentacle! Akalian and Moriel, fall behind me!!"

In The Sanctum of the Meridian, as he sat in on his cobalt throne, Gabriel felt it. His Nexus had arrived. It had been delayed centuries ago when, for a moment in time, the wills of the Adamians and the Heavenly Host aligned to fight against the Darkest infestation since Nero. Lucifer's fascist vessel fell that day, and Gabriel was spared from his fateful event. However, that journey caught up with him now.

"You know what must be done, old friend." The warm voice of the King soothed the anxieties of the Archangel, if only for a moment. Perhaps he now understood some part of what Yeshua felt in Gethsemane all those years ago when he cried, drenched in bloodied sweat and was answered with a similar, peaceful but forceful message.

"We will find you. I promise you that." Those words were enough. Gabriel trusted the sovereignty of his King completely.

He rose from his throne, pulled energy from within him, and placed it above the Aeturnum Stone table. Small beams of Light began to form his Lightblade of the Hafif Kalec, Fisilti: The Whisper of Light. The blue Jian sword, its hooked guard encrusted with bright Shards of Hod–the Glory Stone–lit the dancing glyphs inside the strong blade that now hovered, fully formed, over the Stone table.

The Archangel levitated slightly and entered the beams of blue, slowly approaching the powerful relic that had been a critical extension of his arm for many seasons of his life. Fisilti had spilled more necroplasmic blood than any other blade of the Hafif Kalec, aside from Michael's. Grabbing the guard of Fisilti felt like embracing a family member not seen in ages.

"Once more into the Darkness, old friend."

Afkiel's Staff continued to blast its way toward the Alpha Pentacle in the sky, the legion of holy elohim following her. Light from the Ophanims' multitude of eyes pierced Night Gaunts and winged jackals alike. Moriel spent some of his energy by surrounding him and his accompanying Power with multiple obus set to strike any corrupt creature that came near. He knew that the Alpha Pentacle would completely rejuvenate anyone who traveled through it, so Moriel could use as much energy as he needed until he reached it.

Everything was working. Somehow, this plan, this risk, was turning into the reward they had sought after. A miracle.

Suddenly, they all felt a change, like a fever starting to boil inside each of them. Fear, indescribable and incomprehensible, overtook the Host as streams of black and scarlet matter filled the air around them, traveling ahead at a haunting pace and grouping together about one hundred yards ahead, separating them from their destination. The substance began to grow and form an ominous pool floating in the sky, eclipsing the Pentaclegate completely. Afkiel stared at the forming Necrogate and was the first to audibly acknowledge the horror they were about to face.

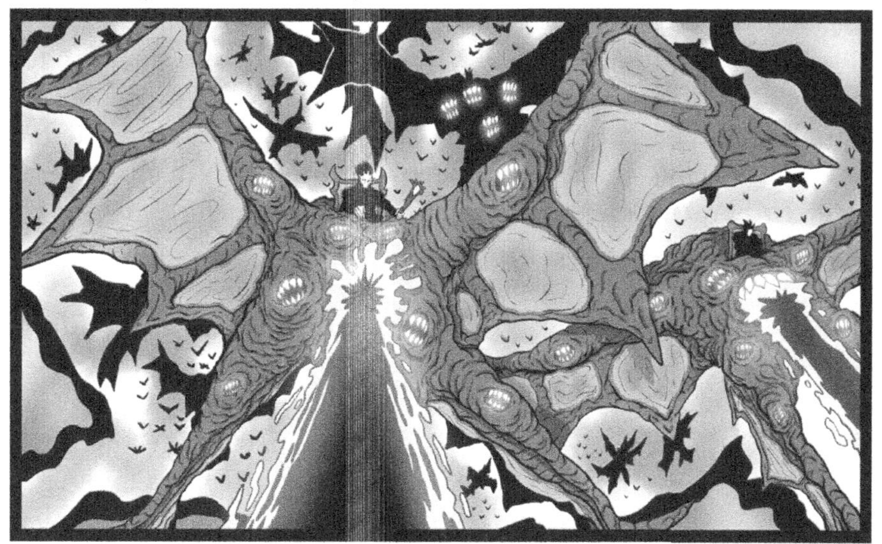

"The Shadow Guard..." she whispered to herself as the tendrils of fluidic nightmare flooded from the hovering pool that dripped with dread and malice. The nightmarish Necrogate expanded throughout the sky like a cancerous plague. The eldritch shapes of the Shadow Guard took the form of mangled versions of the Ophanim: feathers replaced with calloused leathery skin flaps protruding from four or five membranes that were covered, not with eyes of Light, but rather with filed gnashing teeth. The creature's membranes met in the middle of their twisted bodies to form a solid knotted cluster of veiny flesh and bone. Atop these horrid monsters were riders, covered in night and terror with pale, numb expressions. They stared into the very souls of their prey, absorbing the energy vibrating forth from their spiritual bodies like a vampiric disease.

*"Host of The Heavens, evasive maneuvers!!"* Afkiel commanded her elohim, attempting to avoid the piercing gaze of the Shadow Guard. She rocketed upward, trying to outmaneuver and advance the Shadow Guard's position overhead. She could hear her garrison being overtaken behind her as she blasted through the wall of Night Gaunts ahead of them. Moriel and Akalian were still close behind. For now, that's what mattered. She needed to get them to that Pentaclegate. They had come too far to fail now.

Something blurred Afkiel's vision, and she felt a sharp pain engulf her body. Her Staff fell from her hand and she tumbled through the air, head over heel again and again before regaining her balance. As soon as the Chief Power of Gabriel's Order bolted upright, her reflexes activated. Afkiel produced a mirage of counters and blocks against this sinister Shadow Guard Black Knight who had targeted her, the leader of the garrison. The Knight's movements blurred. She had no time to think, only react to the assaults this monstrous creature was throwing at her. So far, she had been able to keep up, but she wasn't going to be able to do so for long.

Moriel and Akalian found themselves in the shadow of the massive, calloused bat wings of a Shadow Guard Ophanim, its teeth bared and veins throbbing. The Dark Rider atop the creature cracked an iron whip on the center flesh sack where it sat. The creature vomited an ocean of necroplasmic bile at the two Powers. Moriel immediately unfurled his wings and slammed his outstretched hands together in front of him.

The energy in his wings surged through the movement in his arms, commanding two of the obus to crash together, forming a blocking shield to protect him and Akalian from the projectile slime.

Joining the action, Akalian summoned tzoharian energy, both from Karaydin and his own body. It shot out of his unfurled wings that stood straight up like powerful antennas and emitted white hot Light. Just as the obu shield was beginning to give out, the shockwave aura from Akalian's wings surrounded the two Powers.

"We can't keep this up for long, Moriel!" Akalian shouted over the buzzing of the tzoharian energy and the warring bodies flying around them. "We have to find a way around this blockade and fast!"

"I think that goes without saying!" Moriel yelled back. "However, I'm afraid the longer we are detained like this, the less *around* space we're going to have." Moriel pointed toward the Shadow Guard's Necrogate. They could see it wasn't just acting as a portal for transportation; it was expanding and enclosing around the entire battle.

"This isn't just a Necrogate for *them*. It's a prison for us *all*," Akalian said in horror and disbelief. The amount of Dark energy needed to capture an entire garrison was unheard of, even in times such as this. This was the power of the legendary Shadow Guard. They now understood the absolute despair that had crippled Joffus and chills crawled down their spines.

Afkiel's arms and legs were numbing. A few of the strong blows from the Black Knight had snuck through her defenses, but it wasn't enough to slow her down. But her pace sadly came to an end. The Black Knight was able to get close enough to slash Afkiel across the eyes with its razor-sharp talons. While it wasn't enough to blind the elohim, it did stunt her reactions. The Shadow Guard creature had time to transform his fluid, necroplasmic arm into a lethal Shadowblade and was now thrashing it at hyperspeed toward Afkiel's abdomen.

Had it been any other being, the stunt probably wouldn't have worked. But indeed, small creatures accomplish great things. All Afkiel understood was one second, she was stumbling backward in mid-air, reeling from the gash across her brow. And the next, the Black Knight had been smacked into oblivion across the battlefield.

The small, bright yellow beam who had just saved her was already rocketing past Afkiel, leaving his weapon of choice floating in the Sheolic wind: the severed head of a Div Sorcerer.

Akalian's shield weakened and Moriel prepared his energy to produce more obus. This, indeed, could not continue much longer. Moriel's power source was mighty but not infinite, and the nightmarish necro-bile of the Shadow Guard Ophanim relentlessly poured on them with full force.

"I'll cover you from behind," Akalian said as he turned, wings to wings against his brother with Karaydin at the ready in his right hand, and a glowing emerald Light force forming in his left. "Prepare yourself!" he shouted. And just as Akalian's wings sparked their last bit of shield energy around them, Moriel slammed his palms together, outstretched in front of him once more, releasing his obus and crashing them together to form a shield in front of him just as Akalian's diminished. As soon as Akalian's side of their defense became unshielded, two more Shadow Guard Ophanim spotted the opportunity and began hurtling toward the two Powers.

"Moriel! I need an obu, now!" he shouted to his brother, but it was useless. Moriel's entire source of energy and focus was on keeping his shield going and producing more obus to replace the dissipating shields. He could neither hear, nor help Akalian.

The Dark beasts were still a hundred yards out but had already begun coughing putrid, black and red bile energy sacks toward Akalian to gauge his reflexes and record his movements so they could outmaneuver him once they gained more ground. This was something Akalian had heard about the Shadow Guard. A soldier could only outmaneuver them for so long because they would quickly learn patterns in defense attacks and adjust accordingly. The Power began slicing through the bags of slime. And although he was a seasoned warrior, Akalian attempted to keep his movements basic so the Guard would not master his defenses. The Power was having trouble thinking of what his and Moriel's next move should be. It was taking all their energy to focus on one of these foul creatures. Adding two more was out of the question, yet that was what they were about to face. Then, hope beyond hope came screaming down towards them.

Akalian had heard about Willow's self-sacrificial standoff with the mighty Cthulhu. Of course, he had. Everyone had. For it was legendary and had earned Willow both his Tetragrammaton and a seat on Michael's Ordering body. However, in all his years, Akalian had never truly seen Willow's full magnificence on display before. So, when through the noise of war and the slashing of sacks of devil bombs, he heard the battle cry of his small brother rocketing toward them and saw the tiny hero's determined face with one blazing eye, white with flame, Akalian knew he was about to witness something extraordinary.

Just as the two Shadow Guard Ophanim reached the struggling Powers and opened their mouths to pour out revolting bile, Willow arrived directly behind them. He let out such an intense cry of war that it seemed to have come from a creature many times his size. The Div Sorcerer had awakened a righteous rage in the choirmite with that final blow of his axe. One that almost immediately cost the wicked wizard his life. The circular wheel of the Tetragrammaton on Willow's stomach blazed with white, hot flames of holy Light. The choirmite's one good eye bulged as fire poured from it and wrapped around the wings at his temples. Then, as his battle cry grew even louder, an ancient prayer, older than the shadowed foundations of the Earth, flowed from Willow's tongue:

"And when dense blackness falls to close,
The day in thickest folds of night,
Let not our faith such Darkness know,
But by that faith let Dark be Light!!"

As the small choirmite shouted the final words of the prayer, tzoharian Light erupted from his Tetragrammaton, completely engulfing all three Shadow Guard Ophanim beasts and riders, as well as the Powers between them. The holy fire of the Tzohar is the very power of The White Throne itself–the King himself–and is completely pure. For a being who wishes to be one with it, the fire spreads overwhelming joy and sustaining life. However, when this holy fire touches Darkness and those merged with The Dark

Kingdom, it does not restore or rejuvenate. It does not help produce growth or flourishing. It annihilates it.

Akalian and Moriel were astonished at what they were witnessing. Both loved Willow with all their hearts and had seen him do great things. They knew he had done even greater things than this, but they were awed by the power surging from their regularly gleeful, whimsical brother. It was beyond impressive. Being caught in the holy fire of the Tzohar rejuvenated not only their energy but their very souls.

However, the same could not be said for the Shadow Guard Ophanim and riders. As their bodies began to disintegrate and burn away, they shrieked in horror. There was no hope for them. Once the purity of the fire took hold, the only thing that would remain would be the part of them that wasn't solidified in corruption, but that part had perished long ago.

As the Light from the fire began to settle, Willow's Tetragrammaton calmed and returned to normal while an unexplainable peace washed over that section of the battlefield. It was as if, even though the war raged on around them, it had already ended in this spot with sweet promises of New Eden. Moriel knew that this meant they had a few moments of rest. For, here in this one hundred yard diameter, new sacred space had been born, and no evil could traverse here—for now.

Through the debris of ash and smoke from the disintegrated beasts, Akalian saw their tiny, teddy bear-shaped sibling. The Power's eyes met Willow's remaining one as a boyish smile spread on the face of an exhausted Willow. As the choirmite fainted, Afkiel caught him from behind, careful to not let him plummet back down to the necroplasmic ground of this unholy land.

"Easy there. I've got you, little brother," Afkiel said, calmingly, to her small orange and yellow sibling, whom she now held in much higher regard. She flew over to Moriel and Akalian, cradling Willow in her arms. "So...he isn't a small bundle of hyperkinetic glee after all," she said with a chuckle.

"Oh, he's definitely *that.* That's just not *all* he is." Akalian winked at Gabriel's Chief Power. After a moment to share in the sentiment, Moriel spoke up.

"I hate to dampen the moment, but we must use this limited space to formulate a plan. It will soon be corrupted once more, and I'm not sure we have many options available to us." Indeed, the options were bleak. With their piercing eyes, the three elohim scoured the battlefield, as they knew their moment of peace and reprieve was quickly ending. The sky and ground were both covered in Shadow Guard beasts, riders, knights, jackals, Night Gaunts, and other nightmares all savagely warring against the remaining members of Afkiel's garrison.

It appeared the only elohim left that still had a chance were the Ophanim still loyal to the King, and even they were beginning to fall. So much death. Would it ever end? Akalian wondered if the Adamians knew that death did not end with them but rather it spread out to all the realms. It seemed death was a grievous doorway to another existence that awaited mortal and immortal alike. And death was certainly on display here on a grand scale.

The Necrogate had by now spread out and engulfed them all entirely, blocking the way to the Alpha Pentacle. With the number of creatures swarming around, they couldn't reach the center pool of the Necrogate, and even if they could, they would be no match against the gate itself. For an elohim to try to prevail against a portal of The Dark Kingdom was to invite chaos inside their very being, tearing their essence into realms unknown. The few elohim of Light who had attempted such a task were rarely found again in one piece, if at all. Defeatedly, Afkiel voiced the only option they had.

"I'm not sure we have another choice, my friends." Afkiel's tone was grave. They had come so close only to fail. "We must fall back...I'm so sorry we couldn't–"

"Wait..." Akalian interrupted the Power and looked around as goosebumps prickled up and down his neck and shoulders. After a moment, the other two felt it as well. Something in the vibrations around them was changing. Something hidden. Something holy.

Amidst a pack of Shadow Guard Ophanim, vibrating energy began to focus and become compact. As the sinister beasts started to feel it as well, they shrieked in fear, but it was too late to retreat. A flash of Lightning split the pack's center. Blinding white fire bolts ripped through the Shadow Guard, eradicating them and simultaneously restoring all the Host. In the middle of the pulsing ball of Light stood a silhouetted figure, his cloak and robes flapping in the wind, and a sword of the Hafif Kalec raised boldly above his head.

*"Isik getir Fisilti!!"* shouted the mighty Gabriel, Son of The Septum Dei. He bolted from the center of the initial blast and began soaring through the air, ripping Dark Ophanim apart with his Lightblade. Everything that stood in the Archangel's path was

instantly torn apart. Gabriel did not come here to merely fight Dark entities; he came for a greater, more threatening purpose. His target was not the Shadow Guard but the Necrogate that brought them there. This mission was now apparent to the three Powers as they watched the Archangel in awe.

"What's he doing?!" Akalian shouted. It wasn't really a question, more of a verbalization of shock and fear. "He knows what that could...what that *will* do to him!"

"He's doing what he's meant to do." Afkiel calmly stated, feeling a sense of resignation and sadness. Gabriel had spoken to her before about his Nexus event and how it had evaded him, or how he had evaded it–the Archangel wasn't sure which–but he knew that eventually, it would catch up with him.

Everyone had a Nexus, and they had to face it. Every mortal would at least face death, but many Adamians had others as well. And although not all immortals would face death–none would face it the way Adamians do–they would face providence in other ways. There is no choice in the matter. A Tzoharian Nexus overrode the Law of Choice to sustain order in The Cosmic Wheel. Gabriel's, it seemed, was finally beginning.

"For Yahweh!! King of Ages!!" he cried. The Archangel reached the pool at the center of the Necrogate and raised Fisilti high above his head with both hands. He arched his back to deliver a fatal blow, then smashed, blade first, into the pool. The Light of Gabriel's essence became one with the sinister portal, transforming every part of the black and red vile Gate into blinding white Light. The Host watched in awe as every member of the Shadow Guard shared the Necrogate's fate, cracking and bubbling over with the Archangel's holy Light. It was destroying the monsters from within.

"The King is with you, my friend," Moriel said somberly as he watched the Light of Gabriel and the blackness of the Gate disappear into chaotic realms unknown.

The two Powers wasted no time and soared; wings outstretched toward the Pentacle of Light. Night Gaunts and winged Jackals attempted to prevent their progress, but the Ophanim made quick work of those lesser devils. As Moriel and Akalian passed through the Alpha Pentacle, the warm glow of The White Throne washed over them and healed them entirely.

"Akalian...Akalian, wake up, brother." Moriel's voice felt far away, as if it were in a distant tunnel. Everything was black. Akalian felt like he was floating in the middle of a sizeable black ocean. Was this the Cosmic Ocean with all the horrors that lived there? No. This was something else. He was on solid ground, or at least somewhat solid. It felt fleshy.

"Akalian, you must get up." Moriel's voice was closer now and was easier to understand. Akalian felt his fellow Power's gentle grip on his shoulder and was able to grasp what the command meant. He opened his eyes to see his brother kneeling over him. Everything was in a green fog. Behind them was a pitch-black, necroplasmic waterfall, dripping and oozing as if it were in slow motion. Moriel helped Akalian sit up, and they both looked out past the fleshy cliff's edge.

"From evil dreams defend our sight,

From fears and terrors of the night..." Moriel said a quick prayer. And as his vision unblurred, Akalian understood why. He could see more clearly through the thick fog stretching out before them.

"There is but one question that has haunted me for quite some time now..." Moriel paused, narrowing his eyes at the ominous Kingdom of Endless Night that lay before them, in complete disbelief at the obstacle that now stood in their way. "...who is this boy?"

# PART THREE

## THE EXORCISM

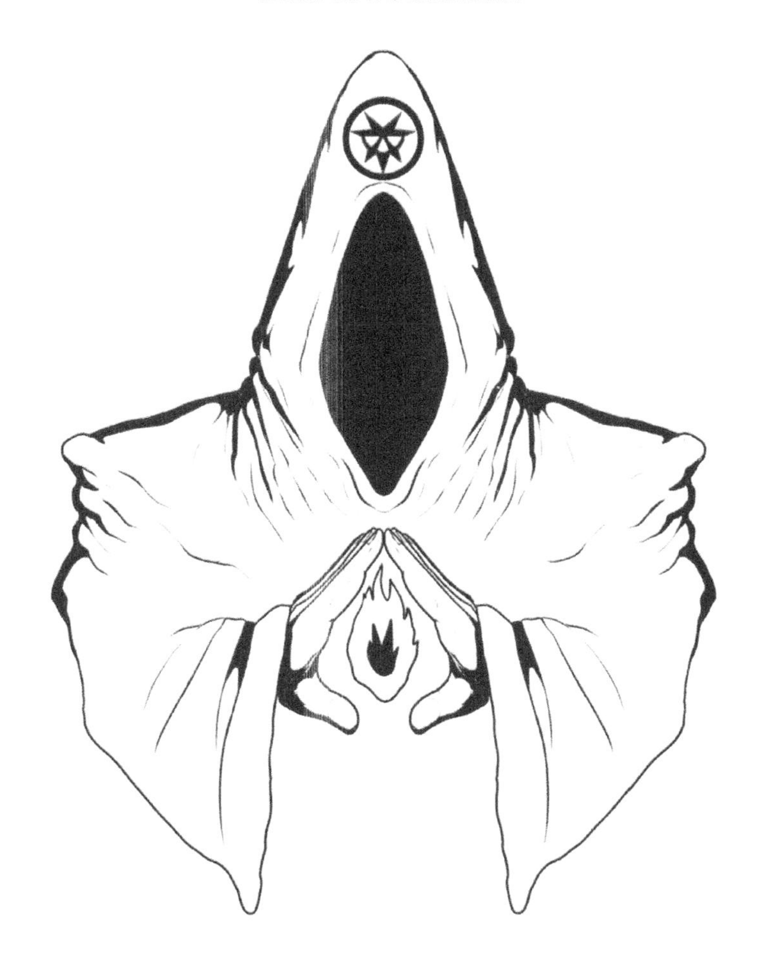

# CHAPTER NINETEEN

## - THE TALE OF THE BLACK TREE -

The sub-realms of The Cosmic Wheel were vast. One could spend many lifetimes traveling the expanse of creation and still not reach its end. It was common for those who walked away from the Heavenly Host—for whatever reason—to search for answers to the new chaotic questions storming in their souls. Much would be learned in this search, but very little life-giving substance was a part of the conclusions they would find. All answers led to Darkness, so much so that one would have thought the Darkness truth and the Light a lie.

Out of all spirits who wandered the realms, the pilgrimage of Baetiel might have been the most extensive and tragic. He cared not for how long this journey would take, only that he needed to find the meaning beyond that of the trivial answers given by the Heavenly Host and his former *tyrant* king. The former Power knew there was more to this life than what he had been told. He felt it in his bones.

Baetiel sought out the most legendary figures of the Dark. Ones whom he knew had walked these paths before him. Elohim he knew to be shrewd and crafty. It wasn't a blind allegiance to Lucifer or Khata that drove him; it was the longing for an inner peace that would finally bring sense into this facade of order he was taught to believe. The former Head of The Order of Michael sat on the Pools of Fanalak's shores, where the ancient Genzarian—planet eaters—disciple of Khata dwelled. Baetiel stared into the enormous, bulbous eye of Fanalak himself, mentally pleading with the sagacious being to share the esoteric knowledge of the Cosmic Wheel. Baetiel was given the knowledge he sought, but not without the cost of madness, for in the lands of Sheol, Dark wisdom always comes with a hefty price.

For many long years, Baetiel sought out the legendary Elder god, Azathoth, the first to find freedom from Yahweh's manipulative control. However, the former Chief Power never found his prize. There were many rumors regarding what had happened to Azathoth once he was violently pulled into the chaotic birth of Sheol, but it seemed no one—not even other Elders from his Council—truly knew what had happened to him. It was said that he had been driven completely mad and had slipped into a comatose state of being, attacking Adamians in their dreams. However, even if that were once true, no one in The Dreamlands could ever recall the Elder god materializing in their kingdom.

In The Dreamlands, the wandering warrior found himself seated in the Court of The Eidolon Lathi, Queen of Thalarion, Sister of Mab, surrounded by all her horrifying glory. Baetiel's years at her side had served his purposes well. It was there that, for the first time, he heard whispers of the whereabouts of Deccal: Blade of Azazel. He knew of this legendary unholy relic and the tree in whose base it had been planted, but until then, Baetiel had always dismissed it as Dark

Kingdom propaganda. He had never imagined the Agacan abomination to be *authentic* or that it held any actual power after the Watchers had been imprisoned in Dudael.

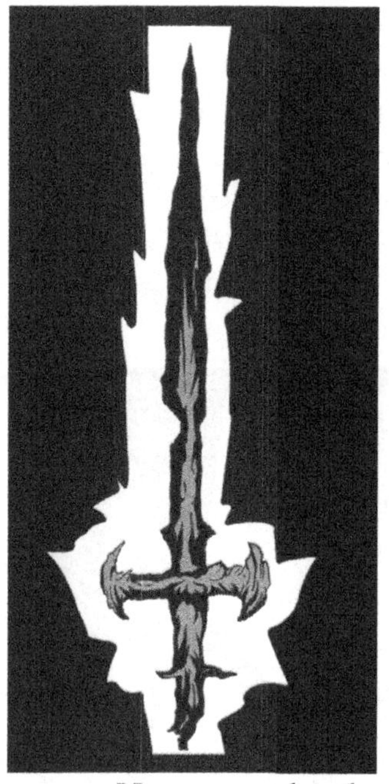

However, now, thoughts of this unholy relic would not leave his mind. It haunted him until he became utterly obsessed. Upon his departure from The Thalarion Court, he was so convinced of the blade's sleeping might that he made an oath to Queen Lathi that, with the power of the blade of Azazel, he would build an army so vast even the tyrant King Yahweh would not be able to withstand its power. With her unholy blessing, Baetiel departed to the Mountain Kingdom of Kadath, where he knelt before Hypnos, Elder of The Cosmic Wheel and ruler of all The Dreamlands. He requested all knowledge regarding Deccal and the haunted Agac it belonged to.

Hypnos, who had remained neutral in the ongoing war between Yahweh and The Dark Kingdom, refused, as he had no desire to fuel the fires of the prophecy of Age End. He was the King of Dreams and was content with such things. Since the Elders had been banished to Sheol, he had wanted nothing to do with his siblings or their Dark allies, nor did he care to aid the King in reclaiming the "perfect" order of The Cosmic Wheel–The Great Téleios of New Eden. Like the Norse descendants of his Elder brother, Nodens, Hypnos had created his own kingdom and would not allow his authority to be usurped by any being, Light or Dark.

However, while Baetiel was supplicating for information, Hypnos' most trusted council was present: The Oneiroi. And on that most trusted council was a being who reveled in fear and chaos and who was constantly at odds with his fellow council members and their king.

Phobetor, Lord of Nightmare, was most intrigued by what could occur if this former Power of the Order of Michael had access to the sleeping might of Deccal and the demons who guarded it. So, in secret, Phobetor met Baetiel in the space between asleep and nightmare: The Valley of Fear. In this place, haunted by the bound spirits of dead giants destined to drift numbly through mist-filled valleys of nothingness until the end of the Age, the Lord of Nightmare informed this former Power, of the black tree: Nefil Agac.

In the days of the Adamian warlord, Tubal-Cain—centuries before The Great Floods—when Father Time and his Order walked a slower path, and months lasted a century, the Chief Watchers of The Eternal Mountain observed the Adamian women of the Corporeum Realm and lusted after their flesh.

Unfortunately, this is where I—your humble host—enter the story firsthand for the first time. Above all else, Adamian, I am the

High Prince of Watchers. We observe all, recording every event so the stories of creation—good and ill—are not lost to time or finite memory. We Watchers were assembled during the Creation Wars and tasked with aiding King Yahweh in gathering information regarding the spread of Khata and his cursed plague.

In the days of Tubal-Cain, my Council of Watchers was governed by The Novem Dei, nine of my most trusted brothers and friends. Each Watcher had his own Order of angels who carefully observed the increasingly hostile activities of both The Dark Kingdom and the Adamian race. They would then report back to their Princes, who convened with me in counsel. Our findings were becoming more troublesome as the wicked Royal Line of Cain—the firstborn of Eve—continued to embrace the ways of Khata.

After hundreds of primordial years wandering through the deep jungle of Karalak—the untamed land east of Sigrafinna Agac—the Tribe of Adam was led by the Spirit of the King to the Mountains of Awlaan. Adam and Eve's corrupt descendants—both physical and spiritual—populated much of the lands to the northeast, pledging allegiance to the Royal Line of Cain and planting the seeds of the mighty Kingdoms of Babylon. Many wars were fought between Babylon and the Tribe of Adam—as primitive as they were—but not once could the line of Cain overtake the

mighty fortress of Awlaan. However, tragically, all of that was about to change.

Through the centuries, Semyazah, Head of The Novem Dei, grieved greatly over the increasing subjugation of the descendants of Eve. Women were no longer considered equals in the Line of Cain but had been stripped of their royal seat and abused as property for forbidden pleasures and comforts of the men who would war, hunt, and rule the Kingdoms of Babylon. Even the most revered descendant of Eve in all the blasphemous kingdom, Jezpirah, daughter of Tubal-Cain, had no say in how her life would be lived.

Jezpirah was betrothed to her cousin, Loch. On her fourteenth birthday, he was to publicly take her as his wife and know her in front of the entire royal Court of Cain. The Court would then partake in her "delights" as they saw fit, as was customary. What was known to the elohim as "nebalah," or what future generations of Adamians would understand as "rape," had become the standard in this declining, debaucherous land. To live as an Adamian woman in the time of Tubal-Cain–and for thousands of years to come–was to constantly walk in fear.

Semyazah's grief toward this ongoing wickedness made him extremely protective of Jezpirah, and he saw her beauty–inside and out–as unmatched in all of Babylon. Therefore, one night, Semyazah gave in to the constant and never-ending itch of temptation. He decided to do something that had never been done before and pursue a desire that was strictly forbidden to act on by all elohim of the Heavenly Host. This Head of The Novem Dei would take the daughter of Tubal-Cain as his bride.

He began in Jezpirah's dreams, slowly turning sweet images into increasingly more sensual and euphoric sensations. Semyazah had watched this descendant of Eve her whole life and knew what she longed for, even her most secret desires. One night, at the height of a particularly sensational dream, Jezpirah awoke to see Semyazah's human form–the very being she had just been physically longing for and dreaming of–standing powerfully at the end of her bed. She immediately invited him inside of her, and in doing so, the two welcomed destruction upon the Earth.

Upon secretly returning to the Elysian Fields where The Novem Dei dwelled, Semyazah was met by his brother, Azazel–second in command of all Watchers–who questioned the Head of the Order over his recent whereabouts. Azazel had peered into Babylon and saw all his brothers at their posts except for Semyazah.

It was no secret amongst The Novem Dei that the two brothers shared an infatuation for the descendants of Eve and had grown to despise the Adamian men of the Line of Cain. Therefore, instead of lying about where he had been and what he had been doing, Semyazah confessed his actions to Azazel and persuaded the second in command to join him in his pursuits. After minimal coercion, Azazel agreed, and together, they conspired to hold a secret council with the remainder of The Novem Dei. They wished to reclaim the world that the Adamian men had led to ruin.

In the dead of night, under the cover of a new moon, the Watchers of The Novem Dei convened secretly on the lonely mountain that had once been Sigrafinna Agac. Upon Mount Sirion, they plotted and agreed to take a sacred oath, pledging themselves with a blood covenant that would bind them all and each of their Orders in this quest to take the Adamian women as their own and become the new Kings of Earth.

On the first day of Jezpirah and Loch's wedding celebration, the Head of The Novem Dei walked in human form into the Court of Tubal-Cain and told the tyrant what had transpired between Jezpirah and himself mere days prior and that the warlord would be wise to give her over to him. Seeing the tremendous stature of the man who stood before him–Semyazah's human form being seven feet tall–

Tubal-Cain not only agreed but offered Semyazah the seat at the warlord's side.

The warlord was no fool; he knew this mighty man must be from the gods. Loch, who stood at an average height of four foot, five inches, felt robbed of his situation and property. So foolishly, the Adamian challenged Semyazah to a duel. The primitive skill of Loch was no match for the Head of The Novem Dei. Without any weaponry–and in one swift blow–Semyazah knocked Loch's head clean from his shoulders. It landed at the feet of Tubal-Cain and ended whatever competition Semyazah may have faced from the rest of the Court.

Through their ability to cloak themselves as mighty men and cast concealing spells between the realms, the Watchers hid their actions from the rest of the Heavenly Host for quite some time. Some wooed women as Semyazah did; some took them by force, or forced their Adamian fathers to give them over. Some Watchers even took multiple wives at a time. Semyazah was the first to plant his seed in his bride, then Azazel soon after. Soon, every bride of the two hundred Watchers who had taken part in the blood covenant on Mount Sirion were expecting offspring of their own.

It was during this time that I began to suspect something. As I was tasked with other matters in the cosmos, I fully trusted my brothers on The Novem Dei to inform me of all that took place in the Kingdoms of Babylon. My trust betrayed me, and months, lasting as long as an Adamian age, passed by without my knowledge of what was transpiring there. Over time, reports from other elohim of the Host began to come in saying the Adamians in Babylon had learned things they should not yet know, if at all. Much like when Adam and Eve took the knowledge of Finna Agac before their designated time, the vibrations of the Corporeum Realm's structure were beginning to shift, forever changing the Paracosmic landscape of the Earth. The Novem Dei and their Orders were too caught up in their lust for flesh and growing power to consider the visibility of this shift, or perhaps, by then they did not care.

The Watchers taught the Adamians various things to help them "grow" as a species. From simple hints, such as using clay to darken the eyes of the Adamian women—making them more seductive, appearing like some of the elohim of the Heavens, so they could entice man and Watcher alike—to the use of alchemy, a mixture of science and elohimic divination, in their everyday lives. The Adamians were promised godlike power that would elevate them to heights beyond their wildest dreams.

However, the Adamian race was not yet prepared to comprehend or utilize these things wisely, for their hearts were too Dark. Regardless, the Watchers had now taken the women as their wives and the entire Kingdom of Babylon as their own people from whom they would shape in *their* image. Very soon, their direct image bearers would be born from the wombs of their forbidden brides.

After an unnaturally long pregnancy, the time arrived for Semyazah and Jezpirah's offspring to be welcomed into this new world. Tragically, not even the tzoharian divination of the mighty Semyazah could save his wife from death during childbirth as the abominable creature ripped forth from her body to wreak havoc upon the world. All in Jezpirah's chambers—except for Semyazah—were torn to pieces by the creature as its wrath raged against the intrusive act of being born. Semyazah fought off the unholy beast, who grew by the minute. It was all he could do to survive as the monstrosity tore a hole through the palace wall and ran out into the night, leaving Semyazah alone with the shredded remains of his beloved and her midwives.

More of the same would occur for the next few, long weeks until the entire Kingdom of Babylon was terrorized by the nightmarish creatures the people named Nephilim: The Abominations of Desolation. They were creatures with consciousness but had been formed from an unnatural rebellion. Like Azathoth's Elder Children, King Yahweh had no direct part in their creation, therefore, they were left to the cold, cruel process of a loveless and purposeless evolution. Their souls were pure malice and greed.

The Nephilim soon grew exponentially–some reaching heights of twenty feet or more–and became all the more violent and cannibalistic. During these days, Semyazah retreated into his despair, while the heart of Azazel grew more corrupt, slowly becoming one with Khata.

Azazel had taken four wives in the same fashion as Semyazah. At the birth of his grotesque offspring, all four women perished. However, Azazel found himself less saddened at the gruesome mutilation of his wives and more fascinated with the abilities of the Nephilim. For, over the previous age-long months, this Second Head of The Novem Dei had been teaching the Adamians of Babylon the art of war and the use of strategy and weaponry. He hoped to inspire this newly reformed Kingdom of Babylon to utilize their newfound skills in overtaking the Mountains of Awlaan so that *his* people could now rule the Earth. However, he soon became disgusted with the primitive minds of the Adamians of Cain. Although some showed promise, nothing compared to what the Nephilim could offer this Prince of The Novem Dei.

It was apparent to Semyazah that Azazel was now more interested in the survival and cultivation of their Nephilim children than he was with the Adamians with whom he had been so obsessed. The Head of The Novem Dei combined forces with Tubal-Cain and the warriors of Babylon to rid the land of the new horrors the Watchers had birthed upon the world's people. But their strength was not enough. Of the two hundred, only a handful of Watchers aligned themselves with Semyazah and Tubal-Cain, leaving the rest to continue taking as many women as they wanted. They even sought out ceremonies provided by the Dark One which saved the women's lives during birth. But it altered their very existence and made them more like cattle ready for breeding.

Like Azazel, the remaining Watchers were prioritizing their new creations over the Adamian women for whom they once longed. This led to a war lasting many months between the Adamians of Babylon, the Watchers, and the Nephilim–who were proving challenging to tame.

During this time of The Nephilim Wars, Michael, Gabriel, Raphael, Uriel, and I ventured to the Hall of Zion and held council with King Yahweh and The Adunalar Elohim. There, we shared information that not only came from the angels in the Orders of the Septum Dei but from the cries of the Tribe of Adam as well. One Adamian in particular, Enoch, and his clan had even slain a few of the Nephilim themselves from the high grounds of the Mountains of Awlaan.

It surprised us to learn that it was all the Watchers in my Novem Dei who led this season of devastation in the realms of Babylon on Earth. I grieved my loss and blamed myself for trusting them so blindly, but the King reminded me that even he, the Creator of all things, had been betrayed by his creations as they continued to invite chaos into the essence of the cosmos. It seemed that with great love came a significant risk of betrayal.

The King explained to us that the actions of the Watchers had set in motion something he wished would never have come to pass. But a mighty purge was sealed in the turning of The Cosmic Wheel. The Great Floods were now a Tzoharian Nexus. No matter what would occur in the long years to come, there was no escaping its inevitability. He revealed that due to the shifting of the Cosmic Tides, many long years would have passed on Earth by the time this meeting adjourned. The Nephilim had now multiplied like vermin upon the lands of Babylon and throughout the Mountains of Awlaan, maturing under Azazel's wicked leadership and causing much of the Tribe of Adam to disperse into the unknown lands of the world. However, many Adamians remained loyal to their first parents, including Enoch and his children. They would all have their own roles to play in the coming Age of floods and ruin.

In this prolific moment, Enoch himself was ushered into the Hall of Zion. He was the first Adamian to take counsel with The Adunalar Elohim since Adam and Eve had left the presence of Eden. We were all astonished at what was happening. King Yahweh decreed that Enoch would be the Herald of Judgement upon Azazel and his Watchers. After receiving the Glory of Yahweh and his Divine Council, Enoch was ushered by Metatron, the great Seraphim and Angelic Dogrudan of the Divine Council, through the lands of Sheol and back to the Mountains of Awlaan, where he would deliver this prophecy of judgment upon Azazel.

Yahweh then turned to us gravely and explained how we would act out the prophecy that Enoch would soon deliver. We each had our own tasks, but the one that seemed most pressing was given to Raphael. For he and his Order were to advance against Azazel, who had usurped Semyazah's rule, cast his brother out of their land and into the wilderness and declared himself a Dark Disciple of Khata. Azazel now lorded over the Kingdoms of Babylon with an iron fist.

Once Raphael left the Adunalar Elohim and traveled through the appointed Pentaclegates to arrive on Earth, many years had passed in the Adamian world. Enoch's return was now a legendary story of heroism and sparked a reverence for Yahweh's protection of the Tribe of Adam. Enoch had walked through a Pentaclegate into the Mountains of Awlaan just as Azazel and his horde were advancing on Adam and his remaining Tribe.

Cloaked in the blinding white tzoharian Light of Eden, Enoch's appearance and the prophecy he spoke struck terror into the hearts of Azazel, his Watchers, and their Nephilim, so much so that they never returned to the mountain ranges of Adam's Tribe. It was now apparent to the Dark Prince that these Adamians had somehow joined The Adunalar Elohim once more–something that was thought to be impossible due to the mark of Khata found in the hearts of all Adamians on Earth. Therefore, Azazel knew what his next move had to be.

It was not in the cities of Babylon that Raphael and his Order found Azazel. On the lonely Mount Sirion, the Dark Prince had built an abominable fortress that doubled as a Necrogate to The Gnashing City of Pandemonium: The Castle of Nefil. The Dark Kingdom, it seemed, had overtaken the grave of Sigrafinna Agac and turned much of the Jungle of Karalak into a wasteland of molten death. The goal was apparent: fight the new Adamian/Edenic alliance by terraforming the Corporeum Realm into a place suitable for chaos to rule once more. Azazel was literally bringing Pandemonium to Earth.

Raphael and his Order grieved upon their arrival, observing so much devastation and needless destruction. This mountain was once their home. Sigrafinna Agac was where the world of the Adamians and the elohim of Eden had come together in joyous fellowship, co-laborship and blissful harmony which lasted countless ages. Now, all that remained was a fiery death that fueled the wrath of the Heavenly elohim even more. This wrath resulted in a surprise attack on Azazel and his horrors of the Sheolic realms.

The battle raged for a fortnight, and the surrounding lands of Mount Sirion were overtaken hastily. However, the mountain itself, where stood The Castle of Nefil, proved insurmountable. The King had explained to Raphael why the fortress was so mighty. In the years since his retreat following Enoch's prophecy–to ensure his victory over any assault–Azazel had fled to the grave of Sigrafinna Agac intending to use the thinner veil between the realms found there to make a kingdom of his own, transporting the very power of The Dark

Kingdom into its vacant space. After turning the surrounding lands of Karalak into a volcanic wasteland, he utilized the power of Pandemonium to forge a blade of hatred and doom named Deccal: The Wicked Maker.

This pitch-black longsword was said to have the very power of Khata in its hilt; it was a force even more significant than that of the ancient Spear of Necrom. The Order of Raphael felt this nightmarish force flow throughout all who defended the mighty Castle of Nefil on Mount Sirion. The Archangel knew he would have to traverse alone, hopefully unnoticed, throughout the belly of the scorched mountain if he wished to reach this Dark Prince before even greater foes arrived.

After three days journeying through the black catacombs beneath the Castle of Nefil, Raphael traveled up to finally reach the mountain's peak. With his tzoharian broad sword, Isik Incindere, he struck down Azazel's giant Nephilim honor guard and faced the horrifyingly grotesque being who stood before him. Azazel, a being who had once shimmered with the Light of Eden, now stood before his ruby throne as a hagged, thorny beast draped in a black cloak that whipped fiercely in the wind. Raphael was taken aback as he stared at Azazel's sharpened teeth and yellow piercing eyes glaring from behind a massive hood.

"Take me if you can, oh *righteous* one of The White Throne," Azazel hissed. And with that, Raphael charged the fallen being. Their blades crashed together with a mighty thunderbolt that shook the skies of Babylon.

Their battle raged like the fierce storm surrounding them. One would gain the upper hand only to lose it to the other. It was clear to the Archangel that Azazel's newfound power flowed from Deccal. Raphael knew he had to separate the two quickly, for he wasn't sure he could outmatch the fallen Watcher otherwise. Azazel's might had grown exponentially since the Archangel had last seen him. As corrupt as it was mighty, a raw power resided in this fallen Watcher of Babylon.

Finally, Deccal won. With the force of a ferocious wind, Azazel struck Isik Incindere, smashing it into a thousand pieces that scattered across the mountaintop firmly lodging it into Raphael's brow.

The Dark Watcher kicked the Edenic warrior towards the cliff's edge, freeing Deccal while white, glowing blood poured from the Archangel's face. Raphael's limp body hit the sticky, necroplasmic earth with a terrible force, sliding to the edge. He would have fallen had he not clutched the side of the mountain's peak at the last possible moment with strength that could have only come from the King himself.

All hope seemed to be lost for this elohim of the Septum Dei. Azazel's power was now too great for him to prevail alone. As the fallen Watcher drew closer to deliver the final blow, sparks jetted from the ground with every step he took.

*This is it now*, the Archangel thought to himself. He would soon join his departed siblings in The White Throne and discover what secrets awaited him in the next cycle of life. However, this was *not* what happened. For in those moments when Deccal was lifted above Azazel's head, a soft whisper of the Spirit of the King gave Raphael reason to hope–to know he had nothing further to dread. A weight filled the hand hanging at the Archangel's side while he hung off the cliff's edge. Yildrim: The Sword of the King had found him in this dire place. As he ran his fingers over the Tetragrammaton etched hilt, its power healed his wounds and eased his exhaustion with the Light of Heaven.

Drawing this newfound power into his essence, Raphael pulled himself up, leaping over the fallen Watcher. The mighty Archangel hurled Yildrim into Deccal, scorching the Shadowblade to death with the White Fire of the Throne. Azazel released a terrifyingly painful scream, as his essence was attached to the Shadowblade. As he fell to his knees in agony, Deccal thudded against the black, slimy ground, steam billowing from its corpse; whatever power it once possessed, diminished.

The soul-broken Dark Prince lay, sobbing rageful tears at his mangled relic that was slowly being swallowed by the necroplasmic earth. As Raphael approached, Yildrim began to fade from his grasp. In its stead was a Shard of Krallik: The Kingdom Stone.

It is said that whoever held this stone and understood how to use it could draw all evil to themselves and bind it to their will. There was a need for caution, however. The wielder of this stone was in

danger of being tempted to use it for selfish gain. Its power was mighty, and, like most things, it could be used to do great deeds, for good or evil. It was clear to Raphael what his next move was meant to be. The Archangel held the holy onyx stone out in front of him, facing Azazel, and through wails of pain and agony, the Dark Watcher was bound by the White Fire of the Throne. The Seal of The All Eye was burned into his brow, enslaving the fallen elohim to Raphael's will.

The power of Deccal flowing through the forces of The Castle of Nefil diminished, and they were soon overtaken by Raphael's Order. Over the next few days, each of the two hundred Watchers were taken captive by various Orders of the Heavenly Host. Most were cast into Tartarus, but the most corrupt of the Novem Dei was taken to the bottom of the known world and thrown into the depths of a prison. It was here Azazel would remain, formless and void. The prison was named Dudael: The Cauldron of The Cosmic Wheel.

Many years later, after The Great Floods had come and gone and the world was again reforming itself, Lilith of The Council of Baal, the current Dark High Sister of Babylon, was visited by the diabolical presence of Khata. During a cosmic alignment of the Cold Moons, Khata spoke to her in a secret Vision and revealed that the blade of Azazel had been locked away in the Caverns of Underearth. It was guarded by a shadow so great that even she would tremble at its might. Deccal had been spirited away, not by any Edenic forces, but by Khata itself. He swallowed it deep into the earth, into the paracosmic places in the planet's core where it waited for a being cunning enough to take it and plant it as a wicked seed in the lands of Dudael. Lilith, who had been quite intimate with Phobetor on many occasions requested his assistance in guiding her through The Cosmic Ocean between the Basalt Pillars and into the Caverns of The Underearth. There, she would recover the hidden Shadowblade of the fallen Watcher.

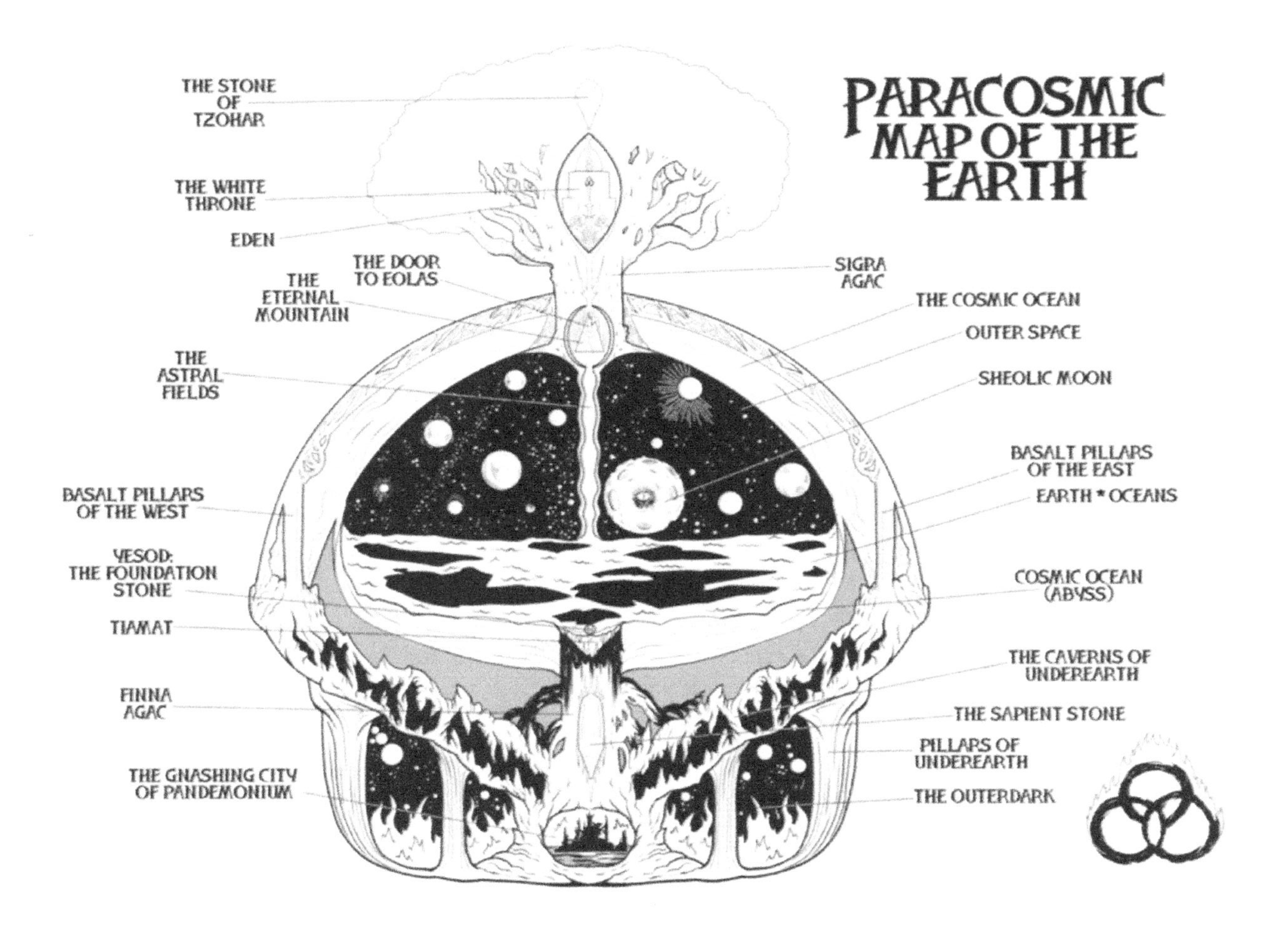
PARACOSMIC MAP OF THE EARTH
THE STONE OF TZOHAR
THE WHITE THRONE
EDEN
THE DOOR TO EOLAS
THE ETERNAL MOUNTAIN
THE ASTRAL FIELDS
BASALT PILLARS OF THE WEST
YESOD: THE FOUNDATION STONE
TIAMAT
FINNA AGAC
THE GNASHING CITY OF PANDEMONIUM
SIGRA AGAC
THE COSMIC OCEAN
OUTER SPACE
SHEOLIC MOON
BASALT PILLARS OF THE EAST
EARTH * OCEANS
COSMIC OCEAN (ABYSS)
THE CAVERNS OF UNDEREARTH
THE SAPIENT STONE
PILLARS OF UNDEREARTH
THE OUTERDARK

Hypnos' Lord of Nightmare guided the Dark High Sister, and also gifted her thirteen dead Nephilim as her honor guard to protect her throughout the Caverns—for there are worse things than ghouls and Night Gaunts in the shadowed places of the paracosmic world.

The terrible will of Khata led the Dark company through desolate necroswamps, undercaves, and murkforests so filled with dread that even Lilith felt a sense of fear. The journey was long and treacherous, and despite their greatest attempts to remain unnoticed, they fought multiple battles along the way with creatures only found in the blackest of nightmares. But, at last, Lilith and her company arrived at the Undermountain Keep of Golge, The Shadow Wurm of Underearth.

Of all the Seraphim in the Tronule Gardinalor who followed Lucifer in his rebellion, Golge was the most ruthless and crafty. Her fall into shadow was legendary. Some said she had even become a skafos—a symbiote form—of Khata as a sinister mockery of the Trinitarian nature of King Yahweh. Lilith was unsure of what to expect from Golge as she alone entered the Keep, but she was prepared to take the blade by force if needed.

Shadow Wurms, like all cosmic serpents who aligned themselves with the Darkness, hoarded treasures in their Keeps. However, the treasures Shadow Wurms coveted were not gold or silver, as some legends would tell, but were souls and unholy relics. Lilith knew that the type of soul did not matter to Golge, for the Wurm hoarded all things, from Light to Dark, from Nephilim and Adamian. It was also not lost on the Dark High Sister that *her* soul would be most coveted in this place, this lair of the beast of the underworld.

As Lilith entered the Keep, the foul odor of centuries-old, molded souls simultaneously nauseated and evoked her desires. Before she set foot on the first step of the necroplasmic staircase, the Wurm was aware of her presence.

"Who disturbs me?" The shadow serpent's raspy low voice vibrated the walls of the Keep. Lilith did not quiver or shake with fear, but boldly faced the disembodied voice that threatened her.

"It is I, Lilith of The Council of Baal, who comes to claim what the mighty Khata has commissioned of me." The Dark High Sister continued up the staircase, her malevolent energy ready to be released upon the Wurm at any moment.

"You wish to *take* from me?" Golge's wicked voice playfully questioned. Lilith knew that if the legends of her being a skafos were true, then the Shadow Wurm was already aware of the reason for Lilith's presence. "How bold of you, little sister, to reveal your hand so quickly."

"Why would I do otherwise?" Lilith continued speaking to the shadows of the Keep while traversing up the slime-covered staircase. "It would be foolish to hide my intentions from you, oh favored one of the Dark."

"Ah. Flattery," hissed the beast. "I expected more from *you,* Lilith of Baal. I know what it is you seek. For the one who has commissioned you speaks alongside *me."*

"So, then the legends are true," the Dark High Sister smiled.

"Truer than you realize, little sister." With that, the necroplasmic staircase that Lilith was ascending transformed into purple and black scales. They were covered with necroplasmic slime that dripped slowly upward toward the head of the enormous Shadow Wurm. The mighty tentacled dragon filled the Keep. Below her rested the chained souls of her damned collection, too corroded and worn to cry for help any longer. Lilith was absolutely in awe of the size of this serpent of the Dark, but she did not allow the glare of the multiple green, bulbous eyes to deter her boldness.

"Deccal. What is its significance? How can the dead relic of an imprisoned Watcher hold any true weight in this world or the next?" Lilith was genuinely asking. Although, she believed the will of Khata did not trifle with hopes, the blade was indeed dead and therefore held no real power that could be used in The Dark Kingdom's war against the Light.

"Azazel was no mere Watcher, little sister. In secret, he shared such intimacy with us that the power he bestowed upon that blade held more weight than even *he* was aware of."

*"Us?"* Lilith questioned.

The Wurm gargled a raspy chuckle.

"Not all mysteries of Khata have been revealed, my pet. But you will discover this one soon enough."

"When?" Lilith's desire to be included in Khata's inner circle was showing.

"In time, little sister. In time. But for now..." The broken and charred sword of Azazel appeared in the thick, moldy air next to the Wurm's enormous, horn-covered head. "...what would you *give* for such a prize as this?"

"I have thirteen Nephilim souls waiting outside your Keep. Take them. They are yours." This was no doubt the real reason Phobetor gave them to her in the first place. Nephilim souls were rare, let alone a collection totaling such a sacred number in The Dark Kingdom.

"Nephilim demons are indeed scrumptious morsels, and that *is* quite a collection you have to offer. However, tell me, my pet, why would I accept thirteen demons over the Dark High Sister of the Court of Baal with eyes so beautiful that songs are sung about them?" It was true, Lilith, with her intoxicating eyes, preyed on men in their dreams and, through nightmares, devoured infant souls in their sleep.

Lilith's eyes were coveted amongst Dark Collectors like Golge." I was commissioned by Khata himself to carry out this task. Why would a *skafos* hinder the will of the one who dwells inside her so intimately?"

"Clever sister. However, there are plenty who could carry out the task Khata has planned. Why *must* it be you? If the great tyrant of the Host can alter his prophets, why could Khata not do the same? Surely, it has seen the endless possibilities available in the turning of the Cosmic Wheel. Come...I would offer you such pleasures while you stay in my Keep."

However, the Sister of Baal now understood she was either already under Golge's spell or was being prepared for it. She had expected something like this from an Underearth Wurm.

She was also well aware that if it was the Wurm's attempt to usurp the will of Khata for her own gain, it was not beyond the knowledge of the mighty Dark force.

There was only one thing it could mean: this was a test. It was a chance for Lilith to prove her worth to the powerful opposing force of the authoritarian order of The Cosmic Wheel. She wasn't simply sent here to gather the blade of Azazel after all. And this thrilled her

wicked soul to its core.

The skafos of The Dark Kingdom were not the same as the Trinitarian unity of Yahweh. The King's Godhead Fellowship, although being three distinct persons, acted with one will. Each skafos within the Dark had its own will, which would often conflict with one another. Genuineness and self-sacrificial unity were not attributes any member of The Dark Kingdom held in high regard. In fact, such traits were seen as pathetic weakness. That kind of feeble interdependence spat in the face of the true freedom of domination and conquest, the heartbeat of the unspoken Creed of the Dark.

Lilith's prideful intuition told her that Khata had appointed this task to *her* because out of all beings whom he would call upon, the Dark High Sister of Baal was the one creature who could stare into the voideyes of The Shadow Wurm of Underearth and not blink.

"A wager then," Lilith said coyly. She knew that such a temptation would master the Cosmic Wurms' vulnerability.

"And what would that wager be, my pet?" Golge's interest piqued, her mouth watered at the thought.

"If I can reach the blade of Azazel before you can ensnare me, for I firmly believe that I am still free from your grasp, then you'll allow me to walk out of this Keep with Deccal in hand."

"And if you cannot reach it?" Golge smiled devilishly.

"Then I...and my eyes...are yours."

Golge's enormous neck snapped backward in surprise at such a wager. Was Lilith *this* bold to assume the Wurm could not ensnare her so easily? For indeed, she could.

"What trickery is this, Sister of Baal? You would risk your very existence for this relic?"

"I am confident in my abilities, oh favored of the Dark. Are you so confident in yours?" Lilith questioned the Wurm. Golge's hubris welled up inside her as her horrific laughter shook the bowels of the Keep.

"Very well, little sister. The wager is accepted."

Immediately, cold dead hands reached from the depths and grabbed Lilith at every limb, pulling her down into the soul-riddled abyss of the Keep. With a broad sweep of her hand, the Dark High Sister released wicked energy, slicing through the arms of death belonging to the slaves of Golge from below. Lilith rocketed through the air toward Deccal but was slapped away by a necroplasm-covered tentacle, sending the Sister of Baal soaring through the air and slamming into the wall of the Keep.

Golge wasted no time in claiming her prize. Her tendrils slithered around the Dark High Sister, and one of her sizeable tentacled appendages with a suction pocket engulfed Lilith's head. As her vision turned to complete and utter blackness, Lilith felt the hideous cackle of the Wurm surround her very soul.

Almost immediately, the Shadow Wurm of Underearth's laughter was cut short as the shadows around her grew thicker until not even Golge could see past her grotesquely horned and tentacle-filled face. The Wurm felt his presence. The fear began to build inside her, an unrelenting horror from which there was no escape. It was here. Khata filled the Wurm's soul and crippled her. The suction appendage fell limp from Lilith's head, freeing the Dark High Sister from her slime-covered prison. She had been counting on this.

"Tell me, Golge of Underearth," the haunting voice whispered through the blackness of the Keep, "at what point did you think usurping my will would gain you favor in the eyes of the Dark?" It was too late for the Wurm to respond; she was petrified beyond movement or thought. It would have done no good if she could answer, for there was no bargaining or pleading with the Dark Anti-Life. Although Lilith's hope was for Khata to intervene, the Dark High Sister was absolutely terrified in the presence of the Anti-Life of The Cosmic Wheel. This was no mere Vision of the Dark force, as Lilith had experienced before. Khata's direct presence was worse than anything she could have imagined.

"Lilith of Baal," the petrifying voice continued, "you risk much to gain the prize you seek. But your risk, as reckless as it was, has brought you favor in the Darkness of the Wheel. I've seen your intentions and found a cunning disposition and one who would be greater than the serpent you were sent here to test. However, as a reminder that risks have consequences, I shall keep what you are so coveted for." With that, Lilith's radiant eyes fell back into her head and out of her mouth. Through her screams, the chillingly numb voice continued.

"I have no room for weakness or egocentric rabble-rousing. Lesser beings allow for rebellion to occur in their fold. Take heed what you've seen here, lest in the future, it be *you* who is found at the end of my judgment."

That day, Lilith was not only given Deccal but also direct ownership over Golge, the Keep, and the treasures the Wurm had collected over the millennia. After being portaled through a Necrogate to the nightmarish lands of Dudael, the Dark High Sister of Baal looked out–eyeless–across the wilderness. On the wind, she could hear the haunting cries of the fallen Watcher, pleading for the blade he once had held. The Sister gazed at the scorched relic within her grasp. She now understood how the power of death, when utilized properly, could start a vibration that would ripple throughout time, corrupting even the most sacred of spaces.

She drove Deccal into the Earth. While the veil between Corporeum and Sheol ripped apart, something new was formed. Something secret. Something that would only be whispered of through the Ages to come.

The energy Lilith had poured into the blade joined with the echoes of the power Deccal once had claimed entered the soil of this newly formed, cursed land, and sprouted an abomination in the Agacan Order. Of all the sacred Cosmic Trees throughout creation, this leafless, sinister, necroplasm-fueled stain upon the land now loomed over the tomb prison of Azazel. Lilith transferred all the haunted treasures of Golge's Keep into the black tree, feeding the wicked, dendritic creation throughout time. She commissioned the thirteen demonic Nephilim souls tasked with protecting her through The Caverns of The Underearth to guard this newly birthed child of Deccal.

Lilith saw it fit to grant the tree a name connected to its ancestor, after the fortress that Azazel had made out of the grave of Eden. The black tree was forever known in the shadows as The Nefil Agac.

As Phobetor completed the tale, he instructed the former Power of Michael that to gain entrance to the realm of The Nefil Agac, he would need to offer a sacrifice to the Dark. Even then, entrance was never guaranteed. Khata held direct dominion over this forsaken realm, and if the proper posture was not taken, then rejection would be the least of Baetiel's worries.

# CHAPTER TWENTY

## - THE BIRTH OF A LEGION -

Baetiel entered the Corporeum Realm in the guise of an Adamian. He would not risk travel in his true form or by portal, for the former Power of Michael did not wish to draw any unwanted attention to himself–from the Light or Dark. Either side would have questioned his motives or attempted to seize him. The wandering elohim first appeared in Ur, then traveled by caravan to the city of Dumah. From that point forward, the locals in Dumah told the tale of the ghostly traveler who haunted the city. No one knew who he was or from whence he came, but only that they felt a great emptiness and sadness in the shadow of the specter's presence.

From Dumah, Baetiel moved only by night through the desolate lava-infested mountain range of Harrat Khaybar–the former Jungle of Karalak. He knew the way well. Although he did not tell Phobetor, Baetiel had come here often to think during his initial time of questioning and doubt. He remembered these mountains from before the first fall of the UcDusme, when they were still filled with the wild spirit of Azathoth and his Elder Children, waiting for a new steward of Earth to come and tame it with a loving hand. But that taming would never come. Instead, the lush jungles and wildlife never had the chance to become anything more than uncultivated landscapes and ravaging beasts before they were melted away by Azazel's wrath.

These thoughts fueled Baetiel's anger all the more. How could the *good* King of Ages allow such horrifying travesties to occur? Now that he knew the *truth* about what The Cosmic Wheel actually was, it was now his chosen destiny to ensure its terrible end.

After a forty-day journey to the bottom of the known world, Baetiel was met by a small desert caravan. The leader was decorated with fine jewels and approached the elohim in the black of night.

"I know why you're here, my lord," the voice was smooth but seasoned, "for it was told to me in a profound Vision." His eyes showed no fear, and Baetiel was conflicted with an utter hatred for this man–simply because he was an Adamian–and a regard for his hubris.

"What is your name, dust creature?" Baetiel asked. He had no patience to disguise his true identity with words.

"My name is Ād, Son of Uz. My people and I are to escort you to the gates of Dudael." The elohim immediately grabbed the throat of the leader and squeezed just enough to let this Son of Uz know that his life very much hung in the balance of the moment.

"Who gave you this task, desert dweller?" Baetiel snarled as spit flung onto Ād's purpling face.

"It..it was a jinn of prosperity and gifts!" The man could barely speak. "She cov...covenanted with me...sa-said that if we met a traveler he-ere and brought him to the gates, th-at...that my tribe would become a...gr-great city of legend! Sh-e gav...gave me these jewels for con-fidence."

"A jinn of *prosperity,* you say?" Baetiel was becoming interested.

"Ye-ess. I sw...swear it on the gods of Baal, El, Marduk wh-whatever holds weight!"

"Tell me," the elohim brought the man close to his face, "were her eyes intoxicating?" Ād's own eyes grew larger with hope.

"*Yes!*" He gasped for air. "The-y were the m...most beautiful things I'd ever s-een!" The former Power began to chuckle. This was no comfort to the Son of Uz, but the grip on the Adamians' throat released, and Ād fell to the ground, taking in deep swallows of air.

"Take me to the gates then, desert ruler," Baetiel commanded as he stepped over the hyperventilating man who was gasping and flailing in the sand.

Two hours later, in the third hour of the early morning, the small group of men halted their horses on a tall dune overlooking a plain covered in a mysterious green-tinted fog. Baetiel looked at Ād with suspicion.

"Why are we stopped, desert dweller?" he asked.

"My men and I go no further, my lord. This place is haunted by devils and ghouls that will draw you into the earth and devour your soul." Ād replied ominously, fear showing unashamedly in his eyes. Baetiel did not laugh or scoff, for he knew the men were right to be afraid. Deep down in his blackened heart, he was, too.

"If you carry on 400 paces into the cursed fog, you will find what you seek. This is where we leave you. Wada'an." The Son of Uz finished his farewell statement. Immediately he and his caravan turned around and they began traveling north, getting as far away from this desolate place as quickly as possible.

Baetiel shed his Adamian guise as he floated down the mountainous sand dune and into the green mist of Dudael. He gathered his energy, ready for a quick release. The former Power knew the Dark Queen of this land was waiting for him, and there wasn't anything he did not anticipate from *her*. The air was thick with a foul odor of molded death, but he could see nothing beyond the cursed fog that swirled around his faded green shades of featherfur.

Since leaving the Host, Baetiel's appearance had changed. His brilliant color had faded into the grayish tones that now covered him, from the four membranes on the back of his head to the bottom of his taloned feet. He almost looked as though his form had faded entirely; like an elohimic corpse being prepared for The White Throne.

However, where Baetiel was headed shared no similarities with that holy place.

The former Power stepped further into the dead silence, dread building in his mind as he continued through the fog. Suddenly, as if the wind carried it straight to him, Baetiel heard a faint wailing. The sound was simultaneously inside his mind and far away as though in a distant land. The combination was discombobulating. He could not hear words, only cries laced with agony and bitter loneliness.

*Azazel's lament is on the wind, and I draw nearer to the black tree,* Baetiel thought as his taloned feet, braver than his heart, carried him forward. The energy inside of him pulsated throughout his body as the wailing grew louder all around him.

"Do you hear your fate, oh weary traveler?" a mocking, directionless voice chuckled. An obu of green energy immediately formed around Baetiel's clawed hands, steaming from the tense power waiting to be unleashed.

"Show yourself, Lilith of Baal!" he shouted. "For I did not travel the vast realms only to be struck down inside your mists of confusion." Immediately, the former Power felt a tingling sensation behind his membranes and through his loosening mane, like a wiry arachnid crawling up the back of his head.

"Lower your defenses, Power, or I will be forced to take them from you," Lilith whispered eerily from behind the elohim. Baetiel whipped around and blasted his obus into the green fog, but the energy found nothing except swirling mists. Lilith's laughter filled the cursed air. "Oh please, Baetiel. Must we continue the skirmish we started when you cast me out of Michael's *holy Order*?" the Dark High Sister's disembodied voice devilishly mocked. "I find it quite amusing that the being who saw fit to banish me to Sheol is now groveling weakly at my doorstep, craving entrance to a realm whose power he knows not how to wield."

"Are you so afraid of facing me that you must remain hidden from my sight, oh *mighty* Queen of The Wild Winds?" Baetiel mocked.

"Such arrogance from an angel whose might has only *decreased* since tearing himself from the opulent teat of the tyrant of The Cosmic Wheel."

As much as Baetiel's pride would have him believe otherwise, he knew this to be true. It made him hate Yahweh all the more. He had discovered long ago that his strength was depleting the longer he stayed away from the direct presence of Yahweh. Independence, it seemed, was an existence his Maker did not wish for him to have; the signs of a true dictator. Knowing this made Baetiel covet Deccal and Nefil's legendary might all the more. He knew he needed this forbidden power to prevent slipping away into nothingness.

"As I'm sure you've been warned already, former Power of Micheal," Lilith's disembodied voice continued, "to gain access to The Nefil Agac, one must provide a sacrificial rite of passage. There is a high price for entering this forbidden realm of the Dark." The Dark High Sister paused, letting out a gleeful giggle. "And I am here to collect such things from you. So, my pet...what have *you* to offer *me?"* Baetiel reluctantly dropped his defenses. When Phobetor mentioned this sacrifice, he knew what he must offer the Dark Queen of Dudael.

Baetiel, unlike many Powers, had two different sets of wings–two on his back and two on the back of his head. An elohim's wings were not used primarily for flight but for added strength. He was gifted the extra set upon becoming the Head of Michael's Order. He knew Lilith had coveted them from the beginning of her dissent from the Light, and to give them up to her would satiate her lust to dominate him. However, removing one's wings was not as simple as removing an Adamian cloak. Like all garments of an elohim, wings were organic to their bodies. And Baetiel knew Lilith was not going to make this process a painless one.

"Well, little elohim? What'll it be?" the Dark High Sister hissed with pleasure.

"I know what it is you want, whore of the night."

"Such language." Lilith playfully observed. Baetiel grimaced. Closing his shadowy, sunken eyes, he unfurled the wings from his back, and braced himself.

"Take them."

"Delicious." The Sister of Baal crowed with sinister laughter as both sets of Baetiel's wings slowly ripped from his body, tearing the fleshy membranes from their sockets. Baetiel cried out in agony and he fell to one knee, grayish-green blood spewing from his back.

Lilith's high-pitched cackles and the howling of Azazel's Lament, rolled around Baetiel's mind, filling it completely.

It was as if Azazel and Baetiel's suffering combined to give the Dark High Sister more power. The gray, faded elohim breathed the putrid green fog into his lungs as he collapsed down onto his forearms while the last bit of his wings ripped free from his flesh and disappeared into the mist. He screamed again, and silver tears ran down the tribal featherfurred markings on his cheeks. Azazel's Lament echoed in his mind for a moment, then began to fade again. The pain was unbearable. As he peered through the fog, Lilith appeared before his broken body.

She looked like a nightmare. Her sagging gray, leathered skin was so transparent that Baetiel could see tar-black muscles underneath. What once had been long, flowing black locks of hair were now thin, greasy strings matted between two enormous horned antlers protruding from her skull. But it was her eyes, or rather where they should be, that made Baetiel recoil in disgust. From the brow bone to the top of her lips was a cavernous hole in the middle of her face. There was nothing but blackness inside her open skull. Lilith noticed the elohim's loathing and smiled with wicked delight.

"Never in all my days did I think *you* would be soaked in your own blood at my feet. Yet here we are, Baetiel of the Order of Michael." Lilith proudly proclaimed.

"That...that's not what I am anymore, wretch." Baetiel snarled at her through the pain. Lilith knelt down close to his tormented and rage-filled face.

"Then what are you?" she probed.

"Allow me entrance to the black tree and you'll find out." He then spat his blood into the imploded vacancy on her face. It steamed as it entered and Lilith breathed it in while swallowing the fluid with pleasure.

"By all means, little elohim. Enter by your own free will." With those words, the Dark High Sister of Baal vanished into the green fog once more.

Baetiel struggled to his knees and paused to consider the blood oozing from the open wounds on his back. He focused his energy on healing and found it much more complicated than it had ever been.

*Temporary,* he thought to himself. *This was necessary. Soon, you'll burn The Cosmic Wheel to the ground.* While these thoughts circulated in his mind, a black void began to pierce the fog. As the green mist parted, the triangular Necrogate opened, not ten yards in front of the broken elohim. No words were spoken, but Baetiel could *feel* the will of the Dark calling to him through the gate. He slowly stood to his taloned feet as his wounds finished healing. The green tints on his featherfur had now faded almost entirely to gray, and his face looked as though it had aged a hundred years since he left the Adamians at the top of the sand dune. None of this mattered to Baetiel, for he knew that whatever awaited him on the other side of that Necrogate was his salvation from the prison and constraints of this order that had kept him enslaved. With that singular thought, Baetiel wrapped himself in his cloak, took a deep breath, and stared unblinkingly into the void of blackness. Slowly, he took a step and walked through it.

Immediately, as Baetiel traversed through the Necrogate, he felt stronger. It wasn't like stepping through a Pentaclegate at all. This process was bolder and wilder. While Pentaclegates were warm and soothing, this was like a burning ice bath. Baetiel felt more alive and invigorated in ways he hadn't felt since his nights in the bed chamber of The Eidolon Lathi. This was the freedom the Dark offered? Yes, and this was the power for which he had thirsted, for so long.

At first, all he could sense was utter blackness. Baetiel was still walking forward, but it was as if the whole world had lost any reflection of light. He knew he was in the silent and terrible presence of Khata. Baetiel's emotions swung from extreme terror to exuberant pleasure to an unquenchable rage-filled fire inside his stomach. It was in this space–the in-between cracks of the realms–that the Dark could be found. It seemed Khata was as omnipresent as Yahweh claimed to be, perhaps even more so, and it was intoxicating.

Finally, a sliver of orange fire shown in the distance. At first, it was a blur to Baetiel's eyes, but as he continued further in the Dark, it became more visible. He felt tall blades of grass underneath his taloned feet, and he slowly turned to take in his surroundings. On either side, far off on the horizons, he saw shades of deep blue and purple fog rolling in and over itself. Turning forward once more, he halted and gasped to view it in all its horrifying glory. Towering miles above him, the black tree loomed–The Nefil Agac.

The orange glow was coming from a vulva-shaped slit at the enormous base of the tree. It seemed as though the fires of Pandemonium might be on the other side, but it was not opened enough for the elohim to tell. As Baetiel's eyes traveled up the black tree, he saw that it was just as Phobetor had said: covered in necroplasm and seeming to branch off in all directions the further up it went. Slime particles broke off and traveled further out, dissipating in the void-filled sky. As Baetiel's eyes explored the expansive field further to his right, he saw his coveted prize. Protruding from a mound of dung and ash, broken and scorched, stood the remains of Deccal: The Wicked Maker.

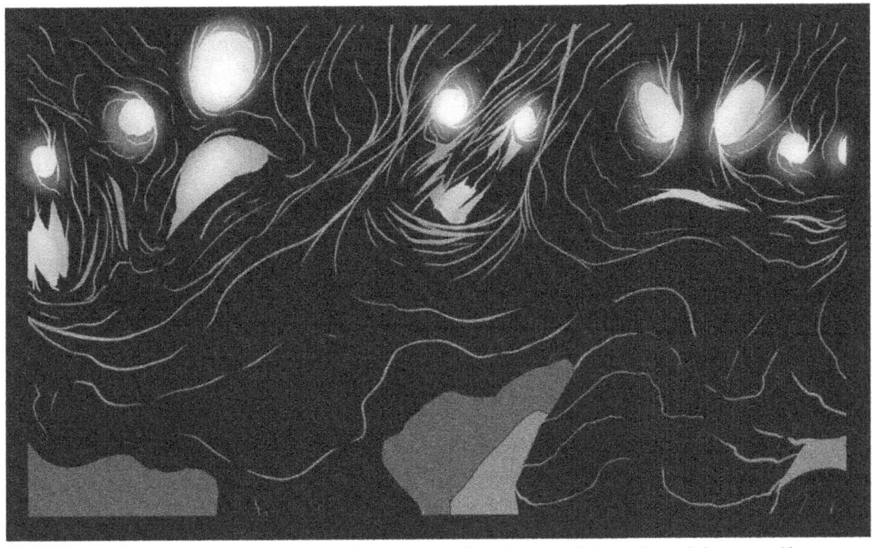

The elohim started through the midnight blue tall grass toward the mound, but he was interrupted by a resounding, howling chorus of voices. They were speaking in unison as though many souls were merged into one and carrying on a conversation within themselves.

"A weary traveler approaches," they howled. "You have traveled far and wide, oh broken spirit." As the voices addressed Baetiel, his deep, sunken eyes found the source of the haunting chorus. High above him, where the necroplasmic branches of The Nefil Agac found their crescendo, the fluidic shapes of Lilith's thirteen

Nephilim guards floated in the abyss of the black tree. "What have you found throughout your journey of the cosmos, enfeebled elohim?"

*Enfeebled?* he thought to himself. Baetiel was already imagining ways to torture these impudent fools. However, it was clear that they did not know who or what he was. Baetiel figured he would play a little game with the demons of the black tree, as he used to with Akalian. For a moment, the heartache of losing his brother twinged inside him, but he quickly put it out of his mind

"Pain. So much pain," he responded, laying on the weariness thick, acting as though he had merely stumbled upon this place—as if anyone possibly could. "I see you have Deccal, Azazel's blade. It was said to have been lost in the realms. Where am I?"

"A better question is, *'how did you arrive here?'"* The apparent lead Nephilim now floated to the forefront of the void appearing like a swimming specter in the shadows. "We are the Guardians of Deccal of the realm of The Nefil Agac, known only to the skafos of the Dark One who has foretold our glorious return as the Sons of The Stars!" They had revealed their hand rather quickly, Baetiel thought. He continued his facade.

*"You are Nephilim??"* he said with an overexaggerated surprise, knowing that the term was derogatory to them. It did its job, and the voices blasted out in rage.

*"We are the great rulers of old!!* Descended from The Watchers!! Before the Baals! Before the rule of *mighty Cthulhu, we were!!* In our extinction, the enemy cast us into the abyss; our race was thought to be no more. But we persisted. We guard the prophecy and await the Final Herald to usher in the days of our return to reign on high!!"

There it was. The purpose that Baetiel had been searching for. *The Final Herald.* He continued to play ignorant.

"I heard whispers of a great purpose at the Tree of the Blade of Azazel, in a secret realm of Sheol." Baetiel could no longer hold it in. His sinister playfulness had reached its peak. It was time to master these pathetic demons. "I didn't know what to expect when I arrived, but I never imagined it would be guarded by *half-breeds."*

"HOW DARE YOU!!" The void of the tree erupted as the thirteen demons joined to become one giant voidbeast, their size dwarfing his. It lunged out of the black tree towards the elohim.

Size was no matter for Baetiel as in an instant he released a terrible blast of green energy. It split the thirteen demons and Baetiel grabbed the leader by its spectral, necroplasmic throat, pulling it close to his own haggard, face. The former Chief Power held a flaming obu in his other hand, threatening the Nephilim spirit.

"Listen to me, half breed." Baetiel's voice was hauntingly calm, and his eyes overflowed with a green necroplasm. The Nephilim had no clue with whom they were dealing. "Whatever purpose you think you have here...it now belongs to me. I led the Order of Michael against the Leviathan, against the Baals, and I helped drive your pathetic race into the depths of the abyss. And now...I am your master."

And master he was. Over time, Baetiel poured all his growing malice and self-inflicted pain into creating a horde of Dark elohim and Nephilim demons, the size of which The Cosmic Wheel had never seen. This Legion's reign of terror plunged the Babylonian world into complete chaos. What felt like random acts of destruction and possessions to the Host of The Heavens were, in truth, strategic–wicked means to an even more sinister end.

Baetiel would no longer be enslaved to Yahweh's order of authoritarian control fueled by deceit. *He* would be the one to bring destruction to the King's precious order, starting with the ones Yahweh held so dear, his treasured Adamians. Only one thing remained. If he were to entirely leave his former life behind, he had to discard the final influence the King had on his life. Baetiel's current form still represented a being molded and manipulated by the tyrant. To completely free his mind from this tyranny, he would need to remove the last remaining obstacle: his very image.

So, on the dark side of the Sheolic Moon, in the Kingdom of Nyarlathotep, Lucifer: The Dark Father, led Baetiel in The Black Mass. He was fully Transfectiated from elohim of Light into the King of Endless Night.

# CHAPTER TWENTY ONE

## - THE LABYRINTH -

From the smallest subatomic being to the largest star in all creation, everything in existence expels energy, sending its vibrations throughout the cosmos. The more intense the vibrations, the deeper their energy imprints on specific places, persons, or things. Events long past leave lasting impressions that even the weakest intuition can sense. Throughout history, Adamians would see phantoms or ghosts of people who often had long since passed into the unseen realms. This was simply because the echoes of their vibrations remained–awaiting the Light or Dark to fill that space if it remained open long enough. These lingering spaces would either become sacred or haunted.

If something tragic happened, such as a great battle or Dark sacrifice–really anything from a simple meal dedicated to a god, to a cannibalistic ritual or Black Mass–the odds of the space becoming haunted increased. Similarly, if exceptionally great joy occurred, reflecting the Light of The White Throne, then the chances of it becoming a sacred space grew all the more.

This process of imprinted vibrations is not exclusive to Adamians and the Corporeum Realm . Every space in all the realms is filled with energy with the potential to create these pockets of transcendence, including the ones inside every being's mind.

Deep in the recesses of Jonathan Young's essence, echoes of his progressive possession screamed at Moriel as the Messenger Power touched the cold ground of the gangrenous reality inside the boy's mind. The elohim felt the pain and anguish of a child ripped from his innocence. The source of this pain was clouded, most likely due to the possession itself, but it was clear to Moriel that Jonathan had suffered severe trauma long before a devil ever showed its face inside his thoughts. However, more disturbingly, in this particular spot, Moriel saw the echoes of a great Shadow Wurm that had wrapped its tentacles around the child and placed him under its Dark spell. The boy's cries of terror brought tears of immense sorrow to Moriel's eyes.

"Oh...this poor child. The fear he felt." Moriel took his hand away and stood from where he was kneeling to face his brother. "Jonathan's astral form was here. This was where...a Shadow Wurm took over his mind. From then on, the boy only saw what it wanted him to see until he was delivered to Xexxus."

*"A Shadow Wurm??"* Akalian was aghast. *"Inside* the boy's mind?"

"At this point, are we really surprised by it? Look around," Moriel replied. "It appears Joffus' words from his prophetic trance were more than just metaphor. I think it's obvious now that the boy *is* indeed meant to be this Manking figure." Moriel paused for a moment and looked up at his fellow Power. "And this was no random possession to be sure...I sense deep historical trauma here that is intentionally clouded from my sight...a trauma that has echoes of thousands of years of Darkness."

"From Xexxus?" Akalian questioned.

"Yes, but more than that. More than *just* the monstrosities indwelling this boy. It's as if a thousand horrible lifetimes are attached to Jonathan's very genetic makeup. I can't put my finger on it, but it's almost as if everything about this child doesn't...*belong*."

"He's not a *godborn* is he?"

"No," Moriel said assuredly and with relief. "*That* would make sense. He *is* an image bearer of the King, but...I don't know...something's...*off*. More so than just this possession."

"Well," Akalian started, "like you said before, Xexxus *has* called himself a Herald in the past. Is Jonathan's essence...in any way similar to Abigail's?" They both paused for a painful moment. The brothers hadn't mentioned Abigail Zahn to one another in a very long time, but her unholy sacrifice haunted their thoughts often. Abigail had been born for one purpose only, to disrupt and temporarily undo the unseen order of The Cosmic Wheel in a plot to destroy the Old World of Earth.

"It's hard to tell. Abigail was chosen as a result of multiple generations of occult consummation and sacrifice. I don't sense that *kind* of preparation here, but it's just as Dark, perhaps even Darker than her trauma and lineage." Moriel even surprised himself by saying these words.

"I don't think I've ever personally experienced a Darker trauma than what flowed in that girl's veins," Akalian said. "The Dark Kingdom uses generational corruption attached to one's essence to bring about catastrophe. So, if this boy doesn't have that, then how could he be their Dark Messiah?"

"Like I said, it's clouded. All I can tell is Jonathan's situation is not like *her* and *he's* a not a godborn," Moriel said, almost defeatedly.

"Then he's something *new*." Akalian grimaced. "Something that Xexxus has been free to concoct and bring to fruition..." The Chief Power trailed off, retreating inside of himself–inside of his guilt. "You were right, you know?" Moriel's head turned slightly in confusion. "What you said at the Pillar of Velkominn. Guilt has haunted me for millennia. If I could but go back to that moment on the cliffside at The Tower of Babylon, I would strike him down. The moment I lowered Karaydin, I fear, could be the genesis of all our undoing."

"I don't believe that you *would* have, Akalian. Nor do I believe that moment is responsible for these events." Moriel lovingly challenged. "If you remember, the other side of my statement in The Great Hall was that your *compassion* led you in your actions. You are so solidified in the Light that I don't believe you could have done anything else in that moment. You were actively losing the *one* brother who meant the most to you. The one being who was of your own flesh...I don't think anyone in all of Eden could have struck him down if they were in your position.

"I know what's been slithering around inside of your mind all these years. I know the weight you carry and the pain you face every single hour. And believe me when I say that if I could take it all away, I would. But I'm not powerful enough to cure the haunting guilt that threatens your peace and clouds your intuition."

"Well, you just see right through me, don't you?" Akalian grimaced again. "To be honest, Moriel, I've held on to this guilt for so long that if my ongoing mission of pursuing Xexxus were to end...I'm not sure who I would *be* on the other side of it."

Moriel put two taloned hands on Akalian's pauldron shoulders and tearfully looked his brother in the eyes.

"We'll find that out together. I promise you." Moriel said with a wink. "However, I meant what I said about your intuition being clouded. I fully empathize with your pain..." he took a deep breath and continued, "but this Shadow Wurm won't. In fact, it will only use it against you."

"That's fair. By all means, take the lead," Akalian said.

"I'll have obus surrounding us on all sides, and let's walk with our blades at the level of our eyes. If the creature's suction appendage comes near us, we'll be all the more ready." As he spoke, he stared at the cyclopean horror towering before them then took a deep, sorrowful breath before facing his brother again. "You know, in all my days, I've never actually *seen* this thing before. And I definitely didn't expect it to be inside the *mind* of an Adamian. An entire stronghold was created to hide this from us, Akalian. It's clear now that Jonathan was *chosen*...but why *him?*"

"Let's go ask," Akalian growled in anger. He lifted Karaydin to the level of his eyes as they began walking toward the monstrous labyrinth that horrified both him and Moriel to their very cores.

Upon arriving inside Jonathan's mind, Moriel was filled with fear. He cried out in prayer to the Spirit of the King for protection and guidance against a *particular* evil, for labyrinths have a long and complicated history in both the seen and unseen realms. Many Adamians over the millennia have utilized this structure in seemingly helpful ways for meditation and for calming their overwhelming anxieties. The Spirit of the King co-labored with them to redeem the idea of this structure for these life-giving purposes, using its disturbing origins against The Dark Kingdom. However, the labyrinth itself, and the ideas that originally sprang forth from this cursed structure, were born in the Darkness.

Born from the bitter fruit of the Great Floods, a new breed of corrupted Adamians began to emerge: The Godborn Children of The Great Serpent, Nachash–Khata's profane mockery of the Spirit of Yahweh. Unlike the Nephilim, these beings were fully human from birth. However, while humans who bore the image of the King had two parents, godborns had three.

Due to the fate of the Watchers, no elohim would dare plant a physical seed inside of an Adamian woman again. Still, there were other methods of corrupting the King's precious children; methods that were practiced by the Watchers before the Great Floods washed away the vileness of the Nephilim. Just as the descendants of the Watchers had shown the Canaanites and the Babylonians before, they taught the elite rulers of the Hellenistic Empire to practice a Dark ceremony to create Necrogates inside their very souls.

This ceremony resulted in the blending of the spiritual biochemistry of a fallen elohim with the physical DNA of the unborn child. During these Orgia Ceremonies, the deified ruler would ceremonially have a mask placed on his head, welcoming whatever entity they worshipped to possess the ruler and spiritually engage in the ritual orgy alongside the Adamians. The resulting birth would welcome a being that was much more than human–a godborn.

Long ago, before the Trojan War, in the land of Crete, this unholy union occurred. King Minos–who claimed to have descended from Zeus and Europa from a similar Orgia Ceremony–had turned away from his god, Poseidon, and started worshipping the god Dionysus. Minos forced his entire kingdom to venerate the animalistic representative for which Dionysus was known: the bull. Bulls were often incorporated into the Orgia Ceremonies of the solstice moons in hopes of receiving a "pure" heir from their god to place upon the Cretan throne. Minos long wished to have a godborn son from Dionysus himself and consulted The Oracle of Crete, who predicted that although it would bring prosperity to the land and favor from Dionysus, the offspring would ultimately be an unstoppable curse upon the Kingdom of Crete.

However, Minos would not heed The Oracle's warning. In preparation for the Anthesteria wine festival, the king ordered a specific bull be kept separate from the others, treating it like royalty for weeks before the ceremony and claiming the gods had sent the creature. In the final days before the festival began, the bull was welcomed into the chambers of Minos' queen, Pasiphae, so the two could become more *acquainted.* She interacted with the bull as if it were Dionysus himself.

The time came for the Orgia Ceremony of Anthesteria. Minos donned his Dionysus mask. He, Pasiphae, and Dionysus' substitutionary bull were the climax of the night's celebrations. Nine months later, the kingdom of Crete received the "pure heir" for which they had longed. However, as with any dealings with The Dark Kingdom, this heir was not what the people of Crete anticipated.

The godborn son of Minos, Pasiphae, and Dionysus appeared to be an average child for the first few years of his life. But, as the child began to mature, his appetites became increasingly carnal. The constant engorging of livestock was enough to starve the people of Crete but insufficient to curb the boy's growing appetite for raw flesh and muscle. Minos' subjects began to question whether the godborn child was a blessing or a curse.

During the Dionysus festival in the boy's thirteenth year, a full moon appeared from behind the clouds. It was revealed to Minos' kingdom that the godborn was indeed anything but a blessing. The moon's light fully awakened the beast within and the boy turned into a raging, cannibalistic terror of the night. It took three days and many warriors to capture and subdue him. The boy had the speed and strength of a raging bull, skin that no man could cut through, and an unholy thirst for human blood and meat.

Minos had the boy locked away in a dungeon, bound by heavier chains than most men could lift, yet the godborn would shatter them within a week's time. Minos lost countless warriors just replacing the boy's bonds. Something had to be done, but the king would not dare kill the godborn son of Dionysus for fear of the wrath the mighty god would unleash upon the kingdoms of Crete. During this time, Pasiphae's Grand Vizier and Architect, Daedalus, approached the king and proposed a plan to use the creature for their advantage for the kingdom instead of allowing it to be a looming shadow of fear.

Daedalus proposed the construction of an enormous labyrinth to imprison the godborn and that every third cycle of the moon they would cast tributes to Dionysus into the maze-like structure to feed the monstrous boy as a prosperity-offering to their mighty god. Much to the dismay of Lady Ariadne, The Oracle of Crete who had initially warned Minos against creating a godborn–she believed keeping the godborn alive would bring further destruction to Crete–Minos agreed, and construction began immediately. However, the boy became a man before the labyrinth's completion. It took two dozen of Minos' strongest warriors to transport the godborn from the dungeons to the center of the giant stone maze, where the people gave the beast seven virgins as an initial sacrifice. In the months after, much prosperity came to the Cretan kingdom due to the sacrificial offerings to Dionysus.

After a time, Crete subdued Athens after war broke out following the murder of Mino's trueborn son, Angdrogeos. He had been killed while visiting the city. As both penance and to pay tribute to the god-king Minos, Athens was required to send fourteen people every six months to offer as a tithe to the horrifying and legendary

"Minotaur of The Labyrinth," the half-man, half-bull monstrosity of Crete. These offerings to the godborn lasted two years, and alternated between Cretan prisoners and Athenian tributes, until one day, a young Athenian warrior named Theseus gathered thirteen of his brothers-in-arms. They all volunteered to act as tributes for

Minos' minotaur and vowed to their fellow Athenians to destroy the beast and end its reign of terror.

Theseus and his mighty men traveled to the Minoan city of Crete and soon found themselves in the labyrinth's depths. In this dark and horrifying maze, the simple plan Theseus had concocted failed quickly as the godborn easily overpowered the warriors who attempted to take the demonic man by force. Two were killed immediately and the monster carried them further into the labyrinth to devour their corpses. Over the next few days, Theseus' men continued to perish as each strategy failed, one right after another.

Almost eight days had passed, and only a handful of the men were left. Just as it seemed all hope was lost, the Oracle of Crete appeared before Theseus in a dream.

"I am Lady Ariadne," the astral form said. "And I come to you now to help end this monstrous nightmare that has fallen upon our great city," Ariadne explained to the warrior that she had been waiting for someone with a heart of conquest, one who could stare the godborn in the eye and not feel fear. The Oracle gave Theseus two items to ensure his victory. First, the mighty sword that had belonged to the ancient giant warrior Goliath: Dev Katili, with which to strike the godborn down. And second, a ball of thin string that when thrown upon the ground inside the labyrinth would glow bright white and lead Theseus and his men out of the wretched structure. Upon waking from his dream, Theseus found the giant sword in one hand and the ball of string in the other. Thus, the hunted became the hunters.

The Athenian warriors attempted to work their way through the giant labyrinth to its center where the godborn beast made its home. The stench is what gave it away. The putrid odor of mangled and decaying flesh filled the labyrinth's air as the Athenians grew closer. They struggled not to vomit. The godborn was in a deep slumber as the remaining warriors entered the atrocious center of the labyrinth. It looked like a massacre. Skulls and corroding limbs lay scattered surrounding a large pile of half-eaten corpses in the center of the room where the "Minotaur of The Labyrinth" lay atop his carrion throne.

**CRACK!**

One of Theseus' men stepped on a bone and snapped it in half which awakened the horrid beast. Immediately, Dionysus' godborn leaped from his carcass-ridden bed and charged at the men in a blind rage. Until now, no one had dared to enter this haunted place, and the minotaur felt more threatened than ever before. Theseus lunged with the enormous Dev Katili at the godborn but he was too slow. The monster dove out of the way and landed on top of another warrior. He ripped the man's jugular from his neck and threw him into the other two horrified men.

Theseus then stood facing this horrifying man-beast who glared with his blazing yellow eyes into the very soul of the warrior. He had never felt fear like this before. Theseus was frozen where he stood, staring at the bulging muscles, the wild hair matted all over the bestial figure in front of him, and talon-like fingers caked with years of blood. This *thing* was far worse than any "Minotaur" legend he had heard. This creature was an absolute nightmare, and now it was charging at him.

*"The heart of conquest."* He heard the voice of The Oracle plainly inside his mind. It shook him from his paralyzed state and gave Theseus strength to raise Dev Katili. With one horizontal slice, he severed the head of the godborn from its grotesque body. The monster fell, limp and lifeless, on the blood-soaked, stone floor. Theseus claimed the head of the godborn, gathered the two remaining men in his troop, dropped the ball of string on the ground, and followed its Light out of that accursed place of death and despair.

Generations passed and the labyrinth was left to rot and fade away into the earth. However, because this place was so horribly and intimately linked to the Dark, as it dissipated from the Corporeum Realm through destruction and erosion, it began to appear in the Sheolic domains, waiting to be claimed by a Dark Master.

Sometimes, places would grow a will of their own and call out to some being to steward it and continue its Dark purpose. On occasion, as a haunted place or object would appear in the unseen realms, it could be redeemed by an elohim of Light. But, like all elohim or Adamians, if the place had become solidified in the Dark, evil was now its only purpose. Therefore, it would be too late for redemption.

In the case of this particular labyrinth, as it began to slowly appear in the Cosmic Ocean in Sheol, it was recovered by a cunning sorcerer of The Dark Kingdom who had been quietly constructing a cult that would eventually change the entire course of history. This sorcerer had many names throughout time and had even split himself into different skafos forms for a season. However, only one sinister group of Adamians knew his actual name: Baphomet.

Controlling the godborn's labyrinth was more than just a simple power play for Baphomet. It was an orchestrated and strategically planned move to allow him to gain the favor of another Dark elohim whose power was now extensive within the ranks of The Dark Father–The Queen of The Wild Winds of Dudael, Lilith. Baphomet and his growing cult of witches from Endor now had the malevolent might of Dudael on their side. They could finally begin the real work of destroying the order of The Cosmic Wheel and ushering in the prophecy of Age End.

Slowly throughout the centuries to come–through the guidance of Baphomet's cult–the symbol of the labyrinth would make its way into circles of worship and sacrifice. Ultimately it became a symbol of a more civilized perspective of *enlightened* society: a society that believed itself to be so much more advanced than its predecessors. In its advancement, it completely blinded itself to the possibility that its very ideals of utopian progression were actually embracing the devil with open arms.

All the while, the Host of the Heavens hunted the haunted dwelling of Dionysus' godborn. They hoped that in destroying the unholy artifact, the idea of the labyrinth itself would begin to lose its persuasive power and one of The Dark Kingdom's most significant weapons in the battle of the mind of all Adamians would be null and void. Alas, it was never found. That is, until Moriel and Akalian arrived inside the mind of Jonathan Young.

Standing in front of the necroplasmic waterfall that was their gateway into this wretched place, they peered through the green mists of the Kingdom of Endless Night and saw Minos' cyclopean labyrinth stretched as far as their eyes could see. They had entered something no elohim of the Heavens had ever seen before in all the cursed lands of Sheol. And it was here in the mind of a thirteen-year-old boy.

"Remember," Akalian whispered as they entered the cursed maze, "Shadow Wurms hide their hearts. The easiest way to weaken

them is to locate the heart and destroy it. That should free the boy's mind to a degree."

"One would hope, but I'm not expecting anything to be *normal* with this one." Moriel replied. "From here on out, we must be as silent as the grave and stay close to our blades, and each other."

The two Powers had traversed through the first ring of the labyrinth. It was too quiet, they thought. The stench of the minotaur's victims still lingered in the air and although there was no evidence of any actual movement, Akalian and Moriel felt the presence of a thousand eyes watching them in the blackness of this horrid place.

After hours of silent wandering through the haunted maze, with only their blades and obus lighting their way, they were surprised and unsettled to see a strange green glow in the distance. As they wound their way around multiple cornered walls shooting out at maddening angles, the eerie illumination grew stronger. Finally, they arrived at an offshoot pathway that led them straight into the labyrinth's center.

As they drew closer to the opening, Moriel saw it first. His jaw unconsciously dropped as they stood frozen in the archway of the center chamber.

"What in the..." Akalian was almost speechless. "Is that what I *think* it is?"

"It's a Shard of the Sapient Stone..." Moriel gasped. In the center of the arena-sized room, suspended six feet from the ground and encased in a glowing green, ghostly shield, was a large Shard–about twelve feet tall–of the Aeturnum Stone of Possibility. The Sapient Stone had constructed things like the Law of Choice and had made true freedom possible within The Cosmic Wheel. However, if abused, it could manipulate this Law and create destiny where it was never meant to be.

"How is this possible, Moriel?" Akalian asked as they entered the chamber, stunned and confused.

"How indeed?" Moriel replied. The admiral blue power reached out to test the aura of the Stone's vibrations. It was genuine. "I can't believe this, Akalian...never...*never* in all my days have I seen an Aeternum Shard *inside* an Adamian's mind. I've never even *heard* of such a thing. The power that must be flowing through this boy is...insurmountable. No wonder Minos' labyrinth is here. They had to have something powerful enough to contain *this.*"

"But *how?* How could they have placed this here? How is this boy still alive? This amount of power alone should have killed him. How could they have kept something like this boy a *secret* from The Adunalar Elohim?"

"I don't know...but if this Shard is fueling the possession...I'm afraid we may be too late here, brother. I'm not sure we can stop this."

"We have to," Akalian said boldly. "This *must* end here. Can we destroy it?"

"Not without killing the boy. Whatever spells are holding this in place must be attached to his very life essence," Moriel grimly replied as he continued walking closer to the Shard, arm outstretched as if he were going to touch it.

"If it is truly impossible for this boy to be saved..." Akalian couldn't believe he was saying this. Tears filled his eyes, and the Power's voice cracked. "If the boy can't be saved, then we cannot allow this future to *happen,* Moriel. We must–"

"Kill him? Yes. You'd like that, wouldn't you?" Moriel uttered softly.

"What?" Akalian was taken aback.

"Anything to win your race with guilt. You didn't care about Abigail, either. Why should you care about *this* one?"

Akalian's heart dropped into his stomach. Visions of the poor girl melting on the sacrificial table all those centuries ago flashed inside his mind. What was happening? What did his *brother* just say to him?

"Moriel..." Akalian realized his fellow Power was touching the Shard. As the admiral Messenger slowly turned to face his brother, ice-cold fear washed over Akalian's body.

"You would *gladly* sacrifice this dust creature just to gain your prize, wouldn't you?" Moriel's face had already begun to twist and warp into a wicked smile. "You're just like *him.* Your king doesn't give a shit about these Adamians. All he cares about is his *order.* All he cares about is control!" Green muck began to pour from Moriel's eyes and mouth. His admiral featherfur started darkening into a calloused midnight blue, and his cloak slowly became a deep, leathery purple.

"All your king has to do is end this," Moriel said from behind sharp, yellowing fangs. "Yet he remains *silent.* Are you sure you can trust such a being? A being who will so willingly send others to do his work for him?"

"Moriel! Fight it!!" Akalian held Karaydin at the ready, and his other hand began to shine with weaponized tzoharian Light.

"Did you *really* think you could *defeat me??* Did you really think I wouldn't know that you forced your way into *my* kingdom!?!" The feathers in Moriel's membrane atop his head were wilting away, slowly being replaced by rigid, twisting horns. His long featherbeard hardened into matted, leathery tentacles. "Moriel is no longer here, oh, holy Power of Michael. Only Endless Night!!"

Moriel leapt toward Akalian. Necroplasm shot from his eyes in a green, liquid lightning, forming two shadow blades that mimicked his twin broad swords, Illeti. Akalian lifted Karaydin just in time for the Shadowblades to crash into it, barely missing Akalian's face as they locked blades. Moriel landed inches from Akalian's snarling expression.

"You will *never* win, filth." Akalian spat at the monster who stood before him. This being was not Xexxus. He knew just by looking into its eyes. But who *was* it? A skafos? Or something else?

"I already have." Moriel mocked with an oozing arrogance. Akalian felt Moriel's Shadowblades pulsate before they began to glow green as if powering up for another strike. The Chief Power acted fast and pushed Karaydin onto his opponent's blades, separating them from their entanglement. Letting out a mighty yell, he push-kicked the counterfeit Moriel directly in the face, sending the monstrous elohim flying through the large open room, crashing into the wall and away from the Shard.

Moriel landed on his feet; blades outstretched on either side of him. The Dark elohim opened his mouth and projected a constant flow of decaying, necroplasmic bile towards the Chief Power of Michael. Akalian dove to the side, dodging the weaponized vomit, and blasted a beam of tzoharian Light from his hand at the Dark being. Moriel held his blades in an 'x' formation before him, absorbing the energy from Akalian's attack.

"Why do you fight for a being who *clearly* leads you into suffering?" the creature taunted. Moriel ran so fast that all Akalian could see was a blur and barely parried out of the way in time to dodge being run through by the monster's Shadowblade. "He could end *everyone's* pain. He could stop me with one simple thought!" Moriel slashed at Akalian's head, slicing through some of the Power's long white hair and just missing his left membrane as Akalian moved to counterstrike with Karaydin. Moriel was too fast. Karaydin slammed into the dark stone of the labyrinth floor, sparks shooting from the glowing Lightblade. Moriel's evil doppelganger continued to taunt the elohim of Light.

"So, he is either playing some sick, twisted game or is *not* who he claims to be. Have you ever really thought of *that!?"* The Dark facade lunged his Shadowblade at Akalian's chest, who, with lightning-fast reflexes, moved into a back-bend as the blade slid through the holy Power's featherbeard before Karaydin knocked it away.

"Silence your tongue, you putrid slime!!" Akalian spun around, Karaydin first, and sliced through–nothing. Green smoke billowed from where Moriel had been. The Dark elohim was nowhere in sight.

"Oh, my tongue shall *persist,* little angel," Moriel's disembodied voice hissed.

Akalian decided to draw him out by taunting him.

"How could you know my King? Whatever you are, you chose your selfish ambitions over alliance with *him* long ago."

"Alliance!?" the Dark being chuckled. "Oh, how *rich.* Tell me, Akalian. How can you *know* your King..." Akalian felt a sharp, leathery talon suddenly slither from behind his head, touching him gently on the forehead. "...when you don't even know who *you* are?" Akalian's eyes began to drown in pools of green energy.

"I know who I am..." Akalian struggled. "I'm... I'm...?"

"Exactly," the wicked Moriel grinned as he materialized right in front of the Head Power. Waving his taloned hands in a haunting motion, Moriel's doppelganger blasted Akalian with an obu, rocketing him across the room and slamming him into the dark stone wall. The Power collapsed onto the floor.

Akalian struggled to sit up as he leaned against the wall, fighting to stay conscious. The attack had been from a fully powered strike from Moriel's obu, one that had ripped lesser creatures apart. He was lucky not to have faded from this form. Moriel walked slowly toward the injured Power with an ominous stride.

"You are who I say you are. And I say, you have *always* been here, *slave,"* he lied, pulling Dark energy from his essence to cast his spell. "Drowning in your cesspool of self-doubt, I look into your pathetic soul and find a child screaming in the darkness for a maker who would rather send him to the depths than rescue him from his desperate and pathetic fate."

"Si...Silence you–"

"You're my *slave.* As it was in the beginning, is now, and ever shall be." The Dark Moriel knelt down and touched Akalian's forehead once more, this time pouring all of the wicked energy into the Power's mind as everything Akalian knew faded to black.

Akalian was lost, drowning in an utterly numbed forgetfulness that was eating away at his very essence. Not only had he forgotten who he was, but *what* he was. The Head of The Order of Michael was now nothing more than an insignificant worm crawling through the fecal muck of the Dark. He had no intuition, no ability or determination. He had no real thought whatsoever. A decaying, lifeless corpse had more meaning in this world than the bewitched Power did right now.

The process being forced upon Akalian was one of the blackest of all rituals. It was the beginning of what was known as an Undertaking, which had only one goal: dismantle and destroy a being's identity, then reconstruct it to serve The Dark Father. Undertakings were different from Transfectiations in one way: choice.

While a Transfectiation was willingly sought after by an elohim, an Undertaking was forced upon a being–seen or unseen–through direct enslavement of the mind so all unique traces of its Yahweh-given, image-bearing qualities were completely erased, and replaced with a slavish demeanor which answered solely to the will of its captor.

As Akalian floated helplessly in the vast nothingness, one phrase echoed all around him, "You're my slave. As it was in the beginning, is now, and ever shall be." Akalian had no reason to disagree with this command, for it was all he'd ever known. This was his name and this was his purpose: Slave. Slave to the Dark.

"Fight it, Akalian."

The warm voice pierced the putrid air of this empty space. Who was Akalian? What did it mean? Why would he ever want to *fight* his Dark master?

"Akalian."

There it was again. That name. Could it belong to him? No. The Master would have told him so and this voice was *not* his Master; and if it wasn't his Master, then it must be the enemy.

A blinding white light suddenly pierced the nothingness in Akalian's mind. He watched as an overwhelmingly bright figure materialized before him. It looked like an Adamian, but one that was united with Light itself.

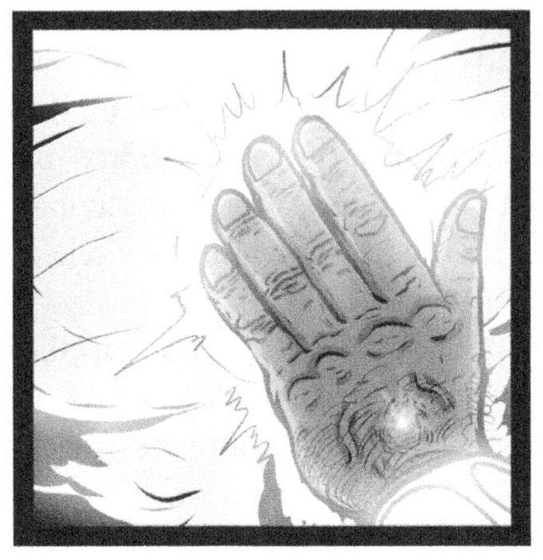

But Light was wrong. Light was the enemy. Light was a prison. The brightness emerging from this being was painful to the Power. He needed to get away. Akalian turned to run, but no matter which direction he faced, this figure stood before him. It was now walking towards him at a calm, but steady pace. Akalian continued turning, attempting escape, but there was none to be found.

"Remember who you are, old friend," the Light figure said. He placed a strong, warm hand on Akalian's chest. The bewitched Power winced in pain at the immense heat of the touch. It was like white hot fire engulfing him. All he'd ever known was cold. Cold was home. Cold and Dark were freedom. This was wrong; this was *enslavement.* He tried to lash out at the Light in front of him, but as soon as his fist struck the illuminated figure, the Power found himself transported to a rainy cliffside overlooking the Tower of Babylon.

# CHAPTER TWENTY TWO

## - THE CULT OF THE GADARENES -

Looking up from the glowing Lightblade in his hand, Akalian peered out across the tempest landscape. He could see the mighty Tower of Babylon in the distance, and he faintly recognized this moment as though it were a distant dream, long forgotten. The Power lowered Karaydin, and with tears running down his crested owl-like featherfur cheeks, he looked out at an enormous elohim floating in the sky not fifteen yards ahead. Silver tears flowed down the being's tribal-marked face.

"Please...don't do this..." Akalian heard himself plead.

"I already have," the other elohim coldly stated through his tears, then disappeared into a cloud of green smoke. Rain began to thunder down hard all around Akalian. The inner devastation felt like he was being ripped apart. It was Hell. He had to end it. He couldn't bear it any longer. The pain was searing the Power's very essence. Akalian had witnessed countless elohim fall to the Dark, but he had never dreamt it would steal this one from him. But who *was* this elohim that brought him so much turmoil? Akalian couldn't remember. Everything was a cloud of confusion.

Akalian screamed into the storm surrounding him and, lifting Karaydin high above his head, the Power smashed his Lightblade into the ground of the cliffside overlooking the ominous, Necrogate fortress of The Tower of Babylon. Lightning bolts from Karaydin engulfed the entire region, hammering into the cursed collaboration of Babylon and The Dark Kingdom, bringing the once mighty Tower to pieces as it crashed into the muddy surface below the cliff where Akalian stood. The Chief Power then dropped to his knees in anguish, his face illuminated by the Lightblade glowing in the shadows of the storm, and sobbed like he never had before, his heart utterly broken.

Years flashed by in an instant as Akalian stood still. The cliffside transformed into the floor of the Citadel of Agios–the highest level of Mount Zion that overlooked the Heavenly City. On this cobblestoned peak, The Power kneeled between the Aeternum Stone Seraphim Wings in front of the white sapling descendant of Sigra Agac. Akalian had just been named Head of the Order of Michael.

A being of Light now stood in front of the small, illuminated tree, holding a long white staff made from a branch from the mighty Sigra Agac. Akalian recognized this being as the one who sparked this memorial journey.

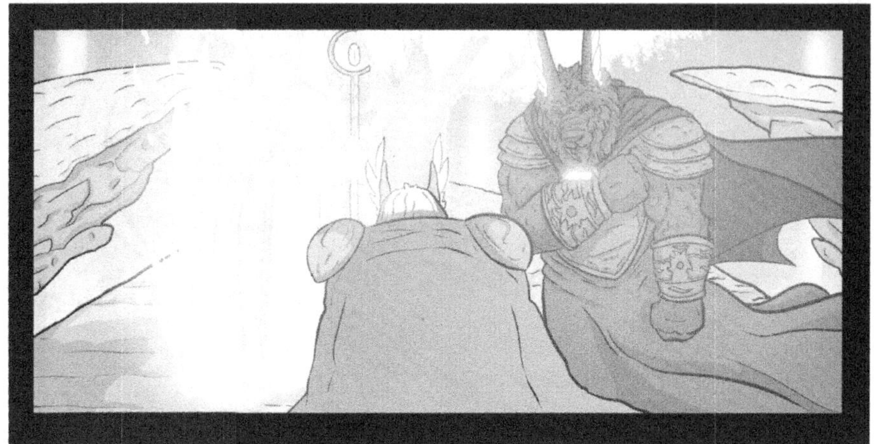

The appearance of this Light-being was different from the start of the Vision. Instead of a more Adamian resemblance, he looked like a creature of pure white flame—a controlled flame that somehow brought life to everything and everyone around it. However, it was the staff that caught the bewitched Akalian's attention. He recognized the Stone suspended in the center of the semicircle, crowning the top of the staff: Tzohar, The Stone of Eternal Light. Just looking at it made Akalian feel as though he were staring at a home he had long forgotten but was now within its reach. Like it was waiting with open arms for him to return.

And return, he did.

Everything began flooding back to him. He remembered the Light-being was his Maker, his King. And next to his King stood his Archangel, Michael, dressed in formal battle garb: gold chest plate and pauldrons, with golden vambraces at the forearms. His purple cape and robes flowed smoothly in the soft, sweet breeze of Zion, City of The White Throne. Akalian remembered this day. It was his coronation as Chief Power. Both of these pivotal figures were bestowing the highest honor he'd ever felt. And yet...a hollow sadness lingered.

Time flashed forward again. Akalian found himself with his closest brothers, the Chief Powers of the Order of Michael. Bradoch, the mightiest of all griffins. Forfax, one of the Evren, whose entire purple and blue body–comprised of constellations and galaxies–remained a mystery to all but the King. Willow, the Silencer of Cthulhu, and the first choirmite inducted into a governing body of the Septum Dei. Raziel, of the Rok Helig, whose very essence is the gaseous form of Krallik, The Kingdom Stone. And finally, Moriel, the brother he held most dear in his heart. These were his closest comrades. All the wonderful memories of times spent with them flooded his heart, and the elohim smiled. Even though he now remembered the joys of who he was, he also remembered the pain.

Baetiel. His brother. The being with whom he was formed out of a single embryo of Light from The Sigra Agac itself.

The King had blessed Akalian with five new siblings to replace what was broken between him and the former Head of the Order of Michael. Through the centuries to come, their bond would become legendary. Akalian's mighty band went on to become the Guardians of the King's Chosen People–the Soma Aedrum. And for a time, the brokenness inside of him even began to heal. But in a cosmos under the curse of Khata, healing was countered by continued suffering and pain.

Time flashed forward once more, and Akalian was transported to the lavender mountains of Aslan Keep, finding himself inside Savas Isigi in Sof Haderech. Raziel, Moriel, and Willow surrounded him as they gathered around the Aeternum Stone table. This band of warriors watched as it illuminated with tzoharian Light, forming a three-dimensional map of Corporeum, honing in on the Sea of Galilee, following a small fishing vessel on the way to the shores of Gadara–one of the ten cities of the Roman Decapolis. The Powers were discussing something dire that had plagued the world for centuries and was finally coming to a horrifying head.

"We've just received word that Legion has been found." Michael was careful in saying these words, for he knew they would sting the Head of his Order. "It appears that Xexxus' horde has grown exceedingly powerful in their union with The Coven of Endor." All eyes fell on Akalian, leaning on the Stone table with his back turned. The Power had not seen his former brother since that night on the cliffside, and only one person in this room–Michael–had witnessed the monster Baetiel had become.

No one quite knew what to say at this moment. On top of causing the overwhelming sorrow and guilt storming inside Akalian, this King of Legion had proven to be one of the most challenging foes the Host of the Heavens had ever faced.

Xexxus had been secretly building an army for centuries in the Sheolic realms. It was apparent that he also included Adamians living in the Corporeum Realm within his horde. The Cult of The Gadarene

Tombs had only recently come to the Host's attention as a real threat, but no one had suspected Xexxus' Legion was behind it.

The Host was aware of the Cult , but in the last five years, the unholy alliance had never caused anything more than minor disruptions in the city's marketplace. It was considered a small cult of Adamians aligning themselves with The Dark Kingdom in feeble ways. No one in the Host had thought anything more threatening was occurring. There were more pressing matters to attend to, for The Word of the King had become flesh, and all attention was on his movements and the unfolding plan in the Corporeum Realm—no one quite knew what to expect.

However, in recent months, a man had begun heralding a great Darkness which he claimed would start in Gadara, then overtake all ten cities in the Decapolis, and eventually all of Rome—the spiritual descendant of Babylon. Terrified whispers turned into prayers to the gods to save the city. The people and soldiers of Gadara tried multiple times to subdue this man and capture him. On rare occasions, they would arrest him, but he would simply break his shackles, overpower the soldiers, and escape into the wilderness of the tombs by the sea, only to return the next day or two. His presence was a plague upon Gadara, as he seemingly could not be stopped.

Upon hearing of the cries of the Gadarene people, Michael sent five elohim to scour the area and report back. When the scouts never returned, the mysterious Cult of Gadara became a priority for the Host of the Heavens. All too late, the Host would find out this cult was in direct league with The Coven of Endor, who had been a horrible thorn in the

Host's side since Jadith, The Unholy Mother–the founding witch of The Coven who conjured a spirit and prophesied doom upon King Saul hundreds of years prior.

The Coven of Endor pledged to assist Lucifer and his forces in bringing chaos into the world in whatever way possible. As far as the Host knew, other than proving to be a manipulative influence on the Soma Aedrum, The Coven had accomplished nothing of *real* significance. Still, things became dire when word arrived that Xexxus and his Legion were now their direct collaborator. In hindsight, it was as if everything The Coven had done up to this point led to this cult at this specific moment.

Thankfully, the Septum Dei put the pieces together rather quickly. The Dark Kingdom knew there was an Adamian who was said to be Yahweh in the flesh. Some of them, including The Dark Father himself, were convinced of this fact and had attempted to destroy the man or, at the very least, corrupt him. Their mission was proving to be useless.

Michael and Raphael both suspected that The Cult of The Gadarene Tombs was attempting to raise their own Dark Messiah in direct competition with Yahweh's Christ, for The Dark Kingdom wasn't entirely sure *what* The Word of the King was doing in the Corporeum Realm. It actually remained a mystery to the majority of all Creation. Even most of the Adunalar Elohim didn't fully understand what Yahweh's plan was in the realm, nor did anyone know how the Cosmic Laws had allowed such a thing to occur. Like the Adamians who followed him, many elohim thought Yeshua–the name chosen for The Word Become Flesh–was going to claim rulership in Jerusalem and bring the Edenic realm to the Temple, allowing the holy tzoharian fire to annihilate all Darkness throughout the world.

Still, others argued that if that occurred, most Adamians wouldn't be left, for the Soma Aedrum was a tiny group within the vast lands of planet Earth; even *they* willingly re-joined the Dark on many occasions. The remaining Adamians throughout the world still very much belonged to The Dark Kingdom. They were Dark property according to the Cosmic Laws set in place by the events of the UcDusme.

In the Great Floods, Yahweh destroyed all the Nephilim and most of their descendants, saving only the ones who aligned with the Light. But that was different. The majority of the beings throughout the known world in those times were either Dark elohim, Nephilim, or Adamians so completely solidified in the Dark that they were no longer even classified as humans–an entirely irredeemable lot. And while it was true that godborns still ruled and roamed the Earth in the days of this Gadarene cult, they were nowhere near the majority.

No, the actions of The Word Become Flesh did not seem to support a political agenda that would result in another genocide. He seemed to only care about seeking out those who would follow him–claiming even those outside of the chosen Soma Aedrum of Israel–teaching them and healing the sick and possessed, all while proclaiming the victory of his Kingdom, turning Dark spaces into Light. It was quite baffling for many, but it was a glorious mystery to watch unfold.

Gabriel–elected to be Yeshua's Guardian elohim on Earth–communed with The Word while he slept in the stern of his disciple's fishing vessel mere hours before Michael's meeting. He had received orders for Michael to set up a battalion of his most skilled and well-rested Powers and gather at the gates of Tartarus. There, they were to await the command of the Spirit of the King for further instructions. Gabriel communicated through his obu that he barely escaped the vessel before an enormous storm hit. He swore that he felt the presence of the unholy, maddening ghost of Cthulhu in the viciousness of the waves. Although the Leviathan had been struck down thousands of years prior, he was still one with the waters, and when the stars were right, his ghost could venture out and cause chaos where he pleased.

From the illuminated map on the Stone table, the four Chief Powers and their Archangel watched this storm unfold, climb to a maddening climax–revealing that, indeed, the colossal ghost of Cthulhu himself was in the waves. Then The Word Become Flesh woke up from his slumber in the stern, crawled out, and immediately silenced the squall and its Dark master.

"That storm was strategic," Raziel stated, attempting to move the moment past Akalian's pain. "For the specter of Cthulhu to assist by attempting to slow the King down...that—"

"That means this is much larger than *anything* Xexxus has been a part of before," Akalian interrupted. "Legion has eluded us for centuries, growing in the shadows like a festering boil, attempting to bring chaos and ruin to the Soma Aedrum. But this is where their reign of terror ends." The whole room looked upon Akalian again as he turned and leaned his heavy, muscular arms on the Stone Table, looking up at Michael with a fierce gaze. "I want to be the one to face him and smite his essence into Tartarus."

"I don't doubt that, my friend," Michael said with the most understanding of tones as he returned the Power's gaze, his bright periwinkle eye almost glowing. "But I need you to be honest with yourself, Akalian. Can you face him and do what must be done?"

"I have to try." A tear rolled down Akalian's cheek. His voice cracked. "I know I'll experience Hell while facing him, but I must be the one to do this."

"Very well," the Archangel responded. Compassion overwhelmed him. "Just know that you won't be alone. We will be there with you when you face him." Akalian began to sob, his muscular arms bowing as he was no longer leaning against the table with control but instead using it to hold himself up. Moriel and Willow rushed to either side of him to support their grieving brother.

*"All* of us will be there." Willow proclaimed, tears welling up in his eyes.

"We will face this...we will face *him*...together as a family," Moriel added. And as Raziel joined them in embracing their brother, Michael stared at the tzoharian map on the Stone table, grimacing at the tombs. The Gadarene people had attempted to raid this haunted land many times, but the catacombs beneath the tombs were vast, and the people were never successful in finding the cult's resting place. Eventually, after enough people were killed and their searches proved fruitless, the Gadarenes simply gave up and stayed away from the area altogether. But on this particular moonlit night, it wouldn't be challenging to find the followers of the cult. For, in the eastern tombs, in the crypt of a forgotten godborn, the cult gathered to hear the Dark prophetic words of their leader and his sorceress.

Through the wailing of nervous swine from a nearby hill, the sound of the stormy waves crashing against the shores of Gadara was music to the ears of the scarred man with the glowing, pale blue eyes. He stood upon the hilltop, on the outskirts of the tombs, gazing out at the raging Sea of Galilee that promised to swallow the would-be Manking of the Host. The pale-eyed man could now run to his master and deliver the victorious news: The Leviathan had answered the call.

Running frantically through the worn, maze-like paths of the hills, he rushed between the basalt tombs that held the decaying bodies of former townspeople whose loved ones dared not visit out of pure and validated fear. These bodies belonged to *them* now. The ancient spirits in feeble Adamian shells would soon know the merged strength of Sheol and Corporeum. The Nephilic demons of Legion had waited thousands of years for this night. This unholy tribe could finally use their vessels as Necrogates, not just in control of the *minds* of these Adamians, but fully merge, making these bodies their own.

In the blackness of night, the pale-eyed man saw the faint orange glow coming from inside the crypt of the long-dead godborn up ahead. He paused for a moment to catch his breath. He hated this dust creature's skin suit with all his might. It was so limited, but it was a necessary means to an incredible end. Soon, he could rid himself of the disgusting Adamian co-habitation and turn the dust creature's soul into a skafos, allowing him to mold this sack of dying flesh perfectly.

The sign of fatigued weakness subsided, and he calmly trotted towards the crypt, ready to please his master. As the pale-eyed man

approached the door of this unholy temple, he heard the words of the High Sister of Endor proclaiming the prophecy of doom upon this land.

"The Moons of Blood across the realms will soon fully align. Then, our final sacrifice will pave the way for The Great Merging–ushering in a new dusk for The Dark Kingdom!" Agora, a sorceress of

Endor, raised her blood-drenched staff in her hand above her cloaked head. "This new dusk will give birth to The Endless Night ruled by The Dark Father *forevermore!"*

The pale-eyed man entered the blood-soaked crypt where thirty possessed Adamians stood, naked and covered in the blood of a child, freshly sacrificed on the fiery stone altar. Inside the Adamian bodies, however, were thousands of Nephilic demons and Dark elohim. Once The Great Merging began, it would be an all-out war to decide which Dark beings would claim these dust creatures, which ones would claim the corpses in the other tombs, and which would find themselves remaining in their disembodied state of blasphemous nothingness.

"My master!" Golgus, the pale-eyed man, shouted. "The Leviathan has answered," he said with sinsiter grin.

"Excellent," a gravelly, deep voice bellowed throughout the crypt. Green eyes pierced the unholy crowd as a man emerged from the shadows. His hair and beard were wild, surrounding open wounds. Chapped lips cracked as he beamed a wicked smile. "You have served me well, slave." And, as if a switch flipped—for there was no transition between expressions—the unnatural grin instantly became a numbed stare. "Now fall in line, half-breed." Golgus twitched at the slur but dared not show contempt.

The green-eyed man turned his attention to Agora and stretched out his hand from inside a rancid fur cloak, revealing scarred flesh plagued by years of untreated wounds.

"And *you* will be rewarded, oh High Sister of Endor, for I have great plans for you and your lineage. Soon, The Age of Endless Night will arrive, and it will be *Agora* who stands at my side in the coming Dark." The witch beamed with grotesque delight. "But, for now," the green-eyed man clapped his hands together, and with a mighty flash, every Dark being–along with the witch–was transported to the Sheolic realm, inside the green smoke-ridden, cavernous throne room of the Castle of Endless Night, "...you will make a delicious addition to my collection of slaves."

Xexxus, in all his leathery, muscular glory, stood before his Legion–the witch at his side–and waved his hand downward, instructing her to bow before him. Agora of Endor was in absolute awe; she was a mere dust creature surrounded by gods. Never in all her wildest dreams had she ever anticipated such an honor. She had been spirited away to join her master at his side in his Castle of Endless Night.

Agora obeyed her master's command and bowed before the green necroplasmic prison that held whatever Adamian Xexxus had claimed years ago. She could feel the malevolent energy building inside of her. There was a *fundamental* transformation happening. Her longing to rid herself of this futile mortal coil was materializing inside her on an intimate and cosmic level. Her desires of no longer being limited to her human state were taking shape, bubbling up inside. Amid these overwhelming sensations, the High Witch of Endor shut her eyes.

"Thank you, my Lord Xexxus." She stumbled through the words, due to both the lustful satisfaction and also the glorious, Transfectiating pain occurring inside of her. Boiling cesspools appeared as Agora opened her eyes, producing putrid gas steaming out and around her head. Her features were the same as before, but that would undoubtedly change over time. This was the unspoken promise of her Dark master.

"Rise, slave." As Agora obeyed her Lord's command, Xexxus turned to face the plague of spirits before him. "We are about to enter a time unknown or unseen since the Nephilim walked the Earth. This region has learned to fear us, but they know not what lies in wait for them. We will consume this world with a mighty, iron fist, bringing the realms to their knees with The Dark Father glorified on high!!"

"And what will you do when the armies of the Host arrive on our doorstep?" All eyes turned to the middle of the cavernous throne room where a grotesque being leaned against a slime-covered stalagmite. The beast had multiple eyes, and skin glowing with vibrant shades of purple, yellow, and blue. A scowl stretched across its calloused, horned face. "Many are thinking this, but I will speak it! There are whispers of an Adamian champion who fights for the enemy. No doubt this is what Golgus meant by his message regarding Leviathan. You have tried to keep this information from us, oh *mighty* Xexxus," the Dark creature scoffed. "But it is said he is–"

"You question me for the last time, Olgoth." As Xexxus stood ominously calm, with his right hand outstretched, fingers in a pinching formation, the middle of the creature's head began to pull inward. "This castle has *never* been breached. Nor will it ever be. Least of all by some worthless carpenter from the West!" Olgoth's head was now being pinched so tightly in the middle that he appeared to have two separate heads stacked on top of each other, a tensed strip of flesh with insurmountable pressure being pulled in between them. Olgoth’s mouth could barely get its words out as his top lip was being pulled towards the center.

"Th-they say he is a *powerful* teacher!!"

*"How many teachers have I eaten alive!?!?"* Xexxus snapped his pinching fingers, and Olgoth's head exploded purplish yellow ooze onto the surrounding members of Legion who, even though many of them agreed with Olgoth, were far too afraid to speak now. Xexxus then addressed the rest of his brood and boomed with mighty hubris. "No. Just like all the dust creatures since the dawn of time...he will fall."

Back outside the tombs, the teacher and his disciples approached the haunted necropolis.

"Uh...rabbi...are you sure about this?" Andraus' voice quivered at the sight of the shadowed tombs up ahead. It had been an exhausting night. They were all weary from lack of sleep and overexertion. However, adrenaline was still pumping through their systems after that storm. A storm unlike any of them had ever seen before had been suddenly silenced by the man to whom they had dedicated the last two years of their lives. It was unheard of. Indeed, it was the most fantastic sight they had ever seen. But even though their teacher proved he was somehow even the ruler over the storms, as Andraus looked out over the nightmare up ahead, he–and the rest

of this small fellowship—felt as though they were about to encounter something *much* worse.

"Yes, Andraus," the teacher said with a playful smirk. "I'm quite sure. We have an appointment to keep." Yeshua, the name on the lips of most men and women in the land of Judea, chuckled to himself. He knew all of his disciples were scared out of their minds. Even Kephas—who was usually quite bold in his hubris and bravado—looked like he might wet himself at any moment. Yeshua loved these men dearly—all twelve of them—and he knew that the last sixteen hours had been a lot for them to take in, but tonight was important. Not only had the Host finally located Legion, but tonight, this wicked horde would attempt another one of their merging ceremonies, ultimately giving birth to the lineage of their Dark Messiah—their Manking. However, the timing couldn't have been more perfect for what this rabbi King had in store for the Decapolis.

This fellowship of men moved into the tombs and onward through them until they saw an orange glow up ahead.

"Remember, my friends, whatever happens here tonight, just follow my lead," Yeshua said calmly.

"I don't think that'll be a problem for any of us," Yochanan nervously stated. Others joined him in his sentiment.

"Quiet now. You've seen many things tonight, but what you're about to see holds greater weight than any of you could know." The disciples took the words of their teacher to heart and remained as silent as the graves surrounding them.

"Master!" Agora shouted in fear. "The teacher...he is here!" The throne room of the Castle of Endless Night erupted in terror. It was at this moment that Xexxus saw a twisted yellow grin in the midst of the panicked crowd. Hastur. He thought he had sensed the odious Yellow King in his midst. Hastur was almost flawless at hiding his essence from other elohim, and Xexxus wondered if he could only see the Yellow King now because the crazed Dark monster willed it to be so. The King of Legion knew he was being weighed and measured. Hastur was a leech but a powerful one. The Yellow King's strategy was to wait for a Dark Dominion to gain strength, swoop in unnoticed, and then usurp its leader. Xexxus would not allow that to happen, not on this night.

"SILENCE!!" The King of Legion erupted, clapping his hands once, and transported his slaves back to the tomb in the Corporeum Realm. Xexxus immediately ripped off the matted fur covering from his possessed Adamian vessel, revealing his horrid nakedness to the world. He grabbed the ceremonial green knife from the stone altar, and charged through the unholy crowd.

"Come," he barked at Golgus. "Let's greet this *holy man* properly." He dragged the possessed man towards the basalt door as if he weighed nothing. Golgus dared not protest but was horrified at the thought of facing this teacher from the West. Both

monstrous figures emerged from the godborn's tomb, raving and growling like wild animals. Xexxus' possessed vessel held the green stone blade pointing at the ground, ready to strike anyone who would dare to come near. The King of Legion chuckled at the terrified faces of the men before him. All seemed ready to flee in fear except this *teacher.*

"Who dares disturb *me!?"* Xexxus howled.

"I do." The teacher's voice was calm but intimidating. Immediately, the King of Legion looked into the eyes of this holy man and froze.

"No..." Xexxus' vessel said aloud. "It's... It's impossible!" In the eyes of Yeshua, Xexxus saw a being of pure white flame. It was The Word of the King. It was true, after all. The enemy had somehow *become* an Adamian. This being was no mere elohim of the Host in human form. The King was now a human but somehow still kept his eternal essence. How could this be?

"Come out of him!" Yeshua commanded.

"Please!!" Golgus–who had also seen the King's holy form–threw his possessed vessel to the ground in a groveling posture. "Word of the King of Ages, please do not send me to the abyss of Tartarus!! Do not torment me!"

"Silence, you pathetic fool!" Xexxus growled, slicing Golgus' shoulder with the green stone blade.

"Tell me your name," Yeshua commanded Xexxus' vessel. Xexxus and Golgus howled in unison with the voice of a multitude.

"I am Legion!! For we are *many!!"* The men surrounding the rabbi shuddered in fear at the unimaginable sound, but Yeshua was unmoved.

"No," Yeshua corrected the King of Legion. "I want *your* name, fallen one." This command was significant, and Xexxus knew it. Since the dawn of time, naming something meant having direct authority over it. Likewise, having someone *give* their name to another showed vulnerability. Knowing someone's name was one thing, but submitting to a command was another kind of power entirely. This vulnerable state was a sign of weakness to the Dark and a diminishment of its conquering power in conflict.

"Xe...Xexxus!!" The King of Legion had no choice but to relinquish his name. The power of The Word's command was too great. Xexxus felt his dominion over his horde loosen. It was both excruciating and humiliating. Golgus, feeling Xexxus' power weaken, continued to plead with The Word Become Flesh.

"Please. I beg of you. Send us anywhere you want! There is a herd of swine nearby! Send us there. Just spare us the horror of Tartarus!"

"Go then," the teacher grimaced. He knew this plague of spirits would drive the poor beasts to their deaths, destroying the herd and damaging the townsfolk's food supply. But, in times of war, casualties such as this were a sobering reality. Again, the rabbi King longed for New Eden and hoped justice would find this horde on the other side of the abyss where Michael and his Order awaited them.

*"No!! What have you done?!"* Xexxus bellowed in fury at Golgus, who had just begged the King to send his horde into a pack of unruly animals. There were likely severely stunted wills in this

livestock of beasts to control. Legion had no time or ability to coerce or usurp the pigs as they had with the Gadarenes. The Dark spirits would be at the mercy of the instincts of the peccary. But worst, this was countless centuries of labor wasted. The Decapolis was lost.

Wrenched from their vessels, every Dark elohim of Legion found themselves flying in a vortex of painful wails through the air, over the tombs of Gadara towards the sea. There, on a hillside not far from where the pale-eyed man stood mere hours ago, the horrible plague of demons and devils overtook a herd of panicked pigs. Absolute terror struck the hearts of the herders tending the swine as they saw their livestock transform before their eyes.

The pigs had been nervous all night, which was unusual, but the men had never seen anything like this. All of the beasts began kicking and biting at each other, and the screams were almost bellows of hatred exiting the peccary. The lead herdsman swore he saw one of the pigs' eyes turn green and, upon seeing this, he began to sprint towards the town. Once the swine started stampeding off the hillside and into the waves below, the rest of his companions joined him.

Back inside the tomb, the formerly possessed townsfolk of Gadara began screaming and wailing at the bloody sight inside the unholy temple. Agora sprang to action, rushing through the traumatized people. She had no intention of facing this teacher or his disciples, but she had to reclaim the green stone blade. Its significance was crucial. As she ran out of the tomb, she avoided all eye contact with the men outside, grabbed the knife, and darted off into the night.

"Never mind her! Go and tend to the people!" Yeshua told his disciples, who hesitated momentarily but ran inside with their lit torches. Kephas and Yochanan had to double back outside to vomit from the sight of the gore they just witnessed. Mattityahu and Bar-Talmai rushed with their cloaks to cover the two naked men formerly possessed by Xexxus and Golgus. Yeshua walked over and sat on a rock to rest himself. He, too, had had a very long night, and even though this body had now been part of him for almost thirty-two years, he still couldn't get over how tired he could become. But, as frustrating as this could sometimes be, it was necessary if things were to be set right. He had so much work left to do and less than two years until this short but monumental season of his life would come to a violent close.

As the herd crashed into the sea, Legion suddenly found themselves splashing through a Pentaclegate and hitting solid, dry ground. Xexxus and his Dark horde frantically examined their new surroundings. Upon gazing at millions of black holes lining the cerulean sky around them, the Dark beings understood where they were. They saw a mountainous structure before them. Its bulbous towers of tzoharian Light pierced their eyes so that they could barely make out the army standing at its base. They had been portaled directly to the gates of Tartarus.

"Now!!" With obus of lavender Light rocketing energy towards the Dark horde, Michael, the Archangel–his enormous Dao Lightblade, Morthwyl, in hand–roared his command as every available elohim from his Order began galloping towards the stunned Legion. Akalian and his garrison led the charge as they collided with the first wave of shrieking devils who barely had time to summon their weapons. Michael's orders were clear: if you can't bind them, destroy them.

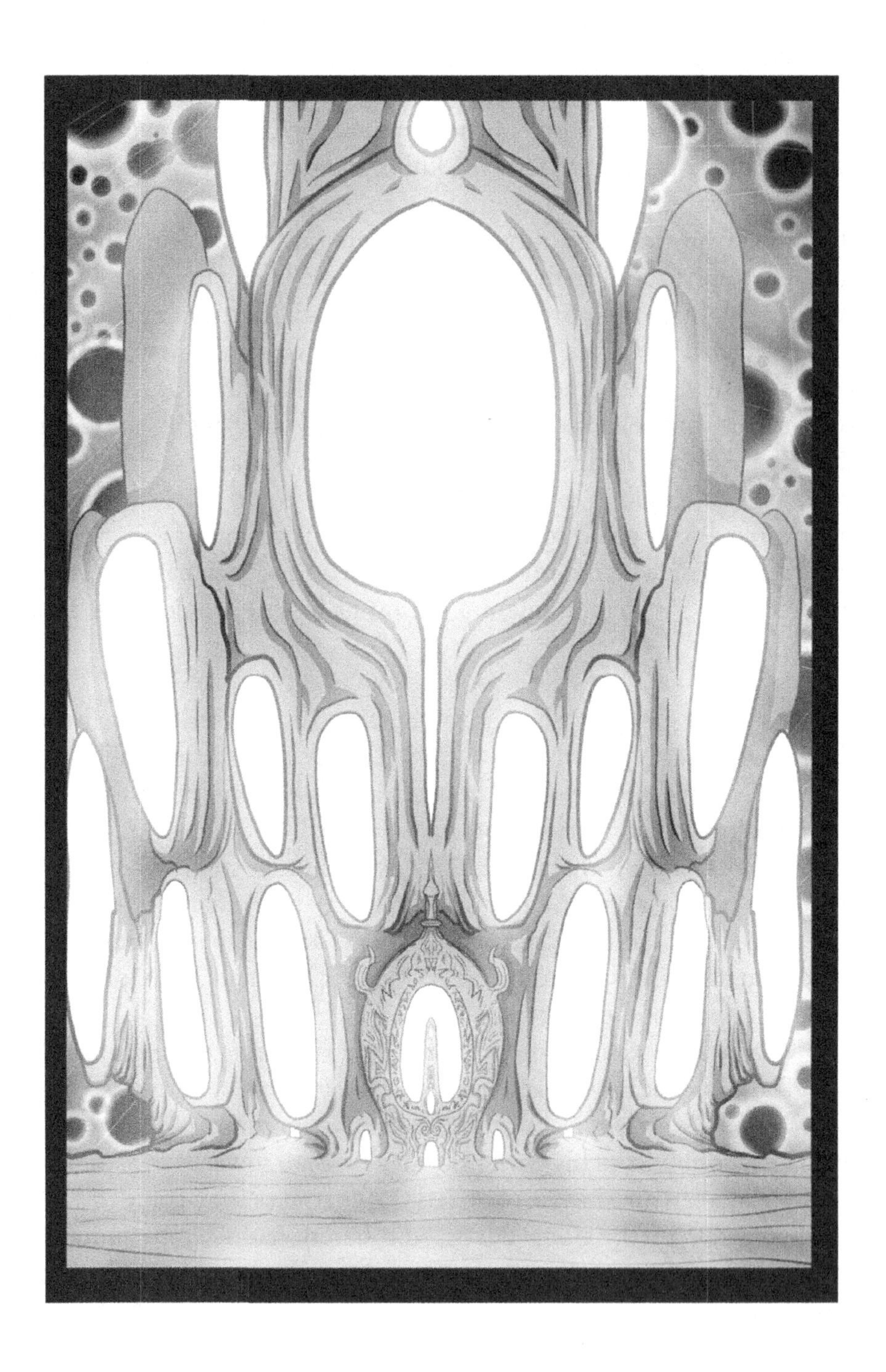

If only they could have matched a Pentaclegate with every member of Legion, placing each one in a tomb inside of Tartarus, but that kind of precision took entirely too much power–much more than they had at such short notice. Also, there was no way to determine which Legionnaire would fall through which Pentaclegate, making it impossible to account for the varying power levels of each Dark elohim.

Out of all of Legion, sights were set on one in particular: its leader. The problem was that Akalian couldn't pinpoint Xexxus anywhere in this sea of insidiousness.

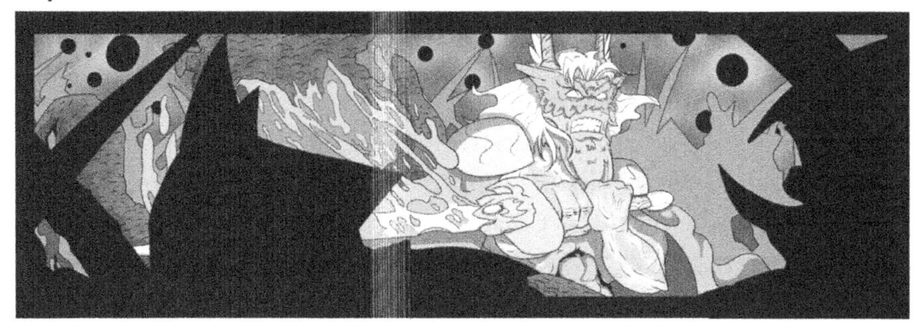

*He won't get away this time!* Akalian declared to himself as Karaydin sliced through the skull of a serpentine warrior, righteous anger raging inside of him. A Shadowblade stabbed at the Power's face with lightning speed, but Akalian caught the sword with a hand coated in tzoharian Light. He ripped it away from its Dark owner, and smashed the hilt into his foe's mouth, tearing it through the other side of the fallen elohim's head. Two more Shadowblades came crashing down upon the Chief Power from the same direction as he swung Karaydin upwards, snapping the blackened steel to pieces. In a blur, Akalian followed through, whirling the mighty Lightblade through the faces of the malevolent elohim in one commanding blow. The Head of Micheal's Order was not interested in binding anyone this time. Akalian didn't know what happened to Dark elohim once they left this form, and neither did he care, for they had made their choice eons ago and caused destruction ever since. Whatever awaited them beyond this form was no more than they deserved.

"Akalian..." The voice was a whisper inside the Power's mind, but he heard it as clearly as if someone was standing beside him. More importantly though, he *felt* it. His heart sank into his stomach and he froze in his tracks. The voice was distorted, to be sure, but he knew it as well as he knew his own. Regaining his bearings, Akalian spun around, Karaydin raised high. Everything was a confusing haze of warring savagery tumbling around on itself in an overwhelming sensation of vertigo. He wasn't sure if this reaction was the result of the power from voice he heard or if it was his body reacting with high anxiety after hearing his brother after all these years. Akalian was tempted to stab Karaydin into the ground and hold on to help balance himself, but that would make him even more vulnerable than he already was.

"See me," the gravelly voice whispered again.

Everything stopped.

Akalian found himself alone in a green, fog-laced space. He could barely see past his hand in front of his face. He also realized that his hand should have held Karaydin, but it certainly did not.

*A spell*, he thought. *Clearly, this is–*

"Hello, brother." The Dark voice was ten paces away from him now. Akalian turned to face what once had been his most beloved sibling in all the cosmos, the one being who was of his own flesh. However, this aged and calloused figure was not something he recognized. Gone was the heroic elohim of Light, draped in silky green and white robes. He was replaced with a Dark creature of the night, covered in tough, scaley, stone-like skin. The figure wore a long bat wing-like cape protruding from his shoulders and falling to the sticky ground at his taloned feet. Instead of four beautiful featherfur membranes with glistening mint-green wingfeathers sprouting from the back of his head, there were now calloused, bone-like horns forming an insidious crown crudely protruding from his brow. It was as if Baetiel's face had been inverted–his face now where the back of his head had been.

Akalian's initial reaction was that of sorrowful horror. He fought the urge to run and embrace his brother in an attempt to cure whatever curse was plaguing him. Tears began to flow freely down his crested owl-like cheeks. However, within a moment, the sorrow turned into a white-hot rage burning in the pit of his stomach. The realization of what this cursed *thing* had done to so many followers of the King–elohim he loved, people he swore to protect–filled him with a searing, righteous anger.

"What have you become?" Akalian sneered in disgust.

"What I wanted to become," Xexxus answered boldly. "Something *greater* than *he* could have ever intended."

Akalian boiled even more.

Back on the battlefield of Tartarus, Willow blocked the axe of a Legionnaire with his tzoharian laced arm and, pointing his other arm at his foe, fired a laser-sharp Light-beam towards its head, severing the gnarled skull from its body. The choirmite immediately flew vertically into the sky above the battle, looking to regroup with at least one of his siblings. He could locate all of them fairly quickly–all of them except Akalian. Willow's heart sank the second he realized that not only was Akalian missing, but also the King of Legion was nowhere in sight.

The choirmite rocketed towards Moriel, who had just run two Dark elohim through with one of his cup hilt, broad swords, Illeti.

"Moriel! Akalian and Xexxus are both missing from the battlefield!" Willow shouted as he flew around the Messenger Power.

"It's as we anticipated!" Moriel shouted in return. "We must find Michael!"

Back in the foggy void, Akalian shouted at his former brother.

"Greater??" Akalian questioned in disbelief. "You think *this* is greater?"

Xexxus stretched out his leathery arms in reply.

"The power gifted to me by The Dark Father is more extraordinary than I could have imagined, Akalian. The freedom found in the Dark, in Chaos, is beyond blissful. You have no idea, my brother." The King of Legion's expression was now almost *kind.* "I have longed for you to join me once again. I've missed you...so very much."

Akalian was taken aback by this. At this moment, he didn't see or hear a diabolical ruler of the Dark. He saw his beloved brother pleading to be loved by him once more. He felt the loneliness in Xexxus' voice, the sorrow of losing the intimate relationship that they once shared. Tears of misery began to flow freely from Akalian's eyes as Xexxus stretched out his cracked and calloused hand toward his brother.

"We can find a greater purpose together. This power can be yours as well if you join me, Akalian. Please."

*Please?* There was desperation in Xexxus' voice, a deep longing for the restoration of their bond. Akalian knew that longing all too well. Xexxus continued as tears now formed in his eyes.

"Please join me, brother. You don't have to follow this king anymore. He has enslaved your mind, and I can help you free it." These words were genuine. Xexxus really believed what he was saying. "It was painful at first, but once I realized how blind I was, the freedom outweighed the grief. There is a *new* world coming. A world with *real* choice and genuine freedom. Not this facade...this prison of Light and order." Xexxus was pleading with all his might, not out of a lust for power but out of longing for his brother to join him. "In Endless Night, you can be whatever you want. I *want* you with me."

"I...I don't..." Akalian stuttered.

"We belong together, you and I. From the very beginning, we were bound together. Let us be bound together once more."

*"No,"* came a voice from behind Akalian. Upon hearing it, Akalian's heart leapt.

"To get to *him*, you have to go through *us,"* Willow growled as he and Moriel stepped between the Chief Power and his former brother.

"You cannot claim him." Moriel grimaced as Illeti shimmered in the green fog.

"Is this what you want, Akalian?" Xexxus asked, ignoring the two intruders, his teary eyes focused on his brother.

This ignited a fire within Akalian that awakened him to the reality of the situation.

"What *I* want?" Akalian saw red. "What I want died *long* ago. *You* did that!" he shouted in righteous rage. *"This* is who I am. I've chosen my path, just as you have chosen yours." Xexxus' expression immediately transformed from sorrowful desperation to cold and emotionless.

"So mote it be, oh Power of Light." Xexxus' voice was more hollow and haunting than ever.

"Enough mind games!!" echoed Michael's voice. "Raziel! Break through!" At that, the foggy space began to tear open, revealing the battlefield around the group of elohim. Michael and Raziel burst through the spell, firing tzoharian Light at the King of Legion. Moriel and Willow joined them while Akalian froze in his emotions. Xexxus immediately formed a green necroshield to block their Light, but it wouldn't hold for long, and the Dark being knew it. But just as Xexxus' shield began to weaken, an enormous, slimy, yellow orb engulfed the King of Legion.

"NO!!" Michael shouted.

A yellow necroshield shot up from the ground in front of Xexxus' protective orb. Behind the shield peered a multitude of glowing yellow, bulbous eyes shrouded by an enormous leathery cloak, slime-leaking tentacles protruding from underneath it.

"Hastur!?" Michael bellowed in surprise.

"Apologies, Michael." The Yellow King's slithery voice hissed. "But we have plans for this one." Two tentacles suddenly smacked together, creating a mighty blast that violently collided with Michael and his elohim, sending them flying backward onto the ground. By the time the Archangel and his Powers gathered themselves, Hastur and Xexxus were nowhere to be found.

Hours later, in the Corporeum Realm, the sun was rising off the horizon. Moriel and Akalian stood unseen, watching The Word Become Flesh comfort the man whom Xexxus once possessed. Yeshua's disciples were feeding the people who had elected to stay after the previous events in the night. The mood was somber but peaceful. There was even some laughter beginning to emerge.

"No matter what The Dark Kingdom does to corrupt the Adamians, his patience and love find a new way to undo it," Moriel said.

"It truly is phenomenal." Akalian agreed. "I wish Baetiel had acknowledged that love and patience. Maybe then...maybe things would be different." Moriel turned to his brother. Grief filled his expression.

"I'm sorry you have to bear this burden." Moriel's compassion was formidable. "I see how painful it is for you and I...I wish I could take it from you. But all I can do is remain by your side as you walk through it. Know that I will never leave you, and I will do everything I can to help guide you."

"Thank you, brother," Akalian replied. "If you all hadn't been there, I don't know what would've happened. And that frightens me more than anything."

"I know what would've happened," Moriel proudly proclaimed. "You would have stood against him, and you would have fought the Dark to whatever end came to pass. That's who you are, Akalian. You aren't defined by your pain, but by the love that drives you to endure it."

Something was happening. Akalian didn't remember this conversation occurring in such a way. He now remembered that they *never* went to the tombs of the Gadarenes. They led an effort to immediately find leads on where Hastur had taken Xexxus, and this moment never happened in history.

Akalian backed away from Moriel as this realization began to solidify in his mind. Before the Chief Power's eyes, a Light overtook his brother. Where Moriel once was, now stood King Yahweh, not as a being of Light as before, but as the Transfigured Adamian form he had been for thousands of years.

Warm tears of joy flowed from Akalian's eyes as his King walked over and embraced him.

"Now that you have remembered where your true strength lies..." Yahweh pulled back, faced the Chief Power, and gave him a playful smirk. "Go and fight."

Everything was immediately engulfed in white, and Akalian woke up as if lost in an age-long nightmare.

"Come slave...let us travel to The Dreamlands and beyond." The Dark Moriel's twisted finger touched Akalian's forehead as he still lay crumpled on the Labyrinth's center room floor.

"NO!" Akalian shouted as he quickly raised his arm toward the beast, blasting white, hot Light from his hand. The Dark being flew across the room, slammed into the Sapient Stone, and landed hard on the disgusting ground.

"I'm not your slave. Nor will I become one." Akalian stood up and faced his would-be captor, now knowing who this was before him. "I am Akalian, a son of Yahweh: King of Ages, Chief Power of the Order of Michael of the Septum Dei, Guardian of The White Throne. And I do not answer to you, *Shadow Wurm!!*

The Dark figure began to shake violently. Green and black slime vomited through mangled, yellow fangs as its mouth began to rip forward, producing countless tentacled appendages. Eyes popped out of its skull like pustules erupting from someone's skin.

"Ymg' ephnaiah megapah' mgehye!!!!" The putrid R'lyehian curses poured from the Shadow Wurm's mouth as this Dark being, and everything around it was pierced with tzoharian Light. The beast let out a final screeching howl as Akalian found his head being released from a suction appendage. The Chief Power let out an agonizing scream; the pain was like having a limb ripped from his body.

As if emerging from a dream within a dream, Akalian exploded forth from the tight grip of a disgusting tentacle–charred bits of the horrible appendage scattered across the center chamber of the Labyrinth. The slime covered Power slammed hard onto the ground, charred tentacle pieces squished and splattered as they landed around him. Akalian leapt to his feet and quickly summoned Karaydin into his outstretched hand.

"Unbind him, you Wurm!" Akalian roared.

In an instant, the Power had surveyed the entire room. It was *much* darker than when he and Moriel first entered. He couldn't tell if they had entered on their own or if they had been brought here, for he couldn't determine *when* the Shadow Wurm had claimed them. The Shard of the Sapient Stone was still glowing green in the center of the room, but surrounding it–in almost every inch of this horrid space–was the slithering, vile, and enormously monstrous Golge. Clutched in one of her odious tentacles was Moriel, imprisoned with a suction appendage tightly gripped to the Messenger's head.

"You may have escaped my clutches, little angel," Golge bellowed telepathically. "But your pathetic crusade ends here!!"

# CHAPTER TWENTY THREE

## - SOMETHING WICKED -

"It's a Shard of the Sapient Stone..." Moriel gasped. In the center of the arena-sized room, suspended six feet from the ground and encased in a glowing green, ghostly shield, was a large Shard—taller than either elohim—of the Aeturnum Stone of Possibility. "If a Shard of the Sapient Stone is being used to fuel this possession...we may be too late. I don't know if we can stop this, Akalian."

Suddenly, Moriel knew something was wrong. Yes, the Sapient Stone was beyond troubling, but the Messenger felt a more profound, more intimate disturbance within his essence. Something sinister was slithering around inside his mind. Moriel didn't know when the Shadow Wurm had claimed them, but the Messenger Power knew they would surely be doomed if he didn't figure something out soon.

"Oh, you cannot stop this, my dear brother, no matter what you do." The voice behind Moriel was one he hadn't heard for eons, and it sent chills down his spine, giving rise to action. The Messenger summoned his obus and spun around, Illeti prepared to strike.

"What have you done with Akalian!? Speak now, or I will strike you down where you stand!" Moriel shouted. Before him stood the slender, sagging, grotesque abomination of Lilith, who beamed a twisted smile at her former brother.

"You always did have a way with words, my sweet," she said, her tone almost melodic. Moriel barely heard the words exiting Lilith's mouth as one of his obus shot across the room, blasting Heavenly Light at the gaping hole where her eyes once were. The Queen of The Wild Winds held up her hand, blocking the orb's beam with little effort. "Please, Moriel. As noble as this is, you couldn't defeat me even if you tried your *very* best. I'm not here to harm you."

The Messenger heard genuineness in her voice. Unfortunately, he also knew she was right. The Darkness had indeed given Lilith enormous amounts of power. Moriel could feel it, but he also sensed something else. She could have easily destroyed him while his back was turned mere moments ago, and what stayed her hand was more than just ego. Lilith had a message to deliver.

"Then why *are* you here?" Moriel lowered his defenses cautiously.

"I'm bored, mostly," Lilith answered in a blasé fashion, turning her attention from him and walking toward the Sapient Stone.

"It's Midsummer's Eve. Isn't there a *sacrifice* you need to be attending?" Moriel's words were as sharp as a knife.

"Oh, there is." She replied. "You *do* know that my Wurm has you and your dense Chief Power under its mind control, don't you?"

"I suspect that's why I'm seeing you. It knows my vulnerabilities."

"Oh, I'm real, my pet. And how *precious* to know that I am your vulnerability." Pride in her victory oozed out of Lilith as she spoke. Moriel winced at her response. "Observe." The Sister of Baal turned away from the Shard and Moriel. Sweeping her hand in one slow motion before her, she revealed the true nature of the Messenger Power's situation.

While what appeared before Moriel and Lilith did not surprise him, he was unprepared for the scope of the monstrous sight he beheld. Almost every inch of the Labyrinth's center chamber was covered in the cruel, slithering body of the Shadow Wurm, Golge. Her monstrous coils heavily shadowed the once brightly-lit green room. Through the darkness, Moriel saw the Shard's light bouncing off two figures trapped in Golge's tentacles. Moriel and Akalian were both motionless in the Wurm's ghoulish prison, her suction appendages engulfing each of their heads. He wondered what horrors Akalian was being subjected to at this moment. The Messenger walked forward to join Lilith as she watched Golge proudly, knowing that this legendary beast was her slave to control.

"Lilith," Moriel boldly said as he turned to face her. *"Why* are you here?" His former sister took a deep breath and lowered her head.

"Because I hate your king. But not *you.*" This response took Moriel aback. Lilith turned towards the Messenger, her faceless void vacantly staring through him, yet Moriel could feel her honesty. "You know what will happen if you stay here. I've foreseen it, just as I'm sure *you* have. There's no need to put yourself through this."

"It's not about *me,* Lilith." Moriel declared. "That's what *you* never understood." The High Sister of Baal let out a howling cackle.

"How regal!" she mocked. "I'd admire you if you weren't so foolish with your loyalties." Lilith composed herself and faced Moriel, her back towards the Wurm and her captives. "I'm here to warn you, Moriel. I'm here to show pity on you, for old time's sake. Don't stay. You're right, I am to be present at a sacrifice tonight–*this* sacrifice. The Fellowship has been overseeing the boy's possession for quite some time now. How do you think Xexxus even got a hold of an Aeturnum Shard or Minos' Labyrinth? He is quite powerful but not as clever as he lets on. Certainly not clever or powerful enough to locate one of the Shards and hold it at bay."

The High Sister of Baal caressed Moriel's cheek. He recoiled slightly from her clammy, cold skin.

"I am saying," she went on, "the work that's been completed here cannot be undone. The amount of power rooted inside this boy is now beyond your control. The message you carry is a *powerful* one, but not powerful enough to save him. Even if Xexxus is removed, it matters not."

"We'll see, won't we?" Moriel sneered.

"Is that *playfulness* I sense?" Lilith dramatically clutched her figurative pearls. "My, my, it seems there might be some personality in there after all!" Lilith chuckled as she circled the Messenger like a shark preparing to strike. "This is your last chance, Moriel. Join me, I beg of you. After this, it will be too late..." The Sister of Baal gently reached her hand out from behind Moriel and caressed his cheek once more while leaning in close with a breathy whisper. "Too late for *us.*"

Moriel calmly walked away from her foul, unwanted closeness and turned to face her in disgust. "What you wanted us to be is never going to happen, Lilith. I will *never* join you." The Dark being backed away, deeply offended at Moriel's words. He thought this reaction

was so foolishly ignorant. After all this time, how could she expect him to say yes to her?

*This is what the Darkness does to a creature,* he thought to himself. *It strips away all reasonable thought and replaces it with a harmful, selfish logic that only produces a cycle of self-destruction.*

"A fool to the end," Lilith hissed. "So mote it be. I'll show you what your foolishness will lead to." In a sudden, twitchy motion, the Queen of Dudael blew a kiss toward the Messenger Power, its energy hitting Moriel like a wall of stone. Immediately, he found himself surrounded by thousands of Visions crashing into one another. It was overwhelming. Moriel could barely distinguish what he saw: familiar Age End flashes of utter destruction intermingled with newer ones he couldn't comprehend. However, through it all, Moriel kept getting horrifying flashes of Jonathan as The Manking figure possessed by whatever Dark Master was behind all this. Could what Lilith said be true? *Is it too late, no matter what?*

**"Unbind him you Wurm!!"**

Moriel suddenly felt himself gasping for air through the hellish muck left behind from the now-severed suction appendage Akalian had peeled from his head. As Akalian flew around the center chamber, hacking and blasting Golge's ghoulish tendrils, the Messenger formed an obu between him and the Shadow Wurm's coils and blasted his way out of the slimy prison. Golge let out a horrendous howl from the

pain, and Akalian took advantage of this opportunity. The Chief Power rocketed towards the Wurm's enormous head and, with one mighty swing, separated the repulsive cranium from its writhing and twisting body.

All at once, the vastness of Golge collapsed, lifeless on the chamber floor, splashing in her own filth. Akalian rushed over to help his brother out of the puddle of black and green slime he had landed in upon being released from the Wurm's grasp.

"Are you alright, brother?" Akalian asked, taking Moriel's arm and pulling him up.

"No physical damage that I can tell. What about you?

"I'm fine...more than fine, actually," the Chief Power admitted with a slight smile. "Something happened to me in there, Moriel. Even though my identity was slipping away from me inside the Wurm's facade, I'm afraid it's been slipping away from me in reality as well. In the black void of that beast's spell, the King found me and reminded me not only who I am but to whom I belong." At this, Akalian wrapped his mighty arms around his brother as though he hadn't seen him in eons. An overwhelming sensation of thankfulness washed over Moriel. The nightmarish surroundings momentarily faded as he returned the embrace with full force, tears rolling down his featherfured cheeks. He had longed for this moment for millennia. He had wanted peace for Akalian for so long, and it seemed as though the Chief Power had finally found it.

"You've stood by me in my darkest of hours," Akalian professed as he released Moriel from his embrace. "The countless times I questioned my worth and ability to go on, sinking further into a pit of despair, you've always been there to pull me out of it again." The Messenger Power beamed a great smile.

"And I'll always be there to do that," Moriel assured his brother, "You can count on it."

Suddenly, Akalian was ripped away from his brother and thrown into the air. Moriel leapt backward, flipping out of the way and narrowly missing being crushed by a rushing tentacle. Gaining his composure, Moriel summoned his Illeti blades and multiple obus, ready for battle. The Messenger Power was in awe of the horror he saw before him. Golge had not only regrown her head but two additional ones as well. The other two were of the same size as their original, but while Golge's main head had multiple eyes and tendrils, these ghoulish copies only had giant, snarly mouths with enormous teeth chomping at Akalian, who was slicing with Karaydin and frantically dodging flailing appendages.

One of Golge's bastard heads lunged toward Moriel but was quickly decapitated it.

"Moriel, find it's heart!!" the Chief Power shouted.

*Right!* Moriel thought to himself. There was only one way to destroy a Shadow Wurm: fatally puncture its heart. As Akalian kept Golge busy, the Messenger scanned the chamber as best he could. It was heavily shadowed, and the Wurm took up most of the space, leaving little room to see past its powerful body. Golge's heart could indeed be hidden anywhere in the Labyrinth, but the likelihood of it being in the center chamber was high. Not only was this clearly where the Wurm had been nesting, but the history of this room was so evil and haunted that it would provide the perfect protection and the chance to feed on the horrible memories of this place. Moriel knew the heart of a Shadow Wurm could consume Dark power just by being in its presence.

"A little swiftness would be most appreciated!" Akalian yelled as a large tendril smacked him, sending him flying across the entire length of the chamber.

"Patience, my friend!" Moriel replied. Moriel now knew that there was no way he could locate the heart by just using his eyes. Although they held much power, the Darkness' shadows were too thick here. One of the Messenger's obus severed a suction appendage tentacle in half as it attempted to close in on the elohim. Moriel knew they did not have much time. He would have to extend his essence and enter the astral plane. As dangerous as this was on a regular occasion, it was almost a direct invitation for possession or imprisonment when used inside the Kingdom of Endless Night. It was especially dangerous if Lilith was near, which he assumed she still was. Regardless, he felt he had no choice.

"There is a time for patience, Moriel, but now is *not it!!*" Akalian shouted as he wrestled with an enormous tentacle while decapitating another head.

*King Yahweh, protect me,* the Messenger pleaded. Moriel calmed his mind and closed his eyes. The obus would give him the protection he needed for now. He felt his astral form slip away from his body and float upward toward the center of the chamber. He reached out with all his senses to every inch of the room. Moriel knew that the longer he stayed in this state, the more vulnerable he would be to an attack from Golge, and from the awful memories of this place. Countless men and women were slaughtered here savagely, and the lingering memories of those events would cause Moriel excruciating pain. Wincing through malevolent Visions of cannibalistic rituals, the Messenger was now astrally touching everything in the chamber. He could feel the Dark power flowing towards one specific place above them. That was it. The heart was hidden well, for the shadows were thickest in the far upper corner of the chamber.

"Gotcha," Moriel said aloud with a smirk.

Suddenly, the skeletal face of Jonathan Young trapped inside Xexxus' throne room flooded Moriel's mind. He felt like he could almost reach out and touch the boy.

*Jonathan...*Moriel thought to himself in horror as he saw the heavily abused and frail form of Jonathan's soul floating inside his necroplasmic prison. *My boy...we're coming for you!*

*"Moriel!!"* The Messenger's astral form immediately returned to his body, and he opened his eyes to find Akalian completely

engulfed by Golge's tentacles. The monster's jaw was opened wide about to close around his brother's head. Moriel shot up into the darkness of the chamber, dodging Golge's slithering and twisting limbs and began firing obus of tzoharian Light all around him. To anyone else, it would have looked like the elohim was firing blindly into the shadows, but Moriel knew precisely what he was doing now. With a swift forward motion, the Messenger slammed his outstretched arms together. All four orbs merged into one massive, blinding ball of Light. For a brief moment, Moriel saw the repulsive sack clinging to the wall from a sticky black necroplasmic web. The heart of Golge was as vast as it was sickening. In a sudden burst of white, holy flame, the large obu engulfed the Wurm's Dark heart, destroying every trace of its nauseating existence.

Golge's head exploded just as its yellow, bile-covered teeth were closing on Akalian's neck. The Wurm's horrid body bubbled and popped. Greenish-black pus and blood flooded the chamber as Golge, the Shadow Wurm, was entirely ripped apart and her pieces flung across the room in all directions.

For a moment, all was quiet. Nothing moved within the inner chamber of Minos' Labyrinth. Every inch of the room was covered in ghoulish guts and putrid liquids. Battered mounds of Wurmflesh covered the floor and walls. Only the Shard of the Sapient Stone was seemingly untouched. Golge's debris had already melted away from its surface due to the heat permeating inside the Stone.

"Ugh..." Akalian groaned as he used Karaydin to help lift himself from under a hunk of Golge's jaw. He was thankful the teeth didn't pierce his head when the beast exploded. Moriel emerged from a large piece of tentacle a few yards away. The blast from the heart had sent him flying through the air, and he had landed underneath the heinous debris. Both elohim were covered from head to taloned toe in revolting guts.

"We've had better days, I think," Moriel said dryly as he stood there covered in eldritch muck.

"Oh, I don't know," Akalian replied playfully. "At least we aren't the ones whose detonated remains currently decorate a haunted labyrinth chamber."

"True. What a charmed life we live." At this, both elohim laughed together. But just as they started to relax in their brief moment of lightheartedness, a low rumbling began to shake the walls of the Labyrinth.

"Yeah, this seems about right," Akalian said exasperatedly.

"The power released from Golge's destruction must have damaged the integrity of the Labyrinth," Moriel exclaimed. The shaking became more violent, and cracks started to form on the chamber walls. "We have to get out of here."

"What are we going to do about this Shard?"

"I'm afraid there's not much we *can* do at the moment. Let's hope it will exit his essence when we exorcise Xexxus," Moriel replied. "Now let's focus on getting to the castle. I know where Jonathan is." Moriel immediately took flight with Akalian following behind him. As they lifted, the ground below them broke apart. The entire Labyrinth was caving in and falling into a black void beneath them.

As they neared the top of the chamber, Moriel shot three obus from his taloned fingers towards the roof. They erupted upon impact and instantly disintegrated the ceiling. Akalian gave one last look below them, and saw the Shard of the Sapient Stone falling into the blackness of the void with Golge's remains and the demolished Labyrinth of Minos.

The two elohim took to the misty, lime-green sky with wings outstretched and Lightblades drawn in anticipation of an aerial attack. But there was nothing. It was deathly quiet. There was no wind. There was no sound whatsoever. Akalian sped up next to his brother.

"You said you *know* where Jonathan is?" He asked in anticipation.

"When I was in astral form looking for Golge's heart, his soul appeared before me, trapped in a necroplasmic prison. I briefly saw his surroundings, and it appears he's in Xexxus' throne room."

"Did you see how to get to his Castle?" Akalian asked hopefully.

"Unfortunately, no. But I have a plan for when we find it," Moriel boldly stated. Suddenly a spine-chilling howl pierced the green sky, followed by a multitude of bawls and roars that sounded like the combination of a wolf, hyena, and a lion. The two elohim stopped mid-air.

"We have to find a place to land. And *fast.*" Akalian whispered. Moriel nodded in agreement, for they both knew what horrible creatures had made those sounds. They certainly didn't want to deal with Night Gaunts if they didn't have to. The two Powers quickly and silently descended, hoping to land on solid ground. As if on cue, the mist parted, and up ahead of them they saw a clearing that led into a twistedly gnarled forest.

"Alright, so we know the skies are being watched," Akalian said as they landed. "It appears as though this is our only path forward."

"Why do I get the feeling that we are being *guided?"* Moriel asked suspiciously.

"I'm sure we *are,"* Akalian replied. "But the question is, by whom? The King or Xexxus?"

Moriel took this opportunity to update his brother on current events.

"Speaking of which. When we were under Golge's spell, I was visited...by Lilith."

*"What?* Was she *real?"*

"I believe so," Moriel replied. "It seemed as though she controlled the Wurm. What is more troubling, though, is that she took ownership of this possession—or at least partial ownership. And Jonathan is meant to be a part of *her* Midsummer's Eve sacrifice."

"So Xexxus is just a puppet for the Whore of Babylon," Akalian declared with a bit of amusement in his voice.

"And he's not the only one..."

A pitch-black arrow made of bone pierced the soggy, necroplasmic ground at the elohim's feet. Four more arrows flew at the two powers simultaneously, one grazing the feathers atop Akalian's head. More arrows came, but Moriel and Akalian had their Lightblades and obus ready this time. In the twisted trees ahead, they saw their hairy assailants gazing at them with yellow eyes.

"Se'irim," Akalian grimaced. “I hate these things." He took two broad steps forward and landed in an offensive power stance, holding Karaydin in front of him. Moriel took his place beside Akalian, with Illeti drawn at both sides, obus blasting every arrow that came near the two towering elohim. Akalian gave a mighty roar. "Come out from the shadows, you bastard beasts! My blade thirsts for you."

# CHAPTER TWENTY FOUR

## - FUEL FOR THE FIRE -

*"Watch them!"* Obadiah shouted back at Bouchard as he ran out the front door of Waverly Hall at Hillcrest Sanitarium. Obadiah had experienced many terrifying things in his life, but what he had just witnessed might have been the worst.

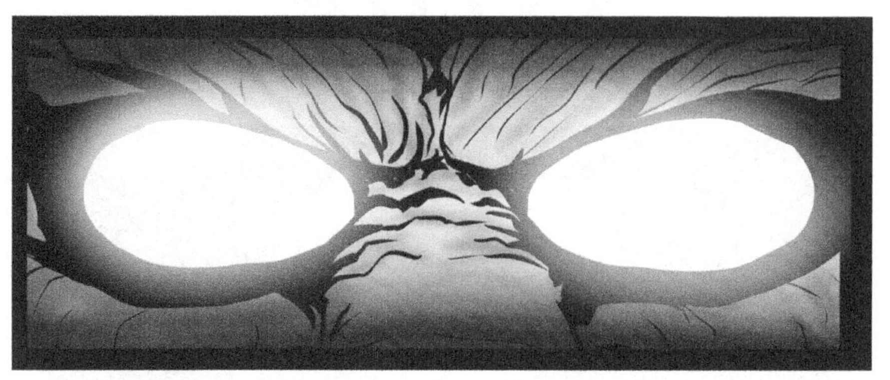

*That boy's eyes,* he thought to himself while running out into the night air. *Those horrible eyes.*

Obadiah had never felt absolutely loathed like that before. It was as if the child was entirely overtaken by *hate* personified. Even coming face to face with Agatha–the Stick Queen herself–hadn't had this effect on him. Obadiah was a brave man who didn't rattle easily, but the hate-filled, ghoulish-green gaze of Jonathan Young made him freeze in fear as though Obadiah were a child seeing the monster in his closet for the first time. He hated himself for allowing that fear to win the moment. If he had been able to prevent his terror from taking over, Mattia wouldn't still be alone with that *thing.*

*Snap out of it!* He exclaimed to himself. *You have to get a grip here. Focus on the task at hand.* The former Cleric recovered quickly from his self-chastisement and circled around the building at a sprint.

*Come on, please still be there,* Obadiah pleaded as he ran. He had been gone for over a decade, and clearly, there had been a lot of remodeling done at Hillcrest. The last time Obadiah was here, the parking garage for the sky-vehicles was underneath the Sanitarium. He was hoping that hadn't changed. Obadiah spotted the lone keypad monitor up ahead and rejoiced.

"YES!" he shouted.

Not only was the keypad monitor still there, but it looked like the exact same model as years before, and he knew how to override it. Obadiah slowed down and knelt in front of the monitor, held his finger on the top left corner of the touchscreen, and typed in the override code on the keypad: 62782099. Immediately, the screen lit up in green.

"**Override Accepted**," the speaker proclaimed, and the outside wall of the Sanitarium began to open, leading down into the garage. Obadiah raced down the ramp to the multitude of skycars, skybikes, and emergency vehicles. All at once, the memories came flooding back.

This wasn't the first time Obadiah found himself fleeing the Sanitarium like this. When he remembered that day over a decade ago, his blood boiled again.

"Obadiah, you can't be serious. This is treason," Gwen warned in an exasperating tone. "I'm obviously serious, Gwen," Obadiah replied. "Children's *lives* are on the line here. There's so much more we can be doing to save them!"

Phillip, who had remained silent for most of this meeting, finally spoke up in frustration.

"What you're asking us to do is to usurp the balance of The Code. To stage a *coup,* not only in The Gathered but also in the very foundation of The Grand Republic."

Obadiah remained calm. He had expected the push-back. When the Cleric called this secret meeting with these two in a vacant bedchamber at Waverly Hall, he knew there would be risks. Change wasn't easy, but if he knew if he could win them over, he could start making real progress for the betterment of the world.

Gwen and Phillip were his most trusted friends on the High Council, and, unlike him, they were on good terms with High Cleric Malcolm. In fact, Gwen and Phillip were both aware of Obadiah's "unknown" missions in The Grey. He'd been flying back and forth helping people in need over there for years. Phillip had even assisted on one of the housing missions, so Obadiah knew their hearts were in the right place. They weren't like Malcolm who was–as far as Obadiah could see–only in this for the power or perhaps something more diabolical. Obadiah wasn't sure. But he *was* sure that the integrity of The Republic Gathered was at stake. He went on.

"Listen to what I'm saying. The Republic Gathered is sworn to uphold the truth of all things. We are supposed to help guide the people of the world to understand that truth, and to care for those who cannot care for themselves. If there are things that could help save and guide the people of our Republic, then it is our responsibility to research those options and determine whether or not they are beneficial tools. As you know, I've been extensively working with the people of The Grey, and...I've seen things. I've witnessed things firsthand that I cannot explain. Things like exorcisms and deliverance practices–"

Phillip interrupted angrily.

"Please, Obadiah, listen to yourself–"

*"Let* me finish," Obadiah sternly said, and Phillip backed off with a twitch. "I've seen exorcisms. I've seen this process of healing *work.* The people respond to it. I...I can't understand it exactly, but that's the point. It's providing results in clients that we would give over to euthanization. Many of our lost causes would flourish under this kind of care, I'm sure of it. We just need the resources for proper research."

"Obadiah, this goes far beyond what The Code allows. It's in stark contrast to the very fabric of reason and logic. You're talking about ghosts and goblins." Gwen interjected.

"I'm aware of this...which brings me to my next point. Are we *positive* The Code is as accurate as they say?"

"Oh, for goodness' sake." Phillip scoffed.

"We don't even know much about its origins other than it was *'written by the forefathers of The Grand Republic.'* This was almost a thousand years ago. I'm asking that we reconsider some things. Things that perhaps our forefathers didn't know. I am asking only that revisions be considered for how quickly a patient is euthanized. I ask that other methods be considered in a patient's treatment plan."

"Dark Magick from The Grey," Phillip spouted. "That's what you're talking about. Look, it's one thing to go over there and bring children food or build houses. It's another thing entirely to bring their superstitious religion *here."*

"It's not Dark Magick, Phillip," Obadiah replied, attempting to keep his composure. "They're just different methods. Some are still experimental in nature, yes, but...we are more than just physical beings. You know this. Medication can only go so far, and it is failing too many clients. You know the progress that 32114 and 32117 showed before their release. They've still been benefitting from some of the practices of the Yeshuite tribes."

"This is dangerous, Obadiah," Gwen interjected. "You're the best elite Counselor we have. Second only to High Cleric Malcolm...some would even consider you his equal. But this is too much. The *other methods* you speak of destroyed the Old World. It's written in our histories."

Obadiah's frustration overflowed.

"The Yeshuite tribes have their *own* histories that add much more clarity to some major inconsistencies found in ours. Practices that saved lives aren't what brought about The Final War! What destroyed the Old World was greed and lust for power! The very same characteristics I've seen in Malcolm!" He paused, seeing the shock on their faces. Never had he lost his temper like this in front of them before, let alone spoken about the High Cleric in such a way. He knew this was no way to convince them to join his cause. Apologetically lifting his hands, he did his best to move forward with a more peaceful tone. "I'm sorry. But we're in the business of saving lives here, right? I say we use whatever methods we can to make that process as successful as possible with or without The Code, if need be."

"Well, I've heard all I need to hear, I think." Obadiah's blood ran cold. The voice behind him belonged to the High Cleric himself. He turned towards the doorway of the vacant bedchamber to see Malcolm standing there with two RPG Officers, electro-clubs drawn and charged, ready to subdue him and his fellow Clerics. Malcolm continued with a smug grin on his face.

"To say I'm disappointed in you is beyond an understatement, Obadiah. However, I cannot say I'm surprised."

"The real disappointment here is you, Malcolm," Obadiah said defiantly. "Why do you think I needed a secret meeting about this? You're beyond reason, and it's costing countless lives."

"Hardly," Malcolm replied condescendingly. "The only evidence which shows that lives are being lost are the lives *you* have damned with your *witchcraft!"*

*"Witchcraft?* What are you–" Obadiah was interrupted by Malcolm's scolding.

"Yes, your *friends* here have been informing me of your activities for quite a while now. All you have done is make your clients accomplices in practicing Dark Magick. They are being rounded up to join The Condemned in The Wastelands as we speak. As is your fate, I'm afraid."

"No!" Obadiah shouted. He flung himself toward the door, grabbed a small chair and smashed it over the head of one RPG officer while simultaneously kicking in the kneecap of the other. The renegade Cleric delivered a powerful right cross to Malcolm's face, sending the High Cleric crumbling to the floor. Obadiah didn't look back to see the reactions of Gwen or Phillip. He didn't care. Clearly, he was alone in this fight.

As he ran out of Hillcrest Sanitarium, he rounded the building, mounted his skybike and rode off into the clouds. He had intended to find his former clients, but that was all for naught. By the time he would have arrived at their homes, they and their families had already been lost to The Wastelands. He had no other choice but to flee into The Grey.

Back in Hillcrest's garage, Obadiah sat on a skybike very similar to the one he had ridden out on all those years ago. The guilt he felt over the loss of his former clients and their families was never far from his thoughts. He couldn't imagine what horrors they had experienced in The Wastelands and often wondered if any of them were still alive.

This fueled the fire of his hatred for Malcolm. Obadiah could never understand how The Coven of Endor always seemed to have endless funds. Lochardt, the leader of the Yeshuite tribes, had told him that Agatha had a backer amongst the wealthy in the Republic. Obadiah always suspected it was more than just money and wondered if Malcolm was involved. He knew Malcolm to be a power-hungry politician who would stop at nothing to secure his seat and stay "loyal" to The Code. But now he was positive that it was Malcolm who funded The Coven. If this was true, The Republic Gathered was simply a more socially acceptable arm of the most diabolical cult this world had ever seen.

"I'm coming for you, you son of a bitch," Obadiah cursed as he kicked the ignition pedal and took off toward The High Temple.

# CHAPTER TWENTY FIVE

## - THE SE'IRIM HORDE -

The two elohim ripped through the flame-infested forest, slicing and stabbing at every rag-cloaked goat-beast that pounced toward them. Neither Moriel nor Akalian were surprised when these haunted woods came alive with nightmarish fire, for these types of theatrics were always attached to a nest of Se'irim. It was intended to intimidate and discombobulate their victims, leading them toward their doom. Many times, it worked. However, it failed to suppress the might of these two Powers, who wouldn't easily give in to fear.

To be sure, Se'irim were nothing to scoff at, and Moriel and Akalian knew it. Their race infested The Dark Kingdom on a vast scale, from mere foot soldiers–as most of this brood appeared to be–to powerful Lords of The Darkness such as Baphomet, who was said to have been the first parent of their race. It was rumored that this specific goat-like appearance–taken on during a Transfectiation–was to venerate Azazel. Although Azazel was not a Se'ir, once a year, the Soma Aedrum of the Ancient World sent a goat into the wilderness–in Azazel's name–to appease the wrath of the Darkness.

"But the goat for Azazel is to be placed living before the Lord, for the taking away of sin, that it may be sent away for Azazel into the waste land." (Leviticus 16:10)

So, with every mangy head that Karaydin split in two, Akalian felt just a little bit better, knowing he was destroying an image bearer of that odious homage.

"There's a clearing just ahead!" Moriel shouted, splintering a blazing tree with a blast from his obu.

"I see it!" Akalian replied. "Remember the Kheynuy!"

"Right!" Moriel started charging a new obu. The Kheynuy were always attached to the foundations of a Se'irim nest and would appear in some form to claim their victim's astral blood, gaining more control over the unfortunate soul's will. Moriel and Akalian knew that this forest led Jonathan directly into the path of the beasts' Kheynuy, who would take a sacrifice of astral blood from the boy, giving more control over to Xexxus.

As the elohim reached the clearing, they leapt off the cliff's edge into the green mist-filled void before them, mentally preparing for the creature they were about to face.

A gigantic claw that seemed part of the cliffside itself erupted through the mist toward Akalian. The Chief Power unfurled his wings, soaring higher up and around the lethal appendage, and dodged its attack. With a ferocious swing, Akalian brought Karaydin down onto the claw, severing it from the Kheynuy monstrosity from which it belonged.

When the Kheynuy screamed in agony, its revolting breath parted the green mists, giving the two elohim a clear view of their current foe. It was literally the foundation of the fiery forest from which they had just escaped. Sticky, jet-black ooze poured from its wound, and the twisted face of the cliffside beast writhed in pain. Hot green and yellow flames spewed from its multitude of eyes and its gaping, sharp-fanged mouth.

Moriel unfurled his wings, giving him an extra dose of power and flew forward a few yards in front of the howling Kheynuy. The cliffside monster roared at the Messenger Power with fierce indignation. In return, Moriel erupted his obu's energy in a ferocious beam of blinding tzoharian Light directly into the creature's mouth.

The entire cliffside detonated. Chunks of slimy, cyclopean rock flew in all directions, while the flaming woods imploded, crashing into the crumbling Kheynuy foundation.

The two Powers landed simultaneously on the ground, a safe distance from the demonic debris.

"Well, that went well," Moriel smirked.

"Indeed. If we were hidden from the sight of the Night Gaunts before, we *certainly* aren't–" Akalian was interrupted by a thunderous roar in the darkness ahead of them, immediately followed by booming drums. The necroplasmic ground at their feet began shaking in a semi-rhythmic fashion. The elohim's gaze pierced the foggy darkness before them and saw a horde of wildly galloping Se'irim of varying sizes and shapes charging forward in the distance.

"Do you have an obu for them that won't deplete your energy?" Akalian asked. He kept his voice calm but he was obviously rattled at the sight of such a horde. "I'm thinking about the same

maneuver we used against that army of ghouls we faced a while back."

"Ah, yes. Give me a moment. I'll signal you," Moriel replied in an almost relaxed fashion. He then walked cooly behind Akalian and began charging a massive orb.

Akalian raised Karaydin with his left hand, and his right began glowing emerald green as he watched the Se'irim army charge toward them. Through the mists, he could see two huge sets of yellow eyes light up the battlefield. Akalian gaped at the two jotunn-sized Se'irim thundering behind the others running like rodents at their feet. One of the giants howled so fiercely that pain shot through Akalian's head, making the elohim wince. Flying around the gigantic Se'irim heads were flocks of Night Gaunts shrieking and snarling as their bat-like wings flapped mercilessly in the revolting air.

"Make it a quick moment!" he shouted back to Moriel nervously. With his glowing right hand, Akalian grabbed Karaydin's hilt, allowing more Light to surge through the blade, then slammed the Lightblade firmly into the putrid ground in front of him. He grimaced as black slime splashed his face. The horde was a mere two hundred yards away now and approaching fast.

"Moriel..." Akalian looked behind him at his brother, whose concentration was focused on the glowing obu that was growing rapidly in front of Moriel's illuminated and melodically twitching fingers. The Messenger was completely surrounded by the energy being pushed into the bright orb.

"You're not helping," Moriel replied agitatedly.

Akalian knelt behind his Lightblade, one hand tightly grasping Karaydin's hilt. He stretched his other arm towards his brother, palm open as if preparing to catch something.

"We will eat the flesh off of your very essence, Lightbearers!!" Akalian whipped his head around toward the charging beasts to see that the foul voice belonged to one of the Se'irim on the front line. They were less than twenty feet away.

"MORIEL!!"

"NOW!" Moriel yelled as the enormous obu exploded forward into Akalian's extended palm. The energy surged through the mighty elohim, funneling through the hand that gripped Karaydin, and exited the blade of the blazing longsword, flooding onto the Se'irim that were now mere inches from where Akalian knelt.

The blinding blast of Light covered the entire battlefield in front of the elohim. From the cursed ground to the heights of the foggy clouds above, every fallen beast was engulfed in the white flames of the Tzohar.

As the Light from Karaydin began to fade, they could see through the decay scented smoke billowing throughout the field. One of the giant Se'irim–half-mangled and completely burnt–was charging toward Akalian, holding an enormous spear in front of it.

Moriel summoned his twin blades, Illeti, and sprinted toward Akalian. As he reached his brother, Moriel stepped onto his bent back and jumped off toward the giant. At the same time Akalian leapt from the ground, giving the Messenger a mighty boost into the air. Swinging Illeti in a scissor motion, Moriel slashed through the Se'ir's outstretched spear then carved the twin Lightblades into the giant's skull, slicing its head into four quarters. The Messenger Power landed on the ground as the Se'ir's lifeless body fell onto a pile of charred goat-beast corpses beside him.

Walking up to Moriel's side, Akalian looked all around them, and saw only burnt, steaming lifelessness.

"Works every time," he grunted with a slight chuckle.

"I need to rest, brother," Moriel said breathlessly. "If only for a moment or two, just to regain my strength."

The two elohim walked ahead about twenty yards and took cover under the dead husk of the other giant Se'ir. Both hoped they would spot Xexxus' fortress soon. Time was running short.

From a bright green obu, Xexxus watched the elohim's progress, studying their moves and preparing for their arrival. The former King of Legion leaned back in his Necrom Stone throne, very pleased with himself and with the events of the evening.

"The Wraiths await your command, my Lord." The ghoulish vizier slithered through the green mist around the giant throne, hoping this news would bring her favor in her master's sight.

"Good, Yagorath." The booming voice of Xexxus echoed throughout the cavernous chamber. He arose from his throne, crossed the stalagmite-infested dais, and descended the wide steps down to his prized possession. Jonathan floated in the necroplasmic cell, attempting not to move or wear any expression that would trigger his captor to torture him. However, Xexxus smiled somberly this time, not at the boy but almost to himself, pondering what was to come.

Yagorath was afraid to speak but needed to know what to do next. The elohim had destroyed their Se'irim army in almost a single blow and had defeated the Shadow Wurm without much difficulty. That was very unexpected, at least to her. But her master seemed unphased and acted like the battle was already won. Xexxus was extremely powerful, more powerful than anything she had ever witnessed. Even when she was his Adamian sorceress in The Coven of Endor at Gadara, she was in awe of the power he commanded. Yet, the two elohim of Light closing in on the castle displayed an extreme resilience to the Dark Warriors of the Kingdom of Endless Night. Other than the wild Night Guants flying around outside, the last defense was the castle Wraiths. They were formidable beings, who could drain one's energy with a single touch.

"M...Master?" Yagorath hesitantly muttered. "...the Wraiths. What shall I tell them to do with the two elohim of Light?"

Xexxus looked down for a moment, keeping his somber demeanor. It made Yagorath nervous. She had never seen her master like this. It was almost as if he was being *sentimental.* Finally, the King of Endless Night looked back at the boy floating in the necroplasmic prison and showed his fangs.

"Tell the Wraiths to let them come."

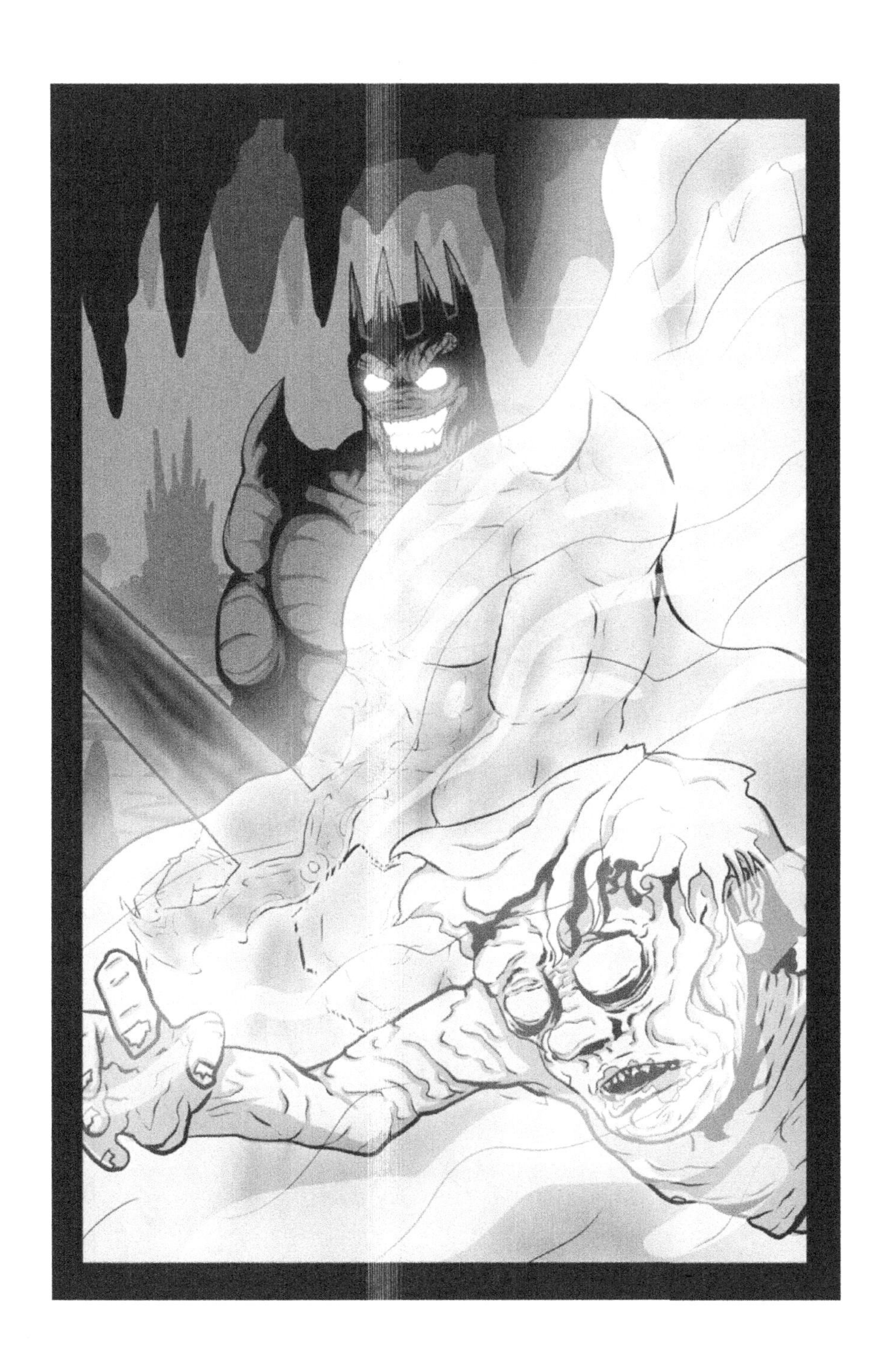

# CHAPTER TWENTY SIX

## - THE BLACK MASS -

As Bouchard watched Obadiah disappear into the night, he did exactly what his former Cleric told him to do: *watch them.* The Headminister looked down at the center screen, trying to make out an image. He could barely see anything through the static, but could have sworn he saw client 43972 floating in mid-air at one point. Bouchard disregarded that thought as quickly as it came. He had seen some fantastically terrifying things tonight, but if he let reality slip too far from him, the Headminister feared he'd be lost to madness.

*Sacrifice? Black Mass? What was happening here?* Bouchard thought. In all his days, he had never experienced anything like this. Sure, he'd heard scary stories from The Grey or The Wastelands, but that's all they were–stories. Things like that–like *this*–didn't happen in the real world. It was all superstitious nonsense. If fairytales were allowed to become reality, the world would collapse. The world *did* collapse almost 2,000 years ago! The Histories were quite clear about that. The Old World embraced unfounded belief, rejected reason and logic which gave way to madness, and was ripped apart.

But what had he just witnessed? Bouchard knew that a person's senses could be untrustworthy sometimes. A shadow here and a trick of the light there could have someone believing in all sorts of things if they allowed their minds to sway too far from reason. But what Bouchard was experiencing wasn't a trick of the light or a straying shadow. He and Obadiah had been flung down the hallway by some invisible force! That had actually happened to him. And whether he liked it or not, Bouchard was beginning to believe in things he would have committed someone for mere hours ago.

Suddenly, the Headminister heard what sounded like cattle being slaughtered from client 43972's room. A blinding white light filled Jonathan's window and Bouchard immediately focused in on the center screen. It, too, was completely white. Then it flickered and all static dissipated, revealing a clear picture. He saw Mattia standing in the middle of the room, looking completely bewildered. Mere feet away lay client 43972, unconscious on the steaming floor.

"Jonathan...sweety?" Back in Jonathan's room, Mattia's voice was trembling. It was a stark contrast to the commanding tone she had used mere moments ago, before the world went white.

The boy's screams were so horrible, unlike anything she'd ever heard. He lay there at her feet, steam rolling off of his seemingly frail, naked body. What had just happened to her? She had just reached out into the ether and asked something–someone?–to save Jonathan and...and it worked! At least, she thought it had.

Her instincts were to reach out for the boy, wrap her arms around him, and carry him out of this horrible place. But something inside of her cautioned such a motherly act.

*How do you know he's not putting on a pretense right now?* she thought. Perhaps he was counting on her doing what she longed to do, putting her in a compromising position so he could then strike a killing blow. He–or whatever was *inside* of him–was plenty powerful and she did not want to underestimate him–or it.

Instead, the Cleric carefully walked over to the door, never turning her back on the boy. She tried her best not to step on the shattered glass scattered across the floor and wake him. Mattia wasn't sure whether she should move fast or slow. It was like being trapped in a cage with a rabid dog that might be sleeping. She successfully made it to the door and opened it halfway, when she glimpsed something on the other side of the room laying at the base of the broken window. It was Obadiah's cross.

Looking down at the center screen, Bouchard was flabbergasted to see Mattia reach the door, then turn away and start walking back across the dark room. He peered down the hallway and saw her slowly creeping behind the broken window.

"What are you doing??" he whispered to himself, fighting the urge to shout down the hallway at her. Bouchard watched her walk to the far side of the window and bend down out of sight. He turned his attention back to the screen and his stomach dropped. Jonathan was nowhere to be seen.

It took Obadiah almost no time at all to reach The High Temple. Most of the usual evening traffic had been nonexistent due to the entire Grand Republic being mandated to attend a local Gathering Chapel for the Gathering Day service earlier in the evening. His only real concern was dodging the attention of an RPG Surveillance Station floating around in the sky like a bird of prey waiting to strike. Thankfully, there were still enough sky vehicles traveling the area that Obadiah's skybike didn't stand out like a sore thumb. He was thankful for these *coincidences.*

As Obadiah approached the empty Observatory level of the sprawling Temple, he could see the light from a bonfire dancing off of the high, monolith-like walls of the enclosed Labyrinth Patio. There wasn't a landing platform on this level, so he had to circle the area a couple of times to locate a surface flat enough to land. Setting the skybike on the freshly trimmed grass, Obadiah made sure he was far enough away from the Patio to not draw attention to the sound of his landing.

Getting off the bike, Obadiah realized that he was acting on pure impulse. He didn't have much of a plan other than he knew he had to stop this unholy ceremony from happening. However, there wasn't enough time to concoct something well thought-out. He knew that, at this point, the boy may not have a shot at staying alive. But Obadiah hoped to be able to give Jonathan's soul a fighting chance and save it from the torture of being permanently transformed into one of those mindless beasts. He wasn't sure what happened to the soul during a merging, but he knew if he could stop this Black Mass, then it would prevent the merging from solidifying.

The former Cleric started to run toward the Patio when he realized his satchel was a lot lighter than normal. He dug his hand into the bag only to find a large rip in the bottom. The Capurro Cross was gone. He cursed to himself, realizing it must have fallen out when the demon inside of Jonathan sent him crashing through the observation window. He said a quick prayer to whoever would hear, that Mattia would remember enough about the Yeshuite customs to know how to use it. Obadiah took off again, knowing that he had lost the best possible weapon he had.

As Obadiah drew closer to the Labyrinth Patio, he could hear Malcolm's voice echoing throughout the enclosure. He reached the edge of one of the tall, monolith walls, knelt down and peered into the opening of the Patio. Ahead of him the High Cleric faced away from Obadiah, addressing the rest of the Council.

"Tonight, we gather together to call upon The Master and his Fellowship," Malcolm bellowed. The High Cleric stood in a long white robe at the entrance to a labyrinth carved deeply into the Patio floor. A stone altar, covered in bloody hand prints stood before him. "We beseech thee, oh great spirits who transcend time. Enter our realm and dwell here with us!"

"We beseech thee!" the Council Clerics chanted in unison. Dressed in hooded robes, matching that of their leader, the High Council formed a circle around the labyrinth. Obadiah could tell the palms of their hands had been freshly sliced, confirming the source of the bloody handprints. At the center of the labyrinth, a large bonfire raged up to the heavens. Malcom continued.

"This night, we give thee a bountiful gift of fire, flesh, blood, soul, and stone!" Malcolm held up a glowing green stone blade. Obadiah froze in fear. He knew this blade all too well. This was the Blade of The Sapient Stone. It had been used in countless sacrificial ceremonies as far back as oral history went. Worst of all, the last time he'd seen it was when he and his Yeshuite raiders beheaded Agnus in The Grey. The blade belonged to The Coven of Endor. This confirmed Obadiah's worst fear: the High Council and The Coven were indeed united. Malcolm wasn't just a backer; he was a disciple.

"Bring forth the sacrifice," Malcolm commanded. Edgar, Malcolm's most loyal follower, began walking toward the High Cleric with a sleeping baby in his arms. Obadiah's stomach turned in disgust. In proper Black Mass fashion, an innocent would be slain as payment to grant the desire of the slayers. In this case, no doubt, the desire was for Jonathan to be merged with whatever pagan god they had chosen for him. But if the High Council themselves were conducting the ceremony, that meant this Black Mass was special. In reality, Obadiah couldn't imagine just *how* significant it was.

"From sky above to earth below. We steward the Blade of The Sapient Stone and remember what has passed between us and The Master. Your promises are true and just!" As Malcolm shouted like a raving madman, the baby in Edgar's arms began to wail and cry. Edgar held the infant out in front of him then knelt before Malcolm, extending the child above his head.

In this moment, Obadiah saw the unexplainable. From the heavy shadows of the Labyrinth Patio walls, two enormous figures emerged. These things couldn't possibly be human. They stood at least ten feet tall, maybe taller; Obadiah couldn't tell through the dancing shadows. One of them was covered in vines, branches, and leaves. The former Cleric thought that this being could be The Oak King himself stepped out from Old World folklore. Next to the giant's side was an equally large feminine figure who seemed to be pregnant. She had what appeared to be a tragedian mask on her face. If the first figure truly was The Oak King, then *this* enormous thing must be Gaia, the fertility goddess of Earth.

Unbeknownst to Obadiah, behind him crept another Dark figure who had slipped through the thinning veil. Had he seen her face, or lack thereof, his hair would have turned white out of fear and shock. But Lilith kept her presence masked from Obadiah as she knelt down beside him, pressed her lips close to his ear, and whispered.

"You know what you have to do," she slithered. "*He* ruined your life. *He* has ruined *so many* lives. Isn't it time he met the swift hand of justice? Isn't it time he met *death*?" As her ungodly breath entered his ear, Obadiah's rage began to rise. It was as if her words became his thoughts, filling his mind with revenge.

Lilith was cunning. She knew if she waited much longer, this fool might destroy everything they'd worked so hard for. So she was

improvising. There was something about The Black Mass that Obadiah didn't know—a fact most Adamians didn't know. The blood of an innocent was standard, but something just as powerful—perhaps more so—was a life taken out of vengeance. The hate-filled energy that flowed forth from a vengeful murder was enough to fuel a generational curse, let alone a sacrificial seal.

As if to solidify the spell, Lilith gently kissed Obadiah's head, sending his fury into overdrive. The former Cleric leapt from his hidden, crouched position and darted towards Malcolm. Before anyone could realize what was happening, Obadiah push kicked the High Cleric over the top of the blood-smeared altar and as though carried by an unseen force, he was flung into the fire pit at the center of the labyrinth. Malcolm landed, impaled by a sharp piece of wood that pinned him down in the middle of the towering flames.

Malcolm's screams were deafening as they echoed against the walls of the Labyrinth Patio, causing most of the Council to scatter. Edgar dropped the infant and lunged at Obadiah, who dove and caught the baby with lightning-fast reflexes, then barrel-rolled into Edgar's shins, tripping the large man and making him fall to the ground. Obadiah rolled to his feet with the wailing infant in his arms and kicked Edgar in the face, temporarily subduing the bald man.

Suddenly, a sharp, blinding pain screamed from Obadiah's back. Gwen had grabbed the Sapient Blade from the ground where Malcolm had dropped it and stabbed her former colleague in the shoulder blade. Phillip saw his opportunity and punched Obadiah in the jaw, sending him down to one knee, still holding the shrieking child.

"Didn't think we'd ever be seeing *you* again, old *friend*." As she uttered the word 'friend', Gwen pulled the blade out of Obadiah's back. Blood flowed from his open wound.

"Well, surprise!" Obadiah yelled. He jumped up from his kneeling position, crashing the top of his head into Phillip's chin, which knocked the corrupt Cleric unconscious and onto the Patio floor. "And don't call me *friend*."

Obadiah backed away toward the wall as Edgar scrambled to his feet. Gwen closed in on him, Sapient Blade at the ready.

"We wondered if that bitch ran off to find you," Gwen hissed in disgust. "She always did have her head up your ass. Of course, we all know you *liked* it that way."

"Shut up." Obadiah barked. "I expected this from 'tall, silent, and stupid' beside you, but how in the world did you let yourself stoop to this level, Gwen? You used to be so much more than *this*. Sacrificing *children??"*

"You have no idea what you've interrupted here, Obadiah. What we've been promised..." Gwen said angrily. "This ceremony was *years* in the making! Just give us the child. You've nowhere to go. Either way, we *will* finish this ceremony tonight."

Obadiah backed against the wall. He was thankful his adrenaline prevented him from feeling much of the pain in his shoulder blade, but he knew that wouldn't last for long. She was right. He had nowhere to go. There was no way he could make it very far with this wound and the baby, and even if he were to get away, they had thousands of children at their disposal. All they had to do was steal another baby from wherever they'd taken this one.

Suddenly, Obadiah realized he no longer heard Malcolm's screams.

At first, he figured it was because the man was dead, but then, between Edgar and Gwen, he saw a horrific, melted skeletal monstrosity quietly standing in the midst of the flames that now flickered a haunting yellow and green.

"Oh my god..." Obadiah was in shock. His two assailants followed Obadiah's gaze behind them to see their ghoulish leader standing in the fire–eye sockets filled with a glowing red hate. Malcolm's bottom jaw dropped and a horrific voice boomed throughout the Labyrinth Patio.

"The deed is done.
The bell's been rung.
The Final Herald is
Placed on high.
The Dark Eschaton is seen,
In the mists of green.
For Age End now is nigh!"

At this, the skeletal creature that once was Malcolm, collapsed into a heap. The flame returned to its normal, vibrant color, its shadow dancing upon the monolith walls of the Patio.

Gwen and Edgar stood there for a moment, completely bewildered and petrified. They had heard The Master's voice before in a secret ceremony with the Three High Sisters of Endor, but neither of them had ever experienced anything like *that*. Not only did it mean that all of this was *real*, but it meant they had somehow already succeeded. *The deed is done*, the voice said. As they wondered how, they turned around to finish dealing with their former colleague. Gwen cursed aloud. Obadiah and the child were gone.

The deed is done.
The bell's been rung.
The Final Herald is
Placed on high.

The Dark Eschaton is seen,
In the mists of green.
For Age End now is nigh!

Moriel and Akalian couldn't believe their eyes. They hadn't been walking very far since breaking for the Messenger to gather his strength. They also hadn't met any more fiends along the way. All was quiet. They could just hear the sound of their breathing and crunching footsteps. Then, as if out of nowhere, the fog lifted and they saw it.

The Castle of Endless Night was a cyclopean nightmare of slimy, black rock reaching miles above their heads. The two Powers were positive Xexxus' throne room had to be at the top of the tallest tower. The former King of Legion's hubris wouldn't allow it to be anywhere else. They were like ants compared to the monstrosity of their destination.

Akalian sighed, worried. "We don't have time for this. Jonathan will be lost before we find our way to the top."

"Also, it feels like reaching this point was entirely too easy. Akalian, it seems obvious that we're expected."

"I know...I can feel his eyes on us," Akalian said.

"Well then, we have a couple choices here," Moriel stated matter-of-factly. "We can fly up to the top, fight off any Night Gaunts that come near us, and blast our way inside, which will, most likely, result in our immediate capture and Jonathan's demise. Or..." Moriel trailed off in an almost melancholy manner.

"Or what?"

"Or we could do what we did when we overtook the stronghold of Jericho."

"Moriel, no. That was one of the riskiest moves you've ever made. We can't do that *here*. This is Xexxus, not some Nephilim demon who's crowned himself king. Plus, we don't have an army of Adamians marching through Pentaclegates surrounding this fortress and weakening its defenses. It's just us against whatever madness awaits within this behemoth."

"Do we really have another choice at this point, Akalian? We've experienced no contests since taking down the Se'irim horde. No obstacles *at all*. Xexxus is playing a game. It's time we play our

own. Besides, you know it's never 'just us.' The King has a thousand pieces moving at once here. We have help we don't know about."

Akalian paused for a moment to think, but quickly realized that Moriel was right. Xexxus probably wouldn't expect something like this, and the Chief Power even said it himself. They were out of time and, therefore, out of options. And, for all he knew, the King *did* have an army of Adamians ready to march around Hillcrest Sanitarium, as unlikely as that may be.

"Alright. Do it."

Moriel started to kneel but Akalian grabbed him by the shoulders and pulled him in for a firm embrace. When Akalian released him, Moriel could see that there were tears in his brother's eyes.

"Please. Be careful, brother." Akalian's voice trembled. Moriel knew what Akalian was really saying. *I can't lose another brother.* The Messenger understood Akalian's worry, but knew this situation was much bigger than their comradery. He placed a hand upon Akalian's pauldron covered shoulder and gave a somber smirk.

"There's nothing careful about what we do. We do it because no one else can." The Messenger stared into his Chief Power's eyes and saw Akalian's fear and pain welling up. He prayed that his brother would have the strength to do what must be done.

Moriel knelt down to the ground and touched it, as he did when they first arrived in this dreadful place. Concentrating hard, he slowly began to release his essence into the ground, hoping to receive the location of the throne room. Moriel carefully reached out into the energy of Jonathan's possessed subconscious and found a connection. Flashes of the boy's life flooded through Moriel's mind. He saw Agatha of Endor holding Jonanthan down and performing some sort of ritual on him. Next, the Messenger saw the boy ritualistically slaughter the Youngs as they knelt down before him. Then, everything began to become extremely disorienting, as if Moriel was looking through some sort of portal. On one side of the portal was Jonathan and on the other side was the shape of an Adamian, reaching out for the boy in desperation.

Finally, when the collage of memories subsided, Moriel's astral form entered the cavernous, mist-filled throne room of Xexxus.

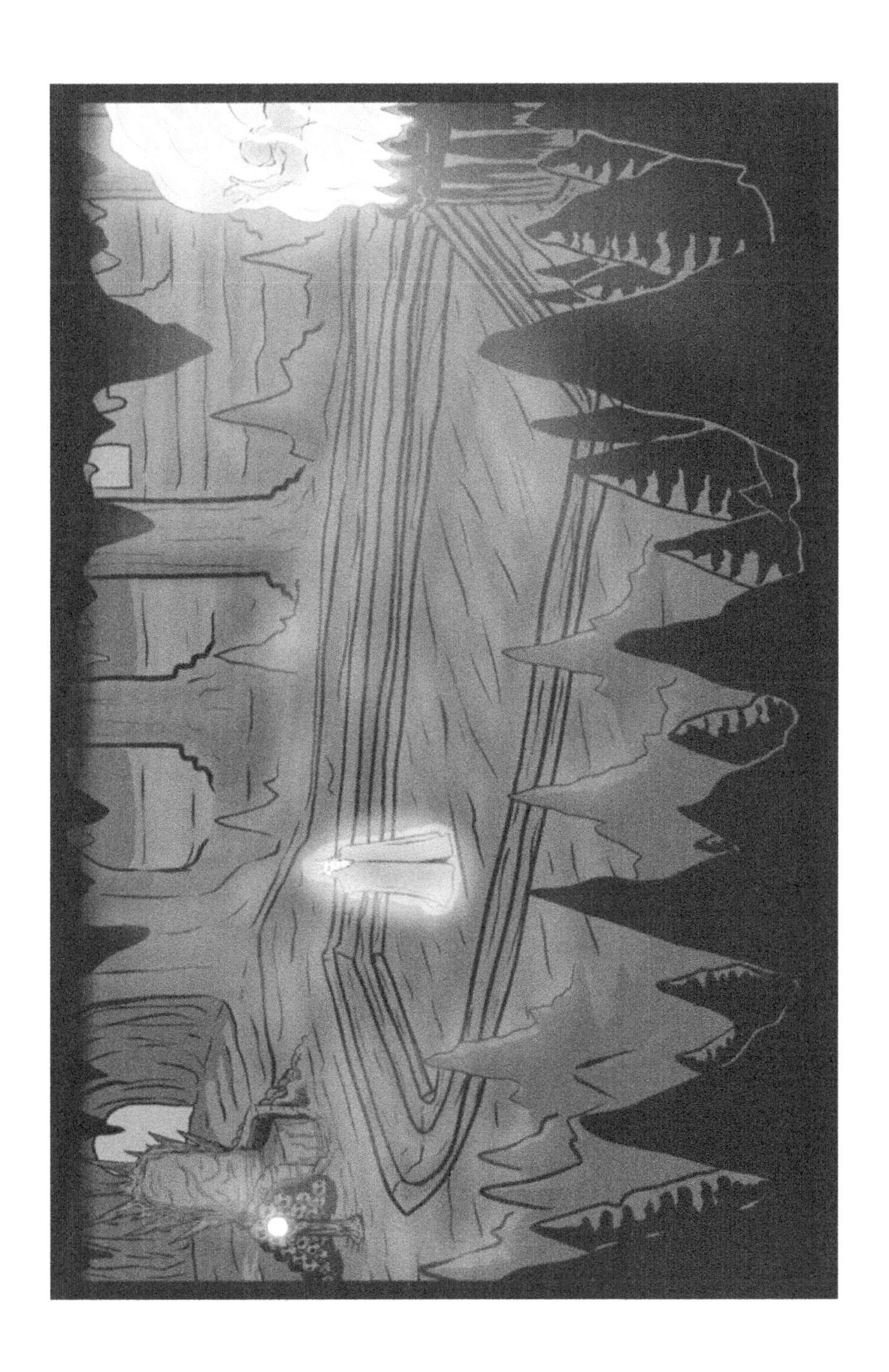

As he peered across the grotesque chamber, the former King of Legion was nowhere to be found, but he saw the boy floating in his necroplasmic prison. Moriel almost sobbed when he saw what Jonathan had become. He was barely recognizable, barely human. The Messenger rushed over to the boy's deformed shape, wanting so badly to reach out, grab him, and run. But he knew he couldn't do that just yet.

"Jonathan. Jonathan, we are here to help you, my boy. Have hope. We're–"

Jonathan lifted his head as if to speak, but, instead, his face transformed into the hideous grin of Xexxus. As the boy's body morphed violently into the former King of Legion, he grabbed Moriel by the throat and lifted the astral form of the Messenger up off of his taloned feet.

"There is no hope here, little angel! We've been waiting for you to sneak in!"

At the base of the castle, Akalian watched in horror as Moriel was engulfed in green necroplasm and completely disappeared in front of his brother's eyes.

"Moriel!!" Akalian shouted in terror. But it was too late.

"Hello, brother." The voice of Xexxus rang throughout his entire wretched kingdom. "It's been far too long, has it not?"

"Where is he!?" Akalian roared in anger at the disembodied voice. Karaydin shot out bolts of tzoharian energy in all directions, expressing his righteous fury. A green, glowing slit opened where Moriel once stood.

"Come and see," Xexxus enticed.

"I intend to." As Akalian entered the Necrogate, one thought rang in his mind. *I sure hope you're right about this, Moriel.*

# CHAPTER TWENTY SEVEN

## - THE THRONE ROOM -

Mattia bent down and picked up the Capurro Cross. It was lighter than she had expected.

*A stone cross adhered to a solid piece of wood should weigh more than this*, she thought as she turned back to where Jonathan was. Except all she found was an empty room. Fear washed over Mattia as her eyes darted around the room, desperately trying to see past the darkness for the shape of her client. She found only empty shadows staring back at her. The Cleric could hear Bouchard yelling from down the hallway to '*get the hell out of there*'. Perhaps he could see something on the monitor that she couldn't?

Mattia darted for the door, holding Obadiah's Cross out in front of her like a desperate life-line. Twenty-four hours ago, she would have been mortified at this act of superstition, but now, the Cross was her only comfort in this dark, forsaken place. As she reached the partially opened door, it suddenly slammed shut. The Cleric turned around, Cross first, frightened, but determined to fight off whatever evil pounced at her from the shadows. But still, there was nothing.

In her panicked state, Mattia never thought to look up. In the top corner, above the door, Jonathan's eyes opened, revealing green globes of flame that pierced the darkness. He dropped down on top of her, tackling the Cleric onto the floor, and sending the Capurro Cross sliding across the room.

"Alright, that's it." Bouchard said to himself as he ran out from behind his enormous desk. The Headminister had sworn he would *never* use this. To him, it was unethical. Even though the High Cleric had told him to use it in extreme cases, Bouchard had never been able to bring himself to do so. He punched in the code to open the safe against the wall, and lifted the lid when the light turned blue. The Headminister reached in and pulled out the six round electro-particle pistol from its charging station.

Every dart in the pistol held enough electricity to kill a grown man. What the Old World knew as guns had been extinct since The Grand Republic had been formed—these weapons were yet another reason for the Old World's destruction. Now the only thing that resembled such *uncivilized* weapons were electro-particle weapons which came in various degrees of intensity. Some of the pistols that the RPG Officers carried were strong enough to cause a person to explode if shot from a close enough range. If anyone other than an official Republic officer was caught with one of these, they were sent to The Wastelands immediately. The High Council was, of course, an exception.

Bouchard knew he only had one shot per minute with this pistol. The gun took 60 seconds to self-charge once it had been fired. If the Headminister were to miss the first shot, it would surely anger the boy and who knows what damage he could do in a minute's time. Bouchard flipped the switch in front of the rear sight of the pistol and felt the weapon hum with lethal energy. He stared at the electric death machine in his hand and felt like one of the "shoot-em-up" heroes of old.

"Hang on, Mattia, I'm coming."

"Welcome, brother." Xexxus' voice was low and crackly, making Akalian's stomach turn. He hadn't heard that voice since the Gadarene ambush. As soon as the Chief Power stepped through the Necrogate, he saw his former brother's *grand* throne room. It was more disgusting than he'd imagined. The entire chamber was filled with a humid, green mist that danced around slime covered stalagmites. To his right, Jonathan was chained to a tall stalagmite protruding from the foggy floor. It was the first time Akalian had actually seen the boy and his heart sank at the sight of the broken and beaten shape before him. On Akalian's left was Moriel, in the necroplasmic prison that had once held Jonathan captive. Between them stood Xexxus on his grand dais in front of his throne of Necromic skulls. Cowering a few steps below the King of Endless Night was his odious vizier, Yagorath, who leaned heavily on her lich staff.

Akalian hadn't known how he'd feel seeing Xexxus again. He had played it out time and time again in his mind. After their last meeting, the Power had been overrun with grief. Right now, however, Akalian felt repulsed at the sight of his former brother.

"I've waited Ages for this," Xexxus said. "Welcome to my kingdom, dear brother." The former King of Legion stretched out his arms directing Akalian to look upon his surroundings.

"I waited Ages for my brother to come back to me," Akalian said numbly. Xexxus seemed pleased at this response. "But he never did. All that remained was *you.* And as I look around this place..." A tear began to roll down Akalian's cheek. "I see that *you* are nothing but a worthless shadow of the warrior Baetiel once was."

"How quick you are to judge me for finding my freedom," Xexxus replied. His grin twitched into a scowl. "And, if I remember correctly, last we met, you spat at my offer to join me in this privilege. So, I'll be sure to respect those wishes now and not make the same offer twice." Xexxus started down the crooked stairs of the dais, his eyes never leaving Akalian's. "I'll take the direct approach and inform you that it is entirely too late.

The *gifts* of The Black Mass have already been given. Fire and soul were given by the High Cleric, stone and blood by the Council itself, and ironically enough, the gift of sacrificial flesh was given by the outcast who attempted to stop the whole thing." Xexxus boomed with a sinister laugh. "He completed the very thing he was attempting to stop!"

While Xexxus was giving his triumphant monologue, Akalian glanced at Moriel who gave him a reassuring wink.

In the skirmish, Jonathan had pinned Mattia down with one hand and grabbed at her throat with the other, choking her. The Cleric could feel things in her neck beginning to pop. As she panicked, her legs started to randomly kick and slide around. Jonathan cackled, his pleasure in taking a life escalating.

"You have been a thorn in my side long enough, you cunting dust creature!" the foul voice inside the boy gleefully shrieked. "Now you will be the first tasty morsel of my hunt. Just as the enemy's Herald proclaimed his Messiah's coming, so shall I proclaim for The Master. There's *much* work still to do, little sow."

Mattia was starting to black out. Her eyes rolled back in her head. This was it. Jonathan saw her life drifting away and his excitement intensified.

He leaned in close to Mattia's face, thick drool dripping from his corroded mouth. "Drift off now, little sow. Give my regards to the Fires of Hell. They're old friends."

"Tell them yourself, you piece of shit." Jonathan looked up to see Bouchard sitting on the ledge of the broken observation window with his pistol pointed right at the boy's head. Jonathan started to roar at the Headminister when Bouchard pulled the trigger. The dart blasted out of the electro-particle pistol and straight into Jonathan's neck. Electricity exploded from the dart, enveloping the boy with a bolt of lightning that sent him flying across the room.

"So, you see, my dear Akalian, there's nothing more for you to do but to submit." Xexxus beamed with hubris. "You've done what the Heavenly Host does best. You've lost. You've–"

Xexxus dropped to his knees, screaming in agony as hot, fiery electricity webbed all over his massive body.

"Now!" Moriel screamed. Tzoharian energy rocketed out of Akalian's hands towards Moriel's slimy prison and the chains that bound the boy. The energies collided, dissolved the necroplasm, and severed the chains, freeing Jonathan and Moriel. Yagorath slammed the bottom of her lich staff on the ground.

"Destroy them!!" she yelled. Immediately, as if from a nightmare, a dozen Wraiths erupted from the mists and began flying around the throne room shrieking and clawing at the two elohim.

"Jonathan, hide!!" Akalian yelled. The boy was weak and could barely stand, but having his astral form freed from the chains gave him enough energy and hope to find shelter amidst the foggy chamber.

As Akalian swung Karaydin through a Wraith's skull, he found himself thanking the King for whatever had happened to Xexxus to distract him. He wasn't sure if his tzoharian blasts would have stunned the creature long enough to free Moriel.

No one quite understood the relationship of spiritual energies in the universe or the rules of how they interacted. No one, that is, except the one who made them. Unfortunately, through the gifts of The Black Mass, Xexxus and Jonathan were indeed merged. The Dark elohim now claimed Jonathan Young as a skafos and therefore the two were intimately connected. Their energies could now affect one another in a more powerful way than before. But the King knew the right combination of energies could subdue them both.

When Jonathan had been choking the life out of Mattia, all of the boy's energy was surging inside of his body. Not only was he feeling the sinister, euphoric victory of destroying someone, but his perverse arousal was peaking. Those high energies were feeding Xexxus, giving him more power and confidence in his triumph.

However, when Bouchard shot the boy, it sent an electric current of pain surging through both Jonathan and the King of Endless Night and overwhelmed them.

Akalian may not have understood what happened on the other side of this event, but it reminded him that King Yahweh was working and that, even in this Dark place, he hadn't left them to their own devices.

"He couldn't have vanished into thin air!" Gwen shouted at Edgar as they looked frantically for Obadiah on the grassy knolls of the Observation Level. Gwen had tucked the Sapient Blade into the belt of her pants underneath her robes. She knew if they lost *that*, they would surely be destroyed.

"We've looked everywhere!" Edgar finally spoke up. "We must get back to the Glass Room and summon the rest of the Council to get ahead of this. We need to call the RPG and have them hunt the bastard down!"

Gwen almost smacked him.

"And what are we supposed to tell them about the High Cleric? We have to get our stories straight within the Council *before* we get the RPG involved. Those sharks get off on sending people to The Wastelands! They don't give a shit about whether or not you're a Council Cleric." Gwen paused for a moment to regather herself. "No. We have to find Obadiah ourselves. If we let him get away, who knows what he'll say about what happened here tonight."

"He's a known outlaw, Gwen. Who's going to believe him over the High Council?"

"You know as well as I do, he still has loyal followers inside and outside of The High Temple. One of them brought him here tonight, for goodness' sake! We can't risk him starting a coup from the shadows. People's fear of Malcom is what's kept it from happening already. But now Malcolm's gone, Edgar. Killed by the very man they would follow. Besides, what would Sister Agatha do to us if she knew we gave up so quickly and allowed all of this to get even further out of hand!?"

That struck a chord with the large, bald man. He typically didn't fear anyone, but Agatha terrified him. Since he was Malcolm's second in command, Edgar knew she would hold him accountable for everything that happened tonight, whether they found Obadiah or not. So, having the outlaw's head on a platter might give him some protection from her wrath.

"Fine," Edgar said. "We'll keep looking."

Just as Edgar spoke, the baby began to cry from somewhere in the knolls. The two Clerics darted in the direction of the wailing and found the swaddled infant in some shrubberies near the open edge of the Observation Level.

"It's very unlike Obadiah to leave a child behind like this, and so close to the level's edge," Gwen said suspiciously.

"Clearly this was where his vehicle was parked. He dumped the infant and left. I guess he's not the hero everyone thought he was after all," Edgar snarked. "Get the child. We'll dispose of it and–"

Both heard the engine revving, but neither of them had a chance to react. In a blur, Gwen and Edgar were hit with the body of a roaring skybike, sending them flying off the edge of the Observation Level. Edgar fell the two hundred yards to the ground below and was crushed by the traffic. Gwen was somehow able to hold onto the skybike hovering in mid-air. Her body was almost completely broken; adrenaline was the only thing keeping her going. The frigid wind whipped in her ears. Below her, hundreds of miles of traffic and bright lights blinked up at her as far as she could see. Gwen looked up in desperation and saw the stoic, haunted gaze of Obadiah, glaring down at her.

"This is for every life you helped destroy. For all the people you led astray. May whatever Hell awaits you greet you with the malice you deserve." Obadiah kicked the Cleric free of the skybike, sending her plummeting to her death. Satisfied, he looked out at the cityscape that surrounded him. Even though it was the dead of night, he knew it was a new dawn for the city of Perethedesh, and for the Republic.

"So ends the rule of Malcolm, High Cleric of The Grand Republic," Obadiah proclaimed to himself. He spat into the wind and quickly flew back to recover the crying infant.

As Moriel and Akalian fought off the shrieking Wraiths, Jonathan's astral form found a large stalagmite a few feet away. As he hid behind it, he realized even though he was surrounded by complete chaos, he felt a joy growing inside of him. He was free. Jonathan knew he still didn't have control over his body, but this tiny piece of his mind was liberated from the grip of pure evil that had held him prisoner for what felt like multiple lifetimes. He began to well up with tears of relief, knowing that his rescuers were in this horrible place with him, fighting for him. But when he looked down at his hands, that joy began to fade. What Jonathan saw before him weren't the hands of a thirteen-year-old boy–not *his* hands–but wrinkled, worn, leathery fingers that were shifting to resemble the talons of Xexxus.

Jonathan could not have been aware of the process occurring inside of him. When a soul was merged with a Dark entity, there were immediate transformations. The body and soul of a person would become a skafos of the Dark being it now belonged to. However, depending on the decisions the Adamian had made prior to the merging, the transformation of the soul sometimes took a little longer to solidify to its new reality.

In Jonathan's case, he was a victim of indoctrination and Dark Magick. He had been corrupted against his will by The Coven of Endor before he had crossed the threshold of the Esad de Yasi–Age of Discretion–that every Adamian must reach before being completely held accountable for the choices they make. The Esad de Yasi was different for each individual. Some–lacking intellectual understanding and comprehension–never reached it at all. Unfortunately, like many before him–and many that would come after–Jonathan's merging was still taking place before his eyes. The Dark Kingdom did not care whether a person intentionally chose them or not; they took what they wanted.

"And where do you think *you're* going, dust creature!?" Jonathan's heart jumped into his throat as he saw the vile vizier, Yag-

-orath, standing in front of him with her lich staff pointed directly at him. Without hesitation, the grotesque, four-eyed creature blasted a beam of sinister energy from the dead Ophanim eye sagging from the top of her staff. Jonathan cringed and jerked his head just in time for the beam to smash against the stalagmite behind him. He jumped to a different slimy protrusion as Yagorath shot another beam at him which slightly grazed his arm. But, after enduring so much of Xexxus' torture, he barely felt it.

Jonathan was panicking, but something inside of him urged him to search for a weapon to use to defend himself. What he found in the muck was the very chain that had bound him mere moments ago. A determined boldness took over the boy's essence. He grabbed the black, necroplasm covered iron links with both hands and swung it wildly at the grand vizier's face, striking her between her two sets of eyes.

Moriel, who had just finished slashing a Wraith in two, saw the boy out of the corner of his eye and smiled.

*The little warrior,* the Messenger thought to himself proudly.

Jonathan continued swinging the chain at Yagorath, who was trying her best to dodge the whipping motions. Finally, she'd had enough. No dust creature, let alone a child, would dare get the best of it. After the chain whipped past her one final time, the vizier blasted the black links from the boy's now fully taloned hands.

"Enough! Now you will feel my full wrath, you putrid little–"

Pieces of Yagorath went flying in all directions. Only a foul stench lingered in the steam that once had been Xexxus' grand vizier.

Jonathan looked across the throne room to see Moriel smiling at him; the obu that had just blasted Yagorath into oblivion floated in front of him.

"Well done, my boy," Moriel said with a smile. Jonathan returned the grin then shifted his gaze over to the second angel on the other side of the throne room. Finishing his final blow to the last Wraith, Akalian beamed at the boy with an affection Jonathan had never felt before. He felt so safe with these two massive beings. For the first time in years–for the first time he could ever remember–the boy felt protected. However, the feelings of safety came crashing down as quickly as they arrived, as he turned to see an enormous Shadowblade erupt from Moriel's chest.

"Yes. Well done," Xexxus mocked. His bulging eyes and teeth glowed in the shadows behind Moriel as he lifted the Messenger up from the floor with his black and green Shadowblade. Moriel's body went limp. "I don't think I could have ever taken him by surprise if it wasn't for your distraction. That's a good 'Little Boy Blue'."

With one hand, Xexxus flung the Messenger off of his blade like he weighed nothing at all. With the other hand, the monstrous figure snapped his fingers, sending Jonathan's astral form across the room and back into the necroplasmic prison to finish his transformation.

"No!!" Akalian screamed, his wrath seething as he saw his dear brother laying lifeless on the floor.

"There." Xexxus' attention focused on the enraged Chief Power. "Now we can be alone at last."

Mattia gasped for air and rolled onto her side, vomiting bile on the floor. Bouchard had entered the room through the observation window and was kneeling down to check on his dear friend.

"W...we ha...have to get out." Mattia scratched out her words. Her throat was on fire.

"It's okay Matty. I got him." Bouchard held up the pistol. "I'm sorry but...this thing...it's lethal. He's dead."

Mattia shook her head violently.

"No...he's...t...too powerful!" As Bouchard heard these words, he looked up to see Jonathan's wild eyes and sharp fangs leaping at him. The boy mounted the Headminister and sank his teeth into Bouchard's neck, opening his jugular with a ferocious rip. Blood sprayed across the shadowed room as the two bodies slammed onto the floor—Bouchard lifeless and twitching.

Jonathan straddled the Headminister's corpse then slowly turned towards Mattia who was sitting up, watching in horror. She would have screamed if her fear hadn't taken the ability away from her. Bouchard may have been a pawn, but he didn't deserve this. He had been loyal to the Republic. His only crime was believing in the system that had indoctrinated him. And although it was the monster infesting Jonathan's mind that did the killing, Bouchard was ultimately a victim of Malcolm. They all were. Including this boy whom she *had* to save.

In a moment of clarity, Mattia realized the Capurro Cross was lying just a few feet away from her. She scrambled towards it, but Jonathan leapt from Bouchard's dead body, landed on Mattia's legs, and backhanded her across the face. She screamed in agony and Jonathan giggled with sinister elation.

"Not so fast, little sow. Apparently, there's still more time to play."

Akalian wasted no time. With the speed of a hurricane, the

Chief Power raised Karaydin and threw himself at Xexxus, blade first. Their broadswords tore through the throne room, blurring and sparking upon contact. For every strike, there was a counter. For every killing blow, a perfect defense. In every way, it seemed these two were equals at their swordplay. As the battle raged on, Xexxus jeered at Akalian, attempting to break his concentration.

"It seems as though I've struck a nerve, putting an *end* to your little Messenger. Careful now, you'll make me jealous," Xexxus taunted as his own Shadowblade–Kasir Karalak–slammed into Karaydin with an ungodly force that would have shattered any lesser blade. In fact, it had done just that, many times. Kasir Karalak was one of the Nectum Ogdre–Shadowblades crafted by Shykal–the blacksmith of Pandemonium. Their number was vast and unknown even to Shykal, but every Shadowblade that Pandemonium's blacksmith had crafted was filled with a hateful and vile power, and was known to be almost indestructible.

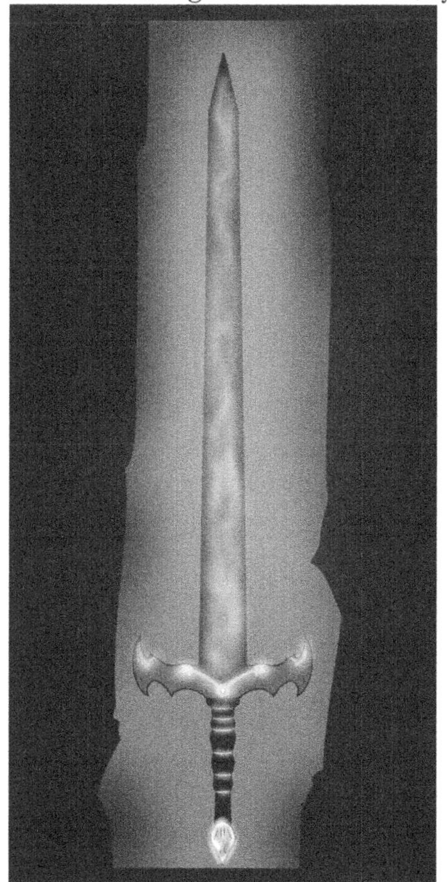

"It was quite clever how the two of you got in here, allowing your brother to be 'captured'," Xexxus continued. "I find that so very uncharacteristic of you. It actually took some *risk!*" Xexxus found an opening and backhanded Akalian across the face. The Chief Power staggered backward. It was the first time he'd ever been physically struck by his former brother, and it hurt. There was no doubt Xexxus was more powerful than the Chief Power. But, Akalian was beginning to wonder just *how* powerful the Dark elohim had become.

"I can be clever too," Xexxus hissed. "And you certainly know that I've taken some risks in my time." Akalian suddenly felt a heavy presence behind him. "Let me show you what I've gleaned from them!"

Akalian turned just in time to block Kasir Karalak from slicing through his back. Although, the Power was not fast enough to block the necroblast that followed. Akalian soared across the foggy throne room, crashing into a thick stalagmite protruding from the ground. Xexxus hadn't just teleported behind Akalian, he had been in front of him *and* behind him at the same time.

"So..." Akalian grunted as he stood. "You've ripped your essence apart to gain dualpresence?"

"It's something I've been practicing as of late," Xexxus said pridefully. "I admit, I've not yet reached my full potential, but I've been promised much more than this."

Only the King of Ages had the ability to be omnipresent–everywhere at once. For a lesser elohim to gain such abilities was unheard of, although it was rumored in The Dark Kingdom that whatever Khata was, he too, was capable of such feats. It was the belief that Khata had accomplished omnipresence that encouraged Dark figures such as Xexxus to aspire to this level of blasphemous power. Only an extreme few were rumored to have multipresence–being many places at once. However, dualpresence–two places at once–though not common, was not completely unheard of among the Dark elohim.

To gain dualpresence, one had to first deconstruct their genetic makeup, then reconstruct it as they saw fit. This practice not only mocked how the King had created them, but it unlocked abilities that were too advanced, both mentally and emotionally for lesser elohim. The power would drive them even more insane than they already were.

"I told you, the power gifted to me by The Dark Father is more extraordinary than I could have ever imagined." Xexxus held out his arms, sheathing Kasir Karalak into his thick, crocodile skin. "Here, let me show you just *how* extraordinary I've become."

Akalian watched in horror as Xexxus' body turned into a fluidic necroplasm which began morphing into a monstrous form, towering high above him into the green mists of the wretched throne room.

Jonathan pulled Mattia close to him and straddled her on the floor of the dark, padded room. His green eyes pierced the shadows as he grinned at her horrified, sobbing face.

"Well, dust creature. You've fought hard, but you will die here in the very room in which your High Cleric created me." Mattia sobbed harder. He took pleasure in how helpless and broken she looked. "Yes, give me your sorrow. It is nourishment to me." Jonathan's mouth began to open wide, his lower jaw extending far beyond the normal limits of bone structure. Mattia was too exhausted to move. She had no hope against such evil. They had failed.

Jonathan's gaping mouth enlarged even further as he bent down toward the Cleric's head to engulf her much like an anaconda would overtake its prey. The Great Serpent, Nachash was joining Xexxus in claiming this freshly merged boy like the Spirit of the King would claim new converts of Light. The boy would soon be solidified. Just as Jonathan's unhinged jaw reached the top of Mattia's hair, the boy felt a sharp pain strike the back of his head. He was knocked off of Mattia and onto the floor.

Obadiah kicked Jonathan in the face, making his jaw retract back into place. The former Cleric leapt on top of the boy, using all of his strength to restrain him.

"Matty! Get the Cross!"

Mattia's adrenaline surged once again. She wiped her tears trying to clear her vision, but everything was still dark and blurred. She could barely breathe because of the congestion built up in her sinuses from crying so hard. Obadiah struggled with all his might to keep Jonathan on the floor. The boy began gargling in a language Obadiah had heard in The Grey, but didn't understand.

"Azanah orahgn ng uh'enyth mgepnog!!" the possessed boy shouted. "Ymg' ch'nglui'ahog gn'bthnknyth!" The floor began to glow green once more and mist erupted underneath them.

As the floor lit up, Mattia saw the Cross and grabbed it before it was swallowed by the billowing fog. Obadiah lost his grip on Jonathan and the boy kicked him across the room. The former Cleric landed hard against the wall and fell on top of the broken glass, hitting his head on the floor. Jonathan leapt to his feet and started toward the stunned Obadiah.

"Hey!!"

Jonathan turned toward the sound of Mattia's voice, eyes blazing in the fog. The boy came face to face with the Capurro Cross.

"Christus Victor!!" Mattia shouted with all her might.

Nothing happened.

Jonathan began to chuckle. "What was that supposed to accomplish, little sow?"

"You don't understand the power The Dark Father gives. He is a gracious ruler." Xexxus' voice boomed from the enormous serpentine monstrosity he had just morphed into. Just as with Jonathan's physical form, The Great Serpent Nachash was fully on display through Xexxus' transformation–giving him power beyond reason. Akalian stared in disgusted awe at what towered above him. Xexxus unfurled immeasurable bat-like wings, unleashing black and green smoke that filled the throne room.

Unfurling his own wings, Akalian immediately took to flight, firing tzoharian energy at the colossal Dark dragon in front of him. In this moment, the Chief Power knew he didn't stand a chance against what Xexxus–his brother–had become. But he clung to the age old saying that marked the archway to the entrance of Gabriel's war room: *The Light shines in the Darkness and the Darkness has not overcome it.* This became Akalian's prayer as he raised Karaydin and rocketed towards the dragonesque head of his foe.

Akalian didn't have to defeat him. He just needed to get Xexxus in the right position. But as he got close, Xexxus swiftly and mightily backhanded Akalian, sending the Power to the ground at a frightening speed. Akalian attempted to gain control, but crashed into the black stone stairs of the dais and skidded across the mist-filled throne room floor, pieces of necroplasmic debris falling all around him. Xexxus cackled, his booming laughter shaking the entire castle.

"I fly as a mighty Seraph before your eyes, yet you still grovel as the lowly Power you are! Submit to me, little angel, and you will find the freedom your heart truly desires. The Dark Father is more benevolent than your King has ever been!"

Akalian found his footing once more and glared at the Dark dragon.

"It's a farce, Xexxus. Your power is only momentary. You've traded your eternal freedom for finite greatness. And it will ultimately destroy you."

"Is that so? And who has told you this? Your *King?* Of course he would say such things!! How else is he to keep you under his control?" Xexxus circled the room, flapping his mighty wings, sending shadows swirling around like smoke. "We found his secret, you know...the source of your King's power. Who he *really* is. The Dark Father has revealed the truth to us. Your King is nothing but a thief and a liar who wants power and glory all for himself!! The Dark Father freely gives power and glory to those who follow him! *He* is a Father of true freedom!"

"The only thing your wretched ruler is a *father* of, is lies. And I'm tired of hearing them!" As Akalian's wings launched him into the air, the Power pulled all of the energy from his essence and poured it into Karaydin, transforming the Lightblade into a pulsing tzoharian torch of power. The Chief Power shot a thundering blast of Light at the Dark Seraph, striking the dragon in the chest. Xexxus let out a howling scream of agony. The serpentine shadow began to fall apart, swirling around Akalian, stretching the Dark elohim's shape. He spun around the Power until all Akalian could see was blackness. Karaydin was the only source of light in front of the Chief Power.

*The Light shines in the Darkness,* he prayed. *And the Darkness has not overcome* –the shadows suddenly broke up ahead, the light silhouetting a tall figure in the distance. As Akalian flew closer, it became clear who the figure was.

Baetiel.

Akalian froze. His senses began to experience a wondrous world long past. He was in Eden. He could smell the newborn trees and the fruits they bore. All of the Darkness surrounding Akalian slipped away as Baetiel walked towards him. Akalian's eyes welled up with tears. He didn't have time to think about what this was. He couldn't rationalize what was happening. All he knew was the one being whom he longed to see again more than anyone else in creation was standing right in front of him. All the wonderful memories of brotherly love, the laughter, the joy, the play–it was all here in front of him. He had longed for this moment for thousands of years.

"Hello, brother." Baetiel's sweet, natural voice rang in the air. "It's been so long. I've felt so trapped in this Darkness and your holy wrath seems to have somehow released me momentarily. Please...please take me back. Please save me from this death."

Akalian's immediate urge was to reach out and hug his brother and welcome him home. But Baetiel beat him to it, and he embraced Akalian with a warmth the Power hadn't felt since before that cursed day at the Tower of Babylon. Tears flowed freely from Akalian's eyes as he closed them, losing himself in Baetiel's embrace. It was everything he'd wished for.

"Oh brother...I've missed you so–"

Akalian was interrupted by Kasir Karalak pushing through his abdomen.

"Pathetic." The voice of Xexxus echoed in his mind as Akalian staggered backwards. The King of Endless Night pulled the Shadowblade out of his prey and push-kicked Akalian across the throne room floor, causing him to collide once again with the sinister stones of the cave-like chamber.

Akalian stood up. His wings had retreated into his back and he was swinging Karaydin wildly, fighting the blinding pain in his stomach.

"You won't win," he said, every movement excruciating. The Shadowblade had released necroplasmic poison into the Power's system and it was infecting him quickly.

"You *fool!!* I've already won!!" Xexxus slammed Kasir Karalak into Karaydin. Akalian's strength waivered from the impact and he lowered his Lightbalde. Xexxus backhanded Akalian once more and the Power flung to the floor, rolling frantically and finally stopping on his back, Karaydin out in front of him in defense.

"I won before you even arrived!" Xexxus pummeled his Shadowblade into Karaydin again. Akalian was doing everything he could to block the behemoth's blows. With every word Xexxus spoke, he smashed Kasir Karalak into Karaydin, forcing the Lightblade closer and closer to Akalian's brow.

"It's time!"

**SMASH**

"You!"

**SMASH**

"Accepted this!!" With this final blow, Xexxus embedded Kasir Kalak into Akalian's face, piercing his left eye completely. White blood poured from the Power's face, turning black upon contact with the wretched fog. In a victorious fury, Xexxus kicked Akalian in the head, sending Michael's Chief Power flailing helplessly across the fog-filled floor. In the violent tumbling, Karaydin shattered into pieces–its stability completely depleted.

Akalian lay there, bloody and broken. He could no longer see out of his eye. The necroplasmic poison from his stomach was working faster than he'd originally thought. He could feel himself fading from this form. Xexxus stood twelve yards away, Kasir Karalak retreating back into his leathery skin. The Dark elohim almost looked as if he felt sorry for the angel he used to call, 'brother'. In a moment of cruel solemnity, Xexxus remembered a fond saying he would tease his brother with all those years ago, and chuckled as he said it.

"My dear Akalian...you're always falling behind."

Akalian rolled onto his stomach with a flop, propped himself up with one arm, and looked up at his former brother with a smirk.

"Maybe so...but at least I look where I'm going."

Xexxus immediately felt the presence behind him, but it was too late. Moriel's taloned hands had latched onto both sides of Xexxus' head and began forming an obu as he delivered the message destined for the King of Endless Night.

"I am Moriel!! Messenger of Yahweh: King of Ages!! I contend with a vanquished foe, who with all his subtlety and strength has already been overcome! When I feel the serpent at my heel, I remember him whose heel was bruised, but who broke the devil's head!!"

Xexxus began screaming in agony and rage as the white hot obu started to form on top of his head, preparing to send him to Tartarus.

*The plan worked,* Akalian thought to himself. *It was the riskiest, most painful plan we've ever had, but it worked.*

Ultimately, the bait was to make Xexxus think the plan was simply for them to enter the throne room and then break Moriel free, allowing them to fight Xexxus together. Of course, the former King of Legion would then believe he'd foiled the plan when it seemed like he was defeating Moriel who would have to allow himself to be run through. While Moriel would lay there, focusing all of his energy on fighting the necroplasmic poison, Akalian would contend with Xexxus and allow the Dark elohim to get the better of him, making Xexxus lower his guard. Admittedly, Akalian did not believe it would go as far as it did–it certainly hadn't gone that far during the Great Fall of The Wall of Jericho. Finally, in the moment Xexxus let his guard down, Moriel was to deliver the message and send Xexxus to Tartarus.

Both Akalian and Moriel knew they couldn't defeat this foe with brute strength. Xexxus had grown too powerful for either of them. However, nothing is more powerful than a message from the King of Ages.

Or so they thought.

Xexxus, in his rage, blindly threw his arms back, his taloned fingers finding their way into Moriel's skull at the temples.

"Tartarus will not have me!!" Xexxus howled. Moriel screamed in pain as green necroplasmic energy began pulling Moriel's hands off of Xexxus' head, diminishing the obu's formation.

"Akalian!! I can't hold him!! He's too strong!" Moriel shouted in desperation.

Mattia stood there holding the Capurro Cross, stupefied. She felt like an utter fool.

"Your petty Magick cannot compete with the raw power of The Dark Father!" Jonathan continued to cackle. "It is everlasting!"

Mattia's mind was a whirlwind. She looked over at Obadiah who had been knocked unconscious against the wall. This cross was her last hope against the demon in front of her. She was out of options.

*Please!! Please help me!!* Mattia desperately pleaded with whatever force had helped her before. If it had helped her then, why wasn't it helping her now? Was there some specific prayer she accidentally prayed to summon it last time? She couldn't remember what she said.

"Come, little sow." Jonathan hissed. "Let us end this." He began inching closer to her when suddenly, he stopped in his tracks and his entire demeanor changed.

Mattia saw sinister confidence transform into raw fear. Then she felt two warm hands firmly grab both her shoulders.

"There isn't much time, Mattia," a sweet voice on her right stated. The Cleric looked over her shoulder and saw a what appeared to be an apparition of a woman, shimmering in shades of white and blue. She wore a flowing robe with a cloak latched at her chest by a

Stone clasp bearing a symbol Mattia had never seen before. Her eyes were glowing flames of starlight, but Mattia felt no fear. Topping the glowing woman's head was a beautiful crown which Mattia would describe later as being made of the stars in the sky. Her kind voice echoed around the Cleric. "My name is Maryam, and this is Yosef. Do not be afraid, we're here to help you." Mattia glanced to her left to see Saint Yosef, who was glowing in shades of deep blue and green. His beard beamed a bright white.

Yosef also wore a cloak, but the symbol on his Stone latch was different, although the Stone appeared to be of the same type as Maryam. He held a long staff that stretched from the top of his head to the bottom of his robes. The staff was one of the most beautiful things Mattia had ever seen. It was made of glistening white oak bearing intricate foliage etchings leading all the way to its top where it sprouted into a carving of an opened flower, a bright Stone shining in its center. Mattia was captivated by its beauty. Unbeknownst to her, this staff and this Saint were a terror for demons. Mattia also couldn't know that the woman who stood at her side was the Queen of The Heavens–Maryam, Mother of the King.

"A mother's love is one of the purest powers in the cosmos. And your love for this child has been felt in the Heavens, dear one," Maryam reassured her, comfortingly.

"Say these words with us," Saint Yosef prodded in a gentle tone. "They will appear upon your heart."

"No!" Jonathan pleaded. "Stop that!! Don't come near me!"

"Silence!" Yosef's shout echoed throughout the room. The possessed boy shrunk back as the tzoharian shard inside Yosef's staff glowed brighter.

Together with the two figures supporting her on either side, Mattia began to say words she had never heard before, but suddenly knew as though she'd recited them every day of her life.

"Saint Michael, the Archangel, defend us in battle..."

Akalian immediately felt power surge through his body as he heard voices on the air of the cursed throne room. He could barely make out what they were saying at first, but then the words grew louder as they continued.

*"Be our protection against the wickedness and snares of the devil..."*

Someone was praying the Prayer of St. Michael. Not only that, but they were reciting it directly to Jonathan's possessed skafos

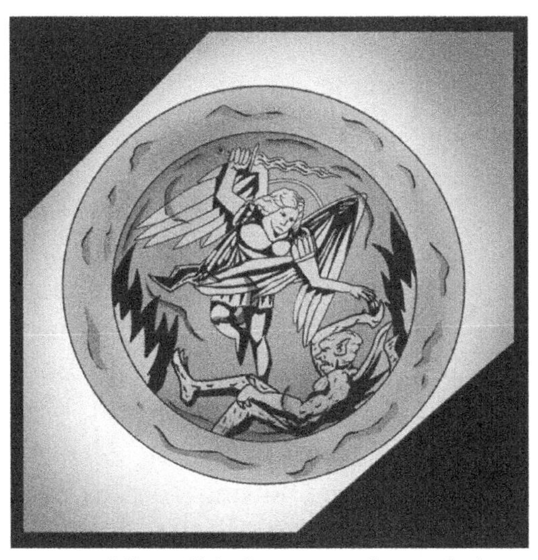

form. The Chief Power looked over at Moriel to see if he was feeling the same effects. Unfortunately, it was clear that the Messenger was not. Xexxus still had a violent hold on him and Moriel was still gripping the Dark elohim's head with all his might. Akalian turned his gaze to the necroplasmic prison and saw Jonathan's astral form immersed in white and blue Light.

The Chief Power glanced down at his abdomen and saw his lethal wound was healing. Akalian now realized what had to be done. It all began to make sense. Akalian's mind went back to the Vision he'd had. To free himself of the evil overtaking him, he had to voluntarily run himself through. Then, Moriel's second Vision showed The Manking being stabbed in the abdomen by a power of Light coming from inside himself. Both Visions of the self-wounded warrior were connected to this very battle. And it was the only way all of this could end. However, one last piece of the puzzle remained.

Akalian and Baetiel were born together from an embryo of Light that sprang forth from The Sigra Agac–The Life Tree. They were more than just brothers. They were twins. In a way, before Baetiel rebelled against King Yahweh they almost had a type of skafos connection–a symbiotic relationship. If something happened to one, the other could feel it in their essence. While that connection was severed when Akalian's brother transformed into Xexxus, the Power still felt that emotional connection. After all this time, after everything Xexxus had done, no matter what Akalian had said or of what he'd tried to convince himself, Xexxus was still very much a part of him. It seemed that even in the Heavenly Host, family would always be connected to one another.

*"God, rebuke him, we humbly pray..."*

Akalian picked up the hilt of Karaydin which still clung to the base of the broken blade. It would be enough to subdue the King of Endless Night. The Power stood and peered at the two elohim struggling against each other. Two brothers: one fallen, one true. Both very much a part of him. Xexxus glared at Akalian, hatred flowing from his eyes.

"His life force is now bound to *me!* If I go, it goes as well!" Xexxus threatened.

Akalian was exhausted in every way possible. What was left of his Lightblade felt heavier than ever. And, although his body was healing, his heart was breaking. He knew what Xexxus said was true. Akalian now knew the true meaning behind the self-wounding in the Visions. He wasn't going to lose a brother; he was going to lose two.

The Chief Power stood in front of Xexxus who was howling and pouring all of his might into fighting Moriel's obu. Green and blue energy were entangled with each other and fired in all directions throughout the throne room. Akalian looked down at the broken Lightblade he held firmly in his hand. As he looked up into the eyes of Moriel, tears ran down Akalian's featherfured cheeks as Moriel spoke through his blinding pain.

"The only way out
Is to move further in.
For even the wisest of all
Cannot go back again."

"I love you, Moriel," Akalian said somberly.

Moriel forced a smile as tears fell from his eyes. "I love you, too. With all my heart. Now do it, brother. Let's end this together."

Mattia, Maryam, and St. Yosef continued to recite the prayer. Mattia was now caught up in their Heavenly energy as it washed over her. She could never put to words just how peaceful that moment felt. But Jonathan, on the other hand, was being physically tortured by every syllable of the prayer.

"And do thou, O Prince of the Heavenly Host, by the power of God, thrust into hell Satan..."

Jonathan's face began to fill with a white Light. Mattia thought it looked similar to the boy-ghoul's reaction to the Capurro Cross in The Grey. As tears rolled down her cheeks, she silently prayed the same outcome didn't await him. Jonathan's demonic voice screamed in agony and the Light emanating from within him flooded the entire room.

"...and all evil spirits who wander throughout the world, seeking the ruin of souls!"

"Amen." Akalian said, as he shoved the base of Karaydin into Xexxus' abdomen.

Xexxus let out an anguished howl as the obu closed over his head. Moriel roared in pain as a bright green energy pulsated into his skull. The entire throne room filled with blinding tzoharian Light. And then the obu exploded.

At first, Mattia couldn't see through the brightness of the room. As things began to dim, the Cleric's senses were on high alert, but she heard nothing. Soon, darkness filled her surroundings and she squinted in an attempt to see. The two bright figures had vanished as mysteriously as they had arrived.

"Cler...Cleric Mattia?" A soft, shy voice pierced the silence. Jonathan Young sat up on the padded room floor, holding his knees up to his chin, attempting to hide his nakedness. "What...what's happening?" he asked in a confused and afraid tone.

"Oh, my boy!" Mattia rushed to him and wrapped him up in her arms as both of them began to cry. "It's okay, Jonathan. It's okay. You're safe now."

As the shadows returned inside the throne room, Akalian watched the green fog dissipate. The walls of the chamber were growing transparent as The Castle of Endless Night faded away from Jonathan Young's essence. The Power looked behind him where the necroplasmic prison had been, and found an empty space. Jonathan's astral form was free. There was no sign of Xexxus, which confirmed that he had been banished to Tartarus. Their mission was complete. However, it's completion came at a heavy cost.

In front of the stairs of the fading dais lay Moriel. Memories of his brother flashed before Akalian's eyes. In his most grevious moments, Moriel had always been there to hold him together and bring him back to reason and Light. The pillar of strength and wisdom who once shone with the very Light of the Throne, now lay there before Akalian, lifeless and gray. Those eyes of life and love that warmed his heart and had always give the Chief Power the assurance of hope and happiness now stared blankly ahead, purposeless and dull.

Something inside the Chief Power shattered and he crumbled to his knees. Akalian couldn't take his eyes off his dear brother as he crawled towards Moriel, sobbing. Reaching the Messenger's lifeless body, the Power cradled his brother's head into his lap and gently caressed his face as tears of sorrow rained down from Akalian's eyes.

"I'm so sorry I couldn't save you...I couldn't save either of you." Akalian lost himself as he wept, lowering his head onto Moriel's, allowing the tears to fall freely onto his brother's cold face. The words Baetiel screamed at Akalian thousands of years ago rang inside his head now. *The King would bring Light out of the Darkness, but the world would then just destroy itself once more.* When would it all end? Why did the King allow it to continue? They'd spent billions of years fighting a war that would seemingly never end. Unending cycles of pain and redemption that led to pain once more. How much more could he take? How much more could any of them take? Akalian wanted to believe that there would be an end to all this. He had faith that the King would make all things new. But, when? How much longer did they all have to endure this?

"It was never your responsibility to save them." The warm voice from behind Akalian brought relief. But also, a twinge of anger crept into the Chief Power's heart as the King's hand landed on Akalian's pauldron covered shoulder.

"Did we do it?" Akalian asked through his tears. "Did we end whatever Tzoharian Nexus this was supposed to bring about?"

"You added variables to the Nexus' equation. Ones that allow for more decisions to be made."

"All of this...for *variables?* So, it's possible that Age End could happen anyway?"

"It's possible, yes." The King's voice was filled with grief when he said this. He knew how much pain Akalian was feeling, and he deeply understood it. "It's possible, but no longer certain. Had you and Moriel not accomplished this, then these new variables would have never existed, nor would the choices exist that could influence and deter the outcome you both saw."

"I don't understand. Why couldn't you have stepped in? *Why?* I know that there are Laws and there are limits to what we can do so the order of the cosmos doesn't break. But...you *made* the order.

You're outside of it *all.* Why did you allow *all of this* to happen? You could have set everything right with a simple thought. The second Azathoth began to have selfish desires, you could have stopped him. So... *why* didn't you?" Akalian's vulnerability had taken over. He was at his wit's end and needed answers. He needed *something* to make sense of all this.

The King calmly took his hand off of Akalian's shoulder, sat down next to him, and took Moriel's faded gray hand in his own. The Chief Power looked at his King's face and was taken aback as he saw tears flowing from Yahweh's deep brown eyes.

"I know you have been holding that question in your heart a very long time. And I know that it has torn you apart inside, fighting back the Darkness that took Baetiel from you...that took him from *me.* And I'm so glad you asked me, because *now* your heart is prepared to know the answer."

Suddenly, Akalian felt their surroundings change. As the Power looked out, beyond where they sat, he saw the vastness of the cosmos. It was breathtaking. The King's strong voice continued.

"The order of the Cosmic Wheel is complicated. Laws that were pre-determined and written into its very fabric affect every being, including *me.* In fact, my explaining this to you now has effects on all of creation that wouldn't have been there otherwise. Everything has a ripple effect."

"But you created it all. How could it affect you in ways that prevent you from acting?" Akalian was trying to understand this personal revelation.

"Yes, I did create it all. But every living thing, if it is truly a living thing, must have an order to it. Laws that, if broken, could undo the very fabric of existence and ultimately cause absolute destruction." As the King continued to speak, their surroundings came to life with the history of the cosmos.

Akalian saw The Creation Wars playing out in front of him. He saw Tiamat emerge from the chaotic waters and swallow the Earth whole. He saw the first Adamians receive ruakh and then saw them take the fruit of knowledge before their preordained time. From that forbidden fruit, Akalian saw Khata emerge out of a Necrogate, causing black, sticky necroplasm to spread forth across the

Corporeum Realm. As the Chief Power sat there watching history pass them by, he listened intently to what his King was saying.

"When Khata first entered existence by the choices of Azathoth, a curse infected the cosmos. It was in that moment that *I* had a choice to make: continue down this path, which would lead to so much pain and suffering, or cleanse it all. But, because of the preordained Laws of order I had established at the beginning, if I chose the latter, I would also end all of you who had not allowed the curse to rule your hearts. The Darkness had in one way or another touched everyone, whether they chose to join it or not. From the beginning, I knew exactly what I must do in this situation. Instead of losing you, I decided to continue on this path *with* you all, knowing precisely where it would lead me." A Vision of the Word Become Flesh dying on a cross flooded Akalian's mind. The King continued.

"I am the course correction. I am why this cosmos did not immediately crumble when Khata set out to rule the hearts of my creation. But it still causes much suffering and pain. In those moments...in *this* moment...it is good to grieve. *I* grieve too," Yahweh's voice cracked when he said this. "I choose to bear this burden *with* you and come alongside you to make a way out of it. It is the only way to keep you all alive and free. I look out into time and space and see so much pain caused by the Darkness but I also see everlasting joy and hope." Yahweh smiled. "I see Eternity with my family; some of whom haven't entered creation yet, and I *can't* leave them behind. I can't leave *you* behind." Their surroundings now faded into a calm light. Akalian heard waves crashing on a shore and knew they were no longer in Jonathan's mind. Akalian then looked upon his King, who was lovingly gazing at him.

"The order of The Cosmic Wheel is broken, but not destroyed. And a part of this fragmented creation is choices. Those choices have consequences that affect everything and everyone around them. In the moments when corrupt choices are made, instead of undoing them, I *use* them to turn the Darkness into Light, so Khata may know it has no victory here. But for me to completely restore the order, change must occur in the most vulnerable place in all creation: the Adamian heart. If *that* changes, then everything else will follow. This is why we continue to fight. We fight to bring change to the hearts of those who would follow me into the Light."

The King paused for a moment and then looked deep out into the distance. "I wish I could tell you more. I wish I could explain *everything* to you, but the weight of omniscience is heavy, and I will not ask anyone else to carry this burden."

Tears continued to flow down Akalian's face, but they were no longer filled with sorrow. They were filled with relief and hope. The King looked down at Moriel's gray body and let out a downcast sigh.

"So, in *this* moment, we sit in grief and pain." Yahweh gently closed Moriel's eyes. "But that pain is not eternal." The King then looked back up at Akalian and placed a warm hand on his Chief Power's cheek, and gave him a hopeful smile as Akalian leaned into this embrace. "This is not the end."

As Akalian and Yahweh sat next to Moriel, the Shores of The White Throne appeared around them. The white sand beneath them warmed Akalian's heart and the sweet aroma of the foamy tide was a balm to his mind. Soon the glistening waters delicately transported Moriel's gray form into the shimmering Silver Sea where he would join the Elohim who had gone before. In the hours after Moriel disappeared from sight, Akalian remained on the shore and the King remained with him.

"Now...let your true form *awaken*."

Etrulia's claw-like fingernails dug deeper into Jonathan Young's scalp as necroplasm seeped through his physical body, pervading his essence. The last twenty-five years flashed before the Dark Sister's eyes and she cackled in delight. Her Coven's allegiance to Xexxus and The Master would ring true this night. She would do what Agatha and Annis never could. She would be the one to awaken the skafos that had laid dormant inside of this dust creature for all these years. Etrulia of Endor would have Jonathan Young embrace his destiny as Manking of The Dark Kingdom. Then, together, she and Xexxus' skafos would awaken The Necronomicon, open The Final Omnigate, and rule as The Master ushered forth the end of The Cosmic Wheel. What her Dark Sisters had begun thousands of years ago, she would be the one to complete. Her essence oozed with victory and pride.

A sharp pain suddenly screamed from the back of Etrulia's head as her vision went black. The witch hit the sandy grass hard. In a panic, she shook her head violently trying to clear the blindness that had just come from the sudden blow to her head. As Etrulia's sight began to clear, she saw Jonathan's limp body twitching on the ground. Had she been connected long enough to awaken the skafos inside of him? Standing above Jonathan was a dark-skinned man draped in a featherfur cloak, waving a white staff in front of him toward the crowd which was screaming and wailing obscenities at the stranger in their midst.

"Back away from him!! He is not yours to claim!!" The stranger commanded, then quickly turned and lifted Jonathan upon his shoulders as if he weighed nothing at all.

Etrulia got a good look at the man carrying her prey. At first, she didn't recognize him. But, once the High Sister gazed into his blazing emerald eyes, she understood who was stealing The Master's promised prize from her.

"I know you can see me through her eyes, Yirah," the stranger bellowed as he pointed the white staff down at the Sister of Endor.

"Do not attempt to follow us. If you do, I will finish what I started with your arm!"

"Akalian!?" Etrulia couldn't believe what she was seeing. As Yirah's skafos, she cowered at this threat. Akalian, the Chief Power of The Order of Michaael was standing in front of her in Adamian form.

"Everyone, kill him!!" The crowd yelled and began running toward Akalian and Jonathan. The Power simply waved his white staff toward them and the front line was instantly struck blind. The crowd was thrown into chaos as the stranger ran into the thick forest with the pilgrim on his back.

Akalian threw the white staff ahead of him. As it landed on the forest floor, it transformed into a large Pentaclegate.

"Hold on, my boy," Akalian said to the unconscious man on his shoulder. "This is not the end."

# PART FOUR

## THE TURNING OF THE COSMIC TIDE

# CHAPTER TWENTY EIGHT

## - THE FELLOWSHIP -

The Village of The Tellyard Bard was quite hidden behind its thick terraformed walls. However, there was much more than terraform technology protecting this nest of evil. For if one were to look at a map of The Grey with all its secrets revealed, they would find that, at any given moment, The Tellyard Bard's location was never difficult to locate even by accident. So, what made the Endorian Coven's Village–like so many other cursed spaces in The Grey–so elusive?

Dark Magick was a wickedness that, at its advanced levels, baffled even the wisest of The Adunalar Elohim. It wasn't that the Dark was more powerful than the Light. It was simply that The Dark Kingdom had consumed the fruit of knowledge out of a selfish desire to gain power instead of waiting for the Deeper Knowledge to be gifted to them by the King at the appropriate time. This chaotic act surely brought them an immediate understanding of the inner workings of The Cosmic Wheel, however it also brought about a horrible corruption that would distort and ultimately destroy them from the inside out.

The Village of The Tellyard Bard was protected by the same Dark Magick that had spirited Yirah away from the Sight of the Heavenly Host twenty-five years prior to Jonathan Young's violent entrance to the Village's tavern. This spell had caused a cyclical manipulation of matter and energy to occur in and around the very fabric of the Village–causing The Village of The Tellyard Bard to actually *move* locations. The spell that orchestrated the Magick was cast by the same ominous being who saved Yirah from Akalian's interrogation. The Dark spell surrounding the Village wasn't a stronghold. That was much too crude and obvious.

Xexxus, in his ego, had made the mistake of creating a stronghold around Hillcrest Sanitarium and boasting his Heralding to whoever had ears to hear. The Master was far more subtle than this. He used the Darkest Magick to cover his tracks and keep his will hidden from anyone and everyone who might attempt to usurp his rule. That included his Council of Shadows. Even The Fellowship–the inner circle of the Council–knew only bits and pieces of what The Master had planned. This left Yirah–whose skafos had just been humiliated by Akalian–completely ignorant of the next steps, now that the Power of Light had taken their Manking from them once more.

Yirah, with his Necromic iron arm that had been gifted to him by The Master upon his merging with Etrulia, pushed the gigantic cyclopean door open, gaining entrance to the Hall of Tamerak, the odious throne room of Dendron: The Oak King.

"You summoned me, my lords?" Yirah's voice quivered in fear. This was not the first time he had been inside the great Hall of The Dark Lord of Summer, but its high arches and black, dripping vines that stretched from one side of the haunted palace to another, were intimidating enough to bring a lowly elohim such as Yirah to his knees. Its odor reeked of rotted pine and mold. However, the daunting sights and smells of the Hall itself almost paled in comparison to what lay at its center.

In the middle of the throne room sat the Goronus Mortem–the Dark twin of the Tamias Mortem which allows this tale to be told. Atop the Goronus Mortem sat a pale blue obu, casting an eerie glow covering the shadows of the room. While the Tamias Mortem is powered by tzoharian Light and life-giving apocalypse (revelation), the Goronus Mortem was powered by Khata and death-seeking apocalypse (the ending of things). This is why the word "apocalyptic" has two meanings, for all creation has experienced both on countless occasions.

Surrounding this glowing fixture of Dark prophecy and doom stood key members of The Fellowship–Dendron, Gaia, Pazuzu, and the mighty Baphomet, second in command of this poisoned brood and High God of Endor. Yirah was thankful that Lilith was nowhere to be found. That was *something*, at least.

"Approach our Council, cowardous sloth." Baphomet's voice bellowed throughout the Hall. The High God of Endor was the largest member of this Dark Council. His eyes glowed a strange grayish blue that illuminated his goat-like head and great horns. Atop his head rested the Endorian god's phallic crown which cradled at its peak a corrupted shard of Krallik–the Aeternum Stone of The Kingdom. Baphomet had two small leathery wings unfurled at his shoulders. His deep purple cloak covered thick, veiny robes of navy blue and black and at his crotch was the insignia of the Thrice Phallic Order of Doom which The Dark Father gifted to all masculine fertility gods of The Dark Kingdom.

Yirah was shaking as he inched forward. His clawed toes clicked against the slimy, black stoned cobble floor.

"I assure you, my lords, my slaves are hunting the wretched elohim who took Xexxus' skafos. Soon we will–" In a blur, Pazuzu, Prince of The Wild Winds, rushed the little devil and snatched Yirah up in a vice grip, bringing him close to his disturbingly pale face. It stood out against the rest of his body which was leathery black that also seemed to shimmer in hues of blue. His two sets of stone-like wings on his back covered his shoulders and the backs of his legs.

The top of his head split into three sections, giving the illusion of a crown cresting around the back of his head. Hovering above this "crown" was a ball of bright blue flame, signifying his clanship with the unholy Order of The Fires of Hell–Commanders of the ongoing torture of Adamian souls. He was a gigantic nightmare to behold.

"You will speak when spoken to, insipid worm," Pazuzu growled. The god of Endor threw Yirah toward the rest of the Council. He landed with a smack at the base of the Goronus Mortem.

"We gave you the dust creature, Jonathan Young, on a silver platter," Gaia hissed through her tragedian mask, which was now solidified to her skull since she had been wearing it for millions of years. She and her siblings Transfectiated into The Facades–an Order of deception and vanity. All of them thrived on the theatrical vice of gossip, slander, and idolatrous beauty, and all wore the face of The Tragedian, the Head of their narcissistic Order. "How could you allow this to happen?"

Yirah began to speak but was immediately cut off by the deep, gravelly voice of Dendron. It boomed through the molded vines, leaves, and moss that covered his enormous body.

"The constellations of The Empress and The Eastern Tower are aligning with Pandemonium on The Winter Solstice in two nights time. We gather here, in my kingdom, to prepare the way for The Manking to rise alongside your skafos, Etrulia, and awaken The Necronomicon. This is meant to be the final victory against St. Nicholas and his Isikaraida as The Cosmic Tide turns to Deep Winter. This is meant to bring about the final Eve of Age End, Yirah. And yet, *the Anak Zaman* is now missing, taken by the very Power who made Xexxus' skafos dormant inside of his own dust creature." Dendron paused and glared at Yirah as if the little devil was now meant to respond.

The Anak Zaman was a term Yirah had heard the Council use only when referring to Jonathan Young. He had no idea what it meant and no one had ever explained it to him. Nor did he have the nerve to ask. In truth, not many Dark elohim knew how to properly decipher the extremely complicated Manking Prophecy that was delivered by The Dark Father so long ago. There were wild rumors amongst the scattered Kingdom regarding the signs of the ancient prediction. Some actually doubted it was real. However, when The Master first appeared after the Adamian's Second World War, secretly forming alliances amongst the scattered Dark Kingdom, the rumors of The Manking began circling again for the first time since the Gadarene Cult was destroyed.

Yirah didn't know *who* The Master actually was, nor was he aware of *any* Dark elohim who did. Some said it was The Dark Father himself, or a skafos, or one of his Dark Princes attempting to rise to power. All Yirah knew was that The Master appeared to the little devil and offered him greatness and The Master had made good on that promise. However, with this greatness came the risk of great failure. The little devil was now being questioned for such failure and had no answer to satisfy his terrifying judges. But he had to give them something or they would soon destroy him.

"We now know what Akalian's Adamian form looks like," Yirah started. "I've alerted all the stewards in the surrounding areas to be on guard and they–"

"*How* was the Chief Power of Michael even *near* The Tellyard Bard Village without you knowing??" Baphomet shouted, his eyes engulfed in flame. "And how did he *enter* the Village and then *escape* without *anyone* following him?!"

"W-we believe he has been in Adamian form for quite some time and potentially has a shield of protection around him that blinds us from seeing him."

Gaia now stepped in to interrogate.

"And how is that possible, worm? Our Orders govern the borders of The Grey. If an elohim of Light crosses into our territory, we are immediately notified and the being is either imprisoned or forced to retreat."

"What of the Yeshuite camps, my Lord?" Yirah questioned hesitantly.

Gaia's pride was struck. Her Order had attempted to rid their lands of the Yeshuites many times and had failed. A green and black necroplasmic blast shot from Gaia's hand and crashed into Yirah's chest, sending him soaring across the room.

"How dare you!?" Gaia screamed.

"No. The sloth is right," Baphomet interjected. "There are seven churches within The Grey that we cannot penetrate. Despite our efforts to corrupt it, the Soma Aedrum is too strong at this moment. It is possible that Akalian utilized those spaces to Pentaclegate from one church to another and then used a protection shield to enter the Village."

"Then how did he escape?" Dendron asked. "Yirah stated that Akalian took the dust creature and ran off into the forest at the base of the Village. There's no way out other than—"

"Other than the Necrogate," Pazuzu growled. "Which Akalian could not use."

"If I may..." Yirah winced as he spoke. He had managed to regather himself and crawl back over to the Council. "It is possible that Akalian carried a Tzoharian Codex with him into the Corporeum Realm."

It was now Pazuzu's turn to blast Yirah across the room. The Endorian god did so with a smile on his face.

"He's right," Pazuzu said in an annoyed tone. "That is the only likely probability."

"Then they are well aware of our plans," said Dendron.

"Yes," Gaia agreed. "However, what could they possibly do to stop the skafos from awakening inside of Jonathan Young? Yirah confirmed that Etrulia did, indeed, stay connected to the dust creature long enough to reengage the Stone inside of him."

"Do not forget, sister," Baphomet reminded. "The Sapient Stone was used to *seal* the dust creature's destiny as The Manking. But it was *Minos' Labyrinth* that kept the Stone's power in check. It was able to hold the Shard's power and direct it toward the will of *Xexxus* who answered to Lilith and The Master. Now the Labyrinth is destroyed and Xexxus is no longer there to guide the Shard's power. Even if the skafos awakens, without Etrulia, there is no one to *guide* it. No *will* to make sure Jonathan Young embraces his destiny."

"What if the enemy isn't interested in *removing* the Shard from the dust creature?" Pazuzu said. "What if they are attempting to *use* it?"

"What if the dust creature were to use it for his *own* will?" Yirah hesitantly mumbled the question. He had once again returned—barely able to stand—to the Goronus Mortem. The little devil braced himself for another chastising blast, but none came. Instead, the Council seemed pleased with this thought.

"Go on," Baphomet uttered.

Relief washed over Yirah, only to be immediately replaced by

anxiety. Yirah knew if he said one thing that displeased any of them, he would be sent flying across the Hall once more.

"Uhm..at this point, we can be *positive* that Akalian has successfully taken the dust creature back to his hideaway and is preparing to master Xexxus' skafos within Jonathan Young. As soon as the skafos awakens, it will fight back, giving off a detectable location. Like a beacon for us to follow. What if, once we locate his whereabouts, instead of trying to face Akalian head on, we simply send someone to covertly *encourage* Jonathan to come back to the Village and finish what he started with his *new found* power?"

"The entire Village will be destroyed," Gaia replied.

"But then *we* could be waiting for him and gain control of the skafos." Dendron declared. "I care not for what happens to those pathetic sows in the Village, even Etrulia. They've all served their purpose. If this gives us our Manking, I'd sacrifice however many dust creatures or skafos it takes."

"And what of the Necronomicon?" Gaia interjected. "Are we to cast this crucial part of the Saturnalia aside? *That* child has been prepared just as Jonathan Young was."

"No," Baphomet countered. "There is *no one* who has been prepared like the Anak Zaman, no one in the entire history of creation. If we lose the child, then we lose the child. If we have The Manking, then we have all we need to begin again."

The Council gave their orders to Yirah and sent him on his way with the warning that if he failed them once more, it would not be The Fellowship who dealt with the little devil, but The Master himself.

# CHAPTER TWENTY NINE

## - DECISIONS & CONSEQUENCES -

Far across The Grey, miles and miles from The Village of The Tellyard Bard, lay a pilgrim. The life of this broken man had been wrought with peril and tragedy. His childhood had been a mystery to him as he had no real memory of anything before the age of fourteen. He was told that trauma from his possession and exorcism was the reason for the memory loss. Memories that, for the majority of his lifetime, loomed over him like a shadow figure seen in the peripheral of his everyday life.

He was raised, in secret, by Mattia and Obadiah, because he had been officially declared dead on the night of his exorcism. Six days after the death of High Cleric Malcolm and other prominent Council Clerics, Grand Chancellor Magnus I—at the behest of his son and successor Magnus II—ordained Mattia Bajuma as High Cleric of The Grand Republic. At her coronation, Mattia was commended for her "*act of bravery and selflessness as she uncovered the heinous plot orchestrated by her predecessor.*" The night was henceforth known to all The Grand Republic as "Reinignacht" or "The Night of Cleansing".

For assisting Cleric Mattia on her quest to bring order back to the High Council, Obadiah was pardoned of his past crimes. Unfortunately, because of those crimes, he was mandated to remain just a citizen of The Grand Republic and was denied access to any Clerical privileges he had once held. But he was granted "Purifican Status" as a reward for his bravery. This status allowed him to remain a societal leader within The Grand Republic. He could still vote and take part in local politics on the Territorial government level. However, Obadiah's trust in The Grand Republic was gravely broken and he believed he was being closely watched by the RPG. Therefore, the former Cleric knew his public profile had to remain as low as possible.

Obadiah also believed whoever had been working with Malcolm would be watching Mattia closely as well, which may have been the very reason why she was elected as the new High Cleric in the first place. She absolutely deserved the honor and he knew she was more than capable, but he didn't trust the majority of the High Elders at all. He often called them a group of inbred vultures. But, he didn't believe that all of them were in bed with The Coven as Malcolm and the Council had been. Otherwise, why would they have rewarded Mattia or himself at all, instead of having them secretly assassinated or cast into The Wastelands?

Obadiah firmly believed that the only reason they were both rewarded and not punished was because at least a few of the High Elders might genuinely be semi-decent human beings. It was even possible that Magnus II was a man of reason despite his debaucherous lifestyle and having come from a staunch, authoritarian father. However, Magnus I had still been in control when Malcolm was killed. Obadiah was almost positive The Grand Chancellor was at least a sympathizer to Malcolm and The High Council's partnership with The Coven. Because of this, Obadiah was easily able to convince Mattia that Jonathan was still in danger.

"Something like this Black Mass came from higher up the food chain than Malcom," Obadiah had said to Mattia after they had settled Jonathan into bed on the night of his exorcism. Mattia wasn't sure whether or not he was right, but she didn't want to take the chance. If Jonathan's whereabouts were known, he could still be in danger, so they both decided to officially end the boy's life on paper. This was a pivotal way to assure his safety.

The official Cause of Death read as follows:

*Client 43972's heart gave out during an attempt to save him from Malcolm's abusive manipulation that fed into the client's delusional and aggressive behavior. Time of death was 0300. Client's body was then promptly incinerated as per usual custom, fearing any contagious contamination.*

Obadiah didn't stop there. He and Mattia both knew that there was a hidden Dark force–something in an unseen realm–that was after the boy. They also knew that The Coven could easily find him through their malevolent divination, so something had to be done to tie up that loose end. Obadiah felt he had just the answer for such a problem. In The Grey, there was a Hoodoo Yeshuite tribe that could place a protection spell on the boy, keeping the Dark Powers from seeing him and then revealing his location to The Coven.

At first, Mattia was skeptical of such an act, not fully understanding how a Hoodoo spell was any different from The Coven's Magick. But Obadiah had explained that there was, in fact, a difference between what was classically known as "white Magick" and "black Magick".

While there was a significant difference between the two, utilizing any divination practice was extremely dangerous for Adamians due to how powerfully deceptive The Dark Kingdom was. Even the most skilled Magician with the purest of intentions could be deceived by a Dark elohim masquerading as an angel of Light. It was for this reason that Yahweh had strictly forbidden divination practices for those who would follow him and call themselves his people. However, in this New World, those warnings found in the Ancient Law of Moses weren't well understood, and, in some cases, long forgotten. Therefore, due to this unfortunate ignorance and the extreme sensitivity of the situation, King Yahweh not only allowed this protection spell to take place, but he guarded it from any Dark Kingdom interference.

In the days following Jonathan's exorcism, Obadiah secretly brought in the Hoodoo Shaman from The Grey to administer the protection spell. Most of the time, a spell of this kind was placed upon an object or an amulet that the subject of protection would carry with them. Nevertheless, Obadiah didn't want to take any chances and instructed the Shaman to place the spell directly upon Jonathan him-

-self. Not only would this cover him wherever he went, but it would also help bury any memories or thoughts of his possession, protecting the boy externally and internally. So, for the next seventeen years of Jonathan's life, neither The Coven of Endor nor The Dark Kingdom knew of his whereabouts, or if he even existed at all.

From ages thirteen to eighteen, Jonathan Young was in training, directly under the tutelage of his new adoptive father, Obadiah. Even though his demeanor became that of a normal teenager, it was clear that the boy was far from normal; his possession somehow had given him *gifts,* as Obadiah called them. Jonathan could move faster than normal children his age and sense things before they would happen, which multiplied his instincts exponentially. His strength also increased rapidly. It seemed as though some of the abilities Jonathan displayed on the night of his exorcism stayed with him. Despite Mattia wanting a common childhood for the boy–as common as possible after such a traumatic experience–she agreed with Obadiah that they had an opportunity with Jonathan that may never occur again.

Despite Malcolm's death, the attacks from The Coven of Endor were worse than ever and the Resistance group in The Grey was wearing thin. This was a chance to build something–an elite team who could lead the Resistance and make a difference in this secret war raging in the shadows of the world. While it was true that Jonathan was a rarity, there were many people–children and adults–who had been rescued from the raids against The Coven, exorcised, and currently going through rehabilitation and being trained to join the fight. It was possible that some of them would prove to have similar heightened abilities or that their traumatic experiences could have increased their drive to fight in ways others did not possess.

Simultaneously, mysterious funding for this secret initiative began arriving in High Cleric Mattia's desk drawer every week with a letter inside the envelope saying, "*Fight the good fight,*" signed only with the letter "Z". Months went by and the currency continued to grow with each letter. Finally, one evening as Mattia was retiring from a long hard day, a shadowy cloaked figure stood in the Labyrinth Room of her High Cleric flat, atop The High Temple. Mattia only noticed him from the corner of her eye as she passed by the double framed opening that led to her space of secluded and sacred meditation.

"*Who the hell are you!? How did you get in here!?*" These were both questions that flooded the High Cleric's mind, but before she could say them aloud, an android-like voice bellowed from a bright blue digital faceplate, illuminating from a cyber-helmet underneath a pulled down hood.

"I am Z," the voice said. "And I'm here to help."

Deep into the night, Z and Mattia met and talked. Somehow this mysterious figure knew more about Reinignacht than even Mattia did. In fact, Z knew things that even the High Elders or Grand Chancellor didn't. As their partnership continued throughout the coming months, and Obadiah was brought into the fold as well, it was revealed that Z was, in reality, a rising member of the Purificans and was well on his climb up the political ladder. His name was Henrik Lazarus and he was the latest rising star in Perethedesh and in most of The Southern Territory.

Both Mattia and Obadiah were shocked at this fact, as Henrik Lazarus was known to be an extremely wealthy socialite who was famous for his more frivolous behavior. He was also known as someone who was not above using his status to get whatever he wanted, whenever he wanted it. A stereotypical playboy type of bachelor. So, to find out that this man—who was soon to be the newest member of The Republic Senate—was secretly investing in their Resistance movement made Mattia and Obadiah confused and more than a bit skeptical.

At first, they thought it might be a trap laid out by the High Elders. But it was Henrik's "Z" persona that convinced Mattia and Obadiah otherwise. Henrik explained that the "Z" stood for "Zion", which they understood to be both a physical hill in the Ancient World city of Jerusalem and a mythical realm of heaven from Abrahamic faiths. Henrik seemed to be using this as a symbolic mission statement.

As Z, Henrik had been building a secret union of shadow

agents all across the Southern Territory of The Grand Republic, and this agency was rapidly growing. He was tapped into every major system, had hidden cameras everywhere, and had even hacked into the RPG surveillance mainframe. When Obadiah would ask him what started his mission, all Henrik would say in response was, "*I saw the corruption beginning to boil over and something had to be done.*"

As it turned out, Henrik had also been secretly funding many of the Resistance's raids against The Coven over the last couple of years. Once Obadiah found this out, he was sold on who Henrik was as a person, despite who the soon-to-be Senator *wanted* the public to believe he was.

Mattia and Obadiah now had a growing team and the funding to finance a brand-new resistance. They built two large headquarters for their base of operations–one in The Grey and one underneath Perethedesh in the Old World abandoned city (Riyadh) that The Lowers was built atop. Henrik had already planted his base underneath the city, so they just expanded it. There were also multiple smaller bases throughout The Southern and Northern Territories, surrounding The Grey. The Coven of Endor and their allies began to feel the pressure inside and outside of their malevolent kingdom.

Ater five years of training and then another six months of directly shadowing Z on his nightly patrols, Jonathan Young stepped forth as the second in command–some would say he eventually became co-commander with Z–of The Resistance Elite. This team of tactically skilled demonologist witch hunters brought a fight to The Coven that hadn't been seen since before The Final War.

For the next thirteen years, it was bloody warfare between The Resistance and The Coven. There were seasons of horror and seasons of victory for both sides. And throughout this time, Jonathan's heart grew darker and more calloused to the war effort.

Even though his courtship and marriage to his fellow Resistance teammate, Lynn Deborney, brought much joy, Jonathan could not shake this *other* side of himself that lived in the darker parts of his mind, eating away at his soul. It was in these shadowy corners that a secret longing for violence and carnage would emerge. Jonathan fought it as best he could and, to his utmost ability, he hid it from everyone around him, including the ones most precious to him

–Lynn, and his parental figures, Mattia and Obadiah.

Then, one fateful night his life exploded. Jonathan's world was ripped from under him and this *other* side of himself began to seep through. For the following six months, he ravaged himself with anything he could get his hands on to escape the pain of loss, anger, and guilt. Drugs, alcohol, and frequent visits to the StagNight bars in The Lowers for a little *R&R* slowly destroyed the man he had once been. Finally, Jonathan did something he would never forgive himself for.

That's when he left. Jonathan left his family, his friends, and his mission. He left it all to chase down the one person he blamed for every horrible thing he'd become: Etrulia, High Sister of Endor, the bane of his existence. Little did he know that six years later he would find her, confront her, and lose.

Still, on this particular night, Jonathan lay unconscious in the cave of a stranger who had risked more and lost more than Jonathan could ever know, just to keep the pilgrim safe. Jonathan's world was about to turn completely upside down.

Dark dreams of nightmarish beasts had been plaguing the pilgrim's dreams in his comatose hours. Jonathan saw a dull shard illuminate to a bright green. He saw flashes of an ominous figure glaring at him, eyes glowing green, and hiding behind thick fog. Etrulia's bubbling, melted face manically laughing as black slime oozed over his soul, leaving a cold wet void in its stead. Cold and wet. Cold and wet. Warm and wet. He now felt this new sensation on his flesh. Warm and wet. A small, prickly tongue. Specifically on his nose. Jonathan's eyes batted open to see a large, orange tabby cat staring at him mere inches from his face.

"Wh..what the–?" Jonathan shot up from his supine position and was met with two realizations. The first was a throbbing headache that distracted him from the horrible dreams he had just been having. The second was the fact that he was stark naked underneath what appeared to be a sheepskin blanket. As Jonathan had sat up, the orange tabby leapt off of him and bounded towards a shadowy figure positioned towards the opening of the cave, on the other side of a roaring fire.

"Uhm. I'm *very* naked," Jonathan grunted through his split-

-ting headache. "Why am I very naked? You didn't do anything... *weird* to me, did you?"

"You stank of witch," replied Akalian. "Your clothes are almost dry."

Jonathan watched as the man came into view from the other side of the blazing flames. It was indeed the dark-skinned man who had accosted him in the alleyway in The Tellyard Bard Village.

"*You?*" Jonathan exclaimed. "What happened back there? Where am I?"

"Those answers will come in time. What is the last thing you remember?"

Jonathan sat up, wrapping himself in the animal skins. He quickly observed his surroundings. There wasn't much to see. It was a small cave, barely enough room for two or three people. In the middle of the cave was a roaring fire pit billowing smoke up into a small opening at the top of the cave. That was it. No furniture of any kind. No cooking utensils to be seen. Jonathan was surprised that he had been laying on an old cot instead of the dirt floor.

"Do you *live* here?" Jonathan asked condescendingly.

"This is not my home. Now, what's the last thing you remember?"

Jonathan massaged his temples, attempting to rid himself of the lingering, throbbing pain.

"Let me think...uhm...I threw holy water on Etrulia and then–oh god. The Capurro Cross...she destroyed it. How did she destroy it?? Why didn't it work?"

"Focus," Akalian said sternly.

"Okay. After that...after that everything goes dark. And then, I woke up...*here.*" Jonathan suddenly stared angrily at the stranger who stood before him. "Who the *fuck* are you?"

"Someone who just saved your life."

"How do I know that's true? For all I know, you work for The Coven and I'm already under some Dark spell. You could be one of her shamans or sorcerers preparing me for a ritual." He gestured down at himself. "I am *very* naked after all."

"You are naked because I washed your clothes. They're drying just outside in the oak tree."

"Oak tree? We're in The Lost Dunes, *friend.* There are no oak trees."

Akalian stepped aside and gestured for Jonathan to see for himself.

"You're free to look."

Jonathan scoffed and stood up, wrapping the covering around his shoulders, holding it tight to himself, making sure the stranger didn't sneak a peek. As he walked closer to the opening, he not only saw the oak tree a few yards from the cave, but it was surrounded by luscious green grass. Jonathan's jaw dropped. It was as if he was looking out onto the gardenesque Observation Level at The High Temple. Even in the darkness of the night, the colors were much more vivid than he'd ever seen before. Sure enough, there were his clothes hanging from a tree branch just outside. Not only did the scenery look gorgeous, but just glancing at it made Jonathan feel completely at peace. A wave of happiness flooded over him and he began to well up inside.

*If this was Dark Witchcraft, it might look beautiful, but I don't think it would* feel *this way. I don't think it could,* Jonathan thought to himself. He had been under Dark spells before and even though a couple of them had made him feel euphoric pleasure, none of them felt this...*holy*. He knew that no matter how much The Coven might try, they couldn't replicate this kind of goodness. There was always at least a slight feeling of cheap imitation lingering around a spell like that. None of what Jonathan saw before him was a facade. This was *real*.

Then, suddenly, a sense of overwhelming rage began to overtake him. Jonathan didn't know where it was coming from, but one moment he felt utter warmth and blissful happiness and, in a split second, he felt boiling hatred and avarice flowing through his veins at the sight of this sacred blooming foliage. Jonathan slowly turned around, pointing all of this newfound fury at the stranger on the other side of the flames.

"What is your name?" Jonathan asked fiercely. It wasn't as much of a question as it was a command. And Akalian knew this. The Power knew that the skafos deep inside Jonathan Young could very easily awaken at any time. Giving Jonathan the power of claiming his name was something Akalian had been careful not to do. He would not allow the skafos to have that conquering power over him. A conquering power that was being ordered of the elohim now. The skafos was clearly emerging.

Akalian quickly reached out and touched the side of the cave wall, sending a ripple of energy toward the opening of the cave directly in front of Jonathan, sealing the entrance shut. Jonathan could sense the change in the atmosphere and attempted to run out of the cave only to have a bolt of tzoharian Light knock him down onto his back.

Jonathan immediately leapt to his feet, unphased by the energy blast, and quickly turned toward Akalian. Madness and loathing poured from his eyes. Akalian had seen that exact expression before, but not on the face of Jonathan Young. It was an expression Xexxus wore all too well.

"What did you just do!?" Jonathan roared. "I knew it. You *are* working with The Coven!" Jonathan Young sprinted towards the stranger before him at a speed Akalian wasn't prepared for. The elohim had never seen an Adamian run this fast, even while possessed.

Jonathan moved exactly like Xexxus. Before the blink of an eye, the wild man jumped through the flames and tackled Akalian to the ground. As they both landed on their sides, the Power held out his hand towards Jonathan and let out a small blast of energy, making Jonathan slide across the dirt floor and slam against the wall. He didn't want to hurt the pilgrim, but he had to gain control of the situation.

"Jonathan Young!!" Akalian's voice boomed with a monumental force throughout the enclosed cave. "Hear me now and heed what I say. The satan inside you is gaining strength. You *must* fight it."

Jonathan roared in frustration as he jerked to his feet, slamming his back against the wall of the cave.

"What's happening to me!? I can't fight it! It–it's too strong."

"Allow me." Akalian quickly approached the pilgrim. The Chief Power reached out his hands to touch Jonathan's head when suddenly a green light flashed in the man's eyes. Akalian went flying through the air, landing hard on the opposing cave wall.

"You will not take me!!" Jonathan howled, green eyes glaring. "I am The Final Herald! Born of The Master! Bringer of Destruction! Usher of Age End! No elohim of Light will prevent the Great Dark Eschaton from breaking forth upon the Earth!!" At this moment, pain screamed from Jonathan's side as he heard a wild hissing sound and felt sharp claws dig into his abdomen. In an instant, the orange tabby cat blasted a bolt of energy out of his furry belly, sending Jonathan helplessly flailing towards the back of the cave. In midair, the pilgrim's shins slammed into the cot. Jonathan's naked body spun head over heel into the back wall and he landed upside down on his head.

"Willow!" Akalian yelled towards his furry friend. "Help me contain him!" The two disguised elohim dashed to Jonathan's stunned body and, by telepathic means, began emitting tzoharian energy from their essences onto the struggling man.

"Jonathan." Akalian took the pilgrim's head in his hands and shook him lightly. "I need you to listen to me very carefully. What is happening to you is hard to understand and those answers will come, but for now, you *must* trust me."

Jonathan was coming in and out of consciousness. He felt as though his soul was being ripped in two.

"O–okay. Just–make this stop!" he grunted in desperation.

"Repeat these words after me. It's a prayer that has ancient weight, but also carries a deeply personal meaning to your heart." Akalian then immediately began reciting the words from the Medal of St. Benedict. A prayer that held more power than Jonathan could know at this time.

"May the Holy Cross be my light.
May The Dragon never be my guide.
Begone satan!
I reject your vanities!
The cup you offer me is evil.
Drink the poison yourself!"

After Jonathan finished repeating the final line, he passed out onto the dirt floor.

Mattia Bajuma stood beside the cyber-window of the hospital room—her now long grey locks fell to her shoulders—looking out across the city of Perethedesh, a place she still loved so dearly. The High Cleric had pressed the shuffle option on the window screen so the thousands of cameras across the vast city would show her the place she called home. And even though she watched the different views come and go, she found little comfort in what used to bring her so much joy and peace.

It had been six years—almost exactly—since the day Jonathan had left. She had no way of knowing where he was, or if he was still alive.

He had been so careful in the last few years not to draw any attention to himself. She knew that no matter how many Resistance agents looked for him, even if it was Henrik himself, Jonathan wouldn't be found unless he wanted to be. And she understood *why* he didn't want to be. Her heart broke for her son. This life had dealt him a horrible hand and deep down she feared that her decision to allow him to become a weapon was ultimately what drove him to spiraling in the dark void he'd fallen into.

Mattia wasn't alone in this decision, to be sure. The man who helped her make it, lay in a coma in the hospital bed next to her, just where he had been for six and a half years now. In all her sixty-five years, Mattia had never found a more faithful and loving partner. She had also never met a more stubborn man than the one who lay in this bed. Being eleven years her senior, Obadiah had no business being in the field the night he was struck down by the High Sister Etrulia, but who could tell *him* that? Especially when his own son had convinced him that night that he wasn't "*too old for this shit*" just yet.

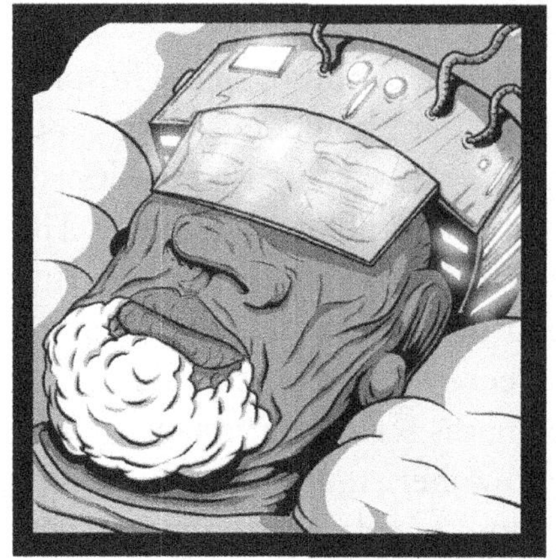

The High Cleric knew this was ultimately what drove Jonathan over the edge. He felt entirely responsible for what happened to his adoptive father that night and for the great tragedy months after. But everything that led up to that tragedy was always something Mattia felt mostly responsible for. Jonathan's actions may have been his own, but she knew everyone was a product of their surroundings. What kind of surroundings had she forced her son into? This question would plague her for the rest of her days.

"Hey, Matty." The deep voice drew her attention towards the doorway. Henrik Lazarus closed the door behind him as he walked into the hospital room deep under the city of Perethedesh. The Fallout, which was the official name of The Resistance headquarters under the city, stretched out at a twenty-mile radius. The hospital wing alone was over two miles of that space. Henrik had funded *all* of this.

"Hi, Laz," Mattia responded as she gently took Obadiah's limp hand. She stared down at both of their wrinkled features and felt loneliness wash over her.

"I come into this room every evening, hoping that he'll be sitting up, smiling at me, cracking some joke about how he'd been waiting over six years for me to come through that door, and what took me so long." She choked up. "But that hasn't happened yet."

Henrik, wearing his jet-black steel-latex undersuit and baggy sweatpants, walked over and sat down on the corner of the bed, taking Obadiah's other hand.

"Knowing this old fool, I wouldn't be surprised if it were to happen just like that." Henrik gave Mattia a slight smile.

"Going out on patrol soon?" The High Cleric casually asked, returning the smile.

"Yeah, but I wanted to stop by and let you know something

first." His expression grew somber.

"What? What is it, Henrik?" Mattia's heart dropped to her stomach. Henrik rarely made a special trip to tell her things outside of their bi-weekly briefings.

"I just got word a couple of hours ago from a Yeshuite tribe in The Grey...they think Jon was there."

"Oh my god."

"The report stated that he stayed for a couple days, filled up on supplies, and departed in an ungravity-pod heading east toward Minasarat."

"What makes them believe it was him?" Mattia was hopeful, but skeptical.

"We have a few covert agents in the tribe. One of them worked with Jon and Dockson about ten years ago and thinks he recognized him."

"Did they say how he was? His demeanor? Anything?"

"It was bleak. The report stated he didn't say much, kept to himself and was hell-bent on reaching The Lost Dunes as soon as possible."

"He found her," Mattia said in shock. "Oh god, Henrik...he found her."

"We don't know that, Matty." Henrik placed a comforting hand on top of hers and Obadiah's. "For all we know, it's just a lead that ends up being a dead end. No one knows where The Tellyard Bard is...and quite frankly, my theory is that it doesn't stay in one place for very long."

"Yes, I know your *'teleportation theory'* all too well," Mattia said half scoffingly.

"How else do you explain how elusive it is? And if it's true, then even *if* Jon found out a location, it's likely that The Coven would know through their divination that he was on his way and–"

*"That's* what I'm afraid of, Henrik. Maybe Etrulia has figured out how to break through Jonathan's protection spell. She's certainly powerful enough to have done so. Maybe she *wants* to be found. It's the Saturnalia. Winter Solstice is in two days. You know the significance he held with The Coven at one point. It's all too possible that they've discovered who he *really* is and want to finish the job they started over twenty-five years ago."

Henrik paused and looked down at the bed. He knew this was a sensitive subject with Mattia and if she wasn't the High Cleric, he probably wouldn't have even said anything, but given her role in all of this, he felt she needed to know. Mattia took the hint and switched gears.

"Have you said anything to Lynn?"

"No. Nor do I think it's wise to do so. The last time we informed her of a reported sighting she spiraled into depression for months. She's tried to use her Sight to find him and failed so many times, I think this would just trigger her all the more. Lynn's in a good spot right now, I don't want to ruin that."

"Alright. I think I agree with that," Mattia responded. "Is there anything else?"

"I think I'm taking Jarren out with me tonight. We need more tactical agents in the field right now and she shows the most promise at the moment."

"She's only fifteen, Henrik."

"And she shows the most promise. I can't help that this war exists, Matty. If we're going to win, we need to take every opportunity we have. When Jon left, he not only left a large hole in The Elite, but he put Lynn out of commission for years. And with the others gone too, our team *still* hasn't fully recovered from that night."

Mattia looked back down at her partner, her husband. Obadiah looked as though he was just sleeping. If it weren't for the wires and head apparatus, she could almost convince herself that he was just taking a nap in a spare hospital bed like he'd done so many times before between double shift missions. Henrik was so much like him. The mission *always* came first. It *had* to, no matter the cost. Mattia understood that drive and respected it, but she also hated it. It took everyone she'd ever loved from her.

"Fine. Take the *child* out into the night and turn her into a warrior. It seems like that's what we do best around here."

Henrik didn't respond. He squeezed Mattia's hand, stood up, and left the room. After a few moments, Mattia got up and walked back over to the cyber-window—freezing the screen on a view of the night sky and stared at the full moon shining brightly between the clouds.

"Stay safe my boy. Wherever you are Jon...please...come home."

"Okay. So, let me get this straight. You're an *angel?"* Jonathan Young asked the stranger sitting in front of him. Then he pointed towards the orange tabby sitting next to them. "And *he's*...an angel too..."

"That is a term many have used to describe our race, yes. In reality, 'angel' simply means, 'messenger'. But for our immediate purposes, we'll leave it at that."

"A cat. Weird."

"You have no idea." Akalian responded as he smirked at Willow, who gave a sassy chatter.

Akalian was trying to ease the pilgrim into things. Jonathan had woken up clothed and in his right mind, and needing answers. The Power didn't want to overwhelm him, but it was certainly time the pilgrim understood a few things.

"Alright. Before we get into this, can I finally know your name?" Jonathan asked.

"Not yet, I'm afraid."

"Right. Because of the whole control...*thing*. I didn't realize it would work on creatures other than demons."

"It normally doesn't. Your situation is not a normal one."

"Well, I have to call you *something*. How about, Clarence? That has a nice ring to it, don't you think?"

"I'd rather you not," the elohim said firmly.

"Well, tough nuts Clarence, it's happening."

"Hm," Akalian grunted disapprovingly. Jonathan's flippant sarcasm was already proving to be difficult. Akalian could sense the bitter apathy behind this defense mechanism. It was a means of keeping control of the situation. *This* was not a side effect of the skafos.

"I have to be honest here, I really didn't think your kind existed. And I'm still not convinced. I've heard stories, sure, but I've never met one of you before."

"Not that you're aware of, at least. We normally keep a lower profile. Listen, I know you must have many questions, but it's imperative that we stay on the topic at hand." Akalian was trying to avoid an endless question and answer session that would distract from their purpose here. Time was running very thin.

"Right. Okay. So, let's see...your cat angel used its magic powers to throw me against the wall because this...*skafos*...was trying to take over my mind, body, and soul. Then *you* grabbed my face and said a prayer that I repeated. Then I woke up and felt normal again. Make it make sense."

"I'll try not to oversimplify it, but essentially, you have two personalities warring over your essence–the *being* of Jonathan Young, if you will. One of them is the Image Bearing human you were born as; the other is a twisted bastardization of an evil human-god hybrid left inside you after your possession."

"The prick didn't even buy me dinner first," Jonathan dryly said to himself. Then he let out a deep sigh, accepting the heavy explanation. "Well...that's not something you like to hear."

"Indeed," the elohim said compassionately.

"And...this *Manking* business? What you're saying is, if I *don't* do anything about this skafos and rush back to the Village, they'll just gain control of me again and potentially end the order of *The Cosmic Wheel?"*

"As of now, I don't see an alternative in that scenario. If you face her, you will die—"

"And all of the villagers will die too," Jonathan finished flippantly. "Yeah, I remember your cryptic warning. A little *more* head ups would have been nice though, don't you think?"

"Would you have believed me?" Akalian responded. "You were so focused on your revenge that you would've dismissed *anything* I said. After a few moments with you, that was quite clear. Besides, I wasn't sure *what* would trigger the skafos and what wouldn't. I couldn't take the risk of mentioning it in the moment."

"That's fair, I guess," Jonathan conceded and then paused for a moment before circling back to the topic at hand. "So, this prayer we recited...it what? Subdued this other personality in me?"

"In a sense, yes. The Saint Benedict Medal prayer is a very ancient, very powerful thing."

"I'm familiar with it, but I'm just not understanding how it was able to subdue such a powerful force. I mean, I couldn't gain control at all. It was like I was completely losing myself. It was like...I was being *repossessed.* Then this prayer undid all of that?"

"For the moment," Akalian confirmed.

Jonathan was well versed in Yeshuetic lore and had used many prayers and relics from this faith tradition. However, the true power behind the specific prayers and relics weren't very well understood in this New World, even inside of the Yeshuetic tribes of The Soma Aedrum. Even though Jonathan had been fighting alongside them for his entire known life, he was more of an "*if it works, it works and I don't need to know how it works*" kind of person. Sometimes that proved very useful. Other times it was problematic. The pilgrim was impressively intelligent, but because of his abilities, he wasn't usually as concerned as he should have been with the intellectual understandings of the *"weapons in the field".*

Akalian wanted to help the pilgrim better understand the situation. The Saint Benedict Medal Prayer—among a few others—

had deep roots in Jonathan's soul, but that was a conversation for another time.

"There are particular prayers that hold great power when paired with a specific person. Just as the Dark Curse–what my kind calls *Khata*–or what the Yeshuites and other Abrahamic tribes call "sin", runs through the generations of humanity, a blessing can also course through the physical and spiritual DNA of a person. When that blessing is awakened, it gives off great power that the Darkness cannot hold back."

"Similar to the protection spell placed upon me? I assume you know about that too since you're an angel and all."

"Yes, I'm aware of that. But, no, that's different. Spells are a manipulation of complicated Magickal energies and sometimes entities. With a spell, there's a bargain being made with unseen forces. A blessing is something bestowed upon a person–or a family–from a powerful being, in this case, the *most* powerful being."

"So, can I just say this prayer every day and not have to worry about it then?"

"It doesn't work that way. For a blessing to blossom inside of a person, it has to be received by real faith, and the individual must entrust themselves to the *source* of that blessing. Only then will the blessing have a lasting effect."

"God, you mean? I have to have real faith in *God* for this to work." Jonathan clicked his tongue. "There's always a catch. I guess you specifically mean Yahweh, or Yeshua, or The Spirit of both that actually isn't either one of them, or however they explain that nonsensical Trinitarian bullshit." Willow hissed and Akalian twitched a bit at the flippancy used in describing their King's nature, but Akalian raised a hand to calm his friend. He understood the ignorance driving this Adamian.

"Struck a nerve, I see," Jonathan said with a smirk. Then he had a realization. "Wait–is *that* why the Capurro Cross failed? I didn't have enough *faith?* I know how relics work. I've used them my entire life. I had *absolute* faith that the Capurro Cross would destroy that whore."

"You had faith in the *relic*. Not the source behind it. Relics can and do hold *great* power. However, if that power is not fueled by the wielder's faith in the source of the relic, then its ability to be a useful weapon against the Dark ceases to exist—turning the relic into just another ordinary *trinket.*"

"Like a holy battery."

"Similar, yes."

"And I guess stabbing that guy in the face with the Cross didn't help either," Jonathan confessed. "Or slitting that godborn's throat with it."

"Probably not." Akalian confirmed dryly.

"So, it seems we're at an impasse here, angel. For me to get out of here and go face this monster without me becoming her sick twisted puppet, I have to not only *believe* in Yahweh, but *entrust* myself to him? Seems a little convenient for *him.* There's just one problem."

"You don't believe."

"Oh, I *believe,* Clarence. I believe that *long* ago, something happened that created all this fuckery, and lesser beings have just been fighting for power over all of it ever since. I don't think *anyone,* not even you, knows what's *really* going on here."

"By that statement, you seem to think you have the knowledge you claim no one has," Akalian pointed out.

"Oh, I don't think I *know* anything. That's just my point. I don't have *certainty,* I have observations. I have experiences. And I have opinions about those observations and experiences. For all I *know,* I'm in a lab somewhere, in another universe, living out a simulation. We're all limited to the facts of *our realities,* and the facts of *my* reality have been a bit of compost fire for as far back as I can remember. And *clearly* before that.

"The facts of my reality have been mostly riddled with pain and horror. What little joy there has been, has always—*always*—been smashed to bits right in front of me. I've seen children, after being raped by monsters, forced to join a cult that breeds beastly killing machines. Even on the occasion when those children are rescued, half of them are then forced to join a *different* cult who's at war with the other side. It's an endless cycle of manipulation and lust for power. It's a game of control and conquest that I was forced to play for far too long, until it ultimately took *everything* from me. Hell...now it's even taking *me* from me. If there ever really was a *me* to begin with.

"So, no, Clarence. I *do* believe that it's possible–maybe even probable–that you come directly from Yahweh himself. But from what I've seen, I want *nothing* to do with him. He's either a lesser being acting as though he's something higher, or he just doesn't really give a shit." Jonathan's numbed hatred spat from his lips with that final statement.

Akalian paused for a moment. He heard the echoes of that fateful conversation with Xexxus on the cliffside of Babylon reverberating inside his mind as Jonathan was speaking. It was as if this man before him–this child who had been savagely victimized in more ways than he could ever imagine–had not only been cursed with Xexxus' skafos, but had been indoctrinated with his *reasoning* as well. A reasoning Akalian understood, but knew he couldn't fully correct in this moment, if *he* could correct it at all. There was too much to sift through and not nearly enough time. The Power silently prayed to the King and redirected the conversation as best he could.

"I once loved someone...dearly. He thought as you do now. We walked together in the holiest of places. Laughed together, sang together. Fought the Darkness side by side. But in the end, he allowed these thoughts to go unchecked, unchallenged, and it drove him absolutely mad. Do not let the same thing happen to *you*, Jonathan Young. I understand your grief and your anger, more than you could ever know. But the worst thing you could do for yourself, and for everyone around you, is to allow *yourself* to be the undisputed ruler of your heart."

"What heart? I don't *feel* anything, Clarence. I haven't for a very long time. For years, I clung to the rage, but then that left me too. In the past, I would try *anything* to feel *something* again. Life kept taking things away from me, leaving me empty. Hollow. And if there's one fucking good thing I can do before I leave this literal God-forsaken hell hole," Jonathan pointed out of the opening of the cave, "it's sending *that* bitch back to Hell."

"Do you not see that this is exactly what The Dark Kingdom is using? They *want* you to embrace this destiny of hate and revenge. They've manipulated you for your entire life, pushing you towards this moment where they could remove your very essence and replace it with their will of destruction and chaos. I may not be able to convince you that Yahweh is who he says he is, but can you at least agree that you should try to conceive another destiny for yourself? Something that *doesn't* involve the undoing of the cosmos."

"You *still* want me to spare Etrulia's life? I'll tell you right now, even if I can be convinced that Yahweh is this all-good, all-powerful, all-knowing God, I will still leave this cave and *end* her," asked Jonathan, incredulously.

"How?" Akalian prodded. "How will you end her? You don't have power over her. You've lost the one weapon you thought you had. The only power you *do* have is going to hand you directly over to The Coven and their mission."

"Why don't *you* just go and stop them, then? If I'm supposed to end it all and clearly, I'm not interested in following your God, then why don't you go *do* something about it instead of trying to change my mind *here?*"

"That is a very good question. Unfortunately, there are rules I must follow. Rules that, if broken, could do more harm than good. The fabric of the cosmos is much more fragile than you realize. My task right now is not to stop The Coven, but to prepare *you* to do so. It is *your* destiny that is intertwined with that of The Cosmic Wheel, not mine."

"A destiny I never asked for," Jonathan said, bitterly. "I didn't ask to be brought into all this. What *choice* did I have in the matter? You talk of decisions and consequences, but where was *my* decision to join this nightmare in the first place?"

"That decision was made for you."

"By *your* God."

"By the *enemy*. Despite what many have said over the course of history, including what some would still say in the Yeshuite tribes, Yahweh does not make every decision in the universe. The King does not work through blueprints and puppeteering, although he certainly could if he wanted to. That is probably what amazes me the most about him. He is, indeed, the most powerful being in The Cosmic Wheel. He holds its very fabric together by the force of his will. And instead of *forcing* others to adhere to that will, he allows for decisions to be made. Decisions that can even put an *end* to everything that he's created."

"Why do that?" Jonathan questioned accusatorily. "It makes no sense. If I were going to create something, I'd want it to be good through and through. Why give the opportunity for destruction in the first place?"

"If you were to have a son," Jonathan immediately winced at this. Akalian understood, but continued. "And you wanted him to have a real life with actual love, joy, and reward, would you not cheapen his existence by preventing him from making his own decisions? It is a crucial part of what being an Image Bearer of the King is all about, Jonathan Young. Your kind was *created* to have the ability to choose because *he* has the ability to choose. We *angels* share in this Image Bearing trait. This is indeed a great risk that has brought great evil upon all of Creation, but it has also brought more joy and happiness than we could ever have longed for otherwise."

"Is it real risk if he knows everything already though? Wouldn't that just botch the whole thing? He can see everything before it happens, right? So, the game's still rigged."

"I don't know how everything works. These questions have even plagued me from time to time. But...I've had the privilege of sitting with him and learning more about his heart. From what I've seen and what I've been told, there are limits he willingly puts on himself. He limits himself from being able to accomplish certain things, at least in an immediate sense. He limits himself to provide real risk so that decisions can be freely made and love can truly exist. The King *wants* true collaboration with a family of his own. A family that, together, can cultivate something wondrous to behold."

"Yeah...well," Jonathan gestured wildly around them, "this doesn't look that wondrous, Clarence. It looks more like a giant hellscape. Even the polished parts are like putting make-up on a pig and giving it a beauty pageant award. It seems like your King has failed."

Akalian sighed. His thoughts drifted to Moriel now. He thought of his brother often and it still grieved him deeply.

Sensing the melancholy, Willow got up from his loafed state and snuggled into Akalian's lap, purring as he settled into a comfortable position. Akalian gently petted his friend and looked into Willow's orange eyes.

He remembered the battle of Hillcrest and how Willow's eye had been severely injured. It took a while for that to heal, and even though it had gained all of its strength back, there was still a sliver of a golden scar left inside the choirmite's pupil. It made Willow appear fiercer than before and the tiny choirmite felt great thankfulness that it remained. He would always tell others that he preferred his eye this way. Not only did it make him "look tough", but it reminded him of the sacrifice he was able to make to save his friends.

Akalian's thoughts were then brought to Michael's scarred face and ultimately to the King's scarred body and spike-pierced hands and feet. He thought of the scar he chose to keep on the eye of his Adamian form in remembrance of Moriel.

"Are you familiar with an ancient artform called, Kintsugi?" Akalian asked.

"I've heard of it," Jonathan said confidently. He'd never heard of it. Akalian knew this to be so, as no one in the New World knew of Kintsugi. It was a dead art form long lost to the sands of time. The Power played along with Jonthan's lie, however.

"Then I'm sure you know it was a Japanese method of repairing broken pottery. In their culture–as in many others–certain heirlooms were considered very sacred. These beautifully hand-crafted bowls and plates would be passed down from generation to generation. On occasion, these sacred heirlooms would break, obviously ruining the pottery and rendering it useless. But instead of casting the pottery into the fire, it was handed over to a skilled craftsman who would mend the breakage with a lacquer mixed with gold or silver. Not only would this bring the heirlooms back to life, but it would turn their brokenness into a work of art.

"This world is filled with pain and suffering, Jonathan Young. That's just the way it is right now. It's a warzone and it *has* been for billions of years–long before humans arrived. Unfortunately, because of the Dark Curse that humanity's first parents embraced, every human is born broken. They–like you–have no choice in the matter. This Curse shapes their very basic desires and needs, and forces them to embrace the poisonous chaos of The Dark Kingdom. And they welcome it with open arms without even realizing what they're doing. It's natural for humans to embrace the Darkness. Left to their own devices, humans would drown in an ocean of chaotic madness from which there is no escape.

"The only one who chose to stand in the gap between the Darkness and humanity's utter destruction, was Yahweh. Instead of casting humanity into the fire, he mends them with the very blood of his own body.

"The Light that emanates from his life source is the very healing power that turns humanity's brokenness into shining beacons in the Darkness. Something that, when taken full advantage of, will crush the head of the Great Serpent and usher in something new. Something wondrous.

"There are very few people in history whose destinies have been as intertwined with The Cosmic Wheel as yours is. But *all* of them suffered in *great* ways. Most of all Yahweh, himself. Your life has, indeed, been riddled with pain and horror. You were chosen by evil to do the most destructive thing anyone has *ever* done since the beginning of time. If this is how broken you are, imagine how bright your mending would shine in the Darkness."

Jonathan was staring intently into Akalian. He didn't know how to feel. Was this angel being sincere? Could he actually have another shot at all this? Or was this just another tool of manipulation like he'd been fed his whole life. Either way, the pilgrim had to admit, he had never in all his days heard anything like *this* before. Akalian continued.

"Consider something, just for a moment. Left to your own devices, you *will* destroy everything. But if you give Yahweh a chance to show you what it *could* be if you would just let go of your need to rule your own destiny, then you could truly be free of the Darkness that has *such* a hold on your soul."

A slight breeze whistled through the air. The fire that still blazed blew sideways towards the opening of the cave leading to the oak outside. Jonathan's attention was brought to the source of that gust. His gaze was led behind the cot against the far side of the cave wall.

"What is this, angel?" Jonathan asked. His curiosity was genuine, but he remained skeptical.

"This is not *my* doing. Go and see." Akalian answered. The King was moving and something inside Jonathan's heart was responding.

The pilgrim rose from where he sat, almost transfixed by a light starting to shine in a forming crack on the back wall. Willow looked up at Akalian and they shared a wonderous smile as they watched Jonathan Young walk around the cot and over to the back wall where he was slowly engulfed in the bright tzoharian Light of The White Throne.

# CHAPTER THIRTY

## - WHEN THE WORLD WAS YOUNGER AND YOU HAD EVERYTHING TO LOSE -

(6 1/2 YEARS AGO)

"Come on, old man. You're not too old for this shit...just yet," Jonathan said with a wink. His mischievous smirk was always enough to get the man sitting next to him riled up.

"I could still run circles around you, kid," Obadiah playfully chuckled.

"You couldn't run circles around me when I *was* a kid." The briefing room filled with spirited laughter. Lynn hit Jonathan on the shoulder.

"Leave the man alone! He's the only reason you *have* any skills to begin with." His wife always brought Jonathan's hubris back down to earth in just the right way.

"I knew I liked you." Obadiah laughed as he high-fived Lynn over Jonathan's head.

Jonathan could hear his father's age in that hoarse, gravelly laugh. At times it was unsettling to think that his hero, this man he'd looked up to his entire life, was now beginning to become frail. It was the natural order of things he supposed, but it didn't make the process any easier to watch. Obadiah was almost seventy years old now, and probably shouldn't be going on this raid at all—or so Mattia had said, multiple times. However, his role was strictly on a counseling level and he wouldn't see any real action. Obadiah would be leading the elite counseling team with the children in tow, giving them the immediate care they needed when they were rescued from The Coven's Beltane Celebration.

Jonathan had been working on this raid for months now. One of their shadow agents in The Grey had acquired intel that Etrulia was planning a significantly large Orgia Ceremony for Beltane. This particular celebration was dedicated to inducting The Coven's new child sex slaves into the brood, and would act as a beginning to their Undertaking process. This was a rare opportunity. Most of the time The Resistance was playing catch up after such a significant Sabbat on the Witch's Wheel Calendar. To be able to raid a Beltane celebration could save countless lives and, if their intel was correct, give them the one Sister that had caused The Resistance so much trouble over the last seventeen years.

As successful as The Elite had been—especially in the last decade—it seemed as though they could never get a solid lead on the location of any of The Three High Sisters. Dockson and Grigsby, who were an unstoppable occult tactical force all their own, had come close once to taking down Annis. But that mission had ended in failure, with multiple Resistance agents losing their lives. Grigsby was almost one of them. Still, Etrulia and Agatha had remained elusive over the years–until now.

For the past five years, they heard less and less of Agatha and Annis. Most of the reports of activity in The Coven was surrounding Etrulia. Some rumors even suggested that she had taken Agatha's place as Stick Queen of The Grey, although there were no hard facts to confirm such a pivotal shift in power. Jonathan and Henrik agreed–as rare as that was–that Etrulia was most likely just following the will of Agatha. Maybe her mysterious age was finally catching up with her.

Regardless of Etrulia's leadership status within The Three, she was a pivotal figure of terror and a crucial presence of diabolical authority amongst the lower witches, warlocks, and sorcerers of The Coven of Endor. And Jonathan had his sights set on capturing her for quite some time. So, when word came out of The Grey that the chance to ambush her was upon them, Jonathan jumped at the opportunity.

*"You're sure this is legit?"* Henrik had probed. And, as always, Jonathan was completely irritated a t Henrik for second guessing every single move he made. *Second in command* had become an excuse for Henrik to constantly place Jonathan under the microscope. At least, that's how Jonathan felt about it. It had been frustrating because in reality Jonathan had more skill and instincts in the field, although Henrik's leadership exceeded Jonathan's ability extensively. Once Jonathan had graduated from Henrik's nightly patrols, he had thought he'd be treated as a peer. But clearly, that was never going to happen. Jonathan knew that Henrik not only continued to see him as a brash, sarcastic child, but he also didn't trust Jonathan's gifts as Obadiah did.

Every member of The Elite had gifts of some kind. Those gifts were due to their possessions and/or divination practices that they had been a part of during their time in The Coven. However, Henrik had recently, and secretly, found out that Jonathan was supposed to have become The Coven's Dark Messiah. The vigilante mastermind decided to keep this information to himself for the time being. But this, of course, added to his skepticism of Jonathan's true nature, even though, as far as Henrik knew, Jonthan was unaware of his horrible purpose.

*No one has that kind of destiny placed upon them at random,* Henrik had decided. There was something more to Jonathan Young that the rest didn't see. Henrik wasn't sure what that was just yet, but he had no doubt it would come to light in time. And when it did, Henrik would be ready.

Thus, this evening, The Resistance Elite gathered together in the briefing room of one of The Fallout Outposts within The Grey–just outside the territory known as Tarrytown. Henrik, garbed in his shadowy cloak and cybernetic attire as Z, brooded in the back corner. He doubted this raid was going to run as smoothly as Jonathan promised it would. In the room–aside from Z–sat the most talented and gifted Elite members: Jonathan Young, Lynn Deborney, Dockson, Grigsby, Tobit, and Jackson Murdock.

"Alright everyone, let's settle down," Jonathan said as he reached the podium in front of the room. "I received word about an hour ago from our covert agents inside that The Coven has settled within the ritual grounds and they're preparing for the opening ceremonies. Cameras aren't up due to how sensitive the event is. We don't want to take chances of any of the sorcerers suspecting something."

"Jon, do we have *any* assurance that the agents haven't been detected?" Grigsby asked in his gruff tone. He was a large man, about six foot five inches and weighed about 350 pounds of solid muscle. This behemoth of a man was covered in a mane of red hair and looked like one of the "strong man" competitors from the Old World. "I'd just really rather not show up to this party if we're expected, ya know?"

"Look, I know this seems almost too good to be true," Jonathan said, "but we really do have every assurance we *can* that our presence remains a secret. No matter what, moving forward with this will always be a risk. But I think we all agree it's a risk worth taking. We haven't been able to nail these bastards at a Sabbat Ceremony before. That's *always* where the most destruction happens, especially for their child slaves. We have a real shot at freeing as many kids as possible here."

"I think we all agree with you on the importance of this risk, J." Dockson stated, reassuring their leader. "I think Grigs is just scared of getting chased by their giant rabid dog again," she chuckled at Grigsby's expense.

Dockson was a tall, slender woman with dark brown skin and a large, wispy afro. She and Grigsby had come to The Resistance as a package deal. Unlike most Resistance agents, they had escaped The Coven on their own, using their tactical fighting skills to break out of an enslavement camp. Dockson had been kidnapped as a teenager while Grigsby had been sold into a work camp by his own village long before Dockson arrived. They had formed an alliance and looked out for each other while enslaved, making sure the other one didn't get sold or abused too badly. Finally, during one of The Coven's Full Moon Esbats–worship ceremony celebrating the monthly cycle of the moon–the two of them were able to fight off a few merged soldiers and escape before the local sorcerers knew what was happening.

Grigsby's powerhouse fighting skills and Dockson's precision were unmatched. They had natural gifting in these areas, but being part of the divination ceremonies, they were forced to participate in, heightened their abilities exponentially.

"Hey! Annis is no joke, Dock! You were there! Fuckin' terrifying monster. Not sure how anyone could call that *thing* a human, let alone a *Sister*," Grigsby defended himself playfully.

"Aw, Grigsby's actually afraid of something for once. I'm shocked." Tobit mocked the large man playfully. Tobit was labeled *strange*. It wasn't an insult, nor was it a compliment. Everything about the man was odd. From his exceedingly lank features to his almost blank smile, Tobit made everyone uncomfortable just by existing around them. Also, things seemed to happen around the lanky man that always landed in his favor, almost as if *luck* was his gift. Tobit was in training to be a sorcerer when he was rescued during a raid by Z. Other than Jonathan, he was the only member of the Elite group to have been exorcised upon rescue–which had 'coincidentally' occurred on the night of his scheduled merging. After Tobit was freed from the demons that plagued him, he became a recluse. Even in the presence of others he had a sense of solitude about him. But despite all this, the Elite knew he was a good man at heart and never questioned where his loyalty was.

"Speaking of which," Jackson chimed in. "Is there any word on Etrulia's whereabouts right now? I don't want my astral form getting in there and being blindsided by that gross bitch. I don't think she bathes regularly, and y'all...you don't understand how easily smells can attach themselves to the astral senses." Jackson Murdock was an astral medium. He had never been involved with The Coven,

but instead was naturally gifted.

Jackson had been born to high society parents. His mother was a Senator and his father was COO of The Lassiter Company. Even when Jackson was a toddler, his astral form would leave his body while he slept and travel the Murdock's mansion, getting into trouble. His parents believed the house to be haunted for a time, but their local Clerics got involved when the boy turned ten, and they quickly realized what their son was capable of. Instead of embracing this, Jackson's parents attempted to have him "cured" of this "disease" that was plaguing him. They wanted to save their reputation. It was at this time that word reached High Cleric Mattia, who stepped in and offered to help the boy directly. When Jackson's parents sent him off to The Shorehart Program to be treated and trained to work in The High Temple, they believed he was being cured. In reality, he was being trained by Obadiah, Z, and other shaman scientists in The Fallout. He learned to control his astral form and joined The Resistance in secret. Everyone outside of The Resistance believed Jackson Murdock to be a normal Clerical Scientist working at The High Temple.

"Don't worry, Grigs. Annis is nowhere in sight. And, as of now, we don't have eyes on Etrulia's exact location, but one of the agents informed me that she was there when the children arrived a few hours ago. I'll have her location for you before you go in there, Jack." Jonathan continued on with the plan. "So, we all know the drill. Lynn, Z, and I will arrive overhead via the Z Bomber, repel down to the ritual sight, and take out the major players who will be performing the ceremony. That includes Etrulia, Lynn, so be sure your mind is guarded."

"Got it." Lynn said as she tapped the device on her head. It was a strip of silver wrapped around the back of her head from one temple to the other, leaving the top of her head exposed. Across the device, protection runes were etched into the silver. The device also gave off brown noise at a frequency that was inaudible to the common senses, but it prevented Lynn's Sight from being abused from a clairvoyant, external force. It was truly a work of alchemic genius that one of the shaman scientists at The Fallout cooked up when Lynn started working in the field.

Lynn Deborney had been one of The Coven's Sight Witches from the age of eleven. She had been taken from her family when their village was pillaged by Agatha. She was rescued by Jonathan when she was seventeen after attempting to peer inside his mind, looking for the location of one of The Fallout Outposts. For reasons unknown to her at the time, Lynn's Sight didn't work on Jonathan, giving him enough time to subdue her and bring her back to the nearest Resistance base for rehabilitation.

Now, Lynn was the most powerful Resistance agent with the Sight—a clairvoyant ability that could be weaponized with proper training. Most people who had the Sight didn't even realize they had it, chalking the ability up to good intuition or discernment. In reality, they had an extra sense which could allow them to do a variety of things: communicate with the unseen realms, see things before they happen, even move things with their minds, which allowed for the Sight to take on more of a telekinetic ability. For some, it was simply how they were born—due to elohimic interference within the family's DNA, or of simply a product of the broken order of The Cosmic Wheel.

Due to her abusive experience within The Coven, Lynn had all of these skills of Sight, although the telekinetic abilities took almost all of her energy to utilize. She was very careful to not use them except under extreme measures.

Jonathan went on.

"Alright so while we are focusing on the main players, Dockson and her team will surround the perimeter and take out the merged soldiers from a safe distance. *From a safe distance,* Dock! This isn't a normal raid and we can't afford to have you and your agents playing cowboy out there."

"I got it, I got it!" Dockson said with her hands up in defense. "Safe distance. Check!"

"Grigs, you'll be the juggernaut, as always. Charge in there with your team, take out any soldiers guarding the kids, and get them out of there. Jackson will be ready to safeguard your path as soon as you leave The Coven's Magick circle. Obadiah, your team will meet up with them two hundred yards away at the rendezvous point."

"And that's when *I* come in." Tobit proclaimed.

"Exactly." Jonathan smirked. "Tobit will arrive...in his usual fashion, and escort us out of there. Let's hope your luck provides a good catch this time. Preferably the High Sister."

"I can't guarantee anything. But you know I'll be there with bells on, ready for whatever happens."

"We're counting on it," Jonathan chuckled. Then he cleared his throat and focused on the man standing in the back corner. "Anything to add, oh fearless leader?"

"What of contingency?" the cybernetic voice questioned.

"We use the same contingency strategies as always." Jonathan sneered. "Retreat to the rendezvous using the provided paths on the schematics and attempt to save whoever we can in the process."

"Lynn, have you had a chance to sit and do readings with the agents?" Z asked.

"Yes, Z. They all checked out."

"How about everyone in this room?"

"Z. What are you insinuating?" Obadiah spoke up.

"All I'm saying is, we can never be too careful," Z replied. "This is the first drop we've gotten on a Sabbat and it all just seems entirely too easy."

"I trust Jonathan with all my heart," Obadiah said boldly. "If

he says we're a go, then we're a go."

"And just so you know, *yes*, I have read everyone present." Lynn coldly stated. "Everyone checks out."

"Has someone cross-read you?" Z interrogated.

"No." Lynn was getting irritated. "That's not usual protocol, Z."

"This entire mission isn't usual protocol." The cybernetic voice was like a cold shower on the room.

"Look." Jonathan started. "I know you're skeptical of all this. Of my sources. But believe it or not, we *do* have everything under control here. This isn't my first rodeo, Z."

"This is a Sabbat. It's *everyone's* first rodeo, Jon. And quite frankly, I think we need to call it all off. Have the agents collect all intel they can, report back, and we can plan our next raids accordingly. This is too dangerous."

"I'm overruling that, and I speak for Matty too." Obadiah said sternly. "Jon's right. We all know the risks. This is, quite possibly, the most important mission we've been a part of so far. Jon's done a great job here. We'll move forward with the plan and follow normal contingency protocols if something goes wrong."

Z stiffened at being overruled by the almost seventy-year-old father of his second in command. Mattia had already told Henrik that whatever Obadiah decided, he had her vote as well, so the vigilante was outnumbered. Given the contractual agreement between the three of them, Z had no choice but to see this through.

"So be it," he said. "I'll be in the Bomber." And with that, Z walked out of the room.

"What the fuck is his deal these days?" Jonathan asked Obadiah angrily. The meeting had ended and The Elite members were dispersing and gathering their agents. Lynn, Jonathan, and Obadiah remained in the briefing room.

"I'm not sure, Jon," Obadiah answered. "I know something's been rattling his cage, but trying to get Henrik to open up is like attempting to knock down a brick wall with a water gun."

"You two have always had some tension, but openly questioning your authority in front of the team like that isn't like him." Lynn was concerned.

"Did anything out of the ordinary come up when you did his reading, babe?" Jonathan asked Lynn.

"You know my readings of Henrik are about as productive as my readings of *you.* Sometimes, I wonder if he also has the Sight and is just really good at hiding it from me."

"It's possible," Obadiah stated. "But he's never given us any reason not to trust him, even if half of Henrik's existence is a mystery to us. I think he's just concerned about all this. And we rarely see Henrik get nervous, mostly because I don't think he actually *does* get nervous 99% of the time. So, I really believe we're just seeing this Sabbat business get to him."

"Maybe you're right." Jonathan agreed with his father, but there was something nagging at him that he just couldn't shake. As the three of them left the briefing room, Lynn and Jonathan walked hand in hand toward the hangar where the Z Bomber was parked. Obadiah headed in the opposite direction. On the way to the Bomber,

Jonathan continued to feel that nagging sense. Almost like an alarm going off in the back of his mind. Not that he couldn't trust Henrik, but that Henrik might be right about this whole thing.

Darkness had now fallen across the land of Tarrytown as High Sister Etrulia walked toward the black stone altar at the center of the Thrice Blessed Circle. The Coven had sacked the town two days prior, collecting fresh children for the Beltane Ceremony. They would become a delicious addition to the dozens who had already been collected over the previous month. Etrulia had wondered why Agatha was so adamant that this insignificant town should be the spot for the Beltane Orgia. She wouldn't dare question her Queen's judgement–out loud at least–but her curiosity was peaked. All Agatha had told her was, *there is much power in a name, child, and this name had to be set aside for such a sacred night as this.*

Etrulia understood that this Sabbat held more weight than the others, but she was still confused as to why the location was significant. She decided to stop focusing on that for now. The Master would explain it to her if she needed to know. Otherwise, the High Sister would simply carry out the Ceremony as planned.

The layout of the Thrice Blessed Circle was standard for such a sacred Ceremony. In the center was the black stone altar which sat directly below an Endorian Standing Stone etched with the wretched symbol of Endor. The stone was identical to the one on the ceremonial grounds of The Village of The Tellyard Bard and various structures throughout The Grey.

Leading up to this altar stood the sorcerers, draped in large black robes with raised hoods. Outside of this inner circle stood the lesser witches and warlocks of The Coven, robed in scarlet, and hands interlocked as they wrapped around the exterior of the altar, forming a second circular layer. The final circle was that of protection. Demonic merged soldiers–similar to the one who had attacked Mattia all those years ago–scoured the wooded area surrounding the Blessed Circle. They also guarded the child pen where the "fresh meat" for The Coven waited in fear.

"High Sister. We await your initiation." The voice came from a naked man laying prone atop the stone altar. His body was ready to be mounted by the High Sister, which would initiate the orgy portion of the Ceremony. First, she and the sorcerers would partake in one another's flesh. Then the lesser witches and warlocks would join. Then, finally...the children would be forced to partake as well. It was a horrible, deplorable thing that occurred during these wretched ceremonies.

In the Endorian traditions, sexual vitality was the first of the "sacred energies" to be released and celebrated in an Undertaking process. It didn't matter the age of a person. As long as their body provided sexual energy for themselves or for someone else, they would participate in the Orgia Ceremony. Eroticism was a primary virtue within The Coven–as it was in most Pagan tribes of the Old and Ancient Worlds. However, like with all traditions The Coven shared with other tribes and religions, Endor's practices were the most diabolical across the history of the world, for they embraced The Dark Kingdom with open arms from the very beginning.

"Your High Sister heeds your call, Brother Grosam. Her body thirsts for yours," Etrulia moaned disturbingly in response to the sorcerer's. She sensuously disrobed and continued walking slowly towards the altar. The sorcerers aligning the walkway leading to the altar began chanting in the corrupt and primordial R'lyehian language, anxious to disrobe themselves and begin celebrating each other's sensual desires. Little did any of them know that gliding down towards them, in the full moon lit sky, was swift and brutal judgement.

A scream pierced the darkness as Z's katana sliced through the body of a chanting sorcerer. The velocity of the drop allowed for the cloaked vigilante to cut the wicked man completely in two. As Lynn landed, she let off a telepathic blast, giving everyone in her ten-foot radius extreme vertigo, sending them crashing to the ground, some vomiting from the shock. Jonathan Young landed directly on top of the naked sorcerer on the altar. He pushed his boots fiercely into the man's abdomen as he landed, causing projectile vomit and excrement to fly out of both ends of the man's body.

"Oooh, sorry about that, mate." Jonathan chuckled. "I know *that's* not what you were expecting tonight." He then kicked the sorcerer off of the altar and onto the ground, tripping Etrulia in the process. Jonathan quickly raised his wrist up to his mouth and spoke into the microphone inside his glove. "I've got Etrulia right in front of me Jack. We're at the altar. You're clear."

"*Sounds like you two will be very happy together,*" Jackson's voice mused through the earpiece strapped to Jonathan's head.

"I hate you," Jonathan scoffed playfully. Then he lunged toward Etrulia and tackled her naked body in an attempt to put her in a restraint hold long enough to allow Grigsby and his team to get the children and escape.

Z and Lynn immediately surrounded Jonathan and Etrulia's wrestling match. While slicing another sorcerer's intestines out of his stomach and onto the ground, Z tossed three electric mines in front of him, which caused a voltaic current to flow between the mines to prevent anyone from crossing through. A merged soldier charged fiercely towards Z in a blind rage and was immediately electrocuted to death. He sizzled as he hit the ground at the vigilante's feet.

On the other side, Lynn was forcing her Sight onto other sorcerers, lesser witches and warlocks as they approached her, causing

them to vomit and feel discombobulated from extreme dizziness.

"I've got her!" Jonathan yelled out as he pulled Etrulia's legs and arms taut, placing all of his weight on top of her in a supine position.

Z raised his glove to his blue faceplate.

"Clear the path, Dock."

*"Roger that!"* Dockson replied.

Electro particle darts rained down onto the pack of merged soldiers who surrounded the pen where the children were being kept. The soldiers immediately fell to the ground, bodies seizing from the violence of the electrical current.

Grigsby and his team of extremely large, powerful agents charged through the Thrice Blessed Circle, bodychecking anyone that stood in their path. A group of them formed a perimeter around the entrance to the child pen, fighting off the soldiers, witches, and warlocks who were frantically attempting to prevent them from stealing their prized dust creatures.

With one mighty blow, Grigsby smashed his fist against the lock on the pin and the gate flung open. The children were frozen with fear, so Grigsby's team began picking them up two by two and running into the woods towards Obadiah's transport. A couple of the merged soldiers broke through the agent's defensive line and charged toward the children being taken away from the circle. The soldiers were met with an invisible force that slammed into their chests, and sent them flying into the surrounding tress. Jackson's astral form was manipulating the astral field, weaponizing the energy waves within the field. Merged soldiers weren't powerful enough to
overcome the energy waves, nor were most of them intelligent enough to understand what was happening.

" *The kids are almost home free, guys! It's working!!"* Dockson rejoiced from her vantage point.

Just as the team began to celebrate, Lynn sensed a disturbing shift in the psychic atmosphere. Something wasn't right.

"Hey guys. We gotta get out of here. *Now*!" she said, almost in a panic.

"Why? What's wrong?" Z asked, attempting to keep calm.

Just then, they felt the earth below them begin to shake.

"What the hell is *that!?"* Jonathan yelled from his supine restraint hold. In response to his question, Etrulia began to cackle maniacally.

"Oh, you're about to find out. You're *all* about to find out." Etrulia pronounced through her wheezing laughter.

Fear washed over Jonathan. He didn't need intuition or Sight to know that the tone Etrulia just used was one of triumph. This was a setup.

A horrific howl pierced the night. Annis, High Sister of Endor came thundering through the trees and bounded into the Thrice Blessed Circle, pummeling every agent that stood in her path. Dozens of new merged soldiers following behind her, like roaches at her feet. Lynn was petrified. She had never seen this wretched behemoth in person before.

Annis stood at least ten feet tall. Her skin was a dark, grotesque blue. Her frightening yellow eyes bulged from their sockets behind thin, greasy, black hair falling from her enormous head. Annis howled again as she sank her sharp, gnarled fangs into the head of a Resistance agent, biting through his neck and, then spat out the head, discarding the body–the life–she had just destroyed. Blood poured down her chin and splattered across her stained, navy-blue robes. There was nothing *human* about this thing that was savagely murdering their teammates.

"Abort! Now! Everyone back to–" Z was immediately cut off.

"*It's too late! They've got us all surrounded! Get out any way you can!*" The voice that rang through everyone's earpieces was that of Obadiah. It meant that even the transport location at the rendezvous had been compromised.

"No!!" Jonathan screamed in defeat and anger. Etrulia used this opportunity of his frustration to use her Dark energy and throw him off of her back onto the ground away from her. The witch shot up onto her feet–her naked body covered in dirt–and leapt up onto the black stone altar. Z hurled two throwing stars at her head, but Etrulia easily batted them away at a superhuman speed. It was obvious now that the restraint hold she had been previously placed in was something she allowed to happen. Etrulia threw her right arm down towards Z, telekinetically sending the cloaked man flying through the air towards the raging Annis.

Lynn attempted to counter Etrulia with her Sight, but was no match for the High Sister. Etrulia lifted Lynn off the ground into the air, and pulled her close to her twisted, knowing grin.

"Clever of you, little witch, to have such a contraption preventing us from entering your mind. But I need not read your thoughts to sense that you shouldn't be here, my pet. There's something rolling 'round inside your belly that's much more precious than these slave tots we have here. Am I right?"

"What??" Lynn was in a confused haze. Did Etrulia just confirm what Lynn had been wondering the last few days? Was she really pregnant?

"I'll be gentle," the witch lied. Etrulia tossed Lynn like a ragdoll through the air, towards the woods. Lynn's instincts kicked in and she pulled her energy downward, catching herself in midair and gently sitting herself down far off into the woods.

"Tobit! Where the hell are you!?" Jonathan yelled into his wrist.

*"Jonathan, I can't go in there, man! With Etrulia and Annis?? There's no way my gift stands a chance against two High Sisters! I'm sorry."* With that, Tobit's communication cut out. He was gone and so was their escape strategy.

"That son of a *bitch!"* Jonathan yelled out as he felt himself being lifted off the ground, his muscles tensing up, frozen. He looked ahead to see Etrulia, arms outstretched, hands claw-like. She was cackling as black, necroplasmic slime dripped from her eyes and mouth.

"Come to me, my pet," she hissed as she began slowly pulling him closer to her claws. "I'm, oh, so curious about *you.*"

Twenty yards away, Z leapt sideways and rolled to the ground, dodging Annis' fist as it slammed into the dirt, leaving a small crater in its wake.

He had initially landed directly at the giant Sister's feet and if his reflexes hadn't kicked in immediately, he would have been crushed under Annis' stomping attack. The vigilante unsheathed both of his katanas and began wildly slashing at the blue behemoth, but her skin was so thick, the blades hardly did any damage at all. Z knew this was a losing battle. He'd faced Annis before and had found no physical weaknesses he could take advantage of. His current strategy mostly involved keeping her occupied so other agents could escape her wrath. Z was faster than Annis, so he knew if he kept moving, she could neither physically catch him or have the time to cast a spell.

In the woods, Lynn used her telekinetic energy to slam a merged soldier into a nearby tree. She had to be careful not to use too much of it. While this was certainly the time to utilize her telekinesis, it would quickly deplete her ability to control her Sight if she kept this up. And this was *not* the time to lose control of her gift. She looked back out into the Blessed Circle and saw her husband being pulled in midair towards Etrulia's outstretched arms. Lynn had to think, and fast. For one, she loved her husband dearly and would die before allowing him to be harmed. She also had to stop Etrulia from using a mind control spell on him or they would all be in *big* trouble.

"HEY!" Lynn jumped at the sound of the shout inside her head. It was Jackson's astral form communicating with her telepathically.

"Holy shit, Jack! You scared me."

"Sorry! Look, this is *bad.* Grigs and his team were ambushed and–"

"We don't have time for that, Jack. Look!" Lynn pointed to the center of the Circle, where Jonathan was held in Etrulia's grasp.

Jonathan was fighting the ungodly hold the witch had on him with all of his might, but he couldn't budge. She had complete control over his motor functions. He found himself face to face with this grotesque woman whose forces had plagued him and his team for over a decade. Etrulia's hands began hovering over Jonathan's body, searching his aura, looking for answers. His protection spell–which had been misinterpreted as a powerful defensive Sight ability by everyone except for Obadiah and Mattia– had saved him from being identified by The Coven on several occasions, but Jonathan had never faced a High Sister directly like this before.

Etrulia's concentration doubled. She had sensed something as soon as Jonathan dropped down from the sky. While the man had her in a restraint hold, she had attempted to read his thoughts, but there was nothing. That piqued her curiosity in a very specific way. For seventeen years, The Coven had been looking for Xexxus' skafos, but it was as if the boy had vanished into thin air.

*Could this dust creature be him?* She pondered this while scanning the ethereal energies of his aura. The lack of information present was very telling. This man's Sight was either more powerful than hers–which she knew couldn't be true since she had complete control over his body–or there had been an extremely formidable protection spell placed upon him. The goal of their trap was simply to catch key members of The Resistance Elite, but if *this* was indeed their future Manking, Etrulia's catch was the most meaningful thing she'd ever done for The Coven. For The Master.

Etrulia pulled all the Dark energy she could possibly muster towards her fingertips as necroplasmic ooze began to drip from her long nails. There was only one way to be sure who this man was, but she wondered if her ability to manipulate necroplasm was strong enough. Only that could heighten her Sight and help her break through the protection spell, revealing once and for all who this man was.

Suddenly, a strong invisible force crashed into the High Sister's body, sending her flying off the black altar and causing her to lose control over Jonathan. Etrulia quickly leapt to her feet, hissing and spun around toward where Jonathan had landed. Lynn was helping the man onto his feet. Jonathan was dazed, but in control of his faculties.

"I will not lose you!" Etrulia screamed and began reaching out with her Sight to pull him close to her again. The invisible force slammed into her once more, knocking her into the standing stone above the altar.

"Lynn, take him and run!" Jackson yelled telepathically. Then, in a whipping formation, he flung an energy wave toward Etrulia once more. By now, the witch had figured out what kind of force she wasdealing with and she caught the invisible tethered wave in her hand by the power of her Sight.

"Ahornah ymg' orr'eog ymg' n'gha!" The High Sister shouted her spell in the demonic R'lyehian language. The spell translated into: *May your strength become your death.* It instantly traveled through the tethered energy wave into Jackson's astral form. The ethereal energy surrounding the man began suffocating him as it coiled around him like a python squeezing its prey.

Miles away from the Thrice Blessed Circle, Jackson's physical body–which lay on a cot in a small transport–began convulsing wildly. As Jackson foamed at the mouth, the two agents guarding him were at a loss as to what to do. They had been instructed to protect his body, but had also been told that if something like this were to happen, there was nothing they could do to save his life. Even if they had a clairvoyant present who could attempt to pull Jackson's astral form back to his physical body, the clairvoyant would also become a victim of whatever or whomever was attacking Jackson. So, the two agents watched in horror as one of their leaders suffocated to death right in front of them. With a pop, Jackson's astral form disappeared from the Corporeum Realm.

Lynn and Jonathan were almost to the woods when Jonathan stopped his wife abruptly.

"Z!" Jonathan shouted. "That asshole's still back there!"

"We've gotta get you out of here, Jon! Etrulia's gunning for you!"

Lynn was then thrown away from her husband telepathically. Jonathan's reflexes kicked in and tossed a throwing star towards Etrulia who now stood a mere ten feet from him. The sheer speed of Jonathan's action far surpassed Z's earlier attempt and the blade met its target, slamming directly into Etrulia's forehead, sending her sprawling onto the ground.

*That's only gonna piss her off.* Jonathan thought to himself. He knew that a simple blade to the head wasn't going to do much to the witch for more than a minute or two. Still, this bought him some time. Jonathan quickly glanced over to his wife, who was already pushing herself to her feet. As he started to sprint toward Annis and Z, a firm hand grabbed Jonathan's shoulder from behind.

Z was becoming more exhausted by the minute. He'd thought about leaping backwards and running for the woods as hard as he could, but that would give Annis an opportunity to target his back and cast a spell. He had to stay close and move fast. Hopefully help would come. If not, he'd think of something, he always did. Z sliced downward at one of the witch's toes and something finally went in his favor. The tip of Annis' smallest toe chipped off in a spout of black and blue blood. Annis howled in anguish. Z had been trying to land a blow like this for the last five minutes, but hadn't been able to get the right angle. He also wasn't sure his blade could cut through Annis at all, but thankfully, it seemed he had found a weakness in her rhinoceros-like skin. Z knew no matter how tough a person was, the nervous system would *always* have the upper hand when it came to a blow to the feet.

Before Annis could regain control, Z leapt off of her bent knee, jumped up toward her head and slammed one of his katanas into the witch's right, yellow, hate-filled eye. Annis' agonizing scream pierced the night air as more black and blue blood spewed from her face. It was one of the most horrible sounds Z had ever heard. And the backhand the vigilante promptly received was one of the most painful things he'd ever felt.

Z hit the ground so hard it knocked the wind out of him and made him lose his remaining katana in the dirt. For a moment, Z panicked because he was struggling to keep his consciousness. And this would give Annis the chance to deliver a killing blow. Sure enough, the vigilante hazily looked up and saw Annis' large foot above him, ready to strike his head. This was it. This was how he would go out. His head crushed by a giant foot.

Suddenly, Annis' foot stopped in mid-air. Z looked across at Lynn and saw her focusing with all her might to prevent the stomping attack from finding its target. Then the giant witch lit up with electricity as electro particle darts plowed into her back and neck. As the giant fell, the ground below them shook upon impact. Z saw Jonathan and Obadiah standing nearby, holding smoking electro rifles.

"Can you move?!" Jonathan asked.

"Yes. Finally. Let's get out of–" A bloody blade slammed into him between his shoulder and underarm, piercing his exoskeletal suit between the armored pieces, and driving into the flesh underneath. The sheer force of the impact caused Z to fall backwards onto the ground again.

Etrulia suddenly leapt onto Obadiah's back, her claws latching onto his head, necroplasm oozing from her fingers into his skull like black eels boring into the ocean floor. She sank her gnarled teeth into the nape of his neck and pulled out a chunk of meat. The older man screamed in pain and fell to the ground as the witch pushed off of his back, flipped backwards into the air and landed firmly on the ground five feet from Jonathan. He darted toward her in a blind rage but Etrulia reached out a hand toward him, stopping him in his tracks.

Lynn threw more of her telekinetic energy toward the witch, making Etrulia stumble ever so slightly, but it wasn't enough to break her Dark grip on Lynn's husband.

"So *spicy*, my dear," Etrulia mocked. "But you have quite a long way to go before you can best *me*." The High Sister reached out her hand towards Lynn and hissed a spell. "Twist."

Immediately, Lynn's stomach felt like it was turned inside out and she felt blood gush out of her vagina. She screamed and fell to the ground.

"Nnn....oooo!!!" Jonathan could barely release his cries for his wife.

"Shhhh." Etrulia put her finger to her lips as she brought Jonathan close to her again. "We have some unfinished business to attend to, don't we? Who *are* you, my pet? Why can't I see your essence? Why is it that I feel my memory of you trying to escape my mind from the minute I see you?" As the witch began to draw more Dark energy to her fingertips, two electro particle darts entered the back of Etrulia's skull. She fell to the ground, convulsing and writhing in pain, her connection with Jonathan finally broken.

"Get up, Jon!" yelled Dockson who was running to Lynn's side. Grigsby ran to Obadiah's body–now limp and seemingly, lifeless–and hoisted him onto his shoulder. Jonathan pushed himself up and saw Z running toward him, throwing blade still embedded below his shoulder.

"Run! Annis is stirring. We can't do anything more here," Z commanded. Jonathan allowed him to take command for the rest of their escape. As they ran for safety, he looked out across the massacred Thrice Blessed Circle and saw countless bodies belonging to The Coven and The Resistance littering the ground. He didn't yet know that Jackson had been killed. He had no inkling of how many casualties this botched mission had stolen from them. But there was one voice ringing in Jonathan Young's mind, and it was a voice that would haunt him for the next six and a half years.

"*You're sure this thing is legit?*"

Within a few days' time, the survivors had made it back to The Fallout underneath Perethedesh. Of the fifty-five agents who had gone on this mission, only twenty-three remained. Jackson had been killed in action and Tobit was AWOL. Dockson and Grigsby suffered minor injuries from their attacks and chose to go back out into the field mere days after they'd returned. Lynn was immediately rushed to an Outpost medical facility the night of the Beltane ambush. Thankfully, the doctors discovered that Etrulia's spell didn't leave any permanent damage to Lynn's body–the purpose seemed merely to inflict pain and fear in the moment. But most importantly, Lynn discovered that she was indeed pregnant and the baby wasn't affected by Etrulia's spell.

Lynn's celebration was cut short when she and Jonathan received word that Obadiah had slipped into a coma and neither the doctors nor the scientists could understand why. The wound from Etrulia's bite was healing as it should. There had been a slight infection at first, but it was quickly healed by a powerful antibiotic treatment. Other than that, Obadiah should have been back on his feet. Yet, for reasons unknown to any of the experts on site, he was completely unresponsive to the outside world.

Even with the news of his wife's pregnancy, Jonathan slipped into a deep, dark depression.

"It's not your fault. You were betrayed by a fellow agent." Lynn had said, attempting to comfort her husband. But her words fell on deaf ears. Jonathan *knew* it was *all* his fault.

*How could I have been so stupid? So blind?* he constantly berated himself. Jonathan had sunk into in a despondent pit of insurmountable guilt and shame from which no one could pull him out.

The source of the corrupt information was a shadow agent named Karlo Fultrof. The man had been a loyal and reliable source for over ten years. Unfortunately, The Coven discovered Karl and threatened to butcher his wife in front of him and then turn his children into merged soldiers if he didn't go along with their plan to set up the false Beltane Ceremony. Etrulia herself had placed a prot-

-ection spell upon him so that Lynn couldn't detect anything false about his claims. After the Beltane ambush, Karl took his family and ran, knowing that both The Coven and The Elite would be after him. Nevertheless, the family didn't get far before a group of sorcerers caught up with them and The Coven made good on their initial threat.

It had now been six weeks since the Beltane ambush, and Henrik still refused to speak to Jonathan. The only thing Henrik had told him was that Jonathan was on mandatory suspension from duty until Henrik and Mattia could agree on what to do with him. Jonathan knew what Henrik wanted–severe corporal punishment. Jonathan also knew he didn't deserve anything less than that, but doubted Mattia would allow such a thing to occur to her own son. He knew his relationship to the High Cleric was the only thing preventing him from being locked in a holding cell.

Lynn continued reminding Jonathan that he was going to be a father soon–attempting to encourage him and snap him out of his despondency. She pleaded with him to see that there was certainly great Darkness in the world, but they were about to bring light and life into *their* world and the lives of their family. To this, Lynn only received grunts and blank stares.

Mattia had mandated Jonathan to go to daily counseling sessions. At first, if he went at all, he was mostly unresponsive. Then after a few weeks he became manipulative, he said all the "right" things which didn't allow the counselor to make any kind of progress with him. Eventually, he stopped going altogether. While on the

outside, Jonathan had turned into stone. The Darkness inside of him was festering.

Three months after the Beltane ambush, Jonathan's spiral sank to a new low. At night, he began roaming the bars of The Lowers, ending up in the StagNight district, paying for artificial pleasure from artificial women. Eventually–just as all who embrace rock bottom–Jonathan found a place to call home. A debaucherous sanctuary.

**THE ELECTRIX** was one of the most popular StagNight bars in The Lowers. Like most "synthetic pleasure taverns" in this red district, one would enter the bar and be fitted with a cyber-helmet device. The large, bulbous helmet fit snugly onto the person's head, covering their eyes, ears, and nose. To complete the full sensory experience, cyber-gloves could be worn to give the sensation of touch during intimacy. Once a person entered a private Electrix Pod, the synthetic pleasure would begin. It was every forbidden desire a person could ask for.

Although the physical gratification inside the Pod was ultimately a farce, the euphoric escape that this place provided Jonathan was *very* real. After only a few weeks, he began mixing his time in the Electrix Pod with "live-dust", an extremely potent and addictive enhancement drug that stimulated the mind in ways that surpassed the efforts of Old World cocaine. After his time spent in the Electrix Pod, Jonathan would drown whatever sorrows remained in the best corn whiskey The Lowers could offer. He never talked to anyone. No one asked him any questions. It was just Jonathan, his shame, and his ever-growing rage. Every night, Jonathan focused all of his anger, guilt, and shame into fantasizing about killing the High Sister Etrulia with his bare hands.

He heard her cackling in his nightmares as he replayed the scene of Etrulia latching onto Obadiah over and over in his mind. His father. She had done *something* to his father to cause his coma, but what was it? For the life of him, Jonathan couldn't figure it out. This was his fixation, his obsession. Jonathan had visited Obadiah in the medical wing of The Fallout countless times by this point. He had even taken it upon himself to do his own anatomy check on Obadiah, but found nothing out of the ordinary. The wound on his neck had even healed by now–there wasn't even a scar because of how masterful the surgeons had been. So, what in the world caused this coma?

He would mutter this to himself at the bar while downing glass after glass of corn whiskey. Eventually, as the months passed, Jonathan would become violent after a few drinks couldn't help him solve this poisonous riddle. Because he was such a regular at The Electrix, the staff, at first, had catered to Jonathan's outbursts. But, after he had slammed a fellow patron's head into a barstool and broke the man's jaw, Jonathan was barred from drinking there again. From then on, after partaking in his nightly dose of pleasure from the Pod, he would leave The Electrix and barhop, visiting every tavern until someone would kick him out.

One night, after six months of drowning in the Darkness, Jonathan came home from his usual barhopping to find Lynn walking up the stairs from the sublevel of their flat placing clothes in her suitcase.

"I didn't expect you home for another few hours." She said coldly. The last three months had been a living nightmare for her. Lynn was now seven months pregnant and almost every night she was left alone. She had been too proud to ask for any kind of assistance until her doctor's orders finally made her accept Dockson's offer to stay with her and Grigsby, at least until they could all try to convince Jonathan to get some real help. Dockson and Grigsby had wanted to have an intervention, but Lynn wouldn't have it.

"He'll just fight you and leave, and, this time he may not come home," Lynn had said. And besides, even though Jonathan was showing extreme neglect and apathy towards her and their unborn son, he had not shown any violence towards her. So, she knew that

she and the baby were safe, at least.

"Wait...are—are you leaving me?" Jonathan said in a semi-drunken slur. He wasn't nearly as far gone as usual that night when—for some reason—he decided to call it quits early and go home.

"No! I'm just, Jonathan, you're never here anymore. Even when you *are* home, you're not *present*. Dr. Jumilla is putting me on bedrest. The baby's fine, but she said too much activity could cause unnecessary stress on my pregnancy and—"

Jonathan was staring at her stupidly.

"Did you even remember that I had an appointment with her today? My god, Jon...do you even know how far along I am?"

"Of course I do...you're..." he trailed off.

"Fine. Look, I'm going to stay with Dockson until the baby is born, okay?"

"Why can't you stay here? We can get someone from Dr. Jumilla's staff to come stay with you."

"You're gone every night, Jon and no one is available to give that kind of care right now. All of the medical staff at The Fallout are dedicated to pre and post mission work. They can't spare someone just to babysit me while you're out, God knows where, all the time."

"So, it's my fault that you have to leave," Jonathan said, mockingly. "You're 'a grown-ass woman with gifts no one else has.' I thought you could take care of yourself? Isn't that what you've said a thousand times in the past??"

"You're drunk. I'm not having this conversation right now.

Look, tomorrow when you sober up a little bit, come over to—"

"No." Jonathan said numbly.

"No, what?" Lynn questioned in an annoyed tone.

"No, you can't leave. I need you here."

"To do *what?* You barely speak to me anymore. You won't spend time with me. You don't even touch me. You have your *synthetic bitches* to do that for you. What do you need me for anymore?"

"What's *that* supposed to mean?"

"Oh, come on Jon!" Lynn was exasperated. "Did you *really* think word wouldn't get back to me about your asinine behavior these last few months? We're the literal fucking surveillance team of the whole damn city!" She was shouting now. "I knew where you were going within the first *week!* The only reason I didn't stop you was because I had *hoped* it might give you some sort of release and snap you out of this fucking pity party existence you're in!"

"My father is lying in coma because of something *I* did!" Jonathan yelled back. "Forgive me for throwing a bit of a *fucking pity party* about that! I'm trying to figure out how to help him!"

"By screwing imaginary computer whores and drinking yourself stupid every night?! Oh, sure, that's gonna snap Obadiah right out it!"

"Shut up." Jonathan said as he moved toward his wife.

"No. I'm not shutting up! I didn't want this conversation to happen this way, but here we are! You're lucky I'm *not* leaving you because I have *every* right to do so!"

"Shut up."

"But I am going to take care of our baby! I say *our* baby very loosely by the way. Because, so far, the only thing you've done to contribute is the sperm that you so freely give to a fucking video game console!! You should be *glad* Obadiah isn't here to see what a piss poor father *you're* turning out to be!"

"I said, *shut up!!"* Jonathan swiftly backhanded his wife so hard that it broke through her instinctual telekinetic defense. She slammed into the wall, lost her footing and soared head over heels down the stairs to the sublevel of their flat.

"Oh god...Oh no..." Jonathan panicked. He ran over to the top of the stairs and looked down in horror. Lynn had fallen down the entire flight of stairs and landed on her stomach on the concrete floor below. She was unconscious, and blood was flowing between her legs.

Jonathan sat in the waiting room of the emergency section of The Fallout medical wing. The coffee he had been given by the staff was now ice cold and untouched. The shock of what he had done was enough to sober him up and give him all the adrenaline he could handle. Dockson and Grigsby were across the room from him, staring into their hands, filled with concern for their dear friend and her baby.

"What the fuck have you become?" Jonathan whispered to himself.

"That's exactly what *I* want to know." Henrik's voice boomed over his head. He had just entered the room quietly.

"Not now, *Henrik.*" Jonathan growled.

Henrik went on, ignoring Jonathan. "Lynn's saying she fell down the stairs while bringing laundry up from the sublevel. I don't believe her. I've seen plenty of injuries in my life, dealing out a lot them myself. So, I know what a black eye from a sucker punch looks like when I see one."

"You don't talk to me for six months and *now* you decide to become a fucking chatter box? Well, I don't have the time for you at the moment I'm waiting to hear–*from a doctor*–how my wife and child are doing."

Mattia cleared her throat from behind Henrik.

"I'm not a doctor," she calmly stated, "but I think it would be better if you heard the information from *me.* Excuse us Henrik."

"Oh god..." Jonathan's breath left him. Mattia knelt down at eye level to where Jonathan was sitting, as Henrik walked to the other side of the room. Mattia put her hand on her son's knee and looked him in the eye. He could see she'd been crying.

"I want to start off by saying Lynn is going to be okay. She has a broken arm, a sprained ankle, and bruises all over, but she'll make a full recovery. But..." Mattia's voice began to break. "But...the baby didn't make it, son." With this, tears rolled down the High Cleric's face. "I...I'm so sorry." She reached out to touch Jonathan's face, but he stood up in a rage and started punching holes in the wall.

Henrik leapt into action and tackled Jonathan to the ground. Henrik would later say that this initial course of action was an attempt to restrain his suspended second in command and calm him down, but no one believed that. Henrik had been waiting for an opportunity to lash out at Jonathan for quite some time–this was merely the excuse to do so.

Jonathan slammed his elbow into Henrik's face, breaking the vigilante's nose. Henrik muscled through the pain and maneuvered himself in front of Jonthan, securing him in a grappling choke hold. In response, Jonathan started landing a barrage of punches into the vigilante's abdomen, cracking Henirk's ribs, sending pain shooting throughout his body. Jonathan may have been out of training for months, but the man still hit harder than anyone Henrik had faced, aside from Annis.

"Enough of this shit!" Grigsby yelled, lifting both men up off the ground and separating them. Henrik began shouting.

"Grigs, I order you to arrest Jonathan Young for the assault of Lynn Deborney and the murder of their child!"

"Stand down, Grigs!" Mattia countered. "Henrik, you're out of line. Get out of here and cool off!"

"I will *not* get out of here, Matty!" Henrik retorted, pointing at Jonathan. "He's been a one-man wrecking ball in The Lowers for months now. He's irresponsible and he's become a danger to other people. You *know* Lynn didn't just accidentally fall down the stairs. When has she ever tripped, let alone fallen by chance? Her gifts prevent these things from happening. And you saw the bruise on her eye and cheekbone. Jumilla already confirmed Lynn didn't hit her head or face during the fall. *That* blow to her eye *caused* her to fall and the fall caused her baby to die! And Jonathan was the only person who was with her tonight. So, you tell me, *oh High Cleric*. What would you do if this man *wasn't* your son!?"

Mattia was taken aback and conflicted. She knew what Henrik was saying was true. Jonathan had caused this. Maybe he shouldn't be held responsible for the Beltane ambush, but this? This was something completely different. She cleared her throat.

"If Jonathan wasn't my son, I would have him arrested for suspicion of accidental homicide and for assault. But he *is* my son. And I've already lost my husband to a vegetative state." At this, Henrik backed away, feeling the sting of her pain. "So, before any action is taken..." Mattia walked over to Jonathan and looked him in the eyes, tears flowing from her own. "I need you to tell me if what Henrik is saying is true...or if Lynn fell down the stairs by accident, as she claims."

Jonathan looked into the big, deep, sad brown eyes in front of him. This woman standing before him had gone through Hell for him. She had risked everything for him. She may not have given birth to Jonathan, but she had loved him as though she did. And he loved her as though he had spent the first nine months of his life inside her womb. And even though Mattia didn't give Jonathan life at birth, she *did* give him life when he was thirteen years old. A life that he had robbed his son of tonight. He couldn't lie to her.

"Yes...I was drunk...and I slapped her in anger. I wasn't in control of my strength, so I slapped her so hard that she hit the wall and fell down the stairs." For the first time in months, tears rolled down Jonathan's cheeks. "I did this. I did this to my wife. I killed my son." In this moment of confession, Jonathan looked upon his mother and saw disgust in her eyes–disgust that was directed at him. It was true. He did do this. He was, once again, responsible for significant destruction of life. He was responsible for turning his family against him. He was disgusting. He was a freak. He was a villain. But he knew he wasn't the only villain in this horrible nightmare that his life had become.

As if on cue, Jonathan heard Etrulia's cackle reverberate inside his mind and knew what he had to do. He knew what his life's mission now was. His life was over in this place. There was nothing left for him here but imprisonment and death–both of which he deserved. Jonathan looked at the repulsed expressions from everyone in the waiting room. He looked at Henrik's bloodied face and said one final statement.

"And, if any of you follow me. I'll kill you too." Then Jonathan raced toward the door across the room and charged through it.

# CHAPTER THIRTY ONE

## - THE RAG MAN -

As soon as Jonathan ran through the doors, he found himself in an eerily familiar environment. The cold, gangrenous ground squished below his feet. Looking ahead of him and then behind, he saw nothing but a vast wasteland of corrupted desert, enormous broken pieces of cyclopean masonry scattered as far as he could see. Everything was dripping with a mysterious black ooze—as black as the sky above him.

This place seemed evil, yes, but it also felt dead. He had a feeling he'd been here before. Was this a nightmare? Had he died? Panic threatened to overtake him. Jonathan felt confused, seeing flashes of some alternate version of this horrible place—what it looked like when it was still *alive*. A place that stole his memories, then replaced them with fear and pain.

Jonathan tried to regain control of his mind and organize his thoughts. He knew he had just darted out of the emergency section waiting room, but at the same time, he was also aware that moment had occurred six years ago. Simultaneously, the pilgrim remembered that just a few moments ago he had been talking to the angel in a cave. Had he just relived the events leading up to his AWOL? Yes, he had. But how? Why? And why did he suddenly enter this place of nightmarish familiarity? Jonathan knew that in reality, when he had burst out of the emergency room doors, he had fought his way out of

The Fallout. He certainly didn't randomly enter this horrible place back then.

"I know you're confused, Jon," a calm, deep voice came from behind him. Jonathan looked over his shoulder to see a man standing there. Jon? Only those closest to him called him that. Who was this? The man had a wild, unkempt beard. Dirty locks fell at his shoulders. The man's clothes were ragged, stained, and torn. He looked like one of the "rag people" who roamed the alleyways of The Lowers, begging for a hit of live-dust or some spare macecoins they could use to buy a drink. Jonathan swore he'd seen this man before on a street corner, but the man had a slight accent Jonathan couldn't place. It certainly wasn't Perethedeshian.

The rag man continued.

"What you're about to go through cannot be avoided, I'm afraid. But I can guarantee you something, I will be with you every step of the way. If you trust me, I will guide you through this."

Jonathan physically winced at the amount of comfort these words gave him. He had no clue who this man was, yet every word that came out of his mouth felt as good and pure as the oak tree outside the angel's cave.

"Alright," Jonathan said hesitantly. He didn't know why he trusted this man, but he did–with all his heart, he did. He was still afraid though–of his surroundings, of what this place might do to him. "What's going to happen?"

"Follow me," was all the rag man said before he started walking in front of Jonathan toward a hauntingly burned forest. The whole thing looked as if it had fallen from a great height and slammed into this slimy terrain–large chunks layering one on top of another, only connected by oozing muck and fallen trees. Jonathan knew this jagged, charred forest hadn't been there just a second ago. But, at this point, he tried not to make sense of things. He was clearly out of his depths now.

As they entered the forest, the smell of decay overwhelmed Jonathan's senses. With every step the pilgrim took, flashes of short, hairy beasts with numb expressions, carrying large torches of green and yellow flame appeared in his mind.

He shook his head in an attempt to stop the intrusive thoughts then looked ahead at the man in rags. The man's feet were raw, and were being scorched with each step he took. Jonathan looked down at his boots and saw that *he* was unphased by this toxic ground.

"Uhm, excuse me! Don't you need coverings for your feet?" Jonathan asked. The man just kept walking, giving no response. "...alright then..." Jonathan muttered to himself.

The two men hiked through the extremely treacherous terrain. All the while, Jonathan struggled between his thoughts of the Se'irim and watching the rag man's feet blister and boil as they walked. No matter how much Jonathan wanted to stop the man and ask him what in the world was happening and where they were going, something inside of the pilgrim silenced those urges. Despite their horrible surroundings, the ghosts of devils, and the deteriorating state of his guide's feet, Jonathan obeyed the impulse to remain quiet. This was odd to the pilgrim, because he was extremely self-aware that this impulse was very unlike him. Yet, Jonathan didn't feel as though he was under a Dark spell, which troubled him all the more. That meant all of this was *real.* Not a Vision. Not a dream. But he was actually in this horrible place with this mysterious person.

As the two reached the end of the haunted forest, they slid down the mucky slope that led to a large, black field. For a brief moment, the pilgrim heard a whisper echo throughout the foul air.

"*Join us...*" the demonic whisper said. Jonathan felt a nostalgic fear wash over him. Like remembering a long forgotten, child-like terror that overwhelmed his adult reasoning.

Suddenly, the man in front of Jonathan shouted in pain, although, the cause wasn't the rag man's feet. The pilgrim could see blood was beginning to seep through the tattered shirt on his guide's back. Then he heard a pop of flesh and saw blood spewing forth as part of the man's spine protruded through his skin. The man doubled over in pain, dropping down to his knees. Jonathan rushed to his side.

"What's happening to you?" Jonathan asked in desperation.

"Help me up," the man gasped. "We...we have to get to that house up ahead."

Jonathan looked out into the field. In the distance, he could see the silhouette of what looked an Old World two story suburban house. Jonathan recognized it immediately from the Histories in The Code. There were some homes in The Grand Republic that were built this way as well, but mostly in Terraforming Outposts or more rural communities.

Even though Jonathan had barely been around them, he felt an unexplainable attachment to this particular building. He couldn't even see the details of the architecture yet, but the silhouette alone made the man almost well up with emotion. Suddenly, the light in the top room turned on. Like a lighthouse shining over a wild, chaotic ocean, the light illuminated the darkness of the field.

Jonathan lifted the man up by his underarms for support. He had no idea how this man was still able to walk with an injury like this, but again, given his surroundings, he accepted that logic didn't work the same way here. Together, they began walking through the field towards the house. Sticky, tar-like ground squished below their feet. The smell of the tall, slimy black grass was rank. As they drew closer to the house, Jonathan realized it was covered in what appeared to be

rotting, human flesh. The nostalgia Jonathan felt for this house *increased*, which disgusted him. But he couldn't help but feel a kind of loving embrace wrap around his mind as he looked upon this grotesque home.

"What–what is this place?" Jonathan gasped as he questioned, almost rhetorically.

"Listen...to me...very carefully." The rag man was understandably struggling to speak as they walked. "When we...open the door to this house...you're going to remember things. Things that will horrify you. When this happens...just keep your eyes on me. I'll guide you...to where we have to go."

"What?!" Jonathan stopped walking and looked ahead at the house, then at the man next to him. "I...I don't want to do this."

"Neither do I," the rag man replied. "But the only way out...is to move further in. You must...face the Darkness inside of you, Jon. That is the only way...you can be freed from it."

Jonathan was genuinely terrified. He knew he had once been possessed. He knew the trauma from that possession had made him lose all his memories from before his exorcism. He knew that Obadiah's protection spell not only helped keep his identity a secret from The Coven and their gods, but it also protected him from whatever terrors still lurked inside his subconscious. This is why Jonathan *never* went looking into his past. The spell blocked things that could creep into Jonathan's mind in his sleep or when he experienced any kind of déjà vu. He didn't want to spark anything that could potentially break it.

The Pilgrim also knew that whatever Etrulia had done to him during the Beltane ambush left a Dark mark on the spell, tampering with its ability to cloak him completely from the most powerful people within The Coven–he assumed this was how she found out who he was while he was wandering The Grey. So, if entering this decaying house were to undo the already weakened protection spell completely, he had no idea what would happen to him–to his mind, and to his defense against The Coven and their gods.

Then, for the first time, the rag man looked into Jonathan's eyes. The pilgrim was unexplainably overcome with relief. It was like looking into a portal filled with hope and life, but there was also great sadness there. As if Jonathan was simultaneously immersed in joy and pain intertwined in a mystifying birthing of something new.

The man spoke clearly and uninterrupted, as though the pain he was experiencing had completely subsided for a moment.

"Your life has been wrought with heartbreak, with Darkness so overwhelming that others would have been crushed under the weight of its burden. You have, indeed, been wounded under its weight. You have become one with Darkness in so many ways–sometimes as a victim, other times as a willing participant. Both of these truths have brought you here. Your life has been shifting sand.

You cling to anything that might give you purpose, only to find that *nothing* will.

"I am here to give you the ability to choose a purpose that will not lead to destruction. So, do not fear what is about to happen, Jon. You may fear the ones who would bring you to your Dark destiny, but take heart, for I am the one who has overcome them."

"Who *are* you?" Jonathan asked. His tone filled with wonder and fear.

"I am the one who would lead you to the Darkest parts of your soul, and save you from the death that lurks in the shadows." A tear rolled down the rag man's check and disappeared into his wild, dirty beard. "When you face this Darkness ahead, *you* must be the one to make the choice. Only then will the transformation from Darkness to Light become a reality."

In this moment, Jonathan was sure who this man was. And he was *nothing* like the pilgrim expected. The rag man gave him a warm, knowing smile.

"Are...are you–" The man put held his hand up to stop Jonathan.

"Not here," he whispered. "Now...open the door."

Jonathan looked ahead of them, realizing they were no longer in the field, but on the disgustingly rotten front porch of the house, standing directly in front of the moldy, flesh covered door. The pilgrim reached out, hesitating at first, then grabbed the slime covered handle and turned it.

Immediately, in a wild gust of odious wind and shrieking howls, Jonathan was overrun by countless thoughts and memories moving so fast he couldn't make sense of them. He saw flashes of his possession invade his mind. The pilgrim remembered being trapped in the coils of Golge and her putrid appendage engulfing his head. He saw himself being chased by the Se'irim through the flaming forest, his feet being scorched the entire way. Immense pain flowed through his back as he remembered the Kheynuy ripping his back open, causing part of his spine to protrude out of his flesh. He remembered the song, the field, and this awful house.

The pilgrim doubled over from the pain of experiencing all of this at once. Now, it was the rag man's turn to lift Jonathan up onto his feet.

"Look at me, Jon! Look at me!" The rag man yelled over the shrieking winds from the house attacking the pilgrim. Jonathan managed to squint his eyes open though the pain and focus as best he could on the man in front of him. When he did this, the noise seemed to dissipate enough for him to regain his control. The pilgrim and the rag man leaned into one another as they struggled up the stairs together, fighting blasting gusts and the relentless pain that both of them were experiencing.

As the two men reached the top of the stairwell and rounded the corner, they faced down a long dark hallway. A faint green light was shining from a door that began opening slowly. Suddenly, a powerful burst of foul air slammed into them, almost knocking them over the fleshy banister of the top landing. The formidable gust was accompanied by a horrible, ear-splitting, high-pitched shriek that pierced the men's senses, causing them to drop to their knees, desperately covering their ears in an attempt to muffle the pandemonium.

Visions of a demonic creature with bright green eyes filled Jonathan's mind. It was dressed in a nightgown and had ferally mangled hair on top of its head, wildly reaching in all directions.

"*Little Boy Blue has come home at last!*" A deep, gravelly voice echoed inside Jonathan's head. The pilgrim screamed in fear, dropped onto the fleshy landing and curled into the fetal position.

"No!!" screamed the pilgrim. "I can't do this anymore!! I won't go!! Just let me die!!"

"Fight it, Jon!" The rag man yelled. "Get back up and focus on *me!*" The wind howled and whipped around them all the more.

The sound of the man's voice brought Jonathan out of his petrified state, but flashes of the creature continued as the pilgrim grabbed the rag man's hand and allowed himself to be pulled to his feet. The pilgrim felt an enormous amount of pressure covering his eyes. No matter how much he tried, Jonathan's couldn't open them. All he could see what the bright green glare of hate coming from the creature. Jonathan felt the rag man grab his face and pull it towards him.

"Open your eyes, Jon! We're almost there!"

Jonathan felt instant relief and opened his eyes. Once again, he looked into the deep brown gaze of the man in rags. He felt hope return to his soul. The horrors were still present, but clarity came back to the pilgrim once more.

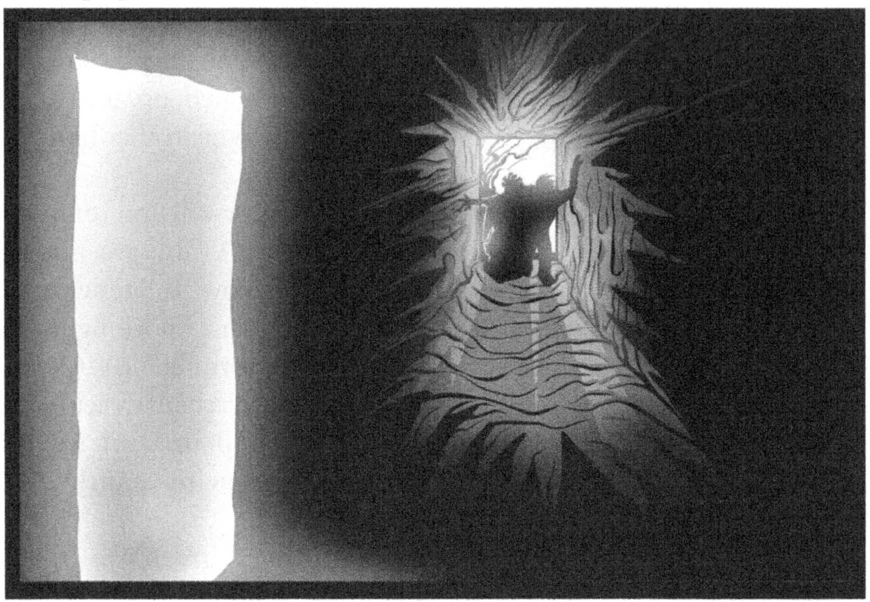

"Come on, my friend! Only a few more steps to go!" the rag man said. They began their journey down the long, treacherous hallway toward the opened door.

The two men fought hard against the wind and the shrieking; they grabbed onto the slimy, grotesque walls and pulled their way down the hauntingly dark hallway. Leaning into one another the whole time, they finally reached their destination, and stumbled across the threshold of the open doorway.

As soon as Jonathan and the rag man entered the room, all the noise and wind stopped. It was unnaturally quiet. Across the room stood a tall, broad man draped in a large featherfurred cloak with his back turned–staring out of the window Jonathan had seen from the field. In the middle of the room floated a large Stone Shard, glowing green and illuminating its surroundings.

"Welcome, Jon," the cloaked man said. His voice was raspy, but eerily familiar. "I've been waiting for you for a *long* time."

The rag man immediately cried out in pain. Jonathan looked

over to his guide and gasped. The corroded, fleshy floor was slithering up the rag man's legs, lifting him off the ground, pulling him into the corner of the room. It was overtaking his body, and breaking every bone in the process. As the rag man screamed, his eyes lit up—a hauntingly bright green. Soon the man's entire body was engulfed in the rotted flesh that covered the house. Sharp, calloused spikes emerged from the back of the rag man's prison, mercilessly stabbing into his head, silencing him. The only part of him that wasn't immersed in the cursed and corrosive tissue were his eyes—they were shining green in the darkness.

"No!" Jonathan yelled. He tried to rush to the man's aide, but found that he couldn't move.

However, it wasn't the floor that had a hold of him. Jonathan looked back to the cloaked man who was still turned away from him, staring out the window.

I had to be sure we'd have an *uninterrupted* conversation." The raspy voice explained. "I don't mean to be so controlling, but you've got to understand a few things." The cloaked man finally turned toward Jonathan and the pilgrim's heart dropped to his stomach. It was *him.* Jonathan was staring at *himself*; or at least a version of himself. His hair was matted and his beard overgrown; his olive skin was pale and calloused. His eyes were dark and tired, and the featherfur cloak looked oddly similar to what the angel in the cave had worn, but it was gray and aged.

"Oh my god..." Jonathan uttered.

"Yes. I can imagine this is pretty strange for you."

"Wh–what are you?"

*"Who.* Not 'what'," the cloaked Jonathan corrected. "And I'm the person whose been feeding you power all these years. That little *piece* of you that remained after your exorcism. I've been trapped in here...in this shit-hole...by myself, for twenty-three years. Only the ghosts of our demons to keep me company." He began walking toward Jonathan, but stopped next to the Shard and ran his long, dirty nails across it. "I'm going to let you move now, but just know you can't do anything to save *him.*" The cloaked Jonathan pointed at the rag man. "He's fine by the way. He's been pretending to be in pain this whole time so he could manipulate you into doing what he wants you to do. Shared trauma bonds people and all that."

"And what are you doing, then, if not manipulating me?" Jonathan asked.

"Great question." The cloaked man snapped his fingers, allowing Jonathan to move freely. "I'm not going to manipulate you. Honestly, I'd let you walk out of here right now, but I need you to hear something first."

"And what's that?"

"*I'm* what they've been keeping you from. And I can give you what you seek."

"*They?* They who?" Jonathan asked.

"I'm not going to speak to you in flattery, poetic words like Mr. Martyr over there. I'm going be straight with you. Everyone around you, from The Coven and their gods, to Obadiah and The Resistance, to the angel in that damn cave...to *that* man hanging there; everyone wants you to follow *their* version of *your* destiny. Doesn't that just sound a little...I don't know...like a bunch of bullshit? They've all tried to manipulate you. Every *single* word they've said is a strategic move to get you and your powers to do what *they* want you to do. I mean, am I wrong?"

Jonathan thought about this for a minute and he couldn't deny what this other Jonathan was saying to him. On the surface, it sounded very true.

"Alright...so is this where you offer me *your* version of my destiny and say its actually the right one?" Jonathan scoffed.

The cloaked man laughed.

"I love you. I really do. That sass. It's great. I'm *you*, twat-face. How am I gonna offer you *my* version of your destiny when *we're* the same person? No. Look–what I'm saying is simple. What if we don't embrace *anyone's* version of our destiny and just make one for ourselves? You're in charge of your own destiny, Jon. No one else is. Reunite with me and we can finally fulfill our deepest longings. And *this...*" the skafos slapped the side of the bright green Shard, "is what's going to help us do *just* that."

"Tempting," Jonathan said. "But how does that work exactly?"

"Another great question. This is a Shard of an extremely powerful Stone–one of twelve actually–that created everything in existence." The cloaked Jonathan pointed to the rag man once again. "That's right. The Aeternum Stones created everything, not *him.* This particular Stone is called The Sapient Stone. It helps govern all possibilities within existence. For a person to wield it takes great strength and willpower. However, *you* have had this Shard within your very essence since you were a small boy, well before your possession ever occurred–"

"What? How is that possible?" Jonathan interrupted.

"That *particular* detail is for another time. You're not quite ready for that answer just yet. We'll get there though, I promise. Just know that you have an intimate relationship with this Shard and you can learn to control it to help you construct whatever future you wish to have. Not just a *chance* at that future, mind you, but the Shard will actually *guarantee* it."

"If that's the case, then why haven't I felt any of its effects? If it's a part of my essence, then how come the direction of my life has become the exact opposite of what I've wanted?"

"After your exorcism, Obadiah had that Hoodoo priest cast a protection spell on you, right? Well, that locked a lot of things away inside your subconscious, this Shard being one of them. Me too, for that matter." The cloaked man paused for a moment, stepped away from the Shard and closer to Jonathan. "*I* am the missing piece that completely unlocks your abilities. Everyone wants to have control over *me* so they can do whatever they want with *you.* So, if we unite and use the Shard on *our* terms and not *theirs,* then we can do whatever the fuck we want. All this power available for our *every* desire."

"You're the skafos." Jonathan stated.

"Yeah. I am. But that doesn't mean what that angel told you it means. I'm not some demonic monster waiting to reclaim your soul. I may look scary and I may act like a caged animal, but that's because I've literally been a prisoner in this *open wound* for over two decades. I'm pissed. And I want out. I want to be back with you. Back where I belong. You've not felt whole since your exorcism, right? Well, it's because a literal piece of you was missing."

This hit Jonathan like a ton of bricks. Had he been lied to by everyone?

The skafos continued.

"I know Obadiah meant well, and honestly, good on him for taking care of you for so long. His intentions were to protect you and he had no idea that it would lock crucial parts of you away like this. But now, we can correct that mistake. We can even set him free."

"What?" Jonathan asked in desperation. "What do you mean?"

"I didn't really want to lead with this because it sounds *very* manipulative, but the truth of the matter is that if we unite, you'll have the power to undo what Etrulia did to him."

"How? With the Shard?"

"We actually wouldn't need the Shard for that. Being a skafos, I have the ability to control Dark energy called, 'necroplasm'. She implanted her necroplasmic seed inside of Obadiah's mind on the night of that Beltane ambush. It lays dormant as we speak, waiting to be controlled. We can simply remove it." The skafos explained.

"By using *Dark* energy..."

"Yes, by using *Dark* energy to undo the *Darkness* done to those we love. It's a weapon, Jon. One that we can utilize *however* we want. We can use it for evil, sure, but if we want to use it to help people, we can do that as well." The skafos pointed to the rag man again. "Using something bad, to produce something good is basically *this* fucker's entire strategy to keeping everyone under *his* version of order and control. He says all these flowery things about freedom, but all he really *wants* is to place everyone in another form of slavery that *he's* in control of."

Jonathan intentionally didn't look at the rag man in this moment. *Look at me* was starting to sound like a way for this being–this God–to control him.

"How do you know all this? Why should I believe you?" he asked.

"I'm a skafos; meaning the Dark elohim that possessed you passed on some of his knowledge and power to me. Normally a skafos would connect you directly to the possessing Dark elohim, but Xexxus was transported out of here and imprisoned, so you don't have to worry about that any–"

"Xexxus..." Jonathan shuddered in fear. He hadn't heard that name in twenty-three years. Memories of the large, terrifying elohim flooded the pilgrim's mind. So did the fear and the pain. Jonathan dropped to his knees as he remembered the torture, the assault, and the humiliation he endured. But, most of all, he remembered that sick, twisted, maniacal laughter. *You are mine* Xexxus had said time and time again while cackling in Jonathan's face. That act of conquering intimidation always left Jonathan feeling completely and utterly helpless.

Memories of the night of Jonathan's exorcism engulfed him. He remembered what happened to Mattia. He remembered torturing her. He remembered murdering Bouchard. He remembered having so much power surging through him that he became something less than human. And he remembered, during all the carnage, an ancient, malevolent power overtaking him. Nachash: the spirit of The Great Serpent–an invisible, twisting, hate-filled *thing* that started turning Jonathan into an abomination. But most of all, Jonathan remembered that *he* wasn't the one doing all of this. He wasn't the one inviting this horrible spirit inside him–the skafos was.

"*You.*" Jonathan said with rage-filled disgust. "You destroyed people I loved...and you reveled in it. You would have me turn into a literal *monster*, just like you did all those years ago!" The pilgrim looked up from his kneeling position to see the skafos walking towards him, eyes glowing green.

"It's better than the pathetic little shit I see before me now!" Instantly, the Blade of The Sapient Stone materialized in the skafos' hand. In a blur, the green-eyed man raised the blade and brought it thundering down toward Jonathan.

The pilgrim's instincts kicked in and he grabbed the skafos' forearms, stopping the blade within inches of his face.

"This blade was the key to my freedom all those years ago. Your *father* thought it was lost when he foolishly sent those Clerics plummeting to their deaths. The Master brought it back to its rightful owners. And now, it will finally finish what it started so long ago! You will not prevent me from escaping this prison, you disgusting little dust creature!" the skafos snarled as the green blade glowed brighter. Jonathan's fists were shaking and he was losing his grip on the skafos' arms. "We are meant for greatness, you and I! Why won't you just accept it?! Can't you see that the last six years have led you to our unity?! You're already a monster, Jon! You fucking *killed* your own son! *I* am your destiny!! I am the key to destroying your *greatest* enemy. I am the key to making you the most powerful being in the *world!* Together, we can set everything the way *we* want it to be! We

can bring about the Dark Eschaton of Age End and *rule* this world alongside the one to whom it *truly* belongs!"

The green blade inched closer and closer to Jonathan's face. If he didn't think of something fast, he was going to lose much more than this battle. He may have caused many horrible things to occur in his life, but it was clear that whatever destiny involved this side of himself, was going to bring complete chaos and destruction to *everything*; not just the things Jonathan cared about.

"*I am here with you. Look to me.*" Jonathan heard the rag man's voice inside his head. Through the straining and the struggling, Jonathan slowly turned his head just enough so his eyes met the man completely immersed in rotted flesh. The green haze covering the rag man's eyes lifted, as bright tzoharian Light began to shine forth instead.

"*Take heart, Jon. And believe.*"

Jonathan felt strength begin to build in his grip as his hands started glowing with the same Light he saw in the rag man's eyes.

"No–No!" the skafos shouted.

"Yes." Jonathan said firmly. Then, with new found strength, the pilgrim pushed the skafos' arms, sending the green-eyed man crashing into the Sapient Shard and onto the moldy floor. While scrambling to get back onto his feet, the skafos realized the Sapient Blade was no longer in his hands. He quickly scoured the floor, then looked up to find the Blade in Jonathan's white glowing grip.

"You were right about one thing," the pilgrim said. "I *am* in charge of my own destiny. And so far, I think I've fucked it up enough already. So has everyone else." Jonathan pointed the blade at the rag man. "So, I think it's time to give *him* a chance. He can't do any worse, that's for sure."

"You *fool!*" The skafos leapt towards Jonathan, his teeth transforming into large fangs. His nails turned into sharp, glowing green talons. The two Jonathans fell to the ground and wrestled ferociously on the rotted floor, each one fighting for control of the Sapient Blade.

Finally, the skafos grabbed the wrist of the hand holding the Blade and slammed it onto the floor. He pinned down the pilgrim's glowing white hand. Quickly, the skafos brought his free hand down–

glowing talons first—at Jonathan's face. The pilgrim caught the skafos' free wrist, preventing it from finding its intended target.

"Everything in your life has been under the control of *that* man hanging there!" The skafos hissed. "He could've stopped it all at any moment, but refused to do so! Why align yourself with a being who causes you to experience such pain!? He can't give you the desires and freedom you seek! *I* can!! Yield, and we can rule this world as we see fit!"

Jonathan's strength wasn't waning, but neither was he able to gain the upper hand. He couldn't move against the weight of the skafos pressing down upon him. Suddenly, the skafos' glowing talons began to grow, inching closer and closer to Jonathan's face. The pilgrim knew he had to think of something, and fast. Brute force clearly wasn't going to win the day.

The glowing green nails were now centimeters away from Jonathan's forehead.

"You cannot get rid of me, Jon." The skafos grinned, revealing his green fangs covered in grotesque necroplasm. "I'll always be here, scraping and clawing inside your head, inside your soul. No matter what you do, I will *always* be with you, waiting for my moment to grab hold. And I *will* grab hold, Jon. You can count on *that!"*

The green nail on the skafos' middle finger pierced Jonathan's forehead. Fresh blood trickled down the pilgrim's face.

"You don't trust in a God," the skafos said. "You never have, no matter how much Mattia or anyone tried to coerce you into doing so. You saw the world for what it was: a hellscape of destruction. Even the polished parts are like putting make-up on a pig. No. This world is exactly what it looks like—creatures in all the realms fighting for power and control. Dominion and conquest. That's the only thing steering the ship. It's *your turn* now, Jon. Join me and claim your rightful place. It'll be a moment of pain from this Blade and then we'll be united, ready to embrace the destiny we make for ourself."

Then, as if the clouds parted inside of Jonathan's mind, he heard the words the angel had said to him.

*For a blessing to blossom inside of a person, it has to be received by real faith, and the individual must entrust themselves to the source of that blessing. Only then will the blessing have a lasting effect.*

Jonathan searched his heart. He may have said that he would align with the rag man—with Yahweh. But did he truly mean it? Did he truly believe that Yahweh was something other than what the skafos was describing? Something other than what he had believed this God to be his whole life?

The pilgrim looked into the glowing green eyes of this thing on top of him. But in this moment, Jonathan didn't see the skafos. He didn't see the potential for conquest and rule. He saw his true self. He saw the thing he had become. The thing that had destroyed his wife's life and killed his son. He saw the hatred that drove him to the brink of utter destruction. And he remembered that through all of it, the rag man still took on every bit of pain that Jonathan had experienced in this subconscious nightmare they were in. That wasn't manipulation. That wasn't conquest. It was love. It was sacrifice. It was a father saving his son. And that was something he could have faith in.

"May the holy cross be my Light," the pilgrim said, staring into the face of evil. "May the dragon never be my guide..."

Where the skafos' nail had pierced Jonathan's forehead, tzoharian Light began to shine, causing the evil being to retract in pain.

"No! Stop it!" the skafos growled in fear.

"Begone satan! I reject your vanities..."

Jonathan began gaining leverage with his Sapient Blade hand, slowly overpowering the skafos and bringing the Blade towards its pale abdomen. The skafos attempted to leap off Jonathan, but the pilgrim's grip prevented him from escaping.

"The cup you offer me is evil..."

The Sapient Blade drew closer to the skafos' calloused waist. No matter how much he tried to fight it, the glowing tzoharian hand of Jonathan Young persisted.

"Drink the poison yourself!"

With the final words, Jonathan buried the Blade of The Sapient Stone into the skafos' abdomen and twisted the thick knife with a flick of his wrist.

Jonathan woke up with a sudden jolt, holding his abdomen tightly. As he looked around, he saw that he was back in the angel's cave. But he was now alone. There was no cot underneath him this time. There was no fire—or any sign that there ever was one. The dirt on the cave floor appeared to have been untouched as if no one had been there in ages.

The pilgrim stood up and looked down at himself. He was still fully clothed—and thankful for that. Jonathan walked over to the opening of the cave and realized he was able to exit freely, but also saw that there was no oak or lush green grass as there had been before. Only coarse, cold sand under a dusky sky.

Then, out of the corner of his eye, he saw something leaning against the side of the cave wall. It was the white staff the angel had carried with him. The pilgrim slowly walked over and picked it up, finding it was much lighter than it appeared. He noticed a carving on the cave wall, that looked as if the engraving had been there as long as the cave had. The carving read, "For the pilgrim who carries a heavy burden."

Jonathan chuckled to himself.

"Alright, Clarence. Thanks for the walking stick. An ungravity pod would've been nice though."

Suddenly Jonathan realized something. He had no idea how long he had been inside this cave. It felt like he had traveled a lifetime before waking up just a moment ago. His mind drifted to Etrulia and The Tellyard Bard Village. The rage that drove him had dulled some, but it still remained. He longed to hold the witch accountable for all she had done, but for the first time in his life, he felt conflicted about the thirst for revenge. Besides, how could he even get to the Village? He had no idea where he was. The pilgrim knew he was in The Lost Dunes, but that stretched on for miles within The Grey.

Then, as if responding to an audible voice inside his mind, Jonathan felt the urge to tap the white staff three times on the ground. He had no clue why this urge was so strong, but he couldn't ignore it, and obeyed.

Tap, tap, tap.

Jonathan heard the sound of rushing wind from inside the cave behind him. His mouth opened in astonishment as he turned to see a portal of Light begin to form out of nowhere. Jonthan's heart started to race. Not only was he unsure of where the portal would take him, but he didn't know what would happen to him if he traversed through it. Clearly, this staff was an angelic relic of some sort. The pilgrim was beyond hesitant to pass through the portal, unsure of whether or not his body could withstand it.

Still, just as he was about to tap the staff again–hopefully to close this portal–an overwhelming urge of comfort and peace overtook Jonathan. After everything he'd just been through, he was sure he knew that this feeling was telling him to utilize the portal and travel to where it led him. This staff had been given to him for a reason.

"Well...alright. Here we go," he said to himself. "If this rips me in half, it's your ass, Clarence." Then, the pilgrim walked through the Pentaclegate and disappeared from the cave.

As soon as the Pentaclegate closed, the elohim leaned against the cave wall, satisfied with a job well done. Lilith beamed a prideful smile, knowing that The Master would be well pleased with her for guiding their prize back to his proper destination.

FOR
THE PILGRIM
WHO
CARRIES
A HEAVY
BURDEN

# CHAPTER THIRTY TWO

## - SO MOTE IT BE -

As the villagers marched through the Lichgate, carrying torches and chanting in the esoteric language of their gods, a ghoulish chill settled on the Village of The Tellyard Bard. Night had fallen and the full moon shone brightly overhead. The path leading to the black altar situated at the base of the Standing Stone was lined with sorcerers and priests. The villagers were forming the Primary Circle around the altar and their leaders–everyone's faces were painted with skulls. Over the course of the last two days, each of the villagers had undergone a spiritual transformation. The fear that the pilgrim observed upon his arrival had now dissipated, leaving behind a powerful determination that they had been chosen.

Two days ago, after Akalian had taken Jonathan into the woods and disappeared–interrupting Etrulia's awakening of the skafos within the pilgrim–the Village was left in complete panic. The dark-skinned sorcerer had bested their Mistress while the olive-skinned man had destroyed their giant chief priest. A few villagers had even been struck blind by "*the sorcerer with the white staff.*" Those particular villagers knew they were doomed, for the Purging Ceremony had been upon them–the final Ceremony of conquering triumph within the Bard Village.

This Ceremony–lasting six hours–of destroying one's neighbor not only had empowered the villagers' confidence, but it had literally transformed their souls, hardening their hearts all the more toward goodness and Light, and causing them to embrace the Darkness. It refocused their attention on why this *particular* Winter Solstice was so special. Many of the recently blind committed suicide to prevent themselves from becoming a sacrificial offering the next day. The others who were truly loyal to the Endorian gods accepted their fate and gave themselves over to the Purging, allowing themselves to be hunted down and killed so that the rest of the village could become one with the heart of the Endorian gods.

The remaining villagers had conquered the weak amongst them and would be the ones to form the Primary Circle during the sacrifice–the Awakening of The Necronomicon. Finally, they would partake in their last Orgia Ceremony of Saturnalia, celebrating one another's fleshly desires, and the coming of Age End. This was not just an annual celebration of the Dark New Year. It was a celebration of the looming Dark Eschaton.

Of all the dwelling places belonging to The Coven of Endor, The Tellyard Bard Village was the only one to never keep children within its walls. Any child born in this place was given to the sorcerers, who would ultimately decide their fate–being sold into sex trade or work camps, or chosen for merging. However, *this* child was different. Her fate had been sealed in the stars the night she was born–six years ago.

Now–on this most Dark prestigious night–with a cold, blank stare on her face, the girl walked through the crowd of chanting villagers forming the Primary Circle. She had been set apart her entire life, never having left the High Tower until this night. Her lineage had been confirmed by High Sister Agatha herself. And, if the High Sister was correct, it was this girl's ancestors who had welcomed The Coven into The Grey hundreds of years before this night. The family Alhazred had a great and terrible history deeply rooted in events like what would soon occur in this horrible Ceremony.

Etrulia, draped in a black Saturnalia robe bedecked in silver Endorian symbols, followed closely behind the girl–Blade of The Sapient Stone clutched in her fist. The High Sister's face had been repainted, but the scars from the holy water remained. The witch's yellow eyes glared around her surroundings. She was waiting for Jonathan Young to emerge from the crowd at any moment. She had received knowledge from her symbiotic master, Yirah, that Xexxus' skafos had awakened and was on his way. Yirah also informed her that the pilgrim was not under Dark control yet and Jonathan Young would be entering the Village, ready to destroy her with his newly found powers. Her job was to carry on with the Ceremony as planned. Then, when Jonathan appeared, she was to hold him off until The Fellowship could claim the skafos for their own. The Primary Circle of Sapiential Offering could then continue with the Manking at her side, just as The Master had promised.

"Nog Necronomicon ahch' bthnkor! Nog Necronomicon ahch' bthnkor!" The villagers, priests, and sorcerers continued chanting in the gutteral R'lyehian language. They cried out to their gods to bless this sacrifice and awaken the crucial piece of Age End that had been kept secret from the Heavenly Host for thousands of years.

If the Manking Prophecy was the Dark Father's contribution to the Dark Eschaton of Age End, then The Awakening of The Necronomicon was The Master's. Even though all Dark elohim were attempting to counter The Great Téleios of New Eden with that of Age End, The Dark Kingdom was always at odds with one another, constantly changing each other's prophecies and striving to overthrow one another within The Dark and be the ultimate victor of the realms. Unlike the grand, prideful fashion in which Lucifer announced the Manking Prophecy, The Master chose to be much more covert, knowing that the fewer elohim–Dark or Light–who knew about the true purpose of The Necronomicon, the more chance of success the prophecy had.

In 730 A.D. of the Old World, The Master appeared before a lowly poet of Sanaá, a haunted city in Yemen, very near the gates of Dudael. It was there that The Master was welcomed into the body and soul of Abdul Alhazred, who was known for his extreme and total devotion to The Elder Gods. For forty days and forty nights, he penned the unholy text of The Dark Kingdom: The Necronomicon. Since then, the grim tome had been used by many who aligned themselves with The Dark Kingdom, but most completely by The Coven of Endor.

However, the true purpose of this wretched tome was far more diabolical than anyone understood. To all, except a select few, it was simply a response to the holy Scripture of Yahweh–some even calling it "The Devil's Bible".

That select few had not only received the revelation of what the grimoire truly was, but they had been sworn to secrecy under pain of eternal torture by design of The Master himself. The dreadful book was now in the hands of the last known descendant of the mad poet Alhazred. The tiny six-year-old clutched the grimoire to her chest as she reached the black stone altar and placed the ancient copy of The Necronomicon upon its cold, rough surface.

The young girl walked around the altar, stopping between it and the Standing Stone, and faced the sorcerers and priests–her blank, glowing eyes glaring numbly. Etrulia stood next to her, raising the Sapient Blade high above her head towards the full moon above.

"Tonight, we gather together to call upon The Master and his Fellowship!" The High Sister's voice boomed throughout the ritual plains.

"You have been chosen to witness this secret sacrificial rite and partake in the glorious reckoning of all things!" The R'lyehian chants grew louder, more emphatic than ever before. "With this blade of sacred Stone, I call out to our gods, our masters, our sacred ones! We beseech thee, oh great spirits who transcend time. Enter our realm and dwell here with us!"

"We beseech thee!" the villagers chanted in response.

"I know I'm not *exactly* who you beseeched just now, but I believe you and I have some unfinished business to attend to, *witch!"* The voice of Jonathan Young boomed throughout the ritual grounds, as he pulled off the hood of the black Saturnalia robe that he'd *borrowed* from one of the villagers. As the pilgrim stepped into the clearing between the sorcerers and faced Etrulia, the torch he was carrying transformed into Akalian's white staff.

*I think I'm getting the hang of this thing. I could definitely get used to it,* Jonathan thought to himself.

The Pentaclegate had brought him into the woods by the edge of the solidified dune walls of the Village–the exact same place Akalian had Pentaclegated prior. At first, the pilgrim wasn't sure where he was, but he knew the feeling of overwhelming peace and comfort had left him as soon as he walked through the portal. Everything had suddenly felt wrong. Like he wasn't supposed to be here. Jonathan was utterly conflicted in that moment. He was so sure that he had listened to what Yahweh or the angel was telling him to do, but the feeling of uncertainty now overwhelmed him. He *knew* the staff was given to him by the angel, but perhaps what brought him *here* was...something else. When he finally realized where the Pentaclegate had taken him, that familiar feeling of rage began to bubble inside of the pilgrim.

Jonathan heard the words of the skafos inside his head.

*You cannot get rid of me, Jon. I'll always be here, scraping and clawing inside your head, inside your soul. No matter what you do, I will always be with you, waiting for my moment to grab hold. And I will grab hold, Jon. You can count on that.*

Standing in the mirky woods of the Village, haunted by what was echoing in his thoughts, Jonathan prayed. He pictured the rag man and asked what he should do now. Should he tap the staff again and hope it would take him somewhere else? Or should he continue onward and finally bring Etrulia to justice? *Justice.* That was now the second time he had thought of Etrulia in these terms. It wasn't *just* about revenge anymore, even though he certainly yearned for it. Now, the thought of bringing the witch to justice for all the horrible things she'd done was present and equal alongside his vengeful longings. His thirst for revenge was tantalizing, but wrong. But *justice* felt right–less about him and more about bringing an ordered consequence to a vile being. He felt a change and knew he would wrestle with the intermingling of these two desires until the bitter end of his conflict with the High Sister.

This realization would have been enough for him to move forward and find a way into the Ceremony. However, Jonathan also remembered that there had been talk of preparing a child for sacrifice on the final night of Saturnalia. To his shame, he admitted that he honestly hadn't cared about that before, but now, he felt a new motivation building inside of him–the need to save the young life. That impulse was something he hadn't felt for years.

Whether or not he had been brought here by Yahweh, the angel, or something else, Jonathan knew what he had to do. The pilgrim ran off towards the ritual plain, hoping a plan would come to him.

Thankfully, it did.

"I formally challenge you, Etrulia, High Sister of Endor, to a *witch's duel*," the pilgrim announced with a smirk on his face. Etrulia and all her sorcerers began laughing.

"I'm impressed that you came back to me. But, I'm sorry to disappoint you, my pet. You have to be a witch or warlock to participate in a witch's duel." Etrulia scoffed, condescendingly, at the man.

"You just saw my *Magick!"* Jonathan held up his staff toward the witch. "I even have a staff that performs great deeds. I believe that makes me a sorcerer. Does it not? Or are you just too scared to face me now?"

Etrulia snarled at his taunt, but she was also apprehensive. She had no idea what this pilgrim was capable of now. In truth, neither did *he*, but she didn't know that part. In fact, Jonathan wasn't quite sure how any of this worked. He had figured out that the staff would obey his will, but he wasn't sure how the Magick, or holy energy, or whatever it was actually *worked.*

He felt as though he was making things up as he went.

"Your taunts do nothing but make you look desperate, my pet." Etrulia forced a mocking smile. "You don't even belong to The

Coven, or *any* coven for that matter. Why should I take your challenge seriously?"

*Where is The Fellowship*, Etrulia thought to herself. Yirah had told her that when Jonathan arrived, they would reclaim the skafos for themselves. Why hadn't that happened yet?

"Because, if you remember, witch, there are *laws* within the world of Magick. And while The Resistance Elite may not call themselves a coven, we are a group of people who have gifts that many would call Magickal. I co-led them for almost two decades. I believe that makes you and I *equals* within the Hierarchy of Magick. Therefore, my challenge is legitimate." Jonathan knew this would pierce through her ego.

"You *dare* equate your pitiful band with *me* and the great Coven of Endor!?" Etrulia knew he was baiting her, but this was going too far. Jonathan wasn't just challenging the High Sister in front of her Coven; the pilgrim was *degrading* her status in front of them. In The Coven, this went far beyond disrespect, it was a blasphemous act that had to be dealt with on the fiercest level. She wasn't sure why The Fellowship hadn't claimed the skafos yet, but she could stand this insolence no longer. Skafos or not, Etrulia was High Sister of Endor. She couldn't allow for her subjects to see her dismiss such heretical ridicule.

"I do not accept your *challenge*, you pathetic boy! But I will destroy you, nevertheless!"

Etrulia's shriek pierced the foul air. A black and red necroplasmic blast spewed from her mouth towards Jonathan. This time, the pilgrim was prepared for it and leapt out of the way just in time, rolling sideways onto the sandy grass of the ritual plain. When he gained his footing, Jonathan pointed the white staff toward Etrulia and willed an energy blast to shoot from it.

*I hope this works*, he thought to himself. White energy blasted from the end of the staff and hit the witch, causing her to fly backwards into the Standing Stone.

"Seize him!" Etrulia shouted, her voice supernaturally amplified.

Jonathan slammed the end of his staff onto the ground. A wave of energy thundered around him, pummeling the sorcerers near him, and preventing any others from approaching.

Etrulia hurdled over the black altar and landed on top of Jonathan, tackling him to the ground. She plunged the Sapient Blade down toward the pilgrim's neck, but her wrists were stopped by the white staff, preventing the witch from hitting her target.

"Nice face paint." Joathan taunted. "Although I don't think that'll hide those god-awful scars from the last time we met. No antiseptic available in this dump? That's a pity."

"Shut your trap!" Etrulia screamed, necroplasm dripping from her mouth like oozing saliva.

"Ugh. You're so gross."

Suddenly, a flash of green emanated from Jonathan's essence and punched the witch off of the pilgrim's body, launching her twisting chaotically across the ritual grounds. In mid-air, Etrulia regained control of herself and landed in a power stance, blade held steady in her outstretched hand. The witch knew Jonathan couldn't possibly have gained enough knowledge about his new found power to best her. He obviously had an enormous amount of might now, but she was positive it didn't match hers. She'd been a skafos of Yirah for twenty-three years. Jonathan had been an unclaimed skafos for less than a day. Etrulia knew things this dust creature hadn't dreamed of yet, and she was tired of dealing with an insolent boy who'd been annoyingly buzzing around her Coven for far too long.

"R'luh Sapientus throdog ah'mgehye!" Etrulia bellowed from the depths of her throat.

Jonathan watched in terror as slimy, black necroplasm appeared at the inner crease of Etrulia's arm and slithered downward over her fist and onto the Sapient Blade. The jet-black ooze began merging with the thick green knife, causing it to twist and prolong itself until it transformed into a vast, long broadsword. Jonathan took a step back, holding his white staff out in front of him and willing it to become a broadsword as well. Only this time, nothing happened.

"Well, shit." Jonathan said in disappointed desperation. He had no idea why this relic wasn't doing what he wanted. He believed in the source. He had faith in Yahweh to help him. So, why wasn't it working?

Etrulia sprinted towards the pilgrim at an alarming speed, slicing her necro-Sapient broadsword at him. Jonathan slammed the end of his staff on the ground once more, hoping that it would have the same effect as it did on the sorcerers. A blinding flash of white energy blasted forth from the staff, but Etrulia jumped into the air. With her broadsword, she sliced through the pilgrim's energy blast like a hot knife through butter. In an instant, Jonathan instinctually brought the white staff above his head in a defensive motion and, surprisingly, it blocked Etrulia's broadsword without being sliced in two. Bright white and green sparks flew off the staff when the sword crashed into it, but there was no damage at all.

Etrulia suddenly spat necroplasmic discharge into Jonathan's face, which sent him crashing onto his back. It felt like someone had sucker punched the pilgrim.

"How does it feel to be bitch-slapped like that, little boy?" the witch mocked. She brought the broadsword down with a terrible force, crashing into his staff once more–causing green and white sparks to fly. "Now you know how your little whore felt before you sent her soaring down the stairs, killing the leech inside her belly!" The broadsword crashed into the staff again.

Jonathan's vision blurred with rage. The necro-Sapient sword smashed into his staff another time, sending sparks flying into Jonathan's face. Etrulia began striking the staff at multiple angles every other second, attempting to either break through the relic or crush the man holding it. Jonathan did all he could to keep up.

"It's better this way though, trust me!" The witch cackled as she relentlessly attacked the pilgrim. "No child should ever have *you* for a father! You pathetic, weak, impotent thing! Better yet, I would have loved to see you try and fail at something else!" Etrulia's laugh echoed throughout the ritual plain. "Failing others is all you're good for anyway! Just ask your *own* father!"

Suddenly, the rage overtook Jonathan completely. Etrulia stopped laughing as she saw the pilgrim's eyes illuminate with a bright green light. In shock and fear, the witch halted her attack and backed away. The pilgrim jumped to his feet–green eyes blazing.

"What's wrong, oh High Sister of Endor?" Jonathan said with a devilish grin on his face. His voice was gravelly and guttural. "You seem afraid." Green and black necroplasm shot from Jonathan's free hand and struck Etrulia in the chest, flinging her backwards towards the black altar. The witch landed hard on her back and groaned in pain as the wind was knocked out of her. She had dropped the necro-Sapient sword upon impact. With her symbiotic connection broken, the necroplasm seeped into the ground, leaving only the Sapient Blade lying four feet from the witch's stunned body. She reached out intending to grab it but her hand was struck by another blast of green and black necroplasm. She screamed in pain. It was unlike any affliction she had felt before. Etrulia hugged her hand close to her, quickly assessing the charred hole in her palm.

"Behold, villagers of The Tellyard Bard!" Jonathan's guttural

"Behold, villagers of The Tellyard Bard!" Jonathan's guttural tone echoed throughout the ritual plain. "Your High Sister has been defeated. She cowers at my feet! She *fears* me."

At this, Etrulia shot her own red and black necroplasmic energy towards Jonathan, but the pilgrim simply caught the assault in his glowing green hands, balled it up, and absorbed it into himself.

"Ahh. That feels wonderful." Jonathan moaned with pleasure. Suddenly, the pilgrim doubled over in pain, grabbing at his abdomen. Etrulia wasn't sure what was happening. She knew this wasn't her doing. Was The Fellowship finally claiming the skafos as their own? Jonathan vomited red and black necroplasm mixed with green glowing ooze.

"No!" the pilgrim shouted. "You can't have him! He belongs to me!" Jonathan dropped to one knee. "No!!"

Etrulia smiled in relief. The Fellowship *was* claiming him at last. This was over. Age End could officially begin tonight!!

Silence covered the ritual grounds as Jonathan stilled, eyes closed. The pilgrim slowly rose and faced Etrulia.

"Yes, my pet," the witch mused as she stood to her feet. "Let us carry out the Awakening together and usher in Age–"

Jonathan's eyes opened and Etrulia immediately stopped talking. Instead of green or black, his eyes blazed with gold and white tzoharian Light.

"No...how...how is this possible...*no!"* Etrulia grabbed the Sapient Blade and sprinted back to the six-year-old girl. She held the thick knife to the child's throat. The girl remained in her trance-like state, unresponsive to anything around her.

"If you take one step closer, I will *end* her pathetic existence!" The witch was fully prepared to do so. She chose not to think about the repercussions of killing the only known descendant of Alhazred in this moment. She didn't care if this ended all the progress made over the years, leading to Age End. She was terrified of whatever *holy* thing Jonathan Young had just become. Yirah and The Fellowship be damned, she would do anything right now to survive.

"No. You won't." Jonathan said calmly, his voiced echoing with the sound of a rushing waterfall. He lifted his free hand gently into the air. Etrulia's arms grew limp. She dropped the Sapient Blade onto the sandy grass at her feet as she began floating into the air over the black altar towards Jonathan. The High Sister attempted to scream orders at her sorcerers and priests to attack the man, but she could not speak. Everyone on the ritual grounds was terrified. They wouldn't have gone anywhere near this man. Silently, Etrulia pleaded with Yirah to help her, but she received no response. She was alone.

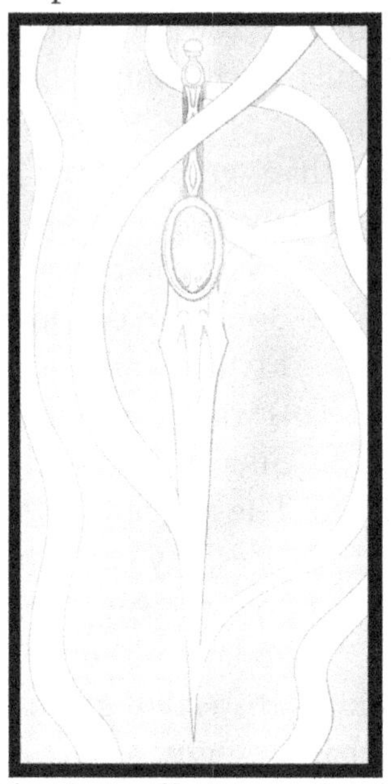

Etrulia stopped in front of Jonathan and she found herself being forced to stand before him. The witch still couldn't move her arms or legs, but she could move her eyes. They looked down at Jonathan's right hand that held the white staff. Only now, the staff was no longer there. It was Yildrim, the Sword of The King. Fear washed over Etrulia. Desperation surged through her body; she screamed internally, silently pleading for help from her Endorian masters. But no help came.

"Etrulia, Sister of Endor," Jonathan began. "You have done horrible things. You have destroyed the lives of the just and the unjust alike. You have reveled in the suffering and pain of children. You have sat with the Darkness and drank the wine of its bitter fruit. You have rejoiced in its pleasures and defilements upon the cosmos. You would have seen the world come to destruction and danced upon its ashes. Instead," Jonathan brought Yildrim up to his chest, the bright white blade pressing against his brow, "you will now suffer the fate of your choices. You will dissipate into nothingness like the wind-driven chaff." Jonathan raised the Sword of The King high above his head, ready to deliver a killing blow. "This judgement is true and *just.*"

Yildrim sliced across Etrulia's body, from her right shoulder down to her left hip. White hot pain surged through the witch as she writhed in agony. She could feel the very fabric of her soul twisting and burning until nothing remained. It was as if she were shrinking into herself, soaking in the white flames of annihilation. All the horrendous acts she had committed flashed before her eyes as the witch relived every single moment, except this time she felt the pain and suffering she had wrought upon her victims. As Yildrim sliced through her body, Etrulia lived an eternity of anguish and torment brought on by her own doing. Then, it was over.

Etrulia opened her eyes and saw a man in white standing before her. There was nothing and no one around them. She was no longer in the Bard Village, but on a white shore with a cool silver tide gently washing over her feet.

"Where–where I am I?" Etrulia nervously questioned. She felt lost in a sea of confusion. She looked down at her hands. She had a scar on her hand from her battle with Jonathan. It felt so long ago. Her dirty black and silver Saturnalia robes had been replaced with a white, cotton gown. Her tribal skull paint had been cleaned from her scarred face.

"Do you remember when you used to talk to me on the hillside where you lived as a girl?" The man asked her.

"What? I've...I've never seen you before in my life." Etrulia answered the man. Yet, tears began to roll down her cheeks as if she was talking to a long-lost friend.

"You used to sing to me on that hill, too. I cherish those memories." The man began to cry a little. "Then...then one of the elders of your village took you and...and did secret things...terrible things."

"Who are you?" Etrulia cried harder. "How...how do you know this?"

"You felt abandoned by your family when they didn't believe you. They even ridiculed you for attempting to 'besmirch the good name' of the man who hurt you. You became an outcast of your village–a village that was supposed to be following *me*. But in their blindness, they ignored me and my guidance. After that...The Coven found you. They lured you in by promising you vengeance for the deplorable things that had been done to you." Etrulia was sobbing by now. "So, you ran to the wretched Coven with your arms wide open. You knew that if *God* was anything like what your village had shown you, then you'd rather give your allegiance to *anything* else. You were deceived. And even though you willingly accepted the Darkness and have, indeed, done terrible things, you were robbed of the chance to know me for who I truly am."

"Oh...oh my..." Etrulia couldn't speak through the tears. The King walked over to her and wrapped his arms around her–giving her the warmest embrace she'd ever felt. Her fears, guilt, and shame melted away while she was lost in the arms of this man. She never wanted him to let go.

"I'm giving you that chance now, child. Go back to the hillside and sing."

Etrulia dropped to her knees. She was back on the sandy grass of the ritual plain. Her white gown had returned to the black and silver robes. But the scar on her hand remained as it was on the white shores. The sorcerers and priests were staring at her. She looked up–tears in her eyes–and saw Jonathan Young. His eyes still glowing gold and white, he now held the white staff in his hand once more.

"The skafos inside you is now dead." Jonathan said plainly. "You're no longer a witch of Endor, Etrulia. You're something *new*." The pilgrim reached out his hand for her to take.

The former High Sister took the hand of the man whose life she'd helped destroy and stood to her feet. She leaned in close to him and whispered.

"How am I to leave this place? These people will surely kill me."

"You'll come with me through the woods one final time. Once we reach our destination on the other side, you're free to go wherever you choose."

Etrulia stepped back and looked Jonathan in the eyes.

"Thank you. Thank you so much–I...don't know how to say..."

"You're welcome." Jonathan said with a slight smile on his face. "Now. Go get the girl and come with me."

A tear rolled down the woman's face. She wiped it away, smearing the skull paint on her cheek. Etrulia turned and walked towards the girl behind the black altar.

"What are you doing? We've sacrificed *everything* for this!" a sorcerer shouted in rage. "We're not going to just let you leave and take The Necronomicon with you!" The sorcerer tried to dart toward Etrulia but then quickly found he could no longer move.

"Listen to me!" Jonathan shouted. His tzoharian eyes blazed in the darkness. Everyone's attention focused on this man who was tearing down their Village, one word at a time. "After we leave here, there's sure to be chaos and violence within this Village. I know, despite the atrocities you've committed over the last few days, some of you do not want to be here. You've longed to escape this place–this Coven–for *years*. I'm giving you the chance to do that now."

Jonathan tapped the white staff on the ground three times. A Pentaclegate appeared next to him. He continued.

"You can walk through the portal and be taken to a safer place. From there you can decide what to do with yourselves. *Or*, you can stay here and fight each other to the death for control over this wicked kingdom that will ultimately be destroyed. The choice is yours."

Etrulia reached the girl whose glowing eyes still stared blankly ahead, and guided her over to Jonathan's side. She had also taken the Dark tome of The Necronomicon from the black altar and placed it under her arm–preventing anyone here from using it again.

Of all the villagers, only twelve people walked through the portal. The rest remained–unable to move–coldly staring at Jonathan and Etrulia, as they took the Saturnalia sacrifice and their unholy text into the woods, disappearing into the fog and overlapping branches of the mirky brush.

Far above The Tellyard Bard, The Fellowship gathered together, and watched Jonathan, Etrulia, and the sacrificial child walk into the woods, through the Pentaclegate, and beyond their sight. Then, they watched the villagers begin to destroy themselves. Some tried to take Etrulia's place out of what they'd just witnessed. In minutes, the Bard Village was lost.

Suddenly, a Necrogate appeared before them in the night sky, Pazuzu charged through it, carrying Yirah by the neck, and threw him in the center of the unholy gathering.

"You have *much* to answer for, impudent worm," Baphomet snarled fiercely. Far above The Tellyard Bard, The Fellowship gathered together, and watched Jonathan, Etrulia, and the sacrificial child walk into the woods, through the Pentaclegate, and beyond their sight. Then, they watched the villagers begin to destroy themselves. Some tried to take Etrulia's place out of a conquering lust; others had been driven to sheer madness over what they'd just witnessed. In minutes, the Bard Village was lost.

Suddenly, a Necrogate appeared before them in the night sky, Pazuzu charged through it, carrying Yirah by the neck, and threw him in the center of the unholy gathering.

"You have *much* to answer for, impudent worm," Baphomet snarled fiercely.

Yirah was a shell of his former self. Not only had Pazuzu beaten him ferociously when he found the devil limping through the Village, but Yildrim's power had depleted Yirah almost completely. When the Sword of The King sliced through Etrulia, it did not harm her physical body–for Yildrim destroys the Darkness, not flesh and blood. Nonetheless, it did kill the Darkness inside of her that was connected to Yirah; annihilating the skafos that she had become, and leaving only the Adamian behind. Because the skafos connected Yirah and Etrulia so intimately, he felt every bit of pain she did. It took all his strength to survive that kind of symbiotic attack. The little devil was charred and broken

. "Speak, Yirah." Gaia spat on the broken elohim. "Tell us *why* you failed."

"I...I have no...I don't know what to say my Lords." Yirah muttered through his pain. "How–how could I defeat that damned Sword?"

Dendron flew over and kicked Yirah's face. Necroplasmic blood flew into the night sky.

"More importantly," Baphomet boomed. "Tell us why your skafos was prepared to kill *both* Jonathan Young and The Necronomicon, completely undoing *all* we'd accomplished?"

“Y–you know a skafos’ will is fickle when it–its existence is threatened.” Yirah was desperate. There was no reasoning with this miserable council. “My...my Lords...why–why didn’t you take control of Jonathan Young? You said you were going–"

In a blind rage, Pazuzu grabbed Yirah and lifted him up over the powerful elohim’s head. He brought the little devil down with a mighty force and split him in two. Pazuzu tossed the mangled halves out into the night.

“What is our next move, then?” Dendron asked The Fellowship, ignoring the fact that Pazuzu had just ripped Yirah in half.

**“Your next move is to do what I tell you to do.”**

Every member of The Fellowship fell to their knees at the sound of The Master's voice. As he walked through a Necrogate and into their presence. Lilith followed behind the large, scarlet draped elohim and closed the Necrogate behind her.

"*Hail The Master! Hail Azathoth, who was, and is not, and is to come!"* The Fellowship chanted in unison. Azathoth, the first of all Creation, stood before them in all his terrifying glory. He ignored their groveling and continued.

"Before you flippantly severed my Messenger in half, he had asked you a valid question, did he not?" Red fire blazed within the copper crowned, half skull of Azathoth. "Why was it that you did not gain control of the skafos? Lilith brought him to you on a silver platter."

"My Lord," Baphomet spoke, still facing downward in submission. "We planned to do so, but the Spirit of the enemy was dwelling inside the Adamian."

"Ahh...I see." The Master said. "Well then. That *is* reasonable. But...did I not *command* you to gain control?"

All members of The Fellowship remained silent. All feared of what would happen next. Lilith beamed a wicked smile from behind the enormous elohim. She fought with all her might not to giggle at the sight of her fellow council members groveling in fear.

"My Dark Lord..." Dendron pleaded. "We would have been destroyed, just as Yirah's skafos was."

"So, I should rip *you* in half too, then." In the blink of an eye, The Master appeared behind Pazuzu and sliced him in two, horizontally with his lethally taloned hands. He then grabbed Pazuzu's head and spun the elohim's top half around to face his Master.

"How's that *feel*, Prince of The Wild Winds?" The Master boomed.

Pazuzu, like Yirah, was not dead, but he was in *severe* pain. So much pain that he could not speak.

"If you don't answer me, then I'll be forced to crush your skull."

All Pazuzu could do was plead with his haunting white eyes. Azathoth brought Pazuzu's face close to his.

"Retrieve my Messenger, *Prince*," The Master growled, the holes in his skull illuminated with red and yellow flame. "And remember, *you* are no authority here in *my* Council."

Azathoth grabbed both halves of Pazuzu and slammed them back together, cauterizing the Dark elohim's wounds with his Hellfire. Pazuzu's screams pierced the night above The Lost Dunes, giving nightmares to all Adamians in the region. The Master shoved Pazuzu into the sky. The large, scarlet cloaked being turned to the rest of The Fellowship.

"Rise."

They did as he commanded.

"What *is* our next move, my Lord?" Lilith's sly voice entered the conversation.

"It is quite disappointing that the enemy has claimed Jonathan Young." Azathoth relented. "However, he and The Necronomicon are now together...which is what was needed all along."

"But..." Baphomet spoke. "If the enemy has claimed him, isn't he *lost* to us?"

"The seed of the Spirit has indeed been cast upon Jonathan Young, but it is not yet known what soil that seed has found. The Time of Testing has begun for the Anak Zaman and the Sapient Shard is *powerful* within him. The very destiny of The Cosmic Wheel is attached to the decisions this Adamian makes. And he is *far* from being owned by the enemy. The skafos still very much dwells within him. His essence has not yet been fully solidified to either Dark or Light." Azathoth shifted his gaze from The Fellowship toward The Lost Dunes. The Dark essence of The Master smiled inside his putrid half-skull. "I'm positive the Adamians will attempt to exorcise the child. And when they do, they will receive something they've *never* encountered before. That may be enough to turn Jonathan Young to the Dark. But if not, our next step towards Age End certainly *will*."

The Fellowship looked at each other excitedly. Lilith stepped forward to address them.

"My brothers and sister. The Unspeakable One's mission was successful." The Queen of Dudael beamed in delight as each member of The Fellowship grinned sinisterly at this news. "We will now go forth and prepare The Omnigate."

"Yes," The Master concluded. "and I will awaken my vessel from his slumber and find you at Gollum Madara. Once again, it is time for The Fellowship to be made known across the Adamian world."

"So mote it be." Lilith announced, wildly grinning.

"So mote it be!" the others responded.

Azathoth then disappeared through a Necrogate.

Hundreds of miles away, for the first time in six and a half years, Obadiah's eyes opened.

# CHAPTER THIRTY THREE

## - THE ADUNALAR ELOHIM -

Akalian and Willow were quite nervous as they walked through the Pentaclegate. When they arrived in Sof Haderech–after leaving the Lost Dunes–they were greeted by the Archangel Uriel who'd informed them that their presence was requested before The Adunalar Elohim. Extremely sensitive matters had to be immediately addressed.

Akalian's first concern was how urgently their presence was expected. He knew that in different Seasons of The Cosmic Wheel, time worked differently in the Hall of Zion. Sometimes, with every minute that passed in the Hall, years would pass in the other Realms. But now, the Turning of The Cosmic Tide and Deep Winter was upon them. Corporeum moved slower during this Cosmic Season, allowing for Eden to interact with the Adamian realm, in tandem with Corporeum time.

Still, Deep Winter would last quite a while, so the urgency had to be more than time differentials. It had been a thousand years since either of them had been harkened to Yahweh's Divine Council.

"Do you think they found him?" Willow asked his brother, hope sparkling in his eyes.

"It's certainly possible..." Akalian was more concerned with *where* they'd found him.

As the tzoharian waves of the Pentaclegate parted, the two

leaders of The Order of Michael found themselves in the center of the Hall of Zion. They were immediately filled with joy and gladness. The very air in this place produced such feelings. The King's presence always contained an overwhelming sense of happiness. Even when grave things were discussed, nothing could overcome the holiness of this place.

"Welcome Akalian, Chief Power of the Order of Michael of the Septum Dei, Guardian of The White Throne. And welcome Willow, Commanding Power of the Order of Michael of the Septum Dei, Slayer of Leviathan!" Maryam, Theotokos–Mother of The King–Queen of Eden, gave a warm and hearty welcome to the two elohim.

She sat upon a white aragonite throne. At her chest, a latch made from a chrysolite Tetragrammaton emblem closed a cloak covering her flowing blue robe, which shimmered throughout the Hall of Zion. Willow was immediately lost in her eyes which shown like the stars upon her holy crown. It was always a wondrous delight to see the Queen Mother–the first Adamian to officially be crowned in The Adunalar Elohim.

"Hail Maryam, Full of Grace." The two Powers held their fists to their chests, and bowed their heads.

"Thank you for your kind welcome, Queen Mother." Akalian said with a smile.

The Hall of Zion stretched out for miles, both upward and outward, yet everyone was seen and heard with no effort whatsoever. Far above them, behind the brightest Light in all creation, dwelled El, The King–The Father of All Light. He was sitting upon The White Throne. Outward, as far as their eyes could see, Akalian and Willow were surrounded by Adamian Saints and elohim alike. They were all gathered for one purpose: shielding as many as they could from the flaming arrows of The Dark Kingdom.

Their intercession was especially important during this Cosmic Season, for while Eden was intimately aligned with Corporeum, so was Sheol.

"And thank *you* for coming so quickly, my friends." The voice of the King filled both elohim with awe and wonder. The two Powers bowed their heads toward the Word Made Flesh who stood,

suspended, above them. Atop his brown, scarred brow, the King wore a diadem made from the Tzohar: Stone of Eternal Light. The Tetragrammaton symbol rested in its center. His flowing white cloak and robes were trimmed in gold and shone as brightly as the sun. The glow from his golden breastplate reminded Willow of the wondrous Solar Dragons playing in Creation's End.

"Kadosh uckez, my King," they said, worshipfully.

"What news brought us here with such haste?" Akalian asked humbly.

"Wonderful, but grave news comes from The Dreamlands, my brothers." From the feet of The White Throne, in a beautiful, gliding fashion, Metatron, Angelic Dogrudan of The Adunalar Elohim, spiraled down to address the two Powers. The mighty Seraphim's enormous serpentine body was covered in featherfur and wings, all shimmering with a palette of countless shades of blues, purples, yellows and reds, hues changing depending on the angle from which he was seen. Metatron, as were all Seraphim who resided in The White Throne, was a mesmerizing sight to behold.

"Upon your command, King Yahweh." Metatron humbly bowed his enormous wing covered head.

"Thank you, Metatron. Proceed." Yahweh replied.

"Welcome, St. Nicholas, Father Christmas, Slayer of Krampus, and King Horseman of The Isikaraida! You and your guest are most welcome in this place!" The Seraphim joyfully boomed.

All attention focused on two figures walking through a Pentaclegate next to Akalian and Willow. The first was a large man, almost as tall as Akalian. He wore a flowing, dark green cloak and robes decorated with red and gold Edenic runes.

His great beard reached just below his chest and was as white as snow. Atop his long white hair was a holly crown with featherfur antlers protruding from its top. St. Nicholas' right hand held one of the Sigra Kadro–tzoharian staffs made from saplings of the great Tree of Life. It stood as tall as he was, and was carved beautifully with Christmastime images. At its top, the staff branched out like antlers from a Lightsteed. Just below the branching, it cradled four small Aeternum Shards–Radost: Stone of Joy, Umut: Stone of Hope, Chesed: Stone of Love, and Baris: Stone of Peace.

The second figure was the first of her kind to enter this holy place. Indeed, she was most welcome and the entirety of the Adunalar Elohim was in awe as she walked through the Pentaclegate. The King beamed a kind and satisfied smile as an Ultharian Cat walked into the Hall of Zion. She stood upright on two legs and wore orange and black royal garb with the crest of Ulthar, The Feline Kingdom of The Dreamlands, on her chest. Her soft fur was a mixture of orange and white with black patches and stripes all over. Luna had the typical tribal marks of her Tabby race beautifully designed on her face. Her large, curious eyes eagerly took in the sights around her. Never, in all her days–from house cat to Ultharian Guardian–did she believe she would be in such company.

"Before I give my guest her introduction, First Things must be addressed," Nicholas said.

The large man walked over to Yahweh, and placed his holly crown at the King's feet. Father Christmas then placed his fist over his chest and bowed his head.

"Kadosh uckez, my King."

The King placed a hand on Nicholas' shoulder.

"It's *so* good to see you again, my dear friend."

Nicholas walked back to his guest and gave her introduction to the Hall.

"My fellow Adamians! Elohim of the Most High King! I present to you, Luna, Chief Guardian of Ulthar!

The Hall of Zion erupted in celebration. Akalian–without even looking down at his choirmite brother–reached down to hold Willow back from flying over and hugging Luna. They had never had an Ultharian Feline in the Hall before, and this was a beautiful evolution of the miracle of Image Bearing. While Adamians did not have the ability of Ex Nihilo–creating something from nothing–as Image Bearers of The King, they could imprint their Image Bearing gift upon creatures placed under their stewardship. For example, when an Adamian welcomed an animal into their family or home and gave it a name, that Adamian endowed the beast Image Bearing purpose–imprinting the holy gift of The King upon the creature. As time progressed in the Corporeum Realm, the animal's personality would grow and the bond with its Adamian family would strengthen. Upon their Earthly death, the animals who had received such Image Bearing purpose would live on, eventually growing into fully evolved, sentient beings. While Adamians went on their walkabout type journeys in Purgatory when they died, animals had no moral sin to work through, so they immediately entered into the Realm of Eden, waiting to greet their Adamians upon arrival.

Ulthar was a safe haven for members of the Feline race who had fully evolved and embraced the mission of claiming Sheol for The King. For thousands of years, Luna and her family had kept Ulthar from slipping back into the hands of The Dark.

"I am so overwhelmed and overjoyed to be here with you!" the Cat said in response to the cheering. Luna had never felt happier. She looked upon King Yahweh, and like the others, gave her worshipful tribute.

Nicholas then raised his hands to quiet the cheerful gladness of the Hall.

"My fellow members of The Adunalar Elohim...Metatron was correct in saying that we have wonderful, but *grave* news." Father Christmas motioned for Luna to step forward and speak.

"A little while ago, word had reached Ulthar that the Archangel Gabriel had been found near the Basalt Pillars of The West where The Cosmic Ocean meets the Seas of The Dreamlands. However, we discovered that the Archangel wasn't just *found...*" Luna pulled out the remains of Fisilti–Gabriel's Lightblade–from within her robes. "He had been *captured*."

Gasps and murmurings resounded throughout the Hall. Akalian and Willow walked over to Luna and gazed down at the broken Lightblade.

"How did you get this?" Akalian asked.

"When I heard news of his finding, I led a small team to the Pillars to see if I could find anything. As you know, we Cats have heightened psychic abilities. When we arrived, I felt this calling to me from deep below the surface of the Cosmic Waters. We were able to retrieve it and when I grasped the blade, I could see *who* took Gabriel."

"Who was it?" Willow asked in desperation.

"Hastur. The Yellow King."

The Hall of Zion collectively held its breath. An eerie silence fell upon The Adunalar Elohim as all eyes moved to their King. The Yellow King was madness incarnate. No elohim of Light who had faced the Old god had been able to best him. Of all the Dark creatures to capture one of their Archangels, this being was one of the most frightening. Who knew what diabolical plan Hastur had in store for Gabriel.

"Go on, my dear." The King said to Luna.

"My siblings and I believe that Hastur has Gabriel somewhere in The Dreamlands. Our environment is becoming more wicked than usual...and The Yellow Sign has been found in the surrounding lands of Ulthar. I informed St. Nicholas as soon as he arrived on The White Ship with Saints Kefas and Andraus."

The King turned to Akalian and Willow.

"It is because of this that *you* are here, my friends. I wish for you to lead a team into The Dreamlands with Luna here as your guide."

The Dreamlands. Akalian's heart froze in terror. It was true that there were now tamed cities in that wild, dreadful realm, but the majority of that eldritch place was filled with madness so contagious that many who traversed there for more than a few days had been driven insane and were beyond any help found on this side of New Creation. Regardless, his King had just commanded this of him. And he would answer.

"Of course, my King. But...what of Jonathan Young? I had thought that...that *I* would become his Guardian now since I have been involved with him so pivotally, and especially since he has entered his Time of Trial and..." Akalian trailed off, but gave a knowing glance at his King. No one else knew just *how* important this man was. Not even Willow.

"I understand completely why that was your expectation, Akalian." The King assured. "I even had planned on that happening for a time. However, *this* task must be yours to take."

"If I may ask, then, who will you choose for his Guardianship?" Akalian was concerned for Jonathan.

"Oh," the King chuckled. "I have someone *very* special in store for our boy."

"I will be his Guardian." Maryam said from her aragonite throne. Akalian was taken aback. This was most irregular.

Yahweh then rose into the air and addressed the entire Hall.

"What I'm about to say to you must not leave these walls." He paused to glance around. "Jonathan Young is not just the skafos of Xexxus. Not only has he been claimed by the Dark as The Final Herald of Age End. He is also the Anak Zaman."

Willow gazed shockingly at Akalian who gave him a humble nod.

*Oh my!*

*How can this be?!*

*He's been found!*

*It's been so long!*

*So, this is it!*

Whispers and conjectures bounced throughout the Hall.

"My King..." Nicholas interjected. "Does–does she know?"

"No, Nicholas. She doesn't. Nor do I want her to know just yet. It isn't the right time for these things to be revealed outside of the Council." The King answered with care in his tone. He knew Father Christmas didn't understand the secrecy, but that Nicholas also trusted him with all his heart. With a nod, Nicholas assured his King that he did.

A hush fell over the Hall of Zion as the Theotokos walked toward Akalian and placed her warm hand on his featherfured cheek.

"Above all things, Jonathan has responded most readily to a mother's love. I was there when you saved him from Xexxus' grasp," the Queen Mother said gently. "I led Mattia Bajuma in the prayer that gave you strength to do what had to be done. I know how much Jonathan means to you. And I promise that I, alongside the Saints and the Spirit of The King, will be sure he makes it home."

Akalian leaned into the Queen's palm.

"I know you will, my Queen. I have no doubt of that."

After a moment, Maryam removed her hand and stepped back to address Akalian and Willow.

"Now you two..." she smiled, "go back to Sof Haderech and get some rest. You're certainly going to need it." Then, turning to look lovingly at her Son, the King of all things, she gave him a soft smile–a mother's smile–and waved her hand. A Pentaclegate swiftly opened and she walked through it.

As Maryam's portal closed, the King glanced at Michael's Powers lovingly and gave them a reassuring smile.

"Well, you heard your Queen. Go and get some rest...and then, go Light up The Darkness and bring Gabriel home."

After Metatron had assigned tasks to all Saints and elohim present, the meeting of The Adunalar Elohim adjourned. Akalian and Willow departed to Michael's Kingdom. St. Nicholas and Luna left to convene with the Riders of Isikaraida. All other Saints and elohim dispersed to prepare their Orders, as the most pivotal turning of The Cosmic Wheel ushered them all into Deep Winter.

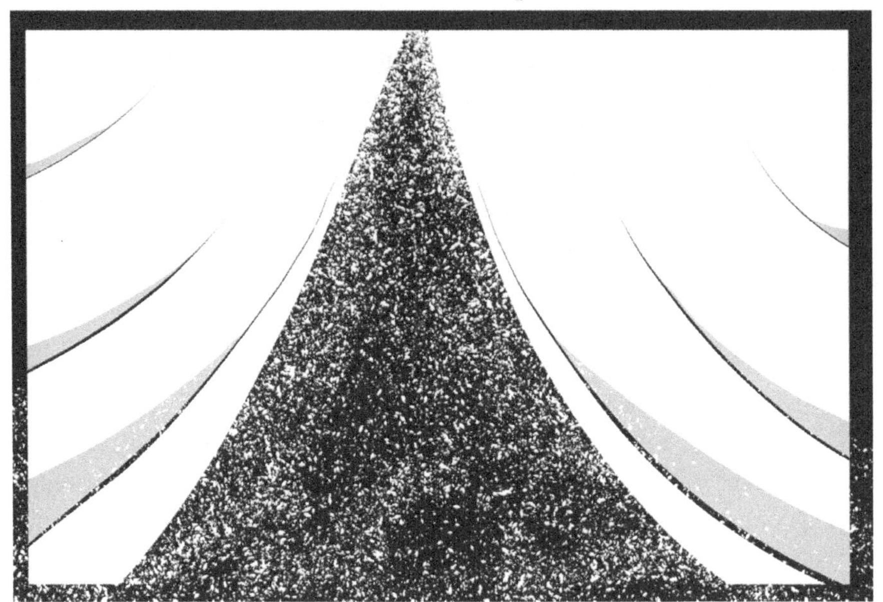

# OLD WORLD
## MAY 1, 1991

The night was a cold one, not necessarily due to the temperature outside, but more because of an ominous specter that loomed over the city. The wind howled and carried the pouring rain this way and that, complimenting the chaotic aura of this night in the city of Louisville, Kentucky.

Traffic was sparse on Interstate 65. Even though that was normal for 3:30 in the morning, it still added to the ghostly atmosphere that crept inside the unmarked patrol car and up the spine of the man driving it towards downtown.

Detective George Aniceto had been awakened from a deep sleep–as deep as a homicide detective could sleep–to the strangest news he'd heard in years. This was impressive due to the direction his work seemed to take him. George never went looking for the weird and unnatural things of the world, but they always seemed to find him. He'd guessed that of most of the homicide detectives in the region, he'd probably experienced the most of what they called "paranormal activity" in his cases. His partner, Dan, always told him it was because he kept company with that weird old woman off of Tenney Ave. But George couldn't help that she always seemed to have answers for him and half the time cracked his cases wide open—for better or worse. But this morning, or night, or whatever you call this ungodly hour, felt different. George was scared.

Through the rain beating against the windshield of the Crown Vic, the detective saw a sea of red and blue flashing lights from Broadway below the interstate as he took his exit. Running the red light and turning left, he saw the news crews of the three different local stations, at least a dozen patrol cars, and his partner's unmarked vehicle that matched his own. Detective Dan O'Neil held a megaphone pointed at the Save-A-Stop which was the focal point of everyone's attention. George noticed that multiple patrol cars had their spot lights shining on the inside of the gas station store. Apart from these lights, the entire facility was dark. This, of course, added to the chill running up his spine.

George parked the cruiser, leaving his flashing lights on, and stepped out of the vehicle into the rain. He immediately heard the haunting sounds of a woman screaming for dear life from inside the store.

"I said shut up, you sow!!" George heard a guttural, almost inhuman, voice howl from the darkness.

"Al! This doesn't have to continue, man! Just let her go and we can talk about all this." Dan O'Neil pleaded over the megaphone.

Detective Albert Burgess was a good cop. He was a veteran Louisville Police Department officer who became a detective on the force back in '70. He had been a mentor/big brother figure to George and Dan ever since they graduated from the Academy fifteen years ago. Al was an old school cop who had barely missed a day of work in twenty-five years. He also had very little patience for officers who "dicked around" on the job or used their power to lord over people, especially those who had very little of that power themselves. But he was also superb at spotting the good patrol officers who would make even better detectives.

Al had clout, and the ear of the Chief of Police, and he used it for the good of the department and the city. When George and Dan applied for Detective together in 1980, Al's word was as good a reference as anyone could have. The two officers swore they wouldn't let him down, and Al's proud, beaming smile gave them even more motivation to keep their word. So, when Al Burgess didn't report for duty on the morning of Wednesday, April 8th, people noticed and they rapidly grew concerned as the hours dragged on.

Even though it wasn't a homicide, George and Dan had volunteered for the case on Thursday morning after Al had been gone for almost twenty-four hours. According to his wife, Deborah, Al never came home the prior evening and had been acting "a bit off" the week leading up to his disappearance. Friday night at 7:30, Al's car was found in the back of The Silo Microbrewery parking lot near the woods. There were no signs of struggle. Nor was there any evidence–fingerprints or foot tracks–found to give them any real leads. They all knew that Al had been twenty years sober and wouldn't have stepped foot in a bar to save his life.

Over the weekend, search parties were scouring the region for the father figure of the LPD. The local news stations were flashing his picture on television and running radio ads every other commercial break. Downtown based restaurants were even giving major discounts for those who joined the city-wide search. But Saturday and Sunday passed, and they found nothing. Weeks passed.

Detective George Aniceto knew all too well that with each day that left them, the odds of finding Al alive were dwindling. So, when his head hit the pillow on Sunday night, April 30th, he prayed to whatever was out there that Al would be found soon. Unfortunately, that prayer was answered with a phone call at 3:10am–merely 20 minutes ago–saying they had not only found Detective Albert Burgess, but that he was holding a cashier at knife point at the Save-A-Stop on the corner of 1st and Broadway. And it looked like he had killed others already.

As George walked up to his partner, he glanced inside the darkness of the Save-A-Stop. Al's face was heavily shadowed, except for his eyes–which somehow looked like they were glowing yellow.

"Hey, Dan," George said somberly as he put a comforting hand on the cold, wet, padded shoulder of his partner's khaki trench coat. "What exactly do we have here?" Dan got right to the point in his faded Boston accent.

"It's Al, George. He's in there and he's acting *nuts!* Witnesses who fled the store and called the cops said that Al began laughing maniacally and then just started slashing people's throats with a knife. Apparently, the cashier was able to get a shot off and hit him. But by the time the first patrol got here, the power was out and he was holding her hostage and raving about some *box*."

"Box?" George questioned, trying to make sense of everything he just heard. "What box?"

"I don't know, man. He's not makin' any sense and I can't get him to talk to me."

"Here, let me try." George offered as Dan handed him the megaphone.

"Be my guest. *Please*," Dan pleaded, desperate for some kind of progress. A sniper was getting into position on the roof across the street, but no one wanted it to come to that. George had been in a few standoffs before. He figured that particular protocol was already in place, therefore he also knew he didn't have much time. He had to get Al talking some sense. George put the megaphone up to his mouth and clicked the trigger.

"Hey, Al. It's George. Look, man I don't know what you've been through over the last couple weeks...I'm sure it's been hell...but this *isn't* the answer, okay? You know that. Every man and woman out here owe you something. We love you. You're our hero...and we don't want this to continue to escalate. So please, just put the knife down and–"

George was interrupted by the megaphone screeching and whining so much that he had to remove his finger from the trigger and pull it away from his face. When he brought it back to his mouth, the megaphone no longer worked. As this realization dawned, they heard a wheezing, gargled laugh echo out of the heavy shadows of the store through the steady, forbidding rain. The yellow eyes of Albert Burgess seemed to glow ragefully at the man who called him mentor and friend.

"Albert Burgess is no longer here, dust creature," the voice bellowed.

"What the fuck..." George said out loud, uncomprehending. That wasn't Albert's voice. Not even close. The detective knew that in moments of heavy psychosis, it was possible for a person to switch personalities to the point of being completely unrecognizable. He'd seen it before, but he *knew* Al. Not only did Albert not have a history of mental problems, he was probably the most level headed guy George had ever met. In fact, he was a devout Catholic whose moral fibers were stronger than a steel trap. None of this made any sense. The bellowing voice continued through dry, wheezing breaths.

"Our time has come. The days of The Yellow King are upon you all...and from his chaotic pleasures, there is no escape. For the *box* has been found and it has heard The Master's call from the depths of the cosmos." The cashier whimpered as Albert Burgess pressed the knife into her throat, piercing the outer layer of skin.

"What the hell's he talking about, George?" Dan said, fear and sadness thick in his voice.

"How the hell should I know?" As George responded, a dark blue 1986 Ford Taurus pulled up amongst the slew of cruisers. "You called Father Deon?" George asked.

"Yeah. I figured if anyone could get through to Al it would be his priest. Plus...I mean...you heard his voice..." Dan said, with that look in his eye that let George know they were out of their depths.

"Yeah...I heard it."

"Morning, Officers," Fr Deon's somber, calm tone brought hope to the two detectives as he approached them, holding an umbrella in his left hand. "So, I see you've found him."

"Hi, Father. Thanks for coming so quickly," Dan responded, extending his hand to the clergyman who reciprocated the greeting. "Yeah, we found him...and in a terrible way, too."

"He's talking nonsense, Father," George chimed in. "And...he's doing so in a voice I've never heard." Fr Deon's posture straightened, his expression turning deathly serious.

"What do you mean?" he asked. At that moment, the wheezy laugh began again followed by shouting that almost seemed to be coming from inside everyone's head.

"You brought this piece of *shit* into *my* presence!?" the gargled voice boomed. "He isn't prepared for this. None of you are!! What happens here now heralds the coming of The Unspeakable One. Few know his tongue, but soon all will bow to wonders of The Yellow Sign."

"Detective O'Neil, I'm in position." The grave voice of Sergeant Larry Gordon, sniper for LPD's SWAT team, came over the radio. "It looks like there's some sort of ritualistic marking on the floor in there. And it's drawn in blood. I can't get a better look due to the darkness, but I think he's going to kill the hostage soon."

"Noted. Hold your fire, Sergeant," Dan replied. The chances of them not using Gordon's talents were dwindling. Fr Deon spoke up ominously.

"Fellas, I don't want to cause more harm here, but I don't think that's Al in there–ya get me?"

"Look," George said urgently, "I know there's clergy-penitent privilege here, but has Al mentioned anything to you regarding occult activity or anything out of the ordinary in confession or in conversation?"

"Nothing." Fr Deon responded. "He came to confession two weeks ago and everything was normal. Boys, I don't know what to tell you here...but I *do* know what a demon sounds like when I hear it."

"Father, you know George and I are both Catholics. And I'm not necessarily questioning this possibility," Dan said. "But isn't that a bit of a jump? Especially if Al's been acting completely normal. I mean, these types of things...they take time, right?"

"Mostly, yes. But as we all know, it's been three weeks since anyone's seen him. Who knows what's happened during that time."

"Regardless of what's actually going on here, if he's really possessed or if Al's just under the *assumption* that he's possessed, why hasn't he killed her yet? Why kill all those people, take a hostage, and then *wait* for the cops to show?" George asked.

"Spectacle," Fr Deon said. "The demonic love attention. Especially if this is supposed to be some sort of 'Herald' as it stated."

"Then if that's the case, let's give him more of a spectacle to buy us some time to get a clear, non-lethal, shot off." George suggested. "Are you comfortable with talking to him, Father?"

"I'll do my best." the clergyman agreed.

"George," Dan interjected, "the news is here. *All* of them. We're gonna catch hell if we have Fr Deon acknowledge a *demon*."

"Looks like we already caught it." George said definitively. "Plus, playing along with whatever is happening in there may be our only way to save them both." Dan nodded an agreement, then he radioed Sergeant Gordon.

"Alright Sergeant. We're going to try and buy you some time for you to get a non-lethal. But if the suspect makes any kind of move with that knife..." Dan looked at George and closed his eyes, "take whatever shot you have. Over." Gordon agreed and the three men walked over to a patrol car. George handed Father Deon the car radio, switched it to external, and gave the father a nod to go ahead.

"I'm addressing the being inside of Albert Burgess. I command you to speak to me in the name of The Father and The Son and The Holy Spirit." the Father said in a commanding tone.

The wheezy, monstrous voice spoke up.

"I was hoping someone like you might show up." Al chuckled, sinisterly. "It will certainly make this moment sweeter for those watching from the other side."

"What is your name, demon?"

"Ah, the direct approach. I'm the Devil. Nice to meet you."

"We both know that's a lie," Fr Deon played along. "Why would the Devil himself be interested in a man like Albert Burgess?"

"There are secret things which go beyond your reasoning and understanding, dust creature. You do not need to know *why* such things happen, only that they do."

George leaned and spoke in a hushed tone. "Keep him talking, Father. You're doing just fine." He turned to Dan. "What's Gordon's progress?"

"Sergeant. You got anything non-lethal? Over." Dan asked over the handheld.

"It's the damndest thing, Detective," the Sergeant stated. "I don't know how to describe it...but, ever since that priest started talking, my visibility on the target darkened to the point where I can barely see the suspect at all. Over."

"The lights are directly on him, Sergeant. How do you not see him?" Dan asked, shocked. Gordon was the best sniper on the force. If he said he couldn't see his target, he meant it. But, from their perspective, there was no way Gordon's view was obstructed.

"I can't explain it Detective O'Neil, but I no longer have a clear shot at all. Over."

"What the hell is happening here?" George said to himself, beginning to slightly question reality. He had seen weird things before, but nothing quite like this. He wished Eula was here, although he didn't know what more she could do. His attention turned back to the priest.

"What is your goal here tonight, demon?" Father Deon prodded.

"What I do now will open the gate."

"The gate to what?" The Clergyman didn't like how that sounded.

"Madness." The thing inside Albert Burgess began cackling. Every single radio in every single patrol car began screaming loudly with static until each one sparked and died. Suddenly, flames erupted inside the Save-A-Stop.

"I got it! I got the shot!" Gordon yelled over Dan's hand-held radio–the only one that still worked.

"Is it non-lethal?!" Dan asked.

"Negative!" Gordon replied. That next moment would haunt Detective George Aniceto for the rest of his life. He knew it was over. Al–or whatever this was–was simply playing games. George silently promised his mentor that he would find out what happened to him and how it got to this point, but he knew they no longer had a choice. Maybe they never did. He grabbed the radio from Dan and yelled over the increasing flames and whining radios.

"Take the shot, Gordon! That's an order!" Immediately, the sound of one terrifying shot rang out from the rooftop across from the Save-A-Stop and the bullet found its target in less than a second. The cackling Albert Burgess now had a gaping bullet hole in his forehead. But, unexplainably it didn't faze him. The cashier had been too petrified to speak, but now began to scream, pleading for help as the flames inched closer to her and her assailant, who began to shout towards the ceiling.

"Let the flames of Pandemonium baptize thee into a blackness that shall rule forevermore!! Ph'nglui mglw'nafh wgah'nagl fhtagn!!" Albert Burgess then slit the throat of the cashier and tossed her twitching body onto a bloody sigil on the floor.

"Fire at will!" shouted Dan O'Neil. Bullets ripped through the blazing Save-A-Stop and into Albert Burgess. The possessed man continued laughing maniacally as the fire swallowed him whole.

Across town, in a quiet little house on quiet little street, Eula McDowell sat at her large, wooden, dining room table and looked up from her steaming cup of coffee. She closed her eyes in despair. Whatever had awakened her at three in the morning had now welcomed something horrible into the astral atmosphere of the city. She wasn't sure just what that *something* was, but she knew it wasn't anything she was ready for.

The gray-haired woman looked down at her cat, Luna, and sighed.

"Weell...I guess it's time for me to go work."

**The Cosmic Wheel is turning...**

The Cosmic Wheel is turning...
The Mysterious Adventures of Eula McDowell
A Cosmic Wheel story
Written by Brian Rodman
Brian K. Morris
& Clyde Hall
Coming Soon

## THANK YOU TO OUR KICKSTARTER BACKERS!!

Adam Flener, Adam Pryor, Alyssa Dolan, Amanda Elswick, Amanda, Andrew Morris, Angi Dudas, Benjamin Rasche, Beth Clark, Blythe Conover, Bob, Brannon Hollingsworth, Brian K. Morris, Brianne Case, Bureen Frankenberger, C. Christian Scott, Campbell Royales, Carlos Phillips, Casey Jo, Chad Nuss, Charles F. Millhouse, Cheryl Davis, Cheryl Miller, Chris & Andrea Gillespie, Cindy Koepp, Clyde Hall, Corey Greco, Corinne Brucks, Corinne Roberts, Craig Hackl, Crystal Young, Cynthia Lee Rose, Damion and Lauren Waldbrunn, Dani, Darice Hancock, Dave, Dave Davis, Dave Swartz, David Berry Jr., David Macauley, David and Lydia Sherrer, Dawn Dulas, Dawn, Dee Sarah Fish, Diana Rodman, Donna Carlene, Doris Bachman, Dottie Smith, Eads Family, Ed Hillenbrand, Eric L. Collette, Etwoine, Gary Phillips, George Sirois, Gerald von Stoddard, GMarkC, Grant Lankard, Greg Tjosvold, Hannah, Hannah Garrity, Hannah Ratliff, J Mills, Jack Brannen, Jackie Villamor, Jake Anderson, Jamaal Williams, Jason Kane, JD Calderon, Jeff Gollaher, Jeff & Lydia Walker, Jencie Brown, Jennifer Brown, Jenny Miller, Jeremy & Sara Woodring, JES, Jessica Branham, Jim Stitzel, Joanna Skinner, Joe Bachman, John Dudley, Jonah, Jon Gentry, Juan Calle, Judy Chism Wegenast, Justan Stratton, K. Lynn Smith, Kasey McCoy, Kayla, Kayla Biddle, Keith, Kellie Austin, Kelly Guentner, Kenneth Myers, Keri & James Witmyer, Kim & Luke Bray, Kim & Kendall Cox, Kimberly Bowman, Kristopher Jerome, Kyla Curtis, Lesley Ailiff, Linda J Wakefield, Linda & George Rodman, Liz Corwin, Lori Droege, Luis A Jaramillo, Marcus McNeal, MarkAdam Miller, Mary, Matt Norhrup, Matthew Harris, Matthias, Megan & James Tindle, MGSpear, Michelle Buchanan, Mihail Braila, Mike Coonrad, Mike Nash, Mike Paul, Morgan S. Comnick, Ms. Davi West, MTS Comics, Nikolas Everhart, Paul & Heidi Woelm, Paula Tirey, Peter Wiggins, Pull_Out_Queen, Queen Empress Sugar Baby, Ray Coffman, Rene & Bert Breland, Rick Bradley, Robert C. Worstell, Rogulynx, Ryan Permison, Sarah Thrasher, Sarah Mayer, Sarah Allen & Mina Thrasher, Scott Casey, Scott Jones, SeerNova Comics, Shashidharan N Subramaniam, Sheila Johnson Musick, Simian Circle Games, Sir Brenton & Dame Kathyrn of The House of Ziva, Space Chimp Comics, Stedmon, Stefani Manard, Stephen Coenen, Steven Byrd, Tammy Walker, Tasha Irving, The Bouchards, "The" Eric Hawkins, Todd Daniel, Vibbs, Victoria Adams, Whitney Cook

**To get the latest updates on The Cosmic Wheel books and other works from B&R Publications, visit brianrodman.com**